PN
6014
.N457
no.3

New world writing

OAKLAND COMMUNITY COLLEGE
ORCHARD RIDGE LIBRARY
27055 ORCHARD LAKE ROAD
FARMINGTON, MICHIGAN 48024

OAKLAND COMMUNITY COLLEGE
ORCHARD RIDGE LIBRARY
27055 ORCHARD LAKE ROAD
FARMINGTON, MICHIGAN 48024

To the Reader

Three issues of *New World Writing* have now appeared—distributed, along with our other Mentor and Signet Books, in cities and towns throughout the United States; in bookstores, drugstores, supermarkets, cigar stores, variety stores, department stores, stationery shops and on newsstands; in prairie towns, mountain villages, industrial cities, on islands off the coasts of Maine, Florida, California and Washington; where people farm, fish, manufacture, go to ball games, watch television, read books, and live—in short where almost every American can meet his fellows and think and buy something. Mentor and Signet books are sold in South America, Europe and Asia as well.

For the United States, this easy access to such good books at a low price is something new and welcome. The semi-annual publication of *New World Writing* (and the enthusiastic response it has brought) is only one of many developments, one aspect of the whole evolution of books and the reading of books in the modern world. Though classics were available in paper back editions a hundred years ago, and "dime novels" in the less distant past, it is only in the last ten years or so that fiction and non-fiction of genuine quality have been offered for sale in paper-bound editions by corner shops and newsstands. While there are some who believe that the reading of books should be restricted to those who can afford to pay $3.00 or $4.00 or more for the privilege, most Americans have applauded the wider reading that the best inexpensive paperbacks have made possible.

And it is in the short span of a year that you—our readers—have made *New World Writing* one of the most influential of literary publications. You have joined with us in a kind of literary salon, to honor and enjoy a gathering-together of the work of the young writer making his first bow, the promising writer, and the recognized or established writer. You have sensed with us also that in attempting to reflect the creative genius of other countries along with our own, we have helped to encourage not only a diversity in creative expression, but also a closer communication between nations.

As the largest and most selective publisher of inexpensive editions, we must confess that when we launched *New World Writing* we were somewhat fearful lest it might to some extent displace on the newsstands some of the invaluable little magazines that were providing important and stimulating vehicles for criticism, scholarly publication in the field of the arts, and, to a lesser degree, fiction and poetry. Your response to *New World Writing* has had exactly the opposite effect. By proving that a larger audience exists, you and we together have inspired a number of other projects which will, we hope, further extend the creative activity—of both readers and writers—which we envisaged. *discovery*, edited by John Aldridge and Vance Bourjaily, is now being published twice a year by Pocket Books. Established literary journals are planning to enlarge their audience by periodic anthologies in inexpensive book format—notably the *Partisan Review* anthologies to be published by Avon Books. And *New Voices*, consisting of material produced by the creative writing group at the New School in New York, has recently been published by Permabooks in paper-bound book form.

To us, as to you, these developments represent a heartening and historic trend. At the very time when writers and critics were regretting the decline and fall of so many fine literary publications and the apparent preoccupation of those remaining with criticism at the expense of fiction, we felt we had a special opportunity and responsibility to use the vast publishing and distributing system at our command to provide a new medium for creative talent.

We are happy, as you must be, and as all poets, critics and writers of fiction must be, that *New World Writing* is a success, and that it has stimulated other publishers to emulate its approach to the problem of the writer and of you, the reader, at the very time when mass media of every sort appear to be threatening not only the little magazine but the book itself. Essentially the material of *New World Writing* is book material, or the beginning, or the promise, of writing which will eventually be published in book form. It seems appropriate therefore that we present our literary publication as a book—even though it may appear to be conceived as a "little magazine."

In this volume there are twenty-six contributors from the United States, and twelve from other countries. The literary gathering in which you are participating has been made possible by the cooperation of trade publishers, writers, translators, critics, literary agents and teachers, under the editorial direction of Arabel J. Porter, who has coordinated the joint efforts of the editorial staff of The New American Library of World Literature, Inc.

John Malcolm Brinnin has served as guest poetry editor of this issue.

THE PUBLISHERS

New
WORLD
WRITING

THIRD MENTOR SELECTION

PUBLISHED BY

THE NEW AMERICAN LIBRARY

New World Writing, COPYRIGHT, 1953, BY
THE NEW AMERICAN LIBRARY OF WORLD LITERATURE, INC.

Evening in Madrid
Copyright, 1953, by Alfred A. Knopf, Inc.

The Visionary Farms
Copyright, 1953, by Richard Eberhart

The Temple and the City
Copyright, 1953, by Christopher Tunnard and Henry Hope Reed, Jr.

Alfredo and the Engineer
Copyright, 1953, by Harper & Brothers

Four Lost Souls
Copyright, 1953, by Dylan Thomas

Sermon
Copyright, 1953, by John Lee Weldon

The Anatomy Lesson
Copyright, 1953, by Evan S. Connell, Jr.

Miss Emily's Maggie
Copyright, 1953, by Jay Leyda

He
Copyright, 1953, by John Ashbery

*All Rights Reserved under the Pan-American
Copyright Convention and the International
Copyright Convention.*

*Published as a MENTOR SELECTION
First issued, May, 1953*

PN
6014
N457
NO.3

OR"/72

Manuscripts will not be returned
unless accompanied by stamped,
self-addressed envelope.

Designer: Ernst Reichl

*New WORLD WRITING is published by
The New American Library of World Literature, Inc.
501 Madison Avenue, New York 22, New York*

PRINTED IN THE UNITED STATES OF AMERICA

Table of Contents

To The Reader, i

MARGARET MEAD
Sex and Censorship in Contemporary Society, 7

HOLLIS SUMMERS
How They Chose the Dead, 24

JOSÉ SUÁREZ CARREÑO
Evening in Madrid, 32

PEGGY BENNETT
The Bronco-Buster, 47

RICHARD EBERHART
The Visionary Farms, 63

CHRISTOPHER TUNNARD and **HENRY HOPE REED, Jr.**
The Temple and the City, 98

DAVID DEMPSEY
Valse Triste, 110

IGNAZIO SILONE
Alfredo and the Engineer, 122

LOUIS AUCHINCLOSS
The Gem-Like Flame, 136

M. R. KADISH
Anthem for French Horn, 154

POETRY: *Selected by John Malcolm Brinnin*

EDITH SITWELL
From The Road to Thebes, 170

SACHEVERELL SITWELL
Mrs. H. or a Lady from Babel, 174

WILLIAM H. MATCHETT
Packing a Photograph from Firenze, 175

SPENCER BROWN
Candlemas, 177

ALEXANDER TROCCHI
He Tasted History with a Yellow Tooth, 179

GALWAY KINNELL
First Song, 180

PATRICK BOLAND
Trials of a Poet, 181

HOWARD MOSS
Venice, 182

SYDNEY GOODSIR SMITH
    Credo, 183

BYRON VAZAKAS
    Skating at Versailles, 184

JOHN ASHBERY
    He, 185

HARRY DUNCAN
    Monodies, 186

HERBERT MORRIS
    Suns, 190

DYLAN THOMAS
    Four Lost Souls, 192

JOHN LEE WELDON
    Sermon, 208

HAMDI BEY
    The Indian Intelligentsia and the Western World, 213

GENE BARO
    Bereavement, 218

ROBERT PINGET
    Mahu or The Matter, 233

LUCINDA COLLINS
    The Conquest, 240

EVAN S. CONNELL, Jr.
    The Anatomy Lesson, 241

JAY LEYDA
    Miss Emily's Maggie, 255

R. S. NIEDELMAN
    Alex's Fun: Well Boiled, 268

ALBERTO MORAVIA
    Consuelo, 291

JOHN HOWARD GRIFFIN
    Sauce for the Gander, 313

PETER MATTHIESSEN
    Late in the Season, 320

B. RAJAN
    None Shall Escape, 329

MALCOLM LOWRY
    Strange Comfort Afforded by the Profession, 331

ALBERT J. GUERARD
    The Ivory Tower and the Dust Bowl, 344

SEX AND CENSORSHIP IN CONTEMPORARY SOCIETY

Margaret Mead

A noted anthropologist, psychologist, author and lecturer, Margaret Mead is Associate Curator of Ethnology at the American Museum of Natural History in New York City. Among her books are COMING OF AGE IN SAMOA, SEX AND TEMPERAMENT IN THREE PRIMITIVE SOCIETIES, *and* MALE AND FEMALE —*all published by William Morrow. Since taking her Ph.D. at Columbia University in 1929, Dr. Mead has made many field trips to Samoa, New Guinea, Bali, the Admiralty Islands and elsewhere. She has been a close observer, as well, of the cultural patterns of the contemporary United States and Great Britain.*

Every known human society exercises some explicit censorship over behavior relating to the human body, especially as that behavior involves or may involve sex. Where there is no written literature and no representational art, this censorship may be limited to the prohibition of the use of certain words, the substitution of words from another language, or the restriction of the use of these words between men and women or between the parent and the child generations. The presence of certain restrictions on bodily behavior is equally widespread. It may be leaving off an earring rather than leaving off corsets, or even putting on earrings after marriage, which is the focus of feeling and taste, but even the complete absence of clothing does not prevent the exercise of certain canons of modesty and shame.

The phenomenon of censorship, as we know it, occurs when certain constituted authorities (usually prodded by other self-constituted authorities) use the power of the State or the Church to forbid the manufacture and sale of certain kinds of publications or pictorial representations. Such censorship not only depends upon the existence of such an organized state or church; it is usually, also, a response to the presence within the society of heterogeneous groups of people with differing standards and aspirations. What is literature to one group may be merely provocation to another, and a medical textbook written coldly and carefully may nevertheless be salacious reading for the adolescent. It is easier for the purveyor of pornography to flourish within the framework of such differing standards than when he is up against a single standard of what should and should not be said, written and drawn. Because this is so, because censorship by one group or authority over another, instead of by all the responsible members of a group of people, is a special circumstance of large organized societies or the small religious enclave within a large society, light may be thrown on the whole question by looking broadly, first, at the ways human societies have tried to regulate the ways in which sex is experienced.

So, for the moment I shall not discuss censorship itself except to state my general position: that I feel that censorship is always to be deplored in a free society. Those interested in freedom of thought must inevitably be interested in freedom of expression, in broadening the areas of exploration and understanding. Particularly is retrogressive censorship to be lamented. Men who have not known freedom are limited but not irretrievably damaged by its absence, but such studies of Nazi Germany as Erich Fromm's *Escape from Freedom* suggest that freedom once glimpsed and valued cannot be denied without severe mutilation of the human spirit. Only in those instances where freedom has been feared rather than valued, regarded as anarchical rather than responsible, can men ethically justify to themselves its increased restriction. As a test of whether such ethical justification is possible or not, one may consider the acts of those in power who are enforcing the new disciplines. If those in power are driven to excesses of cruelty, such as concentration camps and mass murders, which the bulk of the population under control have to repudiate, it is probable that the whole new order is causing a serious ethical strain on the society. The contrast is very striking between the small righteous German burgher who continued to deny the gas chambers of Belsen and the Soviet D.P. who demands that the United States treat all Communists as the Soviet Union treated all non-Communists. In the one case, Western European standards of humanity and justice, of treating each person as an individual, had been violated; in the other, the Soviet D.P. simply thinks the contemporary Soviet government is using right methods (methods of mass accusation and punishment which have always been a part of the Russian police state) for wrong ends. Abandoning one's grandmother may be merely a lamented necessity among a nomadic people with insufficient food, but it becomes murder and remains murder, unless there occurs again a necessity as urgent as that which faced the nomads, as soon as one has some method—dog sled or boat or horse—to transport Grandmother without danger to the food supply or to the younger members of the group. Probably the exercise of freedom is in somewhat the same category. Those who have never been able to exercise it can lead dignified human lives within very narrow confines, but once a society has achieved the self-discipline—both in those who wield power and in those who obey laws—necessary to exercise freedom, then a return to more restrictive measures necessitates the payment of an ethical price, often a price that involves suppression of very valuable and formerly cultivated human sensitivities.

However, our present knowledge does not permit us to extend this statement to the question of sexual freedom. We have no grounds for asserting that in a society where there is less restriction on shared sexual knowledge or experience there is necessarily a better, or worse, set of human values. It can be demonstrated easily that most large societies fail to develop a standard of sex behavior which suits all groups and so often penalize the members of one class in favor of another, just as most small societies penalize a few individuals in attempting to maintain a single standard for the many. From the existing facts we can also easily plead for more kinds of standards, and especially we can argue against permitting children to grow up unprepared for the kind of sex life they will have to live. We know this to be seriously stunting to the personality. To be reared in a Catholic country where celibacy in the service of God is regarded as a high vocation is a preparation for a life of celibacy; to be reared believing in a Protestant definition of human behavior that regards sex as regrettable but inevitable, a low craving that had better be soundly disposed of within the bonds of holy matrimony, mindful of the saying, "It is better to marry than to burn," is a very poor preparation for celibacy. To those so reared, celibacy is neither a privileged nor a tolerable state. The unmarried are suspected of unmentionable vices, or, at the least, of predictable neuroses, a suspicion the more likely to be true as the deprived bachelors and spinsters share the definition of human beings as creatures unfortunately addicted to sexual behavior as long as the human soul is caged, alas, in this low mortal body. The Catholic position that both celibacy and marriage are holy states, that the body is not inherently evil, but that man must fight against himself to use that body wisely and well, permits a different sort of celibate adulthood.

So we know that it is possible for a society to bring up its children either to be helped or hurt by the alternatives offered them, and hurt in different degrees in terms of their innate capacities. As we learn more about those innate capacities—to what extent, for example, individuals vary in their sexual endowment, and to what extent they vary in their capacity to channel their energies into other activities—our sexual standards can be revised to provide a variety of outlets for these so differently endowed persons. Most human societies struggle in some way with the problem of reaching a balance between the demands of an orderly society and the intense capacities for sexual expression of, for example, young adolescent males, soldiers long isolated from women, or sailors ashore. The greater the recognition of intractable physiological appetites which can only be diverted at a price, the more successful social standards can be. Many societies demand that the more successful and energetic men support two wives instead of one, and conversely, in Victorian England a whole bevy of well-disciplined maiden aunts sometimes subsisted emotionally on the marriage of one sister, spending all their warmth and affection on one set of nephews and nieces.

If human societies were faced only with the problem of disciplining sex, of making sure that children were protected from damaging sexual advances, that little girls did not become pregnant too early or young boys have too heavy a burden placed upon their sexuality, and that some orderly division of sexual favors was worked out so that competition for them would not impair the social functioning of the society, the whole problem would take a different shape. But the restrictive side of sexual regulation is only half the story. True, each society has the task of seeing to it that men and women do not have sex relations in socially disapproved ways, the task of bringing up boys and girls in such a manner that they will adopt the socially approved alternatives to sex at any given time, so that in societies with a celibate priesthood a certain number of properly gifted boys will want to become celibates, and so that, in a socially mobile society like our own, many boys and girls will be willing to delay marriage until their education is complete. But in every society it is necessary also to bring up a sufficient portion of the population in such a way that they will want to marry and beget children. In a caste or class society, it is necessary to train children to be positively attracted by suitable rather than unsuitable people, which means in the last analysis that human beings need to be sufficiently interested in the kind of spouses that society approves for them so that they will be continuingly attracted to each other. How attracted members of each sex have to be, what is considered the ideal number of children, how long marriage partners have to maintain sexual interest in each other if the marriage is to be stable—these things vary from one society to another. But the problem is always there. Stripping the body nude, performing all bodily acts in public, divesting sex of all mystery and privacy would not, as the moralists who see only one side of the question fear, result in unbridled license, but might very soon lead to unlimited boredom. Our records of the courts of kings and the seats of tyrants and dictators, of jailers who could abuse their prisoners, and of slave owners who had free access to their slaves give a consistent picture: unbridled freedom to do anything one likes with anyone one chooses, without regard to his or her genuine assent or consent, leads in the end to satiety, to an increasing unreliability of response, to a search for more and more artificial expedients.

Society has two problems—how to keep sex activity out of forbidden channels that will endanger the bodies and souls of others or the orderly co-operative processes of social life, *and* how to keep it flowing reliably in those channels where it is a necessity if children are to be conceived and reared in homes where father and mother are tied together by the requisite amount of sexual interest. If half the members of a society are celibate (because of the religious system or because of a shortage of land, for example), then the other half, charged with producing the children, must maintain a steady sexual interest in their mates if they are to produce and rear properly the necessary number of children. If the social ideal includes the belief, as is increasingly the case in the United States, that people who are not happy together should not stay together but should seek someone else to be happy with, and if "being happy with" is defined either as having children or as enjoying a shared sex life, we see immediately the growth of sterility clinics and the flourishing of adoption, if children are the emphasis, and the growth of books on sex technique and an increasing amount of marriage counseling on sex problems, if sexual satisfaction is regarded as central. Stated briefly, every society has the task of bringing up children who will focus their capacities for sexual feeling on particular persons, with or without overt bodily expression, and who will not only refrain from large amounts of undirected, objectless sex behavior, but will be able to produce the proper intensity of feeling, expressed or unexpressed, for the proper objects.

Seen in this way, the multitude of small and large taboos we find to surround talking about the body, witnessing the bodily acts of others, writing or drawing pictures of bodily acts, can be put in context. These taboos are two-way taboos. They prevent the kind of sex behavior one doesn't want—keep children and adults apart, keep men out of their neighbors' houses when the husbands are away, keep a chance encounter during excretion from turning into a sexual adventure—*and* they provide the necessary stimuli to sex activity in the right places. Where young men grow up with the degree of shyness characteristic of contemporary lower-class English or Australians, with one kind of language and behavior appropriate for the company of men and another for the company of women, where girls belong to a mysterious world, the mere excitement of sitting next to a girl in the movies is sufficiently enchanting to make it expected or usual for a man to marry the first girl he takes out, and with minor and regrettable occasional aberrations (which, however, are usually impersonal, brief and essentially meaningless) to remain faithful to this one girl, as his wife, through life. In societies that depend upon chaperonage rather than shyness, it is the *situation* that becomes the determining factor. After a chaperoned courtship, the young couple are left alone together, a sufficiently entrancing experience to work a magic of its own. In societies like modern America, where young people, unchaperoned and far from shy, are permitted a great deal of both casual and sexually open companionship, the reliance for attraction permanent enough to ensure marriage has shifted to a much more specific sense of "clicking," which often arises from highly accidental factors, such as meeting under circumstances when the good girl of one's own class looks as if she might really be a bad girl, etc. Such an attraction is often hard put to maintain itself through the years of croup kettles and dishwashing.

The question of regulation also comes up in relation to pornography, which manifests itself in some form in every human society—if only in an insistence on a euphemism for the sex organs which, if abandoned, can immediately create sex excitement. The bawdy laughter explodes as often in a primitive society where people wear practically no clothes at all at some pictured juxtaposition, for example, of a canoe prow and a human body, as it does in a men's smoking room in a university town. The sets of taboos and the requirements of etiquette ensure that the unusual or the unexpected which in any way involves the human body will be stimulating and will evoke in a group an explosive bawdy vocal response, usually loud laughter, and a more specific bodily response when the individual is alone or with possible sexual partners. Every human society has room in it for the pornographer to operate.

Every society has, and has to have, standards as to what is private and what shared behavior, what behavior can only be shared decently by those who are equally involved in it. All bodily acts which temporarily blot out other considerations and focus attention on themselves can become to some degree repellent and disgusting to those who are themselves momentarily or completely detached from such desires or urgencies, and all societies prescribe to what degree eating, elimination, courtship, copulation, childbirth, menstruation, illness and death must be sheltered from or shared with spectators. In some societies childbirth is a casual matter until there is danger that mother or child may die, and then the chattering people gathered at the other end of the house become quiet, hurry away to seek protective magic, or flee from the house that may become a house of death rather than birth. In some societies, a sharp difference exists between the degree of excretory freedom permitted males and that permitted females, and females must seek greater privacy, because it is male, and not female, aggression against them that is feared. In some religious groups, men and women who are strangers to each other may kneel close together in a church without fear that the presence of a member of the opposite sex will arouse thoughts and feelings inappropriate to the sacred occasion, but Moslem men, whose women are rigorously guarded from the eyes of strange men, want no women in the mosque to endanger the carefully prepared ritual purity of their bodies. Western Europe has long made a custom of the family meal at which members of both sexes and of all generations may eat together with pleasure and without embarrassment, but there are still many taboos, disguised as etiquette or "consideration," operating against the intrusion of people who are not eating upon those who are ("We'll wait till you finish your dinner"), or against the intrusion of someone who is eating on those who have no food, as for example taking out a large and beautiful lunch in a crowded railway coach on a train without a diner— the situation so skillfully utilized by Maupassant in *Boule de Suif*.

Many societies, especially primitive ones where all human behavior can be more consistently ritualized, have been able to dignify group sexual behavior on certain ritual occasions— a great feast, a ceremony to encourage the crops to grow so that the people may be fed. But here again the question of participation is central. An orgy for all which serves group goals ceases to be an orgy, and so is dignified. Participation at the ceremonial defloration of a bride where all the guests participate, publicly, is an occasion regarded as essential for the well-being of the group. There is nothing secret, nothing shameful. Participation can be quite as solemn as is the non-participation of the men of the Manus tribe, who stay scrupulously indoors and do not peek while a recent widow is walked, by a group of wailing women, naked through the shallow sea. These same men describe with lascivious giggles their spying on similar ceremonies in the neighboring tribe. But the insistence on regulating this question of privacy and participation, and the insistence that where experiences of bodily involvement are shared they must be shared under strict rules, are found in every society. The framework erected is never perfect. There are always chinks behind which the exploiter of inexperience and prurience can beckon and through which the ignorant and the prurient can peek.

And the most available source of forbidden stimulation becomes naturally the behavior of people with different rules, the people of the next tribe: for the Russians, the Armenians; for the English, the French; in a complex society, the people of a different class, a different religious persuasion, a different habit of life. Even in a relatively static society contrasts among rules permit a continuous traffic in accounts and pictures of behavior which is dignified and meaningful for one group and titillating for members of another. Paintings of nude figures, medical works that give detailed descriptions of the body, records of psychiatric interviews, literature that deals explicitly with matters which members of less educated groups are accustomed to refer to only in half-images, half-glimpsed muscular innuendo—these are historically recurrent examples of materials that have a serious meaning for one group and a pornographic meaning for another. The situation is more acute when societies are changing rapidly and when, through translation, the literature of one society is available to another.

As the outspokenness of earlier centuries gave way to the smothering pruderies of the nineteenth, it became apparent in both England and America that young people, especially those in secularized Protestant homes, were not being prepared to deal with sex and that a great many, far too many even in the kind of society that has been content to count its delinquents, its insane, its criminals and its suicides in the millions, were being unnecessarily penalized. City life had replaced country life, the cheerful bawdiness of earlier centuries had succumbed to a primness of speech, families were becoming smaller, stage and music hall provided a less ample verbal and visual education, we were moving toward a single standard and articulate disapproval of a way of life into which men—themselves initiated by "bad women"—initiated their innocent and ignorant wives. There was, and remains, an urgent need for new forms of serious preparation for sexual behavior, for new ways of satisfying the curiosities of the young during the period when they are either physically or socially too immature to experience sex at first hand, for new kinds of instruction for those who are no longer acquainted with childbirth by the first-hand simplicities of the farm, who no longer see a cow bred or a lamb born, who are so unacquainted with the facts of life and death that they may never perhaps even have watched a bird or a kitten die. We need something to replace the warm ties that bound the generations together in the large families where births were frequent and death came to young and old alike, where marriages were greeted with group roistering within prescribed rules that were broad enough to leave the youngsters who wished to know what it was all about in very little doubt that marriage was a state into which bride and groom entered with nervous expectations of delight. The problem of transition from the nineteenth century was and still is acute. How were those who had been reared within one set of taboos to break them without conveying a sense of shock and outrage even as they spoke courageously? How were they to deal simultaneously with their elders and their contemporaries and the children whose eyes they wished to open more felicitously? The whole battle is vividly portrayed in the passionate aesthetic and ethical statements of Havelock Ellis. Thanks to the shock he gave his contemporaries, and to the activities of pandering fly-by-night publishers, his work—so intensely ethical—is still sometimes read for a pornographic thrill by naive and ill-informed college students.

It is fascinating to take up today such a book as *Nature's Truths Told to a Little Maid* by Margaret Irving, published in 1912, with its cover of a little girl with her arms around the neck of her gentle, highly bred mother, and with Longfellow's "Maiden with the Meek Brown Eyes" on the first page. This book explains gently that "Father and Mother Flower sometimes live in the same flower mansion," and "when they do not live together, they have to send their little messages of love and devotion by the butterflies and the bees." Nowhere in the book is there really anything on which a child could build an understanding of the male's role in procreation, although that of the mother is a little more explicit: "She is smaller than the father . . . gentle, patient and loving and . . . watches over her dear babies, feeds them and warms them from her own delicate body." But the sense of danger that every word spoken, even words that seem to us today pallid, cowardly, sentimental and evasive, may be turned into an occasion for snickering pornography or neighborhood scandal shines through the passionate admonition: "*Never* ask a question of a *sacred* nature, such as we have been talking about, of your little companions, or mention *any* of *these* things to them; for you have entered, dear, into the Holy of Holies. The subject is too solemn to be talked about; and the people who do mention these things should be avoided, as their talk is a desecration." Behind that statement stands the kind of father, reared in the late nineteenth century, who would say in a grave rebuke to a younger man, "My boy, that is an awfully nice thing to do, and an awfully nasty thing to talk about."

Precariously balanced as we are at every moment on the razor edge between sex in its place and sex out of place, every change in the treatment of any act of the body—in speech, from the pulpit, in literature, in the theater, in the films, in painting and photography—is bound to encounter fear and opposition from the side of the angels and the side of the devils. Those who have successfully mastered their own wayward hearts cry out against being tempted in places where they had thought they were safe; men who had learned to avert their eyes from women's ankles were singularly defenseless against Annette Kellerman bathing suits, as a later generation, schooled to the frankness of the bathing suit, can be caught again by the witchery of brassieres padded with foam rubber. And those on the other side have an even deeper commitment to the preservation of "decency," to keeping the definition of obscenity wide and loose, so that they may advertise their books in paper jackets, charge immense prices at night clubs where nothing at all happens, sell their packets of postcards of "Great Art." Every shift threatens the safety of those who have learned how to be good—often at a great price, and the pocketbooks of those who have lived parasitically off breaches in the stylized morality of their contemporaries.

Within this situation, the judges who must pass rulings in our courts interpreting the unchanging intent of our society, as of every human society, to protect the inexperienced, the ignorant and the innocent, the weak and the faltering from exploitation and unwanted temptation, have no easy task, beset as they are from both sides by those who do not want standards to change with changing times. New problems arise when radio or television can be turned on downstairs in the living room by a childish hand while mother is upstairs with the new baby, when books that once had to be carried out under the watchful eye of the village librarian or bought for three or four dollars from a meager allowance can be bought quickly, surreptitiously, for a quarter in a drugstore or in a crowded railway station. *Buyer beware* has never applied to children, nor does it apply to adults in any field where we find them incompetent, as in the choice of drugs or preserved foods or the selection of meat or milk. Just because all treatment of sex has to deal with two necessities—the necessity to control it and the necessity to cherish it—and because the releasing stimulus is simply *novelty*, this is a problem as old as human society and one that is likely to be with us always. It will never be solved, as some enthusiasts think, by spreading a "sane, healthy attitude toward sex," summed up in such home truths as "Play, play with boys and girls all *together, live in the sunshine.*"

The nudist cults illustrate this dilemma vividly. Their exponents, while fighting for the right to sell on the newsstands magazines containing pictures the rest of the world finds suggestive, will also assure one that life in a nudist camp is very moral—the boys and girls never even touch each other. So, where in contemporary life there are few taboos on a boy's putting his arm around a girl's waist on the dance floor or on running arm in arm into the surf, provided both of them are wearing appropriate bathing suits, the nudist cults would substitute a world in which one may see but be careful not to touch! Most peoples of the world, having found that the sense of touch is the sense most reliably related to vividness of feeling, would feel justly deprived by such an exchange; they may feel that those who would promote it (having become, by accident or the exploited pruriences of an earlier period, unduly interested in looking) are elevating nudity to a morality, and thus robbing those who can better balance sight and touch in what they feel to be their birthright: the chance to explore the final mysteries of another's body only in the strictest privacy, while being permitted to lay a hand lightly in public on a dancing partner's arm. Some patterning, some mystery is necessary. Different periods, different kinds of work and play, different relationships between the sexes will demand new patterns. Absence of pattern is unthinkable; without it human creatures, hardly to be called human beings, would vacillate between promiscuity and boredom, and society would be impossible to maintain.

But once we recognize that contrasts between the standards of one group and another—between age groups in a changing society, between neighboring countries, between class and occupational groups within a country—create a problem because one milieu will always permit speech, writing, and visual representation which will be regarded as salacious in another, what kind of solution can be suggested? If we grant that we do not want a static, closed society in which every detail of life is fixed and unchangeable (even if such a society were possible), and if we grant that the problem of patterning bodily behavior—treating some aspects as public, some as private—will always be with us, are there any insights which can be offered as background for the style of censorship appropriate to the present period?

One possible contribution to the whole question would be to separate out and get very clear the ways in which intrinsically pornographic material differs from material that the prurient *finds* pornographic and from that which the panderer can *make* pornographic by focusing attention on five pages out of five hundred.

We may define pornography, cross-culturally, as words or acts or representations that are calculated to stimulate sex feelings independent of the presence of another loved and chosen human being. If the original expression was not designed to so stimulate—if, for instance, a book on obstetrics has been written to instruct midwives, a book on biology to describe reproduction, the biography of a poet to throw light on his creativity, or if a pair of lovers have sought what they thought was complete privacy in a country lane—and if it does so stimulate, then the reader of the book or the person who spies secretly on the lovers, hoping to be aroused, contributes his pornographic intent to something which is not itself pornographic. Similarly, the little fly-by-night publishers who sell repackaged serious literary works or serious scientific books with lurid promises of the titillation contained within the covers are comparable to the innkeeper who, unbeknown to the lovers who seek shelter beneath his roof, also conducts a voyeuristic brothel.

The starved, unhappy adolescent, curious, ashamed, afraid to talk to anyone, restlessly lifting books off top library shelves, is a subject for compassion. But those commercial outfits which debase serious work belong in the same class as panderers, exploiting pitiful needs in a way that does not still the needs but makes them all the more insatiable. In addition to the reader or watcher who searches wherever he is able, who finds even the dictionary a source of secret excitement, the bibliographical panderer who includes Havelock Ellis' *Little Essays on Love and Virtue* and a reproduction of Giorgione's *Family* on his lists of publications that will be mailed in a plain cover, and the seeking adolescent—all of whom are using for one special purpose books and paintings designed to meet the needs of men for knowledge and beauty—there is, of course, the *creator* of pornographic art and literature, the writer or artist or photographer who sets out to write or reproduce that which will, by its unusualness, by being something that ordinarily is not pictured or verbalized or done, whet the appetite of those whose desire does not yet have, no longer has, or never had an object.

Consider, for example, this advertisement for *The Whip: A Novelette:*

Showing how a beautiful young woman is seized with the frenzy of her father's great whip so that she cannot love or be loved without it. She methodically sets out to seduce a young English clergyman who is madly in love with her. She torments him with torturing desires and suspense until she has worked him to a point of madness, which is her aim. Then: "She let him see her body. She made him aware of every part of her. She moved her breast toward him with a gentle caressing gesture. She ran her tapering fingers down the length of her body like fluttering birds. And then she froze, and he knew she had done it deliberately. And then his eyes fell on the whip and he saw nothing else." From there on the developments are sensational beyond hint or suggestion.*

The question of intrinsic pornography—whether a book or work simply contains passages that might be regarded by many as pornographic or whether there is anything in the way such passages are handled that provides a clue to the intent of the book as a whole—is admittedly an exceedingly difficult problem. But difficult as it may be to establish in a particular case, in general a discussion of intent clarifies the subject. As one vigorous young American woman remarked of a rather famous literary production containing passages of which the pornographic or the nonpornographic character has been disputed: "It *is* pornographic. For why, because fat little old bald Mr. X is writing about a lot of things he never did."

And she might have added, for people who will never do them.

The character of the daydream as distinct from reality is an essential element in pornography. True, the adolescent may take a description of a real event and turn it into a daydream, the vendor of pornography may represent a medical book as full of daydream material, but the material of true pornography is compounded of daydreams themselves, composed without regard for any given reader or looker, to stimulate and titillate. It bears the signature of nonparticipation—of the dreaming adolescent, the frightened, the impotent, the bored and sated, the senile, desperately concentrating on unusualness, on drawing that which is not usually drawn, writing words on a plaster wall, shifting scenes and actors about, to evoke and feed an impulse that has no object: no object either because the adolescent is not yet old enough to seek sexual partners, or because the recipient of the pornography has lost the precious power of spontaneous sexual feeling. From day-

---

* From an advertisement for Number Seven of *American Aphrodite: A Quarterly for the Fancy-Free* (The Only Privately Published Periodical in the World) in a mailing circular sent out by Lunar Books, 110 Lafayette Street, New York 13, New York.

dreamer to daydreamer the material passes, always bearing the hallmark of a disproportionate concentration on unusual types of recording or representation or action, "in such quantity or of such nature," to quote a legal decision "as to flavor the whole," so that it becomes, in a more direct colloquial definition, "dirt per se."

But if we have defined pornography as that which will stimulate the senses in the absence of an object on the one hand, or the absence of adequate desire on the other, we must then ask whether it is something to be regarded as wholly evil. What about the burning passions of adolescents, the prisoner in his cell, the soldier with his pin-up girl? Aswell's *The Midsummer Fires* describes with convincing clarity the relationship which exists between the haunted painter of the pin-up girl and the old banker who has lived in meager marital fidelity, haunted by visions of pin-up girls.

In a society where there are several religious groups and many millions with no religion at all, can any one religious group demand that the government representing the wider society protect its particular members from temptation? Is it not fair, rather, for the state to reply: Train your young people to be less vulnerable. Do not rely on a degree of ignorance or inexperience which can only be maintained in a closed system. Does not freedom of religion carry with it the obligation of any religious group to educate its members so that they can live in the wider society? (Conversely, how is the secular society to be protected from the products of small self-contained sects —whose shy, innocent girls may safely read sadistic horrors called the lives of martyrs—when their members write and publish the murderous daydreams, which did little harm within the closed enclave of an isolated sect, to be read by millions who were reared in a different way?)

Or a different line of argument may be followed when people wish to make a distinction between children and adolescents on the one hand, and adults on the other, denying to youth that which is designed to corrupt youth, but permitting adults, grown weary and impotent, to make their own choices. Such arguments are reinforced when adults make use of pornographic devices as a way of keeping alive the flickering flame of middle-aged passion within marriage, where the pornographic daydreams become essential to the continuance of the prescribed relationship between husband and wife. Isn't there a difference between the inexperience and immaturity of youth and the conscious choice of adults? Don't we everywhere distinguish between those who are too young and those who are old enough to accomplish their own ruin—or in less extreme terms, to choose the perverse autoerotic daydream rather than a whole living relationship with a real person? If we attempt to preserve this distinction, then mass communications—movies, television, paper books*—bring us up against the fact that in such media it is impossible to discriminate between children and adults. We can keep children under sixteen out of theaters or movie houses, keep their allowances so low that they cannot afford to buy expensive books, and train librarians to hide books that are regarded as unfit for children. But where the child, with a turn of the dial or an easily earned quarter, can listen or look or read, with no adult present to censor, this becomes impossible. Either, in order to protect youth, one must protect everybody, even perhaps to the point of banning serious novels because a class of fourteen-year-olds, quite unable to comprehend the whole, will pass the book around the school room with a greasy little note, "See page 440," until page 440 becomes greasy and ragged, or of destroying the beauty of statues from other lands by adding little false sarongs. We have to choose between bowdlerizing everything and devising some better method. For today youth and age share in the same world; the mass media that have wiped out the difference between rich and poor, so that both may buy *Life* or *Look* for twenty cents, and both may enjoy Rita Hayworth even if one pays $1.50 at the Radio City Music Hall and the other thirty-five cents at a neighborhood movie, have also wiped out the possibility of discriminating between adult and adolescent.

But there are other remedies, and a page might be taken from the practice of the Catholic Church and its Index.† In the days when, and in the countries where, everyone was Catholic, it was possible to ban books altogether. No substantial proportion of the population would defend them, and unsuitable books could be impounded or burned. If the forbidden flourished, as it always does to some extent, it flourished in alleys, precariously, not on bookstalls in a railway station next to a church. But in the modern world where many different religious groups and those who acknowledge allegiance to none must live side by side, it is impossible to ban and burn books as can be done in a state where only one religion flourishes. The Church has developed the Index, a list of books which good Catholics are admonished not to read, except with special permission for scholarly or clerical reasons. This does not mean that some Catholics do not read such books; it is

* For an excellent general comment on paper books see Freeman Lewis, *Paper-bound Books in America*, 16th of the R. R. Bowker Memorial Lectures, the New York Public Library, 1952.
† See Redmond A. Burke, *What is the Index?* Milwaukee: The Bruce Publishing Company, 1952.

quite possible that in some cases unscrupulous publishers are as pleased when a book is put on the Index as they are when it is attacked by the Watch and Ward Society of Boston, for both insure a certain kind of sale, to those who read in hope of finding the forbidden. The Index performs a very important function: it makes Catholic readers aware of the kind of books they are reading. They may read them, but as they read, a persistent sense of alertness to sin defines the situation and to a degree protects them from a loss of values. In fact, it may even sharpen their sense of values, in the sense that Russian Christians used to claim that those who had sinned and repented had a more highly developed ethical sensitivity than those who had never sinned. When I was a child my mother forbade me to read the books of Horatio Alger because they were "bad literature." Of course this stimulated me to read them, but as I read, I searched diligently for some clue as to how the style, the choice of words and themes, constituted something that could be defined as "bad" as opposed to "good" literature. In a world where we are surrounded by bad literature, experience with what is labeled cheap, clichéd, dull, with bathos and synthetic daydream, may be a good insurance against a debased taste—a better insurance, perhaps, than steeping a child's mind only in great and beautiful literature.

The same course of reasoning can be followed in the case of pornography. But legislative decrees on the subject of decency are only half the answer. These will, it is true, ensure that the genuinely pornographic will be sold surreptitiously, and the whispered word, the leer of the vendor or of the schoolmate serves, like the Index, to put the new consumer on guard: "This is pornographic, forbidden." But this is not enough. It is likewise important that the guns of those who embody organized values, those who care about religion, those who care about literature and art, about science and medicine, and about protecting the young, should be trained against labeling anything pornographic when it is *not* pornographic.

Actually, it is as important at present to legislate against false labeling as against the content of a particular book. Every time a publisher puts a cover on a twenty-five-cent edition of a serious and important book promising illicit delights to the prurient, the issue between pornography on the one hand and literature, art, science and ethics on the other is obscured.

The Roman Catholic Church has long recognized the danger of "indifferentism" in religion, a lazy tolerance which casually accepts all religions without feeling any strong sense of the differences among them. Today we face the danger of indifferentism in literature dealing with sex. The serious and the cheap are not adequately differentiated; the great novel of experience in which for the first time a writer tries to deal with some subject which has hitherto been taboo is placed side by side with a book in which the reader is guaranteed a story of rape in a church pew or a set of pictures of nudes in long black stockings. Serious manuals on sex behavior, which are needed in a world where individuals grow up in extreme isolation from the diverse ongoing processes of human life, are placed side by side with primers of exotic forms of eroticism. If every publisher who issued a serious work in a pornographic wrapper was subject to indictment similar—although paradoxically in reverse—to prosecution under the Pure Food and Drug Act, we might begin to steer our way through this maze in which we find ourselves as we obliterate, hastily, without due consideration, the distinctions between the masses and the classes, adults and children, the pure and the impure. To the old abused adage, "To the pure all things are pure," should be added, "To the inexperienced, great confusion is possible."

It is, also, useful to distinguish between the pornographic, condemned in every society, and the bawdy, the ribald, the shared vulgarities and jokes, which are the safety valves of most social systems. Pornography is a most doubtful safety valve. In extreme cases it may feed the perverted imagination of the doomed man who starts by pulling a little girl's braid and ends by cutting off a little girl's head, as each increasing stimulus loses its effectiveness and must be replaced by a more extreme one. This is particularly true of the pornography primarily designed to be brooded over in secret. But it is quite otherwise with the music hall jokes, the folk ribaldry at a wedding, the innocent smut of the smoking room, where men who are perennially faithful to their wives exchange stories which release explosive laughter. Pornography does not lead to laughter; it leads to deadly serious pursuit of sexual satisfaction divorced from personality and from every other meaning. The uproarious laugh of the group who recognize a common dilemma—the laughter of a group of women at the story of the intractable unborn who refused to budge and merely shivered under the effects of the quart of ice cream hopefully eaten by its poor mother, the laughter of a group of men at the story of the bride who asked to be "frightened" a fourth time—is the laughter of human beings who are making the best of the imperfect social arrangements within which their life here on earth is conducted, colonizers of heaven working with recognizable, imperfect equipment for the development of the human soul.

Such laughter is the counterpoint of the good life. Shared,

consecrated by usage and tradition, it is an underwriting of virtue rather than an incitement to vice. Like every other kind of material which deals with the body, and especially with sex, these jokes can be misused, or labeled pornography when they are not, but the criteria of happy sharing and of laughter holds. The difference between the music hall in which a feeble carrot waves above a bowl of cauliflower while roars of laughter shake the audience of husband and wives on their weekly outing, and the strip tease, where lonely men, driven and haunted, go alone, is the difference between the paths to heaven and hell, a difference which any society obscures to its peril.

Hollis Summers

HOW THEY CHOSE THE DEAD

Last year Hollis Summers toured thirty-three colleges and universities by courtesy of the Ford Fund for the Advancement of Education, studying the state of writing courses in American colleges and universities. Born in 1916 in Eminence, Kentucky, Mr. Summers was schooled in Kentucky, and received his Ph.D. at the State University of Iowa in 1949. He has taught high school in Covington, Kentucky, then at Georgetown College in Georgetown, and since 1949 at the University of Kentucky in Lexington. The author of two novels, CITY LIMIT and BRIGHTEN THE CORNER, and shorter pieces that have appeared in magazines, Mr. Summers is married and the father of two boys.

Margaret stuck one candle in the middle of Chip's birthday cake, and I lit it with my cigarette lighter. "Blow, blow, Chip," Margaret said.

But Chip didn't blow. He just held the new plastic ball with both hands and banged it against the tray of his highchair. The bell inside the ball tinkled and Chip laughed. Margaret and I laughed too.

"It's wonderful, isn't it?" I said.

"It's wonderful," Margaret said. She leaned against the sink and watched Chip bang the ball. "He won't ever die, will he? He's so beautiful."

The ball slipped from Chip's hand and clinked onto the floor. It didn't roll far. It only wobbled and the bell rang inside it.

"Damn," I said, and Chip said something that sounded like damn, and then he said, "Car, car."

He never did get the idea of blowing out the candle. Once during lunch he put his chin in the icing and drew back as if he'd been burned. We laughed at that too. The frosting was like lather on his face; he licked his face; he licked his lips and laughed with us and said, "Car-car."

"Chip wants to take a long, long ride," Margaret said. "That's what you want, isn't it, Chip? For a birthday present."

Chip banged the blue plastic ball and the bell rang and we got ready to take the long long ride. I put Chip's mattress in the back of our coupé. I covered the mattress with a sheet and tucked in the corners as if it were a hospital bed. Margaret fixed part of the birthday dinner for a picnic. She had fried chicken and the first tomatoes from our garden and cans of liver and spinach and custard. "And he'll have cake for dessert," Margaret said. "Cake, Chip, you hear that?"

She forgot the diapers and we had to turn around at the edge of town and come back. I wasn't even annoyed with her for forgetting, and she said that I drove better than she did.

"I'm glad we got to see our house again anyhow," Margaret said. "I'm not sorry about leaving the diapers."

"It's a beautiful house," I said.

Chip stood up on his mattress and pressed his face against the back window. He beat the blue ball against the glass.

"Chip's glad we came back. He never heard of its being bad luck."

The motor of the car sounded good. I was listening to the motor. "It's never been bad luck," I said after a minute. "And we're always forgetting things."

"I love you," Margaret said. "I love you and Chip."

"I love you and Chip." I rolled the window up so that there wouldn't be too much air in the back.

Neither of us has any idea how far we drove. I keep trying to visualize the mileage numbers under the speedometer, but nothing comes. We know, of course, that we passed through Carrollton, and that's twenty-three miles from home. It was just two o'clock in Carrollton. The clock over the courthouse said so.

I said, "It's time for his nap, isn't it?"

And Margaret said, "You don't have naps on your birthday, you ought to know that."

Chip came over in the front seat with us. He sat between us and began a lot of talk without words. He didn't look sleepy.

I drove around the courthouse a couple of times and then turned right and went over a bridge. We're both sure we went over a bridge, even though we didn't think anything about it at the time. In a little while we hit a macadam road that had sugar maples along the sides. The road was a cave. The sun shone through the leaves and ran ahead of us. I don't remember being conscious of any fields beyond the trees.

"Maybe we'll come across some place that's just terrific," Margaret said.

"It's pretty, isn't it?"

"Like a bad painting." Margaret began to hum to herself. Chip leaned against her, but he didn't go to sleep. The trees stopped for a while and then they started again. I remember that I kept wondering what it would be like to hear a love song when you were an old man. I wondered if it would be like anything. I started to ask Margaret about it, and then I didn't.

It was probably about three o'clock when we reached the park. My wrist watch had stopped, and I didn't bother to wind it. The time didn't matter.

Margaret sat up suddenly. "What did I tell you? Something terrific."

"You been asleep?"

"No, of course not."

"Damn," Chip said, or something that sounded like it.

The name of the place was Highland Park. We're sure of that. The letters were written over the entrance in electric bulbs. We noticed when we left that one of the bulbs in the G had burned out. I swung the car under the bulbs that spelled Highland Park. A man at the gate came out and smiled at us.

"Thirty cents. A dime for each rider and a dime for the car." The man spoke slowly as if he had all of the time in the world.

"But there are three of us." I nodded at Chip. He sat up and blinked his eyes. The side of his face was red and there was perspiration around the line of his hair.

"You got a fine boy," the man said. "No charge for him."

"But we want to pay for him," Margaret said. "It's his birthday."

"No charge." The man gave me my change, a Franklin half dollar and two dimes. I made the car follow some painted arrows to the parking place.

"It's funny, I wanted to pay for him too," I said.

"We will." Margaret patted her handkerchief around Chip's forehead and neck. "Chip will be a big boy and some day . . ." She wasn't thinking about what she was saying because she stopped and said, "Look, Chip, a swimming pool. A wonderful big swimming pool."

"What do you think of that, Chip?"

"I wonder why nobody's ever told us about this place." Right away Margaret began taking off Chip's clothes.

There wasn't any charge for Chip again, even though we explained about its being his birthday. I told Margaret I'd take him with me, since I dressed faster than she did. Chip wore a pair of training pants. He looked pretty proud of himself. I put him in the wire basket which the desk man had given me. Chip's eyes were big and he said, "Water." Then he said something that sounded like "Oogle," and I said it back to him. We had quite a conversation while I got into the rented trunks.

"Bye," Chip said, and I said, "Bye."

"You're crazy about that kid, aren't you?" A man spoke behind me. I turned around quickly because I had thought we were the only people in the dressing room. The man wore white swimming trunks and his skin was very brown.

"He's a good guy," I told the man. "This is his birthday."

"You can tell that all right," the man said.

I slipped the elastic identification bracelet around my ankle, and took Chip out of the basket. "Is the water good?"

"The water's fine." The man had disappeared by the time I turned to take my clothes back to the desk. I could hear his feet splash through the antiseptic trough outside the dressing room.

The concrete floor was slick. I slipped once. I held to Chip. He laughed as if we had a joke.

Margaret was waiting for us. "Now who dresses fast?" She stood at the edge of the sand which led to the pool. She pulled at the sides of a white bathing cap, and she ran ahead of us over the sand. I was surprised at how much sand they had around the pool. It was like a regular beach. Margaret looked wonderful in the rented bathing suit. It was the color of the yellow sand.

Chip grunted and held to my neck. My shoulder was sunburned from working in the yard and he hurt like the devil. I told him so.

"You know what the last one in is," Margaret shouted. "Hurry!" She beat the water with her hands.

Chip liked the pool right from the first. We stayed in the shallow end the whole time. I don't remember anybody around us, but Margaret says there were some children and a few parents. The place was big though. I told Margaret I ought to go back to the car and get the new ball, but she said there wasn't any need. We took turns swinging Chip through the water.

After a while a wind came up from somewhere. Chip began to shiver a little and we decided it was time to go in. Chip didn't want to get out of the water. He cried and kicked at me, and Margaret kept saying, "Look here, look here, is that our Chip?"

It was almost cold in the dressing room. There wasn't anybody at the desk so I reached over the counter and got the wire basket. A couple of towels with Highland Park written on them lay on top of our clothes. The G was blurred. I dried Chip as well as I could. "Look here, look here," I kept saying. I slapped my foot down against the floor and splashed water. The floor was covered with water now. I wondered at the time if the wind had driven the water out of the pool. Chip sniffed and chewed at his upper lip.

But when we met Margaret we forgot about the wind. We took our picnic basket to a table which was shaded by a red and white umbrella. Chip sat in Margaret's lap. "What shall we have for the birthday boy?" Margaret asked. Chip was frowning and then he began to laugh. He said, "Water," and he patted Margaret's arm with his hand.

I ordered a couple of beers and Margaret asked the waiter if it would be too much trouble to fix the juice of two oranges, no water, and to sterilize the glass. The waiter said it wouldn't be any trouble at all. Generally, when we had Chip out we looked around to see who was watching—that's the way we judged people: if they smiled at Chip they were good characters. But we didn't look at anybody that afternoon in Highland Park. The table was an island. We talked about things which we both knew well; we didn't know at the time that our conversation was important. I didn't pay for the orange juice—that came to me only yesterday. I had looked at the bill that afternoon too. I had noticed that it was written in a small backhand, like a woman's writing. I thought at the time that it would be a crazy joke if God turned out to be a woman.

When we finished eating, we walked around a little. Highland Park was big. It seemed to stretch clear to the edge of the land. There was a pavilion for dancing. The orchestra men were already standing at the gate. They wore white suits and dark blue ties. There was even a theater with "Air Cooled" on the marquee in letters that were covered with snow. We couldn't know what time it was, but we knew it was getting late.

"We have time for a ride, though, don't we?" I said.

"Maybe one. Would you like to take a fun ride, Chip?"

Chip rubbed his eyes with the back of his hand. He looked shy. He had just started looking shy that week.

We decided on the ferris wheel. It was big, like everything in Highland Park, but it moved slowly, the way a sleepy mind moves. I didn't even try to pay Chip's fare to the man who stood at the bottom of the wheel. We told Chip to notice the bulbs, no bigger than Christmas tree lights, that outlined the spokes of the wheel. Chip looked at them, but he didn't say anything.

It was a long ride for eleven cents. The man who pressed the stick smiled at us every time we curved down past him. He was a big man, and he reminded me of the fellow in the white trunks at the bathhouse, or the waiter, but I can't remember his face. Margaret thinks that his eyes were dark, but I can't remember his eyes.

Once the wheel stopped when we were at the very top. Chip pushed against the rail which fastened us in. It was light still, but suddenly the bulbs on the wheel blinked on. They were blinding at first. I couldn't see anything but the lights which were threaded through the wheel. After a minute the Park beneath us came back into place. The bulbs were in soft colors and Chip tried to reach for them.

"We have to get home, don't we, I guess?" Margaret said. She spoke loudly, as if she had to shout above the soft light. I nodded to her. "We're going to have to go home," she said to the man as we swung past him.

The man smiled. He took us around another time, and then the wheel stopped and the seat we were in rocked back and forth like a cradle.

"Thank you very much," Margaret said. "Very fine ride."

"Thanks," Chip said, or something that sounded like it.

The man did not speak. We are sure of that.

When we passed the theater two young people were dancing in the foyer to a kind of Negro spiritual with a heavy rhythm background. It seemed strange for them to be dancing to a hymn. Margaret said that it seemed strange to her too.

Chip was sound asleep before we got to the car. I laid him on his mattress. Margaret and I stood and watched him, our arms around each other. He rolled over once and then he settled on his back, gone to the world. His right arm was thrown above his head, and the fingers of his hands were loose.

"Don't you wish you could sleep like that?" I said.

"Don't I?" Margaret said. I didn't know what she meant.

I helped her in the car and closed the door carefully. Then I got in on my side and started the engine and eased out of the parking lot. No one was at the gate. Margaret said that we had forgotten to bring a blanket. "But we didn't forget much, did we?" She was whispering.

"Not much," I said, and we both laughed.

Margaret stood on her knees and covered Chip with one of the diapers from the basket. "Do you mind putting your window up?" she said. "The air's stronger back there."

I put the window up and we started through the cave of trees. I pulled at Margaret's shoulder and she moved over beside me. "Yeah," I said.

"It's not like any day, is it?"

"That's right."

The road curved. Margaret leaned forward. "You'd think we could see the lights from the Park, wouldn't you?"

"Maybe we've come too far."

Once Margaret said, "I hope I remembered to turn off the gas under the water heater," and once I asked her if she wanted a cigarette, and once she read a highway sign aloud, "Slow Cattle Crossing." I don't remember anything else we said until just before the city limit of Carrollton. Margaret spoke so softly that I didn't hear her at first, then her words sounded against my ear: "I guess nobody could write *Pilgrim's Progress* anymore, could they?"

"Could *he*." Margaret looked up at me. She did not smile. "Sure, sure," I said.

"No, I mean really." Margaret moved away from me. The courthouse was lit up as if it were a funeral parlor or a part of Highland Park.

"There's no point in trying to scare ourselves."

Margaret did not answer.

Beside us was a White Castle hamburger place. Ahead, a street light changed from green to red. A policeman stood on the corner.

I asked, "You want something else to eat?"

"What about Chip?" Margaret placed her hand on the back of the seat to turn around.

"We'll eat in the car." I put on the brakes. Margaret almost lost her balance. "Sorry," I said.

"Why don't you just back up?"

"Isn't there a fire plug?"

"Not much of a one." Margaret was on her knees.

"But there's much of a cop. We'll go around the block." I hummed a tune under my breath. I switched on the dims. The policeman looked at us.

"Chip!" Margaret called.

"Careful, you'll wake him." The light turned to green.

Margaret sucked in her breath. She put her hand on my shoulder. Her hand hurt my shoulder.

"What's the matter with you?" I turned my head. Margaret's face was green in the light. Her eyes were wide and her mouth was opened.

"He's not back here." Margaret spoke softly. The policeman motioned to me. "Chip's not back there."

I reversed the car to the curb beside the fireplug. A sign said, "No Parking Within Ten Feet."

Margaret clicked the light above her head. I put my elbow on the back of the seat, and I leaned on my elbow, and I looked at the mattress. The sheet was rumpled and I could see the outline where Chip's body had been. The plastic ball with the bell inside of it lay in the corner.

I took my left hand and put it on the door handle and pressed down the door handle and the door opened. I stepped on the running board and then down to the ground. I turned around and I pushed back the seat. Chip was not in the car.

The policeman came up to me.

I looked over at Margaret. She lowered her head.

"You havin' some trouble or something?" the policeman said. He was tall and he wore glasses. The right shaft of his glasses was taped with adhesive.

Margaret raised her head very quickly. I could see the pulse beating in her throat. "Could you tell us the way to . . . Highland Park?" she asked.

"Highland Park?" The policeman took off his cap. The cap had left a line on his forehead, and above the line were drops of perspiration. "You sure you got the right name?"

"Highland Park," I said.

"There's Melody Park." The policeman nodded. "You take 32 straight out. You can't miss it."

"No, Highland Park," Margaret said. "It's an amusement park. They have a swimming pool, and a theater, and rides."

"There's Melody Park," the policeman said. "But it's not like that. It's a fine place though. They have bands sometimes."

Tears were in Margaret's eyes, but her voice was even. "It's Highland Park we want. *Highland.* A bulb is burned out of the G."

"If there was such a place around here, I'd know it, lady. I been born and raised here."

"Well, thank you, then." Margaret pushed back the seat and motioned to me. "We mustn't stay here by that fire plug."

I looked at the policeman for a long time. I couldn't see him very well. I wondered if it were the chlorine in the water that made me not see him very well.

"Melody's a mighty nice place," the policeman said.

Margaret held her hands in her lap. The light from the

dashboard showed her hands. She rubbed the nail of her left thumb with the ball of her right thumb.

"God damn." Her words sounded like praying.

But, of course, we couldn't find the road. It was almost daylight when Margaret said, "I guess it doesn't happen to many people . . . this way."

"Margaret?"

"We'd better go home."

She was on her knees. I knew what she was going to reach for. "Please don't. For God's sake, please don't." I didn't mean to shout at her.

She turned around. She hadn't even touched the ball, but the movement of the car made the bell ring.

EVENING IN MADRID

Translated by Anthony Kerrigan

José Suárez Carreño

A resident of Spain since 1920, José Suárez Carreño was born near Mexico City in 1914. He trained as a lawyer in Valladolid and moved to Madrid in 1940. He first attracted literary attention in Spain with a book of poems entitled THE MENACED LAND; in 1944 he won the Adonais Prize with AGE OF MAN. His novel, THE FINAL HOURS, which won the Nadal Prize in 1949, will be published in the United States in 1953 by Alfred A. Knopf. *Evening in Madrid* is the opening section of this novel.

(Evening in Madrid: Copyright, 1953, by Alfred A. Knopf, Inc.)

The girl stopped smoking and stood up suddenly. Her mouth was fixed in a distracted smile, the kind of smile habitual with people who know the necessity of suffering. Making a slight gesture with her head, she shook her hair, a splendid blonde mass falling smoothly to her shoulders. She hesitated a moment, and then picked up a pair of stockings and, with that care and precision of which only women are capable, began to pull them on.

In the bedroom, with the light already switched on, it was quiet, but from another room came the sound of a violent argument. Shocking cries reached the girl, the shrill, nervous voice of a woman, and, now and then, the weary, hoarse voice of a man. While putting on her stockings, Carmen listened to the voices with complete indifference. She had heard them for years, and now they no longer aroused even her curiosity. Like someone silently following a familiar melody, at such moments she sensed, through the outcries, her parents' impatience, exasperation and fury. Abruptly she realized that this was the very despair that she herself had been feeling during the past few quiet hours. "But they have to give vent to it, get it out of their systems." She felt that her own silence of more than a year had been an overwhelming condemnation of them.

Then she began to look at one of her long, shapely, rounded legs poised in mid-air, and she thought of the desire they often evoked. This always filled her with a complex sensation of disgust and pride. She looked at her almost naked body. Her first impression was that its beauty was arid, as the instrument of his craft is for an artisan. She felt everything alive in her being dehumanized, losing all vibrancy. She looked at the room she sat in. It was her own room, and she could detect the peculiarly intimate odor enclosed in it. She saw all the furniture, familiar through years of use. Everything was as always. She was not rootless like so many other girls. She lived with her family. And for a moment she again listened to the voices coming from beyond the door. "They always say the same things," she thought. "I'll never know how much they hate each other. But do they hate?" And she recalled how often after they had exchanged insults and blows she had heard them lock themselves in their room to make love, making her sense the physical bond that held them together. "They are young," she thought, "too young to be my parents. Or perhaps it's that I'm too old to have parents." And suddenly she was aware of her age: nineteen.

The telephone rang. The girl hurried to finish dressing. Through the door she heard her mother's shrill voice. "Señor Aguado is calling you." And then, making the tone of her voice almost confidential, she added: "Carmen, don't forget that we have to pay the rent tomorrow."

"I'm coming. Tell him so. Go on," the girl heard herself say.

The man for whom she was dressing this evening was calling her. She knew in advance (she was well versed in his habits) where they were going to dine and even the courses they both were going to order. She recalled what her mother had just said. "Tomorrow the rent will be paid. And tonight I'll be with this man." And it struck her as strange, as though in a sort of nightmare, that she, the daughter of an ordinary clerk, would find herself in a few hours in a luxurious room in a house of assignation with a fifty-year-old man, a millionaire, seeing him enjoy himself and suffer at the same time.

"Come on. Don't take so long."

It was her mother's voice again. For an instant Carmen recalled that voice as it had sounded years earlier, when she herself was still almost a child. Then it had reached her in the cold of early morning, and Carmen had known that it was time to get up and go to school. Now it was night, and a man was summoning her. Well, he and her parents knew why. And, pulling down the skirt of the black dress she had just put on, she left her room.

2

The man waited at the telephone with intense expectation, as if within that black bakelite apparatus which he had so often used with indifference his destiny itself was now being shaped for him. He, Angel Aguado, was waiting in the cramped confines of a telephone booth for something false and useless, but absolutely necessary to him. He could not hate his wife, though perhaps he despised her. He could not be a normal husband to her, and he had to feel the loathing that he inspired in her—but neither could he break away from her. His desire or love for her was a dead thing, something empty and horribly sweet which he would never stop feeling until he died. It seemed to prove, tragically now, what the dark pain of his childhood as a healthy, rich little boy had been. "You're a girl," other boys had said who got the best of him in fights. He knew that it was not so: he had often pondered the question in terms as pure and cold as a scientific problem. For a long time he had considered himself effeminate. But he was an intelligent man, and he no longer had these doubts. After a strange enough conversation with his wife—at the time they had been married only one year—he had sought out another woman to be his mistress. That would be his liberation. His marriage had been a mistake, like many another. He would leave his wife at once. She had already proposed a separation. But his mistress, after knowing him a few days, ran away. When Angel Aguado knocked on the door of the apartment that he had rented for her and no one answered, he felt—as a dying man perceives things in one prodigious montage—that he, the man knocking on the door for his beloved to open, was dead, would now always be dead to what men call happiness.

He had gone back down the stairs calmly, with terrible calm. On reaching the street door he was conscious of hurried footsteps behind him.

"This letter. The young lady gave it to me for you."

Aguado took it from the woman's hands. For an instant he noticed the cold, penetrating odor of a dirty body and old clothes. The smell revolted him. Nausea rose to his mouth. And he opened the letter.

> Angel:
> I'm leaving. I am lost, but I can't see you any more. You are good, but you are repulsive. I know I'm doing wrong, that you would give me lots of money, and that I am losing this apartment and this security. But I can't stay here with you any longer. I don't believe that any woman could do it for very long. You are— But I am going away without knowing the truth, whether you are what I was going to write, or if, on the contrary, you are greater than other men. What else can I tell you? Nothing. Isn't that so?
>
> Pilar

The letter said exactly—he realized it suddenly—what Aguado had expected. For a long time he had been awaiting this letter, which now surprised him brutally. And he understood that in the midst of his despair he felt a sort of liberation, as if the knowledge that he could never be linked to a woman —neither lawfully nor illicitly—freed him from something that at bottom made him wretched. With indifference, almost as if remembering someone known superficially in a time long gone, he recalled the woman who had signed this letter with the name Pilar. It was as though each day this woman had offered him a different body, now all coalesced into one. And he felt the promiscuousness of flesh asserting itself shamelessly through all those naked bodies as if, in losing this woman, he was letting the entire world slip from his own limited, weak grasp. The indifference with which he remembered her was like a preparation for his torment. The feeling that, in relation to his wife, had been sorrow, and therefore more bearable, in this case was the pure, hopeless indifference of having proved by means of an outsider—this Pilar who signed the vulgar letter of farewell—that his problem, he himself as a problem, without knowing why, was insoluble. Aguado walked away in despair, as though in that apartment rented for mercenary love he had left behind his last hope of existence.

He walked about the streets, concealing his agitation in the silent appearance of a hurried passer-by. "And I can't be pure. If I could achieve that, everything that now seems horrible to me would end. I must try for chastity, find a way of being chaste, come what may." And he tried it. Devoid of religious spirit, this man sought a purity based on frustrated sexuality, sought it like someone looking for the birth of a child from a woman's dead body. There began for him a period of retreat and solitude, a formidable thing in the midst of a Madrid springtime, gentle and caressing in its warm, sensuous atmosphere. Lived in continually, solitude ceased to be solitude in some way that he could not explain. What at first had offered itself as calm ("Here it is," he thought. "Now I have a quiet that women cannot disturb by their presence") quickly turned into a new reality that—perhaps because in truth it was unreal—disturbed him more profoundly. Until then his problem had consisted of something certain which he had to face involuntarily. But when he found that the solitude, by the mere fact of being solitude, produced a modification of what for everyone else was reality, he understood that what up to then had concerned him was merely the surface of something more rich and disturbing. For him reality had ceased to be real. Life, naturally, continued to be the same as always. There were his house; all the long-familiar comforts; the maids silently going about their efficient business; his wife in several different dresses and with varying gestures, as though showing the distinct aspects of someone who would never allow herself to be fully known. Madrid was outside, the entire city, with its inhabitants unceasingly on the move and the diffuse noise of its traffic. But this, which existed for him too, could be annulled as it was by the solitude and the silence. It was not a matter of dreaming. In his experience dreams were a sort of existence in a vacuum, in which—insubstantial, lacking reality—things meaninglessly displayed their potentialities. Dreams had the sadness of insufficiency. But Angel, on the contrary, at last, found in his unreal existence the way to satisfy his sensuality.

One day the realization came to him suddenly that his whole struggle for chastity had been nothing but a subtle way of exacerbating—better, perhaps, of creating—his lust. Hitherto, for him, desire had not been something in itself, separable from his own nature. More, he was aware now that often desire as such did not exist in him, and that if he searched for it, he was moved not by the pleasure that desire always carries within it, but on the contrary by the bitter anxiety stirred up in him by this road leading nowhere. Anxiety for its own sake, torturing him and flagellating his spirit, seemed to him the sign of something that had been fighting within him since his childhood.

From then on his life was a huge secret, perhaps from himself too, and—like all secrets—it created a need for confession. During the day his mode of life was normal for a man of his age and station. Although he was estranged from his wife, his relationship with her assumed a conventional air of understanding in the way that relationships founded on good breeding do: in it everything that could be called sentiment and passion had been hidden away. But for Ángel Aguado this paralleled a stratagem that no one could penetrate or even suspect. While at his wife's side, correct in appearance, but withdrawn from her, Ángel recalled his experiences with other women, as if dealing with a series of furtive violations of which—on other women's bodies—he made her the victim. Seated facing her in silence during dinner, sometimes he would smile with mysterious malice as he remembered how on the preceding night he had been with her, weeping, crying out, making her a participant and almost an accomplice in her own degradation. And at bottom it was nothing (he did not know this) but the repetition, again as of someone trying to drag something through time to the present, of the violent, bitter scenes that had marked their marriage at its beginning.

Of all the women he had known and put to use, the one he most sought and needed was the girl he was now calling, Carmen. And not because of her physical resemblance to his wife—now that to Ángel his wife no longer seemed beautiful—but because of the existence in her, whether in her character or in her carnality he did not know, of something able to carry him into that state which in him was substituted for happiness, a state of mind that, had anyone asked him of what it consisted, he would not have known how to explain, inasmuch as while he was living it, it filled him with emotions as different as depression and exaltation. And now, almost in that state, he waited at the telephone for her reply.

"Yes, yes, it's I. Good. We'll dine together. I'll be down in the street in fifteen minutes. I'm very glad too. Good-by."

There it was. The man hung up the receiver and left the telephone booth. He was in an American-style bar on the Gran Vía. Crossing the salon to get to the street, he was aware of the murmur of the people taking aperitifs. The noises of conversation, laughter, the fresh sound of clinking glasses. He also smiled. A middle-aged man, elegantly dressed, tall and rather heavy, he started the motor of his car.

3

When Carmen emerged from her house fifteen minutes later, a man was waiting for her. Not that she knew it, or even knew the young man; nevertheless, he was waiting for her. Swarthy, very young, and poorly dressed, he looked like a tramp. He was standing in shadow across the street, immobile, smoking calmly and with enjoyment. Some yards away, its motor now cut off, was an automobile that had arrived a few minutes earlier. The young man was exhaling the smoke of his cigarette in the manner of someone relinquishing a great treasure, but without taking his eyes from the doorway across the street. Now the girl emerged. The boy watched her without moving. For a moment she stood in the glare of the doorway, as if created by the glow of the electric light. She was beautiful: youth shone from her skin, from the long gold stain of her hair. Her whole appearance had an irresistibly attractive, joyous, shining force. Unable to resist, the boy started toward her. Their footfalls sounded together on the nearly dark sidewalk. By her side, he was now almost touching the black cloth coat that covered her, and he inhaled the perfume emanating from her body. He grazed against her lightly and, as she turned to stare at him with a look of surprise, he stopped and watched her go on. Tall and attractive, she receded from him with the implacable steadiness of a departing train until at last she got into the automobile, which then started up. From its exhaust came puffs of light smoke smelling of gasoline. The car was one of those new streamlined models. Swiftly and smoothly, as though someone were whisking it away, its gray color merged more and more with darkness and distance. Then the youth felt at ease. The girl had gone, and he was again aware of life as it was: something obvious and natural.

Had anyone asked Manolo (that was his name) why he came every day to watch the girl go out, he would have laughed as if at the madness of someone who had nothing to do with him. And if anyone had asked him if he came because he was in love with that girl, Manolo would certainly have spat out a blasphemy. If he came here every night, as he also hung about the exits of dance-halls, this had nothing to do with love. He simply liked to do it; he wanted to do it, and for that reason he did it. His life was nothing else. He was now considering the aspect of the street (one in the Salamanca quarter), trying to penetrate the strangeness that this silent and withdrawn manner of life made him feel. He was perfectly aware that the neighborhood was inhabited by rich people—the houses all had big, sumptuous façades—but the surroundings, devoid of sound, seemed to him sorrowful and boring. And yet the girl lived here. There were scarcely any shops in the high, dark mass of the façades, only a dairy and, a little farther on, a custom shoe shop, both closed. High up, as if weighing on the air, were the projections of bay windows and balconies. Manolo would have liked to know—not for any reason, but simply to know—which window the girl was in the habit of looking out. But he had no possible way of knowing, and anyway, the matter did not interest him too much. He was very well aware that nothing should command too much interest—among other reasons because it was of no use. Manolo had failed to attain too many things that had interested him to have any illusions.

In reality he had never obtained anything he wanted, not even once. He was eighteen years old, and he had never had what he wanted. Women, food, automobiles, cigarettes, suits, were like a heap of frustrated illusions in his memory. And he recalled winning the favors of many girls, tattered street-girls and occasionally even old prostitutes. Manolo had done well enough with them; this very night he would go in search of one of them who went with him for nothing because she was his sweetheart; but that kind of thing was different. Women of that class are not the desired ones. Just as cigar-butts were not his ideal, even the butts of Havana cigars. No. And now he laughed happily. He was laughing at not being the man who had taken the girl away in his automobile. From his pocket Manolo extracted several cigar-butts; taking off their old, burned wrappers, he felt satisfied; in his dirty hand the tobacco became a single mass giving off an acrid, strong odor. Carefully he rolled a cigarette and lighted it, quickly and cleanly thrusting the match into the sheltering hollow of his hand, and then throwing it, still burning, on the sidewalk. The odor of burning tobacco recalled for an instant the automobile that had just sped away; Manolo crushed the match with the sole of his old shoe, as if that memory was within the flame. That was the way he always behaved; that was the action called for.

He had to be on his way. For him the nights were what morning and afternoon hours are to other people. His day began now. He must go to eat at Las Ventas, and it pleased him to realize that it was distant and that he would have to walk along the Calle de Alcalá, filled as it would be with people returning to supper after having been in the cafés and movie houses. Manolo would listen to their talk, he would look with satisfaction at some woman moving along with her sweetheart or her husband. He enjoyed looking at them, and sometimes he would even tell himself that he was the husband, and that just as soon as they reached their home and were alone in their room, he would pull her against his body and kiss her on the lips. And in that thought this young man, walking along behind some elegant couple, managing to follow as close as possible behind the woman, ceased, without being aware of it, to be Manolo the loafer on his way to buy or steal whatever he could—scraps of meat or of fried, half-rotten fish in the street stalls of Las Ventas. He became transformed into a pure human curiosity attempting to fathom, if it was possible, that transient, elegant woman who could never even suspect his existence. At other times he stopped before the windows of restaurants or cafés and stared with serious attention—in which there was no trace of envy or longing—at the food on display, as a traveler lets his eyes wander over an unknown landscape. Manolo knew that these things were to be eaten. Simply seeing them made that obvious; what was difficult for him was to assign to them the odors and flavors that in reality they must have. Lacking that sort of experience, he could summon up only the odors and tastes of what he was accustomed to eat; that food, necessary as it was to him at the moment when he wolfed it, nevertheless never struck him as agreeable. At such times, there took place within him a struggle between something that he could not imagine very clearly and something that he did not want to recall. For though Manolo accepted his life as what it was, it did not follow that he found it too pleasant a companion.

He looked along the street again. Scarcely any people were abroad. A maid walking an expensive dog attracted Manolo's attention. It must be fine to have a dog like that; nor could it be very difficult. The maid and the dog were drawing farther away every moment, without having noticed him. Manolo whistled slowly, softly at first, then louder by the second. What he was whistling was a song being sung all over Madrid. The maid and the dog suddenly stopped and looked toward Manolo. He stared too, straight at them. There were the two gazes: the large, round, somewhat damp stare of the animal, and the other—the dark, ardent, sly gaze of the woman. The boy stopped whistling and strode off quickly in the direction of the Calle de Alcalá.

4

Carmen's parents were eating their supper. Actually, they were about to finish. It was ten o'clock, and they would have to hurry if they wanted to arrive in time for the night's feature film. They were sitting across from each other, both of them still very young. They had been married when they were both not much more than children, a fact that neither of them had ever forgotten. The husband would shout it out when they fought; the wife thought of it constantly. Carmen's father was called Enrique. He was of good family, as he himself said, a well-known family, people of whom one could speak to anybody—except that out of spite Enrique did not speak of them, inasmuch as his father and brothers had not spoken to him since his marriage.

The mother, that is, was not of good family. When Enrique had first met her, she had been an apprentice in a dressmaker's shop on the street on which his family lived. It could not be said that they had married for love, though they had married because of love's consequences. Their relations had had the natural result for couples who conceal their passion in the darkness of vacant lots and trash heaps. For some days (it was very early summer) they had lived out their secret affair, in which common desire mingled with inexperience. One understood love as little as the other. The blind need that they felt for each other when they were together, and which they satisfied with animal speed, had to be interrupted: Enrique's family was going to pass the summer in a Sierra village. At their farewell there were no tears, but only a sensual exacerbation. Painful caresses and all the thick sensuality of two active, ignorant bodies remained in their minds as a memory. A few days after this separation the girl knew that she was pregnant: a friend explained it to her.

When it first struck her, she felt only one thing: curiosity. For several days she had been nauseated and had vomited constantly, as if inside her body something was in commotion like houses and trees in a cyclone. She thought that she was sick, and she had felt a dark, animal fear in the face of these upheavals, which she did not understand. Now it was different. She was pregnant, and she felt the fact almost as a caress. She knew very well what this was. In the street where she lived—the Calle de la Encomienda, in a poor quarter of the city—in the nearly public life lived by the inhabitants of those small, dark houses, old, dirty, and lacking ventilation, the intimacies of the neighbors were always a street matter. One knew that one neighbor was four months pregnant, that another had decided to have an abortion. And when the hour of labor arrived, the women of the neighborhood and the street children would gather in groups in front of the house where the delivery was taking place, listening attentively—as though to a very dramatic scene in the theatre—to the cries torn from the woman, now stretched out on the bed, by the act of birth. Carmen's mother knew this, and had always viewed it, lacking the prejudices of education, as just what it perhaps really is: a natural thing. But this very knowledge made her think quickly of the consequences that it would inescapably bring.

She knew that when her father found out that she was pregnant, he would shout atrocious words and beat her. She also imagined her mother shrieking, calling her a sow and a lost girl. The parents of a girl she knew, who had later had a child, had acted in that way, and she had seen it. And without more thought she decided to conceal the news from her family. She realized that not very much time had passed, and that Enrique would return soon. And in fact he returned. When his girl-friend told him that she was with child, he was astonished.

In the Sierra village where he had been, the memory of the girl had come to him often, especially toward evening when he saw pairs of sweethearts losing themselves mysteriously in the pine grove. Enrique had attempted to prevail upon various girls, but he had not been successful; and therefore his return to Madrid was more than anything a longing to relive and find again what he had left behind in the darkness of unfinished buildings and vacant lots. As he learned that he had made his girl pregnant, two distinct and even opposed feelings contended within him: on the one hand, a puerile, yet male satisfaction at being able to do such a thing, and, on the other hand, a fear that was not less troubling because it did not fix itself on anything or anybody. The girl, meek and anxious, looked at him. He understood her at that moment exactly as she was: a woman handed over to him. And he felt afraid, afraid, within himself, in the blood; he began to laugh. Panic arrived suddenly, as instantaneous and irrational as a stroke of lightning, and Enrique neither could nor knew how to fight against it. He considered running away from his sweetheart's side, but instead of doing that he found himself kissing her mouth, straining his body against hers. The girl whimpered with happiness. And her pregnancy was not mentioned again.

Two months later, she appeared with her father. Enrique, waiting where he waited every afternoon, saw her approaching with an unknown man. He had not yet recovered from his surprise when the man stood in front of him. The man was short, but fat, in his forties. Dressed like a laborer, his face ruddy and weatherbeaten, with thick lips and a flat nose, he aroused a feeling of fear and repugnance in the younger man.

"Is this him?" he asked the girl.

Crying, she said that it was. Enrique was more bewildered than he had ever been in his life. The man stared fixedly at him. For the boy there was something fantastic in the dread he felt before those eyes—they were small, almost expressionless, penetrating—which were fixed upon him.

"You must marry her at once. Marry her—because if not, I'll kill you. Otherwise why did you—" And here the man uttered a graphic and terrible expression. "What's your answer? The same thing always happens. It's very pretty for you to play the fool now. Come on, the three of us are going somewhere."

Enrique did not dare even ask where. They took the subway as far as Progreso. Then they walked along streets filled at this hour with noisy people. In the Calle de Mesón de Paredes they stopped outside a tavern. As soon as they entered, Enrique realized that most of the people there knew that they were coming, and were waiting for them. They all greeted the father as he came in. All of them seemed ordinary people except one, who was wearing the uniform of the municipal guard. Enrique saw that they were looking at him silently as if he were a rare specimen.

"He really is a little gentleman," a voice in the back said.

The father finished drinking a glass of wine.

"All these are friends of mine. You've got to tell them that you're the father of what my little girl is carrying in her belly. Come—answer!"

Enrique's voice could scarcely be heard. It was like a whisper filled with fear and shame.

"Louder. You've got to say it louder. I want everyone to hear it."

Enrique now raised his voice. "I'm the father," he said.

When they heard him, all the men began to laugh.

"They must get married then," said the municipal guard. "They're both minors."

"Well, of course they'll get married," someone else bawled. "If not, Felix here will crack his skull."

The father invited everyone to drink. Enrique and the girl joined in. In the drinking and carousing of these ordinary folk, Enrique felt something healthy and happy. And he foresaw that in spite of his family's opposition, this girl, who inspired no love in him—perhaps not even affection—would be his wife.

Two days after the scene in the tavern, Enrique finally spoke to his family. Having to do so horrified him, but the attitude of Carmen's father allowed no delay. The next day he emerged from his doorway with a small suitcase: his parents had turned him out forever. As his father had told him between choleric screams, his filthiness had stained an honorable name. Enrique was left in a quandary. Until that moment he had been the son of a well-to-do family, studying for a career in law. He had not the smallest idea of what it meant to live on one's own. He set off directly in search of Carmen, and she left work to accompany him to her house. Enrique there met the woman who was to be his mother-in-law; a woman of the Madrid type, dark and with graceful, delicate features, whose prematurely aged face resembled her daughter's. There he lived; from there he got married, discovering things and customs that he had never heard of. Among these people he breathed in poverty and simple habits. He made friends with types whose existence he had not even suspected, and he began to understand their speech, a mysterious jargon both graceful and coarse. Suddenly he found that he was just one more type in that quarter. "El Enrique," as he was called, was now one more comrade among the neighborhood men who drank and played cards in the taverns. He had given up his studies. In reality, he did not like the profession of law, but on abandoning it he realized that he was losing more than some learning of no importance to him: he was losing a way of life as well.

He found employment in a government office. It was time: his wife had just given birth to a girl. The salary was enough. Enrique looked for an apartment—he found the one they still lived in—and they moved at once. He did not want to go on living with his in-laws, against whom he felt an obscure, impotent rancor. He was going to create his life beside his wife and the daughter he had involuntarily acquired. The fact of having an apartment in the Salamanca quarter, just as his family had, seemed to him clear proof that he might still reconstruct his life. He even had another satisfaction, though this was less conscious. One morning his wife's mother appeared, in tears; her husband had died during the night, suddenly. When Enrique beheld his father-in-law dead, a bitter memory returned to him: that man had completely changed his life. And he felt a sort of calm on seeing him rigid on the wooden bed, strangely mute and impotent. He presided at the burial and mourning, and the next day he went home drunk. When his wife cried and screamed insults at him, he said nothing. He himself, in truth, had no idea why he had acted that way.

There was never any understanding in his marriage, though desire continued to be a bond between the two bodies. Without knowing each other more than physically, they had the relations not of husband and wife, but of two lovers. At bottom they went through the years as the two children who had made a mistake in the early days of a summer. Enrique despised his wife as ordinary and ignorant; she despised him as weak. Both felt a hostility that could be expressed only in the most ardent caresses, as if sensuality, blindly manifesting itself, were trying to blot out the irremediable difference between them. Their life swung between these two extremes.

And thus Carmen, their daughter, came to know them. She was from early childhood used to her parents' shrieking and passionate raving. Vile words, charged with strange suggestions to her ears, were what she heard constantly; sometimes as angry insults, other times as raucous expressions of love lavished caressingly. Her parents appeared to her not as those gigantic, perfect beings which parents seem for most children in the first years of childhood, but as a man and woman whose weaknesses and blemishes came constantly to view. When the economic crisis arrived, Carmen one night made an extraordinary discovery. She was lying in her bed, and in the silence of the night she heard her parents talking.

"I can't. I've tried it, but it's impossible," her father was saying.

"Impossible for you, who are a coward. Everybody deals in contraband. Everybody brings home money. Only you can't do it."

"But it's not that easy. You need influence and connections. I've talked to a lot of people, trying to do something. Just today I was with an old friend who carries contraband, and the police have seized the storehouse he had in Madrid."

"Well, we can't go on like this. With your salary we have scarcely enough to eat. And I—do you hear me?—won't resign myself. If you don't know how to earn money, I'll do it."

The building's elevator started up, and for some moments Carmen could not hear their conversation.

"Shut up!" Once more her father's voice was audible. And the dry sound of a blow was heard.

Her mother was crying softly now. In a little while she said: "It's for the girl, and for you too."

"Shut up. Shut up or I'll kill you."

And then nothing more was heard. Silence returned, that silence of Madrid at night, broken from time to time by the noises of streetcars and automobiles.

But Carmen could not get to sleep for several hours. In the darkness she thought of what her mother had been saying. She was eighteen years old. She had received what is called a good education, and now she was attending an academy where typing and shorthand were taught. She wanted to find a job. Then she thought of her sweetheart, a boy who had approached her on the street and with whom she had been going out for two months. She did not love him. She found him childish, stupid. She knew him too well not to despise him. She knew when he was going to caress her, clumsily, when he was feeling the need to kiss her: she saw it reflected in his face in an animal, obvious way. Carmen put up with him because he took her to the movies, because they went to a café frequently. But at bottom she felt only weariness and disillusion in his presence. There was nothing in him to satisfy her intelligent and alert young woman's curiosity. The words she had heard from her mother occupied her like a problem. Without knowing why, she thought: "I'm younger and prettier than my mother. Also, I'm more intelligent. It will be easier for me. I don't feel any need to do it with anyone" (this was true); "it will be disagreeable to do it without desire, but I'll have money." At dawn she fell asleep. And she took the first of her men the next day. Once her initial shame and repugnance were overcome, Carmen found the occupation acceptable, though bothersome.

She began to have enough money. Inasmuch as she could not spend it for clothes, the amount she saved began to be considerable. But the most difficult thing remained to be done: telling her parents. Every day she thought that she would tell them, but, imagining the scene that would result, she would let it slide. It was her former boy-friend who suddenly informed her parents. He wrote an anonymous letter, in which he explained some of Carmen's adventures. As a postscript he asked if it brought in much money, "inasmuch as all the lovers she chooses have the appearance of being very rich." Carmen's mother had no sooner read the letter than she went racing into her daughter's room, overflowing with indignation. She entered yelling, but all in vain: Carmen had already gone out. Thereupon she began to go through her daughter's things. She stood rigid in astonishment: there, in her hands, were five thousand-peseta notes, almost what her husband earned in a six-month period. She did not know what to do. The money proved that what the letter said was true. And she burst out weeping bitterly, but without ceasing to look admiringly at the five thousand pesetas.

Carmen was relieved at realizing that her mother already knew. When she opened the door, Carmen saw the full knowledge in her eyes. "Well, good—that's that," she thought. "Now to see what she says to me." But her mother said nothing. She felt an embarrassment that prevented her from speaking of it to her daughter. That was one reason. The other was her need to wait for her husband to arrive, as is the case on certain family occasions. Finally the father arrived; the mother, who until that moment had stayed tranquil and silent, threw herself into his arms, whining. Enrique did not understand her tears and gazed at his wife mistrustfully.

"What's going on? Tell me why you're crying. Come on now, tell me."

His wife did not answer immediately; it had been an agreeable surprise to her to be able to stimulate such impatience in her husband. But her hysterical agitation was stronger, and in a garbled, incoherent way she told him what she had just discovered. Enrique behaved like a madman. Like all weak people, he was choleric, and his rage came like a maniacal explosion, the only response that occurred to him. Carmen did not wait to be summoned by her parents. When she heard them shouting, she presented herself in the dining room. She was very pale, but her silent posture spoke of firmness. Enrique first struck her and then wept like her mother. Carmen said nothing; she accepted the insults and the blows. When she saw that her parents were crying, she threw the fistful of bills on the table and slowly and stiffly walked back to her room.

For several days Carmen and her parents did not speak to each other. Enrique had told his wife that he would make things right whatever happened, and she waited curiously to see what her husband was planning. One afternoon Enrique came home before his usual hour. He no sooner saw his wife than he said: "The world's a filthy place. Everything in it is swill."

And he told her the news that a family friend had given him: "The daughter of my brother Ramón has run away from home with a married man. And my brother certainly has money and comforts—not like us, who have only worries and poverty."

And from that day forward Carmen's mysterious manner of earning money was accepted at home.

THE BRONCO-BUSTER

Peggy Bennett

Born in Hendersonville, North Carolina in 1925, Peggy Bennett attended the Florida State College for Women in Tallahassee, Florida and Black Mountain College in North Carolina. She now lives in New York with her husband and two children. She has contributed stories and poetry to *Harper's Bazaar*, *Mademoiselle*, *Partisan Review* and *Accent*, and is the author of a novel, THE VARMINTS (Alfred A. Knopf, 1947).

Shackled to the earth, for two or three years Frankie had coveted the Harley-Davidson belonging to Jerry Jenkins, who worked at the radio repair shop across the street where the man once charged Mama two dollars to make a tube snug.

The name Harley-Davidson was a solo Frankie's soul sang: a short, powerful melody, self-sufficient and moving. It acted on his imagination like drums and bugles. Whenever Frankie saw Jerry lunging, bouncing, sputter-popping down Ninth Avenue on his Harley-Davidson, Frankie fell into elephantine reveries of heroics, and finagled against rude awakenings.

But Mama seemed to finagle against reveries. She could think of two dozen intrusions in a minute. He had to take some clothes to the cleaners, shop for groceries, clean the ring from the tub, pick up his clothes, sharpen her pencils, get her a bucket of water for her mop, hand her the scissors, and so on.

As she worked in Aunt Helena's maternity shop for their bread and butter, his conscience did not let him explode in noisy rebellion. She was on her feet all day. Her varicose veins were blue and unsightly. Every time he saw Mama's legs he wanted to bawl like a little kid. Instead he got gruff and jerky, and felt headlessly enraged. One of these days, he realized, moderately tarnished with self-pity that he must be burdened so young, he ought to support her, take her off her feet, put her out to pasture.

She was not the kind of woman who felt that males were gods. Frankie knew a couple of Jewish boys whose mothers worshipped them prostrately, doormattishly. Mama did not have this stimulating inclination. Sometimes Frankie throbbed indignantly, wounded by her lack of enthusiasm for his powers. Yet he admired her greatly because she was so contemptuous, so tough. Mama was boss, and Frankie knew it. His smothered fire gave off damp sighs. "Jeez, I wish I had a motacycle!"

She constantly sniped at him about spending a couple of hours in the bathroom whenever he entered it on business. "What you doing in there?" she brooded. "Can't you do your mooning someplace else? Somebody else likes a chance to get in there once in a while!"

Often, particularly after a boring, irksome day of being considered awkward, adolescent, pesky, inept, and of hanging around nooks and crannies feeling useless and unwanted, Frankie could hardly wait to get into his single bed at night— he had slept with Mama until he was ten—and set himself asail in the dreamy dark. This was incubation with a vengeance.

He became Robin Hood on a motorcycle. He owned the world as he rode a gorgeous mechanical bronco through Europe, Asia, Africa, Australia, North and South America, and, in dreams, where all things are possible, on the moon, Mars, and under the crust of the earth.

He had no desire to tour ghastly Antarctica, which was uninhabitable, unless some scientific gang made it their headquarters and he had to wipe them out. But he did tour Alaska and the Hudson Bay region, skimming ice deserts on his magnificent motorcycle, his hawk eye gauging the midnight sun. In all of his dreams there was a beautiful woman who both hated and adored him and finally shot him, not realizing that he was a noble spy. As he lay dying his magnificent, panting agony of death, the whole wide world, including all the planets in this solar system and a trillion others, mourned him singlemindedly with black-edged newspapers and all that.

And so, having made the supreme sacrifice for the benefit of the incorruptible United States and France, that other most noble nation, his exhausted, pain-wracked physique faltered, failed, and became—Frankie's uncontrollable sobs once again woke Mama from a snoring sleep. "Eh! Eh!" she cried, sitting bolt upright, clutching the bedcovers as if they were reins, and rolling her eyes hugely as if she too had been recalled from far-off lands and was a stranger in her home.

One day Frankie would invent a motorcycle which could climb the air. Then he would invent another motorcycle which could freely enter outer space.

Frankie saw that Jerry Jenkins owned his world when he rode that great insect. Jerry was a solitary figure, king of space. Bicycles might serve old men and nervous girls, but motorcycles were vehicles for young gods. Of all the earth-bound vehicles, motorcycles were indisputably supreme.

Jerry Jenkins was a 5'2" redhead with a sour, priggish face and air for nobodies like Frankie Fleischer. If you are short and slight, a rabbit of a boy, you need a motorcycle to enhance your stature. Many customers hated bitter Jerry during their brief courtship of him. He took cold delight in shearing them down to his size.

During those first months, Frankie had courted Jerry assiduously, hoping for a chance to borrow the beloved steed sometimes, if he ever learned to ride it, but Jerry never weakened. A frown altered Jerry's anxious, pale, pug-nosed face whenever Frankie sauntered tensely into the shop. Frankie sensed the chill, but could not help himself, prevent himself from coming. The motorcycle was magnetic.

He hung around uselessly, dangling, fidgety as a housefly in a summer kitchen, hoping for one chance to straddle that beautiful, synthetic and improved breed of mustang, just to see how it looked and felt from the saddle.

The cynical and secretive men in the radio shop did not encourage him, but only Jerry was rude outright. "Watch it!" he'd belch, coming at a rush, clasping a radio cabinet to his abdomen. Frankie might expect to get stepped on if he didn't "watch it."

"I know what you're after," Jerry would sneer, not lowering his voice, not even looking at Frankie, but brushing by.

Being an only child, Frankie had not developed the art of riposte. He couldn't argue with Mama lest she blister him with her hot tongue. When she wasn't afire, she was usually so damp, suffering, always suffering, that he might as well have been gagged. Never quick with words, Frankie was a snail at his studies, was in the eighth grade again this year. His mind was a baffled mole in rocky ground, but it dreamed of an epileptic seizure of grandeur.

"Aw, I don't want no ride," he answered sluggishly to Jerry, shrugging with embarrassment as he unconsciously revealed he yearned for a ride.

Leaving the shop on wingless feet, Frankie immediately began bettering his condition the only way he knew how. He daydreamed of racing Jerry Jenkins on another motorcycle and beating the pants off him, while a sidelines crowd, the other men in the radio shop prominent among them, roared encouragements, then jeered the fallen, fuming gladiator in his mud puddle.

But even Jerry had his better nature, was reversible at odd moments. On a few soft mornings the second April he had gruffly taken Frankie to the back court of the shop and demonstrated the physiology of the machine in brief tests of its viscera: gas tank, feed line, etc. Frankie memorized parts and functions thirstily. Still, Jerry never gave him the real break. The tantalizing exhibitions were never so elaborate as to include instruction in an actual trial run.

Then Jerry left town to go into the army and sold his cycle to a dealer. The casual hardness of this final betrayal was typical of the city, where too many cynical and wary people lived by the fantastic code of reality, which is: Rob or be robbed. A deep ache occupied Frankie's vulnerable breast. Even if you are born in a city, you never get used to the abuses of yourself. Frankie felt that his dream of possession had meant a lot more to him than the machine had actually meant to sly, sad Jerry, and that Jerry should have offered it to him first at least.

Frankie daydreamed that he bought a tremendous motorcycle, that Jerry came whining to him for a ride one day, and that Frankie licked the daylights out of Jerry right in the middle of the avenue. He daydreamed that he met up with Jerry in the army, had a fistfight with him, kayoed him cleanly, became a colonel on the spot, rode off to war on an enormous motorcycle at the head of his regiment, and, fearing naught, put the enemy to flight. He rode the motorcycle right up on top of an enemy tank and directed the battle from there.

He daydreamed. It kept him out of mischief. Mama had little room to complain.

Dimly he figured that everyone had a similar form of obsession: girls for dolls and movie stars, women for babies, men for automobiles and horses, and so on. Sometimes he even wished wistfully that he did not have to adore motorcycles. It left him hungry and unfulfilled, to be always without.

He had adored them from the neighborhood of his fourth or fifth birthday. Those were the days when his old man quit coming home, preferring that other dame with the peroxided hair and swollen bosom. Mama was a ghost of herself, sick at heart (insulted almost out of her wits). She moaned in her sleep like an invalid, wept incessantly over her dishes and washings, and let the house go to pot out of sheer dissipation of energy in her addiction of grief.

A vision of motorcycles seemed to cancel Frankie's smoking confusion and pain. He watched them excitedly from the windows as they sped out of nowhere and disappeared. He lost pain and anger in their brisk chattering and urgent thrusts.

As he got a little older, capable of crossing streets by himself, he had amorous sessions with passing cycles. When he found them parked, he furtively put forth his hand, lightly ran his fingers over some accessible portion of the magical anatomy. His delight was to be able to tag one while it was ejaculating itself past him. He would run on the sidewalk as fast as he could, trying to keep up with it. Usually, however, he lost a pursued cycle on its first green light. Spurned so efficiently, he felt like a grieving nothing.

It was awkward worship when he was just a kid, but now he was getting a lot older and would have to do something constructive about it. He was wearing long pants and cultivating an impassive air. His downy beard had been mown seven times.

Mama didn't want him to have a cycle. She forbade it. She threatened to send him to live with his father if, within her knowledge, he ever bought, borrowed or stole one.

His father didn't want him. Frankie knew that. The blonde having taken him to the cleaners and flown, the old man was on his last legs. A few months ago a doctor down at Bellevue almost killed the old man by withholding alcohol from him for eight hours while the old man was in convulsions. As it was, the old man nursed the illusion he had damaged his ticker.

When Mama heard about this, she delivered to Frankie one of those long sermons she gestated perpetually in her mind, but Frankie was too bemused, and dismayed, on discovering deep within himself a hidden desire for the old man's death, to hear her preachments.

As for letting him have a motorcycle, when she arrived at that subject she was as final as amen.

"I'm your mother," Mama explained, tipping the black skillet so that the wild, spitting oil ran up and down over the whole dull black floor of the shallow crater, making it gleam with searing power. "I'm the only person on this rotten earth who cares whether you hawk or spit. Nobody is ever going to love you like I loved you, don't you kid yourself. Your wife may love you for what you can get her, but it won't be her what pushed you into this hateful world and sweated and slaved for you when she was so tired she could drop dead . . ."

Watching her capable hands grow so agitated she burst the yolks when she broke the eggs, he wanted to howl with the agony of it, but stared dully until prodded, thinking how hungry he was for excitement, how glad he would be to lock himself into the bathroom after supper, how eager he was to get to daydreaming of his glorious future from the black bed. Only daydreams could mollify his hunger, and they didn't cost a thing.

"Why don't you want me to have no fun?" he said suddenly, sullenly. He did not know what to do for the inflammation of his spirit. He did not know how to deal with Mama. Unfortunately he whined.

How can you tell somebody who doesn't love motorcycles that you adore motorcycles? How can you persuade that person to love motorcycles? Frankie had raved about motorcycles for years. When he was younger, Mama had listened to him with the hurt face of someone trying to protect her child from her hurt. Now older and of necessity less sensitive to his problems, she acted as if she must not have been listening in the old days after all. She obviously had not given his poor words much weight. He'd wasted his breath. His fire had not been contagious. She seemed utterly blind to the pure souls of motorcycles, their sinless speed, their wheels' exalted spinning. What was the matter with her, goddamn her! that she could not see.

Blind, she sighed like a sea, accusing him of thoughts of leaving her for a snip, a parsnip, of a girl—he never even looked at a girl, he didn't like girls any more than he liked pussy cats!—and of being dissatisfied with his blessings, when she ought to have seen that she could have made him satisfied by popping a glossy new motorcycle at him with her blessing. Why did she fight that foolish, losing fight!

"I wouldn't care if you had ten motorcycles and broke every bone in your body, I wouldn't care if they brought you home looking like my old washboard," she rejoined, "if you weren't my son. But you're my son. I don't want my son going around crippled for the rest of his life. I don't want people talking behind my face how I let my own son go to the dogs."

He sensed her selfish purpose to keep him her underling by casting him into the throes of her own woes. He was wising up. He felt disgusted. He gritted his teeth. "There ain't a boy in New York gets inta less trouble than me, and you know it! Why don't you wise up!"

Contempt darkened her face. "You sound like your father," she said, and moved over to the sink as if trying to get as far from a bad stink as possible.

Scraped, like the time he tried to shave with a bad blade, he went to his bed and flung himself down. The trouble was, he loved Mama, even when he hated her. He wanted her to live forever, him tagging around, and he wanted her dead, him grieving, him on a motorcycle tearing past billboards in Nevada, Arabs in Colorado, guerrillas in Mexico.

Even in these late times, every time a cop passed, hard and black as a serpent on his ranting and roomy machine, steering enormous antlers, the smell of leather upon him, and in his goggles omniscient as a God-insect, Frankie was sent into spells of dreaming.

(—spiraled out on an enormous throbbing motorcycle through a timeless, non-spatial, non-biological world where he hungered not, slept not, defecated not, nor felt the corrosive bitterness of his mother's gastric anguish as she ate both his and her hearts out, nor felt the shame of being himself.)

For he was that handsome cop with gloved hands resting majestically, though casually, on the huge handlebar grips. Or, better, since cops were all corrupt, no longer noble, he was a lone wolf of an intelligence out scouting in black turtleneck sweater and black leather jacket lined with fleece. ("Wow, what a man, what a man!")

Or he was a speed cop broken for some framed-up insubordination, ratted on, doublecrossed, and seeking revenge. For they were out to get him if they could, that shadowy gang headed by his algebra teacher and Jerry Jenkins! Frankie was better than noble. He was nobly criminal. In his dreams he designed his tragic death that the whole world might do penance forever.

One day, when Frankie was melancholy sixteen wishing he had a little pocket money beyond the dollar his mother peeled out every week, his mother unexpectedly produced Mr. Murphy for dinner. Mr. Murphy was an insurance salesman, a gray-headed Irishman with tiny blue eyes and a cheerful red face. He talked about the necessity of warming "the cockles of the heart." What a line of bull! Frankie thought contemptuously.

Mr. Murphy was not trying to sell Mama an insurance policy per se. A widower, he was trying to sell Mama an insurance salesman—which was, after all, what every true salesman really has in mind for every potential customer.

Mama looked almost young. Frankie was scandalized. Could she have forgotten the viciousness of man and Papa? She burbled like a sixth story faucet when another person in the building was drawing water at the same time. She actually laughed at Mr. Murphy's silly witticism. It was a mad woman.

Mr. Murphy returned the following Sunday and all Sundays thereafter. Frankie hated him. He wanted to black those tiny eyes, stop that coquettish smile. He wanted to break those stained gray teeth and stop the gurgle of Mr. Murphy's giggling and that running stream of blarney. Frankie got out as soon as he could after dinner and slunk the streets, full of splendid cookery for a change, but as low in mood as a boy could get.

Once, in his haste to leave the room, Frankie collided with a pointed door and broke an incisor tooth. His cusp, with its exposed nerve and slashing pain, was also his hurt heart. For a while it absorbed his attention, for no daydream could siphon off his unexpected misery. He groaned and moaned around the house, but Mama's ear was elsewhere, and he hated her.

Personally Frankie thought Mr. Murphy was the glibbest fool in New York, or wanted to think so, although secretly, alas, he had to admit that Mr. Murphy had a clever insight into the greed of mankind. Witness his power over Mama, who was usually no man's fool and who usually assumed that all men were fools.

With great astonishment and dumb woe, Frankie realized gradually that Mama thought Mr. Murphy sweet, handsome, gallant, clever, dashing, amusing, bold, shy, gay, blithe, boyish, paternal, brilliant, deep, winsome, lovable, loving . . .

Frankie hated both of them.

When Frankie got out of school in June, it was Mr. Murphy who resourcefully pulled strings and got Frankie a job clerking weekday evenings and on the weekends in a grocery delicatessen in the fashionable district just south of Central Park. Frankie had to do remedial courses in the mornings. "He just wants an excuse to get me out a the way," Frankie thought vengefully.

Wild with interior rage that Mama had deserted him for another, Frankie immediately tossed aside his untried plans to succor her and began saving his money for himself, for a cycle.

Somnambulistically he did his tasks. His vacant face brought acid comments from a loveless old shrew in a fur coat as she fished for her hard change. The boss frowned at Frankie in Jovian sternness. "Step it up, young man! Why, when I was your age, I was running things!" he barked for the benefit of the wealthy old goon. She shook with silent mirth of pleasure, her upper lip covering her upper plate with a little to spare. Frankie's ears radiated heat.

He grew sulfurous. Let them persecute him now! Soon he would be riding through the red country of Arizona, through frazzles of sunlight as intense as burning celluloid. Someday they would know their error.

As he mechanically sliced bologna and weighed cheese, he was marking time before he climbed aboard his huffing and puffing porpoise and rode into all the glossy color photographs he had seen in big commercial magazines. Therein, elegant, if Mamaless, he could finally achieve the heaven he had glimpsed so many times, the heaven of perpetual novelty.

Mr. O'Neill was a hard boss on all his help. Smart as a burn, he kept at the boy to keep moving. "They say idleness be the divil's workshop," he warned Frankie solemnly, triumphantly.

During the rush hours he worked his small team like a demon slave-driver. He did a tornado of business in little more than a stall, and the turnover of stock was rapid enough to keep them all panting. Meanwhile he adjured them, "Let's not be gathering dust, now. I want to hear that cash register ring!"

And, "What did I tell you now? Sure, and you think I was spoofing. I want you to play The Star Spangled Banner on that there cash register. We don't want any of those subversive-like fellers working in our store."

His cruel cheerfulness drove the boy ragged. In reprisal Frankie smoldered, dreaming of giving Mr. O'Neill that long overdue shiner. It was not so much the steady gait as the blarney that got the boy fed up. That incessant voice, cutting through Frankie's dreams like a whip, lashing his helpless brain just as it sped him through the famous avenues of Los Angeles or Miami, that constant interference with the nourishing dream, almost drove the boy mad.

Frankie's sidekick for the past few months had been Gitch Bemmelman, a maddening young nitwit whose features combined the shining face of Christ with that of a donkey. Gitch had an outrageous air of saintliness and command, but Frankie realized this covered an abysmal lack of perception.

Frankie liked Gitch almost because he knew Mama would not have. Gitch had a touch of motorcycle to him: he was *verboten.*

Gitch got a lead on a cheap, secondhand motorcycle on Friday afternoon and almost broke his neck to break the news to Frankie. He might have grabbed it himself, but he didn't even have the price of a strawberry soda. He figured Frankie's cycle would be partly his if he tipped Frankie off.

Gitch came to the store at six-thirty. Mr. O'Neill had warned Frankie several times to keep his pals away. "I don't want ya ta think yer gettin' by with a thing!" Gitch stood on the sidewalk and waited until Frankie came up from the cellar with a crate of canned soups.

"Hey, Frank! C'mere a minute! I got somethin' ta tell ya!"

"Can't. Busy."

"You ain't so busy."

"You might not think so."

"I got somethin' terrific ta tell ya."

"Can't you spill it here?"

"Well . . . okay. I got ya a motacycle."

"Golly!"

Gitch's brother-in-law, it turned out, knew a fellow in Jersey City who was getting rid of his motorcycle, selling it cheap.

Frankie wanted to know how to get hold of this guy.

"You got to talk to Scappy," Gitch explained. "Scappy can tell you."

Frankie went down to the warehouse as soon as he could beg an hour off. He had to wait around twenty minutes then for Scappy, but he figured it was worth the gamble of his job. Scappy was a truck driver for a big wholesale corporation. As soon as he hove in sight, Frankie made a beeline for him. "Hey, Scappy! What's the dope on this engine Gitch was tellin' me about?"

Having just loaded up on a seventy-five cent plate of hash, the blue-plate special, Scappy wasn't feeling too benign. "All I know's a feller in Jersey City's got a motacycle he wants to get shut of fast soze he can latch on ta a new Buick. I see him now and then on my run. He's okay. Works in a service station. Says he's gettin' hitched and promised the skirt ta give up drinkin' and the motacycle. I told him I thought he was doin' the smart thing to stay away from those halfbaked engines. I never did understand how anybody with the brains of a pea-squirter would let himself in for one of them foolkillers."

The frank insult was Scappy's forte. He was the kind of fellow Frankie and Gitch liked to describe, with some discomfort, as a swell guy. Having his say was his specialty, and if you didn't like it you could go and shove it. Scappy was a man's man.

He was short, but his upperarms told a story. They bore a bulge of muscle which never went away. He liked to wear his sleeves rolled up, or a sweatshirt, because of them, though he had quiet poise which kept almost everybody from suspecting him of any such vanity.

A crackling voice, a deadpan delivery of opinion, and his

pale and steady glistening eyes gave him an air of tough resiliency and seasoned authority.

"Scappy's a real nice guy," Gitch said of him. "He's very good to Sis. Oh, he'll go out with the fellers and shoot the breeze, and he'll shoot craps sometimes and drop maybe ten or fifteen dollars cause he gets to losing and won't stop, but he don't mess around with loose women none, and when it comes Easter he always goes to church. He never misses a Easter. He's Catholic and Catholics ain't supposed to marry Jews, but he's on the square, he don't feed you no lies."

So Frankie knew Scappy well enough to believe that Scappy wasn't trying to pull a fast one. Scappy had religion. He wouldn't lie if he didn't have to.

"How can I get hola this fella?" Frankie asked Scappy.

"Well, I could maybe pick it up Sunday morning if I got the cash. You got the cash?"

"How muchuz he want?"

"He said he'd let it go for fifty bucks if he had to, but he mighta hiked it since then. I don't know what you can pick up for fifty bucks these days, but it ain't going to be no magic carpet. You ain't got no license for this engine, you know. You gotta get a license. You could get in plenty a trouble without no license. The cops could spot you in a second. How you gonna get a license?"

"Aw, they ain't gonna spot me that easy!" Frankie said hotly, while self-doubt preyed on his mind.

"Sure they will! A kid like you? Huh! Your mother know you're out?"

"Aw . . . I'll get a license. I'll bribe a cop. I'll—anyway it ain't your backyard," Frankie jabbed wittily.

"You got fifty bucks for this fella?"

"Yeah, I got fifty bucks," said Frankie. "I'm willing to cough up fifty bucks. If it's a good one, I mean. I don't want no bum cycle."

"Oh, it looks all right," Scappy said casually, moving aside for the loading men, who were coming in dolly-pushing safari. Frankie felt that he had to talk fast, having been gone an hour already.

"You gonna pick it up for me?" he asked.

"Sure," said Scappy impersonally, lack of enthusiasm being part of his character. "I ain't promisin' it'll be there. I ain't the guy's mother, you know. But if it is, and if he's giving me the straight dope, I'll try to get hola it for you, see?"

"What you gonna charge me for carryin' it?"

"Aah!" Scappy turned away in disgust.

Which was very sweet of Scappy, Frankie thought happily, figuring it was even more of a bargain if he didn't have to pay for its transport. Of course Scappy might have already allowed for his cut when he announced the price was fifty bucks, you couldn't tell, but maybe he really was a swell fella. Frankie was troubled by an odd itch to love Scappy. That Gitch was a lucky guy!

Mr. O'Neill was surly when Frankie came in, but he didn't bother to dock him. He made Frankie clean out the toilet and scrub the floors down. When it came one o'clock, Frankie was so tired he could hardly focus his eyes. His mood gave him a bumpy ride. Part of the time he was under the floor, part of the time up kissing the ceiling.

He slept like a clod, but woke early Saturday morning, so keyed up he could hardly sit down in a chair for levitation. He flung himself about like a marathon dancer. He was hopped up. He bolted food on high voltage. He was souped up. He was not quite sane.

"I may be in late tonight, Sweetie," Mama said guiltily. "Mr. Murphy is taking me to see a radio show."

Frankie felt panicky. Why, that damn fool! He got, he ruined, all the Sundays. Now he was taking over the rest of the week too. It didn't matter that Frankie would be working anyway. The point was, Mr. Murphy was taking over Mama, lock, stock, and barrel. Frankie felt murderous. "I don't give a damn!" he scowled, twitching, his mouth full of bread he suddenly found himself incapable of swallowing.

"What?" said Mama. "What? What?" She gulped, flung down the spatula and the potholder, and tramped heavily out of the room. Immediately she rushed back in, hands on hips, and bellowed a ten minute lecture unhappily. Then she gulped her coffee and left for work, ten minutes late already.

Frankie couldn't touch another morsel. He scraped the egg off his plate into the garbage pail and spat his mouthful of bread into the toilet. His throat ached. He wanted to break down and cry. "You and her are through!" he told himself gruffly.

There was this other problem to sicken him too. He had no idea how to go about getting licenses and permits. There was a United States office somewhere for this sort of thing. He would be grilled. He would have to lie, because he was a minor and because Mama didn't want him to have the engine, but something would have to be done.

At lunchtime he went to the bank and withdrew fifty of his eighty-odd dollars. Mama would sure kick if she found that out, he thought with a thrill of savage pleasure. (He'd show her!)

Gitch was waiting when it came quitting time. "Scappy says he's gonna try and get your cycle," he announced.

They tore down to the warehouse and watched the loaders finish loading and retreat, while Scappy and the warehouse manager sealed the van. Scappy turned toward Frankie as if in afterthought. "Okay. Fork over, Kid," he said fatalistically.

Frankie's hand trembled so violently he turned beet red. The minute he felt the money leave his hand he began to worry as if he'd lost his grip on life itself. He'd disobeyed Mama.

Scappy stuck his head out of the cab. "You know you gotta get this thing fixed up with the government," he warned. "This guy ain't gonna want no trouble with the law."

"Okay," Frankie agreed feebly.

A Negro loader was still standing by, resting from his work pushing the dolly. "You don't like no motacycles, does you?" he called to Scappy with a grin. Scappy slowly turned toward the light to examine his keys, as if he wasn't paying much attention to a mere Negro loader. "Aaah, I seen too many kids make fools of themselves on the crazy things," Scappy snarled. "Oughta be some law makin' em illegal."

The Negro loader, accustomed to white men's uneasy coolness, said with owlish glee, "I think I rememba readin' somewhere how they was over eight hundrit deaths caused by them things one year."

Scappy shrugged. "Yeah. You couldn't pay me to ride on one a them damn pieces of junk." He reached for the ignition. The truck roared. Scappy poked his head around his sill to see what was coming down the street, glanced up front, then into the rear view mirror, climbed sidewise on the great steering wheel to revolve it, and departed serving as the brain of a behemoth.

Frankie spent the night with Gitch, but Mama was heavy in the backroom of his mind. At eleven-thirty he was a hairbreadth from telephoning her, but he didn't quite do it.

The boys celebrated by drinking half a gallon of red wine and studying life in the windows across the street from Gitch's bedroom with binoculars Scappy had stolen when he was a master sergeant in Germany. One girl, who lived in a single room, spent the evening primping before her mirror in the nude. She thought Venetian blinds hid her from view, even when the slats were open. She was wrong.

Gitch studied her movements zealously, giggling as he speculated on the facts of her existence. ". . . now she's going over to the bureau again to fix her hair another way . . . now she's smirking in the mirror . . . hey, look at that! Hey, brother! . . . now she's reaching up in the closet and taking down a, down a, Hey! Frankie! It's a bottle of hootch! Why she's drinking it, honest ta God! Jeez! We oughta go over and introduce ourselves, whacha say!"

"What'sa matta?" he asked Frankie curiously, catching the mute whimper on Frankie's face. Frankie dolefully shook his head.

Frankie woke when the sun first caroled on the sill, and he lay fidgeting, wretched, until Gitch opened his dark eyes.

Sick and trembling, Frankie braced himself and called the warehouse. He was told that Scappy was already late.

"He's getting your engine," Gitch said wisely.

"When you reckon he'll get in?" Frankie wanted to know of the voice in the receiver. It didn't know. He didn't recognize it. It said the company was lax about Sunday operations, reduced to a skeleton shift.

As time went by, and Scappy was still reported missing, Frankie got increasingly depressed. Several times he almost phoned Mama, but then he remembered Mr. Murphy was due there in a couple of hours, if he had not already come, and the picture of Mama being comforted and reassured by Mr. Murphy was enough to paralyze his impulse. Instead, he chewed his fingernails off and started on the little tucks of skin.

At twelve-fifteen Scappy called. "Hey, come get this damn engine out of here before it gets banged to pieces."

Frankie shouted hoarsely, trying his best to sound delighted. He and Gitch swarmed down to the warehouse, puffing and prattling. "Gee, that Scappy's a swell feller! He's a wonnerful guy!"

Frankie was exhausted. His squelched conscience was returning twice as strong. What was Mama thinking, doing? . . . Mr. Murphy . . . Mama . . . Mama in auld lang syne . . .

"You got a bargain here, Son," one of the men squatting beside it announced when the boys galloped, panting, into view.

Sure enough, she looked all right. Worn, but big and strong-looking.

"They just broke her in right for you," another man broke in.

The men stood back and waited for Frankie to take possession.

He couldn't move. The weight in his mind made him sag. The truth was, he didn't like her. It was worse. He hated her. Why, he could not have said, except perhaps that she was a whore, like the woman who got his father, a dirty lie of a thing, and he wished he could pitch her right back where she had come from.

"Seef she can run," Gitch babbled, thrusting Frankie aside and leaping onto the huge saddle.

The men had all risen, and now they stood back. "Well,

now, let's see what she can do," one of them invited, and they all waited, glistening and eager. They loved their machines, these twentieth-century men.

Gitch was getting off to let Frankie on.

"Go ahead, Gitch," Frankie said languidly.

Gitch was astounded. "Yeah? You sure? Oh, okay!" He leaped upon the starter pedal once, twice, thrice, and, marvel of marvels, the ignition caught. She sounded peppery, even to Frankie's leaden ear, but he was cleft clear through.

Gitch got off the motorcycle perfunctorily. "Okay, Frank! It's all yours!"

The men waited for the new owner to take possession of his mercurial steed, to consummate himself. But Frankie had the air of a man who has already consummated himself. After intercourse there is sadness.

One of the men was telling about the European circuses in which daredevils got their machines to ride up perpendicular banks and to whirl on vertical circuits and even sometimes to ride on a concave ceiling, so furious their speeds.

"Why don't you try her out?" one of them nagged Frankie softly from the sidelines. It was the Negro loader.

"You know, I believe the kid is scared," hummed another derisively.

Slowly, as time became slow-motion, Frankie moved. Clumsily, almost falling, tripping over his feet, he mounted the motorcycle. With surprise he noted he was on his motorcycle. He stepped listlessly on the starter pedal. It did not catch.

"You have to jump!" the men started shouting at him. "Jump on it, big boy! Come on, give it a big hop, there!"

Frantically, his head almost flying off backward, he gave a huge jump, and almost lurched to the cement, his motorcycle on top of him.

The ignition caught, and he was trapped on this mad, stammering, mechanical creature. He longed to get off. He tried to, but stopped. It was difficult and his audience was waiting. He had to go through it—had climbed out on a limb, cut off from retreats.

Slowly, but much too fast for his comfort, the machine coasted down the gradual ramp into the street. Now it waddled furiously. He wanted to get off but couldn't remember how to stop her. Furtively he struggled with devices, hoping by experiment to accomplish the matter. It would be horribly embarrassing to let it be known he was on and couldn't get off. But somehow he couldn't gather his wits and take possession. He was riding off down the avenue passively, wondering idiotically what was going to happen next. Could he keep going, maneuvering until his gas gave out?

Prayerfully he watched the lights and hastily followed a truck around a corner into a side street. He ached in every muscle with tension. The buildings which lined the streets thickly as colossal sardines were quaking and swaying in the corner of his eye, as if about to topple on him.

Growing vigorously aware that he needed help, he circled the block back toward the warehouse. As he rounded the third corner he saw Gitch waiting. The other men had already disappeared. Frankie was exhausted; he surrendered. He felt at the mercy of the river, which made the island of Manhattan small, and at the mercy of the blinding sun. As he drew near Gitch he tried to stop the motor once again. He succeeded in almost losing his balance. Badly befuddled, he lost his head. "How do you stop it!" he bawled in terror as he went cruising swiftly by toward the corner again.

This time the ground rumbled and pitched violently as he followed it around the block. When it rose swiftly toward his face, he'd shut his eyes. People seemed to be screaming at him frantically from the pavement. Some men did shout as, in his zigzags, he barely missed colliding with the monstrous tail of a gigantic van. Every second was an age. The buildings muttered as they hung over his nape, aiming for him alone.

He rounded the last corner with a prayer Gitch was going to have somebody from the warehouse ready to help stop him.

Nobody was standing there.

Too late Frankie saw Gitch standing by the curbstone at the corner, prepared to leap on and help him if he could. Frankie had already aimed the motorcycle at the soft bank of fruit and vegetables on the stand across the street.

He was getting off.

A taxi came bearing down the avenue, its skirts flying on its rapid breeze. Frankie pushed the accelerator, trying to beat it across in front of it. Then, getting cold feet, he tried to swing.

There was a detonation like dynamite as the taxi met the hind of the cycle. The taxi cruised brokenly into the fruit and vegetable stand.

Shellshocked spectators, surprised as if by a midmorning sunrise, stood rooted, bulging-eyed. Somebody's Mama in a white rayon slip peered down out of an upstairs window. Two little boys in felt beanies ran up, shrieking and jabbering. An old man whistled between his teeth. Gitch sat down hard on a curbstone and weakly fanned his face with a limp hand.

The sun gloated on the shiny avenue, touching with a gleam the taxi run obliquely into the stand. It caressed a shoved and fallen motorcycle with a greedy light, while a wheel on the cycle spun slowly. It melted on a boy's breathless body lying prone, as if sleeping, about five feet out into the broad street.

Richard Eberhart

THE VISIONARY FARMS

Born in Austin, Minnesota, Richard Eberhart was educated at Dartmouth College, Cambridge and Harvard Universities. He now lives in Cambridge, Massachusetts, with his wife and two children. He has published six books of verse. Later this year a new volume of poetry, UNDERCLIFF, will be published by Oxford University Press. *The Visionary Farms* was first produced at the Poets' Theatre in Cambridge, Massachusetts, in May, 1952, directed by Jeanne Tufts and Frank Cassidy. It was also produced in May, 1953, by Glenn Hughes, in Seattle, Washington, directed by Robert O'Neil-Butler, with music by John Verrall.

Copyright, 1953, by Richard Eberhart. All rights reserved, including the right of reproduction in whole or in part in any form. Caution: *Professionals and amateurs are hereby warned that this play, being fully protected under the copyright laws of the United States, the British Empire including the Dominion of Canada, and all the other countries of the Copyright Union, is subject to royalty. All rights, including professional, amateur, motion-picture, recitation, public reading, radio and television broadcasting, and the rights of translation into foreign languages, are strictly reserved. Permission for any use of the play must be obtained in writing from the author.*

SCENE I   Home of the Everymans

ROBIN EVERYMAN/BERYL EVERYMAN, *his wife*/JASON CURLEY, *a scholar, formerly the Consulting Author*/WENDY CURLEY, *his wife*/CHARLIE WESTGATE, *a scholar; also a poet*/GRAYCE WESTGATE, *his wife*

    ROBIN
Well, here we are for another thrust
And joust against man's ancient adversary.
    CHARLIE
What is that, this time?
    ROBIN
                    The death of his spirit.
For if he has not imaginative fire
He is as good as gone.
    CHARLIE
               Gone where?

ROBIN

                                 Why,
Gone to the devil.

JASON

                Are you still the Devil?

ROBIN

A prince of great price, somewhat angelical.
I'd be a devil to flay his death-like spirit,
An angel to illuminate the affair man.
So let us, in our present enterprise,
Turn time backward, to see what powers,
Forces, circumstances, and chances
Burgeon and develop in a situation,
And tread a little, within our theater,
Some baffled steps of the journey of Everyman.

JASON

I am prepared to order my imagination.

WENDY

Is it going to be a comedy?

ROBIN

Wendy, if you have studied definitions
Practically everything is. We will show
The strong, pervasive reaches of the world,
Conjure a time of massive brightness,
Elicit the hammering flaws, and what time does.

CHARLIE

This sounds pretty serious.

GRAYCE

                     I had hoped
You would make it light and racy.

ROBIN

The past may show an eternal present.

JASON

Take fortune in strong gripe, and break its neck?

WENDY

That is fantastical.

BERYL

             We are bound
On Fortune's wheel. It is not bound by us.
It is always good to gain perspective
In viewing a universal spectacle.

WENDY

What, universal in a little room?

BERYL

                    An everywhere.

GRAYCE

Let's go.

EBERHART / *The Visionary Farms*

CHARLIE
    As if we had not life enough,
We must relive and tempt it forth in imitation.
BERYL
And open our souls to truth's old worst.
ROBIN
You talk as if you had not known of it.
GRAYCE
Of what?
ROBIN
    We are mincing tricksters. Summer's gone.
You have had the blithe, the budding time,
The time of blossoms, then the burning time
To learn your parts by now. Cast off the quotidian
And let us deal with an American scene.
BERYL
The pool of memory, and of our large desire.
JASON
I confess I have not learned my part or parts.
I had to screw the lid on Henry James.
It took all summer with a silver screwdriver.
WENDY
My work on Spanish folklore was exacting.
I am mainly interested in the thirteenth century.
After that, history is not good repetition.
ROBIN
I suspected this. I coped with it.
GRAYCE
Spock and Gesell have exercised my time,
Along with a brace of brassy gynecologists.
CHARLIE
I had to force a course on Melville; Moby Dick
Swallowed me entire. I am pure whiteness.
ROBIN
This is to laugh. It is comedy
Before it begins. We are the comedians
Who do not take our theater seriously,
Arguing that upon our several stages
We like to play our own realities
Compelled by egotistical esteems.
Beryl, could you make us all a drink?
We will sit around and pass the glass of time.
    There is a knock at the door. Robin lets in Consulting Author.
Good evening. You came in just at the right time.
You know all of these people, I believe?

CONSULTING AUTHOR
How do you do. It is good to see you again.
ROBIN
Come in, sit down.
Beryl brings drinks.
                    Here is a glass with whisky.
I want to consult with you, seriously.
CHARLIE
The waters of life.
BERYL
              Would you have charged water?
CONSULTING AUTHOR
It is pleasant to think I might be helpful.
Beryl passes drinks all around.
Thank you.
GRAYCE
      Thank you.
WENDY
              Thank you.
CHARLIE
                    Thank you.
JASON
                          Thanks.
ROBIN
My desire is to show an impossible situation.
CONSULTING AUTHOR
Make it probable. Everything is probable.
ROBIN
It is so real people would not believe it.
CONSULTING AUTHOR
Then you would not have to invent it. Seeing
Is believing.
ROBIN
          I always thought seeing was deceiving.
CONSULTING AUTHOR
Legerdemain and sleight-of-hand are handy.
As a matter of fact, I have powers of divination.
ROBIN
I always suspected you of being a devil.
CONSULTING AUTHOR
I am also somewhat angelical.
I have been operating by thought-transference
Now for quite some time, with respect to you.
ROBIN
Why, this is astonishing.
CONSULTING AUTHOR
                    In fact it is.

EBERHART / *The Visionary Farms*   67

    ROBIN
Do you not think I know what I want to do?
    CONSULTING AUTHOR
You see as through a glass, darkly. Everyone does,
Almost. I have special powers of divination.
I will show you what you wish to show.
    GRAYCE
This is weird. What is he going to do?
    WENDY
It sounds strange.
    BERYL
                Not table-lifting, I trust.
    JASON
I am waiting to see the accustomed rabbit.
    CHARLIE
I would not mind a new kind of parlor trick.
    Consulting Author goes swiftly to the door, lets in six young men actors, three young women. They nod, but do not speak. They stand around in professional ease.
    CONSULTING AUTHOR
I have conjured these, my sprites, from Harvard Square.
They will actuate my airy theater.
If you do not mind our using your other room
We will pass before your eyes some tricks.
The girls will set the stage. Women are always
Setting stages. I will be the director,
And you can be the drinking spectators.
Whenever necessary, I'll be a commentator.
Drink in our merry and sometime festive clarity.
    At Consulting Author's motion of command the actors go out right, reappearing only on stage later as action indicates. The six principals sit as if somewhat spellbound, anticipating and ready for what may transpire.
    Consulting Author takes a wand out of his inner breast pocket. He makes a few passes over the six principals.
I carry a delicate, mystic, silken wand
To clear the air on these cloudy occasions.
I wave this now before your eyes and minds
To purge the qualities of every day,
And take your disbelieving personalities.
Each thus becomes a part of Everyman.
What is, is what might happen to him.
And each can share in the scenes of fabulous life
As if imagination were reality,
For reality is strange as imagination.
    He puts down his wand on a table.
Now I must become a barker. Come all,

Come to see our show, our spectacle,
No furtive side show; big tent events.
The time is 1919. The place,
A small town in the Middle West.
The scene is in the Congregational church;
Within it a little Sunday School.
Thompson Ransome will soon appear,
That shrewd, expansive citizen
Noted as a most quick character
Who will teach the growing youth.

SCENE II   The Congregational Church
Ransome comes into the stage room, dark, dapper, serious, about 35. He stands behind a flat desk upon which are two glasses. Several boys and girls come in after him. They take seats.

RANSOME
Now boys and girls, I want you to sit still.
I am going to talk about good and evil.
We all want you to be good boys and girls,
Grow up to be a credit to our town,
Go out and do something in the world
Worthy of note, and of our care.
You have to be good to do good.
You must develop stalwart wills
To resist temptation and evil.
You must develop the fierce strength
And maintain the ceaseless vigilance
Of our fathers who came to this West country
To build anew the American dream.
Do not deviate from the truth,
Follow the harsh light of its gleam.
Do not lie, steal, be bullies or be mean.
Obey your parents and your teachers.
Work hard in school, labor diligently
To grow up straight, to better your minds.
There is no end to what you can do.
The world is a wealth of opportunity,
If you will do good, and shun evil.
But woe unto you if you do evil.
I am going to show you an experiment,
Something that you will never forget.
Notice these filled glasses here.
I am going to take out a silver dollar.
  He takes a silver dollar from his right pocket.
Notice the brightness of this dollar.

EBERHART / *The Visionary Farms*

See how clean it is, hard and pure,
A symbol of the American dream.
I will drop it in this glass of water.
   *He drops it in a glass of water. The class is all attention.
   Pause. After a minute he takes it out.*
Here it is, I hold it up,
Bright, hard, pure and clean.
Now I will drop it in this glass.
   *He drops it in a glass of transparent, hydrochloric acid. Little
   cries of astonishment as it turns black, fuming. The youths
   are fascinated, somewhat spellbound at the trick. Ransome
   holds the glass with the black dollar at the bottom right be-
   fore their faces.*
See how it is black all over.
Where is its brightness and its cleanliness?
Where is its luster, its bright shining?
It is ugly and impure immediately.
   *He takes the blackened dollar out with a pair of forceps
   from his pocket and holds it before them, menacingly.*
If you do good you will be a shining brightness,
The world will love you and respect you,
You will have a fair name among men,
You will honor your fathers and mothers
And honor your Father who is in Heaven.
If you do evil, your soul will turn black
Immediately, like this hideous dollar.
You will be ruined, ugly and unvaluable,
Of no shining use in the world,
Corroded and lost in damnation.
Do not sin. Do not do evil.
You have within you the power of free will
To be good, or to sink into black evil.
May you never forget this experiment.
Go, and do good. The class is dismissed.
   *The youths sidle out, disturbed and much impressed. Ran-
   some leaves with an air of rather prim satisfaction.*

SCENE III   Fahnstock's House
   *Scene in the sunporch of the new, large house of Adam
   Fahnstock, the secretary and vice-president of the Parker
   Corporation, large manufacturers of soaps.*
   VINE FAHNSTOCK, *his wife/*
   Their children: WILLIAM, 16/ PETER, 15/SUZANNE, 10
   Fahnstock is reading the Sunday paper.
       FAHNSTOCK
What did you learn in Sunday School this morning, Pete?

PETER

Mr. Ransome gave us a lecture on good and evil.

FAHNSTOCK

I trust you profited by the experience.

PETER

He put a dollar in a glass of water.
He put it in another, I guess sulfuric acid.
It turned black. Then he gave us a lecture.

FAHNSTOCK

I have always taught you boys to be honest.
There are three basic rules of life.
If you follow these you are bound to succeed.
Health, honesty, and hard work.
Never do anything to undermine
Your health; you have strong constitutions.
I have told you to be absolutely honest.
Never tell a lie. And always work hard.
That must have been an interesting lesson.
Ransome has proved a good man with money.

WILLIAM

I thought it was a little artificial.
He sounded almost like the minister.

PETER

Bill, come and help me fix my bike.
The right pedal is bent.

WILLIAM

All right, I will.

They leave, right.

VINE

Suzanne, don't you want to go in the kitchen
And watch Inga make the strawberry shortcake?

SUZANNE

Yes, Mother.

She goes out, left.

VINE

You said Mr. Parker was coming over?

FAHNSTOCK

Roger said he would drop over for a visit.

VINE

We must get the new Victrola fixed.
I am anxious to hear the new Caruso records.

FAHNSTOCK

Always something to fix. The new Cadillac
Looks as if it would never break down, though.
I am planning a new silo for the farms;
We need another for the big barn.
I think I will put in fifty new Holsteins.

A bull named Piebe Laura Olley Homestead King
Is on the market. He is worth twenty thousand dollars.
Three of the men at the office each agree to take a fourth.
    VINE
I never could hold you down. You are too heady.
I wanted a comfortable house, just large enough,
Instead of this enormous mansion. Ten acres
Of lawn is too much. I spend my energy
Ordering the servants, instead of enjoying life.
    FAHNSTOCK
You know you love it. It has been my dream.
Think of the success, Vine, we are enjoying
Since the old days when we started on nothing.
    VINE
I tried to keep you from building the Mad House.
    FAHNSTOCK
That house at the bottom of the Grand Canyon
Took my eye. I said I would never rest
Until we had one like it on our forty acres
Where the children could play, and for our picnics.
Thick steaks sizzling over the open fireplace!
Those two buffalo horns I had set in the cement
That I got from Ranch 101 out in Kansas
Are a nice touch. You know you love it all.
    VINE
I love you, but wish you were not so expansive.
We have too much. It may spoil the children.
    FAHNSTOCK
I wanted more than anything in my life
To give them this estate to grow up on,
To give them everything that I did not have,
And build in them such fundamentals of good character
That they cannot but succeed in later life.
    VINE
Think of what we spent on the furniture
And the interior decorators from New York.
    FAHNSTOCK
I wanted to have the finest house in town,
Bar none. Now we have got it. Let's enjoy it.
Of course, ours is not as grand as Mr. Parker's.
    VINE
Mr. Parker owns the Company
You must never forget. I feel somewhat restive
About all of these grandiose developments.
    FAHNSTOCK
Just think, I started from the bottom, on nothing.
Now twenty years later, due to industry

And hard work, I own thirty-five per cent of the stock.
>   VINE

You must be careful, though, about the future.
Son Ted will be coming back from Jefferson.
His father will want him to go into the business.
>   FAHNSTOCK

Young Ted? He's wild, and has shown no ability.
Let us cross that bridge when we come to it.

> *There is a knock on the door. Roger Parker enters, a tall, spare yet full-bodied, intelligent-looking man of 60, the president of the Company.*
>   PARKER

Hello, Vine and Adam. It is a nice Sunday morning.
>   VINE

The summer is lovely. How is Margaret?
>   PARKER

She is not feeling very well, but nothing serious.
I just thought I would drop over for a little visit.
>   FAHNSTOCK

I was just telling Vine about our new plans
To expand the farms, to put up a new silo,
And put in another herd of Holsteins for milk.
>   PARKER

You have quite a place there, a going concern.
I have heard you have bought some adjacent property.
>   FAHNSTOCK

Yes, another parcel, two hundred and forty acres.
We will put it the first year into timothy.
>   PARKER

I never had any interest much in farms.
All you men seem to be going in for them
In a great way in the last few years.
Ransome is developing a chicken ranch
And has already got twenty thousand chickens.
>   FAHNSTOCK

He is certainly aggressive; and very sound.
>   PARKER

Yes, we made a wise move in selecting him.
He was always good at figures, from the first.
You remember, after he was out of business college,
That local one over in Hopkins, when he came to us,
I think I started him at twelve dollars a week.
I came out here from Ohio in 1898.
I was luckiest of all, two years later,
To get you, Adam. You've done a magnificent job;
But I never thought you would become a veritable genius
In promoting and selling the company's products

All over the country, developing branch facilities.
We partake of the greatness of America
And nothing can stop us.
   FAHNSTOCK
                     Yes, it is wonderful
And you are the one with the original insight
Into the almost limitless possibilities.
We neither of us dreamed, not even you did,
That we would be grossing many millions in sales
When we began in that small old factory.
   PARKER
I have had the greatest confidence
In Ransome as the comptroller of the treasury.
He has grown up with it as we have become big,
A very valuable man, thoroughly satisfactory.
He has a passion for modernizing farms, too.
He says he is managing them very profitably.
   FAHNSTOCK
He is capable in handling the Company's money.
It is fortunate for both of us we developed him.
   PARKER
He became so much interested in his work
That he will not take time off for a vacation.
That's real devotion. His farms being near at home
He has no trouble in managing and attending to them.
   FAHNSTOCK
He has set up an office on Water Street
Where he now employs, I believe, twelve girls.
   PARKER
He is interested in developing real estate.
I never objected to the apartment buildings
He put up last year, so long as they make money.
No wonder we like the nickname Hurricane Ransome;
Hurry for short. He is always speeding things up.
   FAHNSTOCK
He is teaching my sons in the Sunday School.
   PARKER
That is good. He was always a moral man.
We are all secure and we have nothing to fear.
I must leave now, just a friendly chat.
We are going up to the Lakes next week.
   VINE
I hope you will catch a thirty-pound musky.
   PARKER
I fish only to order my thoughts, and get a change.
  Good-by.

VINE
> My best to Margaret.

PARKER
> > > Good-by, Adam, Vine.

He turns back.
Another thing I recall about Hurricane.
Do you remember when he first came he was restless
On my twelve dollars a week. We had, I think,
About twenty-two hundred employees then.
Within two months, with his native inventiveness,
He was selling candy at lunch hour to the workers,
Which brought him in a substantial increase.

FAHNSTOCK
> > He then
Set up a stand, and became very popular with them.
They all loved his speedy way of doing things,
Always in a rush to improve things all around.
He made as little profit as he could on each piece
But in doing it he had a lot of fun.

PARKER
Imagine his calling his place The Visionary Farms.
But as long as they pay, I guess it is all right.

> GRAYCE
> > Men, by nature expansive and idealistic,
> > Think to know how to teach us the realistic.

> WENDY
> We are less hectic, and are skeptics.
> But it is the great spring of wildness in the West.

SCENE IV   Office, The Visionary Farms
> *Scene: office of the chicken ranch on The Visionary Farms.
> Thompson "Hurricane" Ransome at his desk. An electric
> fan is running. It is summertime, July. Hurricane is a man
> of quick, energetic gestures, wiry, forceful, direct. He is
> reading the local paper. He rings a buzzer. His manager,
> Jones Taft, comes in.*

HURRY
Taft, this is a sweltering hot day.
I want these farms thoroughly modernized.
How would you like to be one of our cows?
I have to swat flies even in here.
They spend half of their energy swishing their tails
Trying to keep off the flies. I want action.
I want a master fan made with six-foot arms,
Here is a rough sketch.
> *Shows a rough sketch.*
> > > Notice the fine points.

Put plenty of power on it. Blow all the flies
Into and pen them in this metal corridor,
Like this. Set up these elements there
Where they will be automatically asphyxiated.
   TAFT
I will try to have it made in a month, sir.
      HURRY
A month! I want it done in a week.
   TAFT
I'll try, sir.
      HURRY
         Also, I want an electric fan
For each cow.
   TAFT
         Very good, sir.
      HURRY
               I want vacuum cleaners
To keep the cows immaculate, specially made
With heads to make them feel they are being massaged.
   TAFT
We can probably get some blueprints from Chicago.
      HURRY
Chicago, nothing. Adapt them. Have them made here.
I want them set up in a week.
   TAFT
         I'll try it, sir.
      HURRY
If you cannot manage the works to suit me
I will have to get somebody else who can.
How many were there here over the week end?
   TAFT
We served free lunches to ten thousand, sir.
      HURRY
I spent ten thousand dollars on the children's pool.
Was it full, too? Do they use the swimming pool?
   TAFT
It is full every day, sir, crowded Saturdays and Sundays.
      HURRY
It makes me sick and tired to procrastinate.
When I started this chicken farm two years ago
So many visitors came to see the ranch
I had to have a hotel put up to take care of them.
I told your predecessor to build one in two weeks.
He couldn't oblige. I fired him and did it myself.
I made the contractor put it up in two weeks,
Including music room, library and billiard room.

TAFT
And a very commodious place it is, sir.
HURRY
How many chickens have we got now, all told?
TAFT
Twenty thousand is the official count.
HURRY
How many from Japan?
TAFT
                    Five hundred and fifty-five, sir.
HURRY
How many from Brazil?
TAFT
                    A thousand, and as of yesterday, two.
HURRY
What about the new cross breeds?
TAFT
                         Coming along nicely, sir.
We are losing quite a few to an unknown disease.
HURRY
What we need is a chicken physician and surgeon.
Get on long distance, call the State University
And see if you can locate just such a person.
Tell him we will give him ten thousand a year.
TAFT
Yes, sir.
HURRY
      We can easily afford that for the right man.
I must have the best expert in the field
To take care of the prize I got from Java.
I paid ten thousand for that one rooster,
The finest bird in the world, to lead the flock.
TAFT
I will make the call, sir.
He phones.
HURRY
              Make the girl hurry it up.
The only way to make money is to spend money.
There is a knock at the door. An automobile salesman comes in.
SALESMAN
Good day, sir.
HURRY
Good day. What do you want?
SALESMAN
I have a new eight-cylinder Cadillac outside
I would like to show you.

EBERHART / *The Visionary Farms*

HURRY
> What color is it?

SALESMAN
Blue.

HURRY
I'll take it, send it to my home at once.

SALESMAN
Don't you want to see it?

HURRY
> What for? Good day, get out.

Salesman goes out hurriedly. The manager returns.

TAFT
They are flying a chicken surgeon down right now.
They say he is the best in the field. The plane is doing ninety.

HURRY
How much money do we make on milk?
Maybe we had better put on some more herds
To feed the chickens. Is that new mash working well?

TAFT
Very well. We give a lot of our milk to the children.

HURRY
I want everybody in the country
To come and see The Visionary Farms.
I want to show them how we do business.
Look at that stack of letters three feet high,
Inquiries in only one day on our poultry
Which we now ship to every part of the country
For breeding purposes, or even send them abroad.
One of my best schemes was The Visionary Trail.
It will be done very shortly. I am having the V.T. insignia
In great gold and black letters painted on
Every telephone pole from Minneapolis to Chicago,
Deflecting the route to come through the ranch here.
I estimate a crowd of ten thousand on Sundays
And have built up a forty-piece saxophone band
To open up the new dance hall. Quick work,
Especially by the interior decorators from New York.

He takes up the phone, dials a number.

Hello, is this the Valence Syndicate in St. Paul?
This is Thompson Ransome of The Visionary Farms.
Send five hundred dollars' worth of the finest linens
You have for my hotel here. I want them at once.
How should you send them? Why put them in a taxi
And get them here within three hours. Hurry it up.

He puts down telephone. There is a knock at the door. Enter chicken physician and surgeon.

BEANPOLE
My name is Rubin Beanpole, to be your surgeon.
HURRY
Beanpole, listen to this.
He picks up a letter from his desk.
We have twenty thousand
Chickens here, and letters are pouring in from all sides
With checks from every part of the United States
From people who want the Visionary product.
Here is a letter from a man in Kansas City.
He wants a prize-winning rooster to beat a friend
Of his. He says, "I'm willing to pay three hundred and fifty
And split the prize money with you if I get it."
I will take him up.
He rings a buzzer.
Enter Taft.
HURRY
Taft, go out among the flocks
And bring me the best prize-winning rooster we have.
TAFT
Yes, sir.
Leaves.
HURRY
Do you think you will like the job?
BEANPOLE
The danger is to escape the natural plagues.
Often some bug or other gets into them.
It is something that destroys them from the inside.
HURRY
It is your business to keep them looking fine.
I will get somebody else if you can't keep them well.
Taft brings back a handsome rooster.
Is that the best we have got? Like it, Doctor?
Beanpole nods.
Well, this is a very handsome critter, but not
Good enough. I am determined to win that bet.
The comb is not of the proper sort. Alter it,
Beanpole, alter it.
Beanpole opens his case, like a doctor's kit, takes out surgical instruments, alters comb to make it look bigger.
HURRY
The color is all wrong. Taft, get some bleach.
Taft goes out, returns quickly with bleaching materials, hands them to Beanpole.
HURRY
Well, bleach it, Beanpole, bleach it.
Beanpole bleaches part of the rooster.

EBERHART / *The Visionary Farms* 79

> BEANPOLE
>
> Now I think he is bleached to suit.
>
> HURRY
>
> His tail!
> That is not the tail of the best prize winner.
> Taft, go out among the flocks; bring me the best
> Tail feathers off the best roosters you can find.
>
> TAFT
>
> All right.
>
> *Taft leaves. They admire the bird. He returns with a large handful of feathers.*
>
> HURRY
>
> Now, Beanpole, perform an operation
> On this critter and make his tail superlative.
> Take these extra tail feathers, splice them
> And glue them on, make him the handsomest bird,
> Worthy of The Visionary Farms.
>
> *Beanpole operates, splices and glues.*
>
> BEANPOLE
>
> There, there, sir, there is your beauty.
>
> HURRY
>
> Well, maybe. I'll bet I'll win that bet.
> Taft, crate him and send him right along to Kansas City.
>
> TAFT
>
> Very well, sir.
>
> HURRY
>
> That will be all for today.
>
> WENDY
>
> Gaiety lifts the spirit to racy heights.
>
> GRAYCE
>
> Realism makes me feel hot and frothy.

SCENE V   Office, The Visionary Farms

> *One month later.*
> *In Ransome's office at the chicken farm. Ransome is sitting at his desk.*
> *He presses a buzzer. Beanpole comes in.*
>
> HURRY
>
> Beanpole, our rooster won the grand first prize.
> I knew we could put it over on them. Success is a trick.
> I am giving you a thousand-dollar raise
> Because of the success of your operation.
>
> BEANPOLE
>
> Thank you, sir. I need a new laboratory
> To study the evidences of internal destruction.
> There is some bug destroying them from the inside.

HURRY
Have one put up at once to your satisfaction.
Hire as many assistant experts as you like.
We want the land carpeted with chickens.
Don't let anything get them from the inside.
Presses a buzzer. Taft comes in.
Taft, the insignia on the telephone poles
Directing the people to The Visionary Farms
Were completed almost at once.
TAFT
       Very good, sir.

HURRY
How many came to the mammoth celebration
When we opened the new dance hall last week?
TAFT
We expected about ten thousand, sir,
But we clocked in sixty thousand spectators.
HURRY
Fine, fine. I could be here only an hour.
Did Caruso sing?
TAFT
    He did, he sang "O Solo Mio"
Over the loudspeaker I set up.
Everybody was wild about his singing.
The multitude wanted you to give a speech, sir.
HURRY
Speech, nothing. I am a man of action.
What do you think I got the entertainers for?
I ordered thirty special newspaper writers
And twenty magazine writers to spread the word
All over the country about The Visionary Farms.
TAFT
They were much impressed, sir. Have you seen this?
He proffers a large rotogravure section setting forth in page after page the glories of The Visionary Farms.
HURRY
Pretty good. Put it on the stack of them over there.
BEANPOLE
I have to report that one of the prize roosters has died.
HURRY
Died? That's impossible. What did you do to it?
BEANPOLE
It is some bug boring from within, sir.
It is something getting in the inside of them.
HURRY
Which one? Not the Javanese Master, the Leader?

EBERHART / *The Visionary Farms* 81

    BEANPOLE

                                                Luckily not.
It was the Starry Striker from Havana.
    HURRY
Beanpole, I am going to take away your raise.
We do not want death and destruction here.
Furthermore, we have got to treat these birds right.
Taft, what we need is a chicken cemetery.
We are not just going to throw them away.
I want you to set up one on the Ridge lot.
Set up a twenty-ton marble monument;
Have carved on it, "In Rest, Our Feathered Friends."
    TAFT
Yes, sir. I will have it carved in Carrara.
    HURRY
Never mind Carrara. Get it from Vermont.
I want it all set up and placed in two weeks.
A kind of special park for our guests to walk in.
Have sculptures of cocks on marble pedestals.
I want you to install a loudspeaking system
Which can be turned on Saturdays and Sundays
Giving the recorded calls of twenty types of prize roosters.
    TAFT
That will be quite lively, sir.
    HURRY
                      That is what we want.
No death and destruction on The Visionary Farms.
We are showing the world how to manage life.
It is just as easy to have big ideas as little ones.
America is powerful, of limitless possibilities,
All it takes is speed and audacity.
Why, Hell's bells, it's easy, it's a cinch.
    BERYL
      I grew up in a bright and furious time.
    GRAYCE
      Nobody really knows what the times are like.

SCENE VI   Ransome's Office
    Office of Hurry Ransome in the Parker Corporation.
    Alone.
    HURRY
Sometimes I have to think out loud
To keep from sort of getting the creeps.
    He studies the Company's books and ledgers.
I always thought it was easy to juggle books
Since I studied them at Hopkins College.
These double entries balance and check off,

But they didn't think anything about time;
Time is of the essence, and time is the trick.
Funny, it was seven years ago
I borrowed that five dollars from the Company's funds.
I intended to put it right back;
It was easy to get away with, hard to put back.
Once on the books I could not adjust for it.
That was the beginning of my system.
I remember how innocent it all seemed then
And I was drunk with my secret vision.
With the Company growing, so big and sound,
And I controlling the books to the last penny,
I developed a system that worked, a real tap root.
First I drew on a bank in Birmingham.
It always takes a few days for the mails.
To cover that check I would draw on a bank
In Omaha; to cover that, on a bank in Scranton.
If I needed more time, on a bank in New York
Or Boston. With business mounting to the millions
I always had a flock of checks in transit.
Of course they all paid off in time.
The auditors went through the books each year,
Found nothing amiss; they believed in money in transit.
I had it in a delectable state of transit,
Going around in accord with my stratagems
Which were figured with meticulous attention.
If it had not been for that first five dollars
I do not believe I would have done such scheming.
As it is, I have found it as easy to take
Twenty thousand dollars as two hundred
And nobody in the world knows the difference.
I have the figures in my head over the years,
It has been seven years now since I began.
I have kept my secret inviolable,
Inviolable from wife and family, or from any man.
The figure stands at over a million dollars.
I, Hurricane Ransome, am the man.
Everything pays off, everybody is prosperous,
The system itself is as strict and mechanical
As the whole process of making money is.
I am bound upon the wheel of my own design
And force myself into frenzies of activity
In presenting to the world The Visionary Farms.
I am absolutely bound by my own system,
Cannot even take a vacation of a week,
I must be on hand all the time, relentlessly
Fixing the books, covering the checks,

Bedazzled by my big embezzlement.
I have to keep a light shining in the world,
A fierceness of action and of energies
For the frenzies of the darkness in my heart.
As an actor I will not wince, or show a sign
Of the abysmal knowledge fighting in my vitals.
My wife, my child, Mr. Parker, Adam Fahnstock,
How could I do it? How could I betray you?
It is the evil getting me from the inside.
The slightest, innocent-seeming insinuation
When it all began, back in *1914*,
Has grown in my hand to my most monstrous sin.
I am bound upon a wheel of fire,
There is no end to the agony I am in.

SCENE VII   Fahnstock's Living Room, six **months later**
It is evening.
VINE/WILLIAM/PETER/SUZANNE
    VINE

William, you sit over there. Suzanne,
Come and cuddle up by me on the divan.
We are going to hear Peter say his speech,
We will rehearse him for the Declamatory Contest;
Miss Williams chose the title, "The Turk Must Go."
Do you think you have learned it by now, Peter?
    PETER

I have put a lot of time on it. I think
I can say most of it. Just think, maybe
I will get to go to the State Oratorical Contest.
    WILLIAM

I was never good at learning speeches;
Mathematics is much more interesting.
Pete said some of it at the Duo meeting.
Our rivals, the IRT's, have orators too.
They are going to try to win the contest.
    PETER

Duodecim is much better than the IRT's,
We have the best literary society
In high school.
    SUZANNE

What about the Happy Workers?
    VINE

Suzanne, you were certainly energetic and fine
To form the little group of girls your age
And be the leader of the Happy Workers.
    SUZANNE

Well, Pete, why don't you say your speech?

WILLIAM
O, Mother, did Pete tell you he has been elected
To be editor of the next year's Annual?
VINE
Yes, I think it is wonderful. And that you
Are going to be the captain of the football team.
WILLIAM
Fullback. Pete is going to play right halfback.
It looks like we are going to have a heavy team.
If we work together maybe we can beat St. Paul.
VINE
Now let us listen. Go ahead, Peter.
PETER
                          Mother,
I really do not want to say it yet.
Give me a few more days to learn it by heart.
I need to say it to myself up in my room.
VINE
Well, all right, Pete, if you do not wish to.
We will rehearse it some other time, you and I.
Suzanne, you go up and get ready for bed.
I'll come and tuck you in, and give you a kiss.
Boys, you had better go to your rooms and study.
You children are all so fine, I love you so much.
The children go out.
Ever since Peter made that wild left-end run
In the Creston game last fall, hurtling across the sideline,
And knocked me down hard to the ground,
I have had a pain in my chest where his head hit me.

SCENE VIII   Mr. Parker's Living Room, six months later
PARKER
Come in, Adam. It is nice to see you today.
FAHNSTOCK
Roger, things are getting worse. Vine is suffering
Much pain, and has to have hypodermics
Every few hours.
PARKER
            I am sorry to hear it.
I had thought the trip to Chicago would help.
FAHNSTOCK
We took her in a private car, and then
She underwent the highest voltage treatment.
Before that, you recall, we had a machine brought here
On the advice of both the doctors.
PARKER
They are known to be the best in the world.

FAHNSTOCK
They could not diagnose her case for months.
It looked like pleurisy. Then they told me,
Secretly, that it is carcinoma of the lung.
There is no hope. We have not told Vine.
　PARKER
Adam, if there is anything I can do for you at all
I will do it. To think of our close circle of twenty years
Being broken, and that Vine has to suffer so.
I will do anything in the world I can for you.
　ADAM
William is going up to the University,
Peter is going to stay home and help take care of his mother,
I am trying to be strong, to see it through.
　PARKER
Let me know if there is anything that I can do.
Adam goes out.
　　BERYL
　　Through the young streets of the talking town
　　Awareness grows, as in ancient times and places.
　　　WENDY
　　Ted has come back from the East to work for his father.
　　　GRAYCE
　　Handsome and light, he wore a golden key ring
　　When he left. The doors are open to him, returning.

SCENE IX　　　　　　　　　　　　　　The Barber Shop
Scene in Bub Woodward's Barber Shop. There are three chairs.
Ted Parker comes in, now out of college and in the business.
　TED
Hi, Bub, give me the works.
　BUB

　　　　　　　　　Okay, Ted.
We'll give you better than you got back East.
　TED
Have you seen the new roadster I have just bought?
It is a specially built convertible, will do seventy.
　BUB
No, maybe you will give me a spin in it some day?
How would you like your hair done, Ted, the same?
　TED
The same. Don't cut it off too short, though.
　BUB
You know me. I've got some new slickum to put on.
　TED
Give me the works.

Bub starts working on Ted.
BUB
How do you like being
In business? Isn't it kind of hard to settle down?
TED
I like it fine. It takes some time to nose around,
Learn the works, look into all the systems.
I have got plenty of ideas of my own.
BUB
Did you go out to the opening of the new dance hall?
TED
I drove out in the new speedster. We are certainly booming.
Ransome drew about sixty thousand for the opening.
BUB
Quite a guy, Hurry. Since you have been away at school
He has built that place up like nobody's business.
Did you see the head of the flock he got from Java?
TED
Of course, I have seen everything. It seems to work.
It seems rather crazy to call them The Visionary Farms.
BUB
Ted, it's not too bad. Since you were a little kid
Look how we have grown. Really not bad.
Your father was a true visionary,
Ted, when he began the works, and Adam Fahnstock,
Who spread the word to the ends of the country.
The town has boomed. I began with one chair.
I think Hurricane hit on a pretty good title.
TED
Well let me out of here, Bub. I've got
A date to take Molly Catherwood for a spin.
BUB
All right, Ted. There you are. All right?
Come in again.
TED
Sure will, Bub. So long. See you again. . .

SCENE X   The President's Office
*Scene in the president's office, at the Parker Corporation.
Roger Parker is standing by his huge desk. Ted Parker is
talking to him. Roger Parker presses a buzzer. Adam Fahn-
stock comes in.*
PARKER
This is very serious.
FAHNSTOCK
What is the matter?

EBERHART / *The Visionary Farms*

PARKER

Adam, Ted
Has found something irregular in the books.
He has been looking into our various systems,
As you know. Ted, show Adam the papers.
He shows Adam a check and some bank papers.

TED

This looks very irregular to me.
As a matter of fact, it looks like embezzlement.
Where is this money to be accounted for?
You see, this one does not check off. I am
Suspicious. I have studied the matter for several days.

ADAM

It certainly looks out of the ordinary.
Our books have been audited by Smith and Smith,
There has never been the slightest thing amiss.
Roger, I suggest we call in Ransome.

PARKER

That is just what I am going to do.
He rings a buzzer. Hurricane Ransome enters, at ease.

RANSOME

Well, gentlemen, what can I do for you?

PARKER

Taking the papers from Ted and Adam.
Hurricane, this is a very serious matter.
Do you see these figures here? And these statements?
They do not agree. It looks like the Company is short.
How do you account for these discrepancies?
Hurry takes out a 3x5 pad of paper from his left pocket. He takes a pencil from his vest pocket. With meticulous care, and seemingly without emotion, he writes down a figure on the pad, looks at it intently, and hands it precisely to Mr. Parker.

PARKER (*reading*)

One million, one hundred and eighty seven thousand dollars.
Hurricane, what does this mean? What is this figure?

RANSOME

I have embezzled precisely that amount of money
From the Company during the past eight years.
They are all dumbfounded.

PARKER

Hurry, you couldn't do this to the Company!
It is unbelievable. It is incredible.

FAHNSTOCK

Good Heavens, Hurry, how could you do such a thing to me?

TED

I got suspicious when I saw these papers.

RANSOME

Gentlemen, I just got careless. I just forgot.
I forgot to cover the check I had in transit.
I thought I had an unbreakable system.
It makes me feel better to make you my confession.
Do what you will. I am washed up. Eight years.
Bring in the books, and call in the auditors;
I will show you precisely how I rigged it.

PARKER

Where is our reputation for honesty now?
Why this will ruin us all.

FAHNSTOCK

      Think of our good name,
Our sterling reputation.

TED

     I thought there was something
Phoney about The Visionary Farms.

PARKER

Ransome, we will have to call the police.

RANSOME

Of course.

PARKER

  Ted, call Chief Decker.
He rings the phone.

TED

Chief Decker? This is Theodore Parker. My father
Wishes you to come right over.
He puts down the phone.
        He'll be right over.

FAHNSTOCK

This is incredible. I cannot believe it.

PARKER

We have trusted you implicitly for twenty years,
Putting into your charge millions of dollars
Because of our faith in your honesty.

TED

This will change the history of the Company.

RANSOME

I just got started and I could not stop.
Back in 1914 I took five dollars.
I could not justify it on the books
So I thought of a way to cover the withdrawal.
It worked so well I did it again, then again.
After a while I found it just as easy
To take out twenty thousand as a few dollars.
That is why I never took a vacation.

EBERHART / *The Visionary Farms*   89

Fahnstock and Parker look at each other dumbfoundedly. Chief Thomas Decker comes in.
PARKER
Thomas, you have seen much in your time.
I have to tell you the worst that has happened to us.
Ransome has embezzled over a million dollars
From the Company. You will have to lock him up.
Chief Decker gives him a hostile look.
DECKER
Why, Hurry, I wouldn't believe it. Come along, Hurricane.
He takes him out.
CONSULTING AUTHOR
addressing his wand
> Over the entire, the young, the hectic town
> I wave this instrument, projecting news
> Shall hurtle down the years their massive import.

SCENE XI   The Furniture Store
Scene in Jacob Herzog's furniture store. Jacob and his daughter Frieda
JACOB
I am one of the two Jews in this town.
Frieda, it is a long way back to Russia.
You have grown up to be a good girl
Under the aegis of our real democracy.
I am glad that you are on the Debating Team
With Levering Banfield and Peter Fahnstock.
Our store has grown big since you were little,
Since your mother died. I have been honest,
Have won the loyalty of many customers.
Who would believe what happened to Hurry Ransome?
He was always doing people good,
Speeding things up, enlarging the horizons,
Making more work, and urging strenuous efforts.
FRIEDA
He was so serious in Sunday School.
He always preached to us on good and evil.
He exhorted us to do good, to shun evil.
I remember the dramatic experiment he made
With a silver dollar, the pure one, the black one.
JACOB
Yes, who would believe what happened to Hurricane?
The people serenaded him in the County Jail,
Some with guitars and banjos, boys with saxophones,
A voluntary crowd of a thousand townsmen

Came to pay their tribute to the Hurricane.
They raised sums, they tried to bail him out.
The magnitude was just too much to cope with.
They formed a committee of his admirers
Even before he was sentenced, to get him out
As soon as possible from the State Penitentiary.
> FRIEDA

I think he was evil. They should put him away for life.
> JACOB

You are young, Frieda. You do not understand life.
The thinnest line divides the false and true.
It might have happened to your father.
> FRIEDA

                                    No, Father,
Not you. You are as wise as the world. What did he get?
> JACOB

He was sentenced to fifteen years in the State Penitentiary.
His name is broken, his honor is gone,
His wife has died of the shock, and his son,
What can become of his young, his tender son?
Always be a good girl, Frieda.
> FRIEDA

                                    Father, I will.

SCENE XII   The President's Office

Scene: The office of the president of the Parker Corporation. Mr. Parker is sitting at his desk. He rings a buzzer.
> PARKER

Adam, the banks are threatening receivership.
It is a question whether we will be able to carry on.
I command you to turn in your stock to me at once.
It is imperative to cover the deficit.
I cannot cover it all. You own a major block.
I have decided that you must turn it in.
> FAHNSTOCK

Why, Roger, this is inconceivable,
This will ruin me. Would you do such a thing?
Do you understand what you are saying?
The value of the stock is worth now practically nothing.
You cannot do such a thing to me.
The Chicago bankers have withheld receivership
Under the stipulation that I execute
And bring us out of this. You know that well.
They place a most absolute faith in me.
> PARKER

I own this Company, Adam. My word is law.
You will find in footnote thirty-four

EBERHART / *The Visionary Farms*

Of the contract we signed twenty-one years ago
The powers delegated to the President
To call in stock whenever he deems necessary.
  FAHNSTOCK
Roger, my wife is dying of cancer.
  PARKER
Adam, you will turn in your stock by tomorrow noon.
  FAHNSTOCK
Your conduct toward me is intolerable, despicable.
I feel that Ted has put you up to this.
I am the man who has made this Company gigantic and famous.
We have worked together as a powerful team
Through the full years of our maturity.
You know that the bankers believe in me, not you.
You are saving your own face at the cost of mine.
You are making your right-hand man the scapegoat.
Roger, are you capable of such vile trickery?
Neither you nor I was to blame for Hurricane.
You hired him, promoted, believed in him,
I with you. We both trusted him implicitly.
Now that he has pulled the wool over our eyes
So that we have been blind for eight whole years,
You are not man enough to take the rap
Along with me, but you would ruin me.
  PARKER
You will turn in your stock by tomorrow noon.
  FAHNSTOCK
You would do this with my wife on her death-bed?
  PARKER
Money is stronger than life, Adam, much stronger.
  FAHNSTOCK
You are vile, treacherous, you are obscene.
You would trample on every decency,
Every one of our thousands of acts of good will,
Every fine and just and generous act,
You would destroy the home and the family,
You would destroy me when I most need you
For the weak motive of saving your own face.
You put my powerful nature in a frenzy
Against the gross wrong you are accomplishing.
You make me mad and livid with rage.
You are crazy in the head, Roger, you are wrong.
  He makes to rush out.
  PARKER
One thing before you go, Adam Fahnstock.
You have been getting too big for your own boots

For quite a few years now, for quite a long time.
I own this Company. I am the President.
You cannot command me. I am the law.
Fahnstock rushes out in powerful realization.
    FAHNSTOCK
O, whatever gods there are, give me restraint!
Deliver me from the evil power of hate.
        GRAYCE
    I like the idea of violence, not its use.
        WENDY
    What if Hurricane had never been found out.
    He is vital as part of the upsurge of America.
    If he had kept on, only Death would have found him out.
    A curious villain to be such a heady hero.

SCENE XIII   The Apple Orchard
Scene in the apple orchard of Adam Fahnstock's estate.
FAHNSTOCK/WILLIAM/PETER/SUZANNE
    FAHNSTOCK
Suzanne, close the door of the car. Come over here.
They stand under an apple tree in full bloom; it is June, 1922, the whole orchard is in bloom.
Children, I have brought you out here to the orchard
Because there are many things that I have to tell you.
I want to talk to you here in the orchard I planted,
Where we have had the Maypole every spring, so many
Picnics, and every fall the fragrant cider mill.
It is a special place we have loved, since you were small.
I want you to look me straight in the eyes, each of you.
I have taught you to be honest, straightforward and clean,
We have given you everything that love can give,
You have grown up to be industrious and fine.
Now you must steel your souls, for this is hard.
You have heard the story of Hurricane Ransome.
You know that Mr. Parker and I trusted him,
That we saw him as a competent bookkeeper
Many years ago, promoted him, and elected him
Years ago to be comptroller of the treasury.
For eight long years he has betrayed us,
As you know, taking money illegally,
Cunningly and viciously from the Company
Without either of us suspecting it,
So cleverly did he cover it all up.
I married your mother in 1898,
The finest woman that I had ever known,
The finest woman that I have ever known.

We came out here when the town was very small.
Here I began my progress in the business,
Our love was perfect, and here you all were born.
We have had a wonderful and loyal family.
Strong as I am, it is hard for me to go on.
I must tell you the truth, and I will tell it.
While you do not know all of my affairs
You know that I own a great deal of the stock,
Yet a considerable less than the controlling part.
Mr. Parker has seen fit to call this in,
Which means that I have to sell it to him
At practically nothing, at great devaluation,
So that my fortune of twenty years is gone.
   PETER
Father, I have forty dollars in my savings account.
I want you to take it.
   FAHNSTOCK
                         Bless you, son, that wouldn't help.
   WILLIAM
Father, I will quit college and go right to work.
   FAHNSTOCK
Fine, William, but I hope you will not have to.
   SUZANNE
I will do everything I can to help Mother.
I will pick her some apple blossoms, now.
   FAHNSTOCK
                                   Do that, darling.
We will have to live in a different way.
We will have to give up many possessions,
We will have to stick very closely together.
   WILLIAM
The Parkers are the best friends of our family.
I do not understand it, it seems too cruel.
   FAHNSTOCK
The world is a place of struggle. We have to meet it.
Now come close to me here, all three of you children.
I want to put my arms around you, and love you.
This is the hardest thing to do in my life.
Steel yourselves now, boys. Suzanne, come close.
We have done everything we could for Mother
Since her terrible illness began.
You have all done everything you can.
We are up against something beyond us.
I have not been able to bear to tell her
And now I must tell you, I must tell you the truth.
Mother is worse, and has not a chance for life.
  They all weep, restrained by Fahnstock.

Now you children must try to be strong.
While there is love there can be no death
For we carry love with us to our own end.
Love we carry in our memories.
  PETER
Do you think Mother knows?
  SUZANNE
                    Mother is so beautiful,
I love her with all my heart and soul.
  FAHNSTOCK
                    Children,
I do not know. The doctors have advised us
Not to tell her. But about two weeks ago
Late at night she called me to her bedside.
Her suffering was for the moment slightly lessened.
She told me that she had loved none other,
And of her love and devotion to you children.
Then she said nothing, but looked me in the eyes.
We held our hands together a long time.
Then she quietly took off her wedding ring
And silently she gave it back to me.
Then the pains came, I had to give her more morphine.
  *Toward the end of his words he takes out the wedding ring
  and holds it up to them.*

SCENE XIV   Home of the Everymans
  CONSULTING AUTHOR
  Waves his wand
Thank you, ladies and gentlemen, that is all.
We are going to leave the action at this point.
All of these gentlemen have become madmen,
Due to the enormity and gross enchantments
Of the times, astonishing products of America;
Each might soon be at the other's throat
And lay some bloody forms about our stage
Not unlike the old, gross days of Elizabeth.
Now let us enjoy what's done, and let's construe.
Let us keep vile actions off, and bring on thoughts
To estimate these matters to a standstill.
We are not going to have the usual climax;
Originality is to leave it to your imaginations.
Homer is more realistic than Shakespeare.
You continue beyond the high peaks to the lowlands.
Violent actions are flattened out by the years.
  ROBIN
You pay a tribute to the time's confusions.
We confess our lethargy and inability

To conclude the action dramatically.
Do we not owe fidelity to action?
    CONSULTING AUTHOR
No, we owe fidelity to talk.
It is the temper of our times to rage
And talk tragedy into comedy.
Now Adam Fahnstock could kill Mr. Parker,
But all these men were too intelligent,
The matters too complex, too thoroughly understood
In one way, yet not understood in others,
As, that Ransome did not estimate himself,
The compulsive vessel of universal evil,
Yet understood well the actions of the world.
Adam we see in a Homeric rage
Who could heap coals of fire on adversaries,
Yet we contend he was too pure a man
To venture murder. Ransome will not break jail
And shoot the town up in a Western riot.
You know his character is such that soon,
The model prisoner in prison, soon
They will have him keeping the penitentiary books,
A true-to-life pure comic touch, is it not?
    ROBIN
He's much too smart for fifteen years in jail.
By good behavior, that irony and mockery,
They will let him out in seven years or eight,
A halfway measure suiting our society.
Parker, the man of the letter of the law,
We may assume will feel no guilt, but go
In due time to his sixty-two-foot tomb,
The largest in the local cemetery,
Unblamed, the dauntless American Millionaire.
Or if guilt stung him, he would never show it.
    CONSULTING AUTHOR
And Adam, by being too good would not be downed
But change his life and live in militant ability.
The Greeks would show one of his enraged sons
With purpose growing like a power in his vitals
Who, twenty years later in a red rage,
So pure and implacable a lover of justice,
The elders dead, would kill the son of Parker.
    GRAYCE
I would like to see you work that out.
I would like a just action, less that's theoretical.
I wouldn't mind seeing some accurate shooting.
    CHARLIE
I keep the emotional feeling of the conflict.

It is the new play to indicate, not overstate.
> WENDY

Just a little like my Spanish folklore.
> BERYL

Life's complex enough. Who'd think to tie it up
Into a neat dramatic package? Life is cloudy.
> CONSULTING AUTHOR

I will put my wand back in my jesting pocket.
We see that everyman's both good and evil,
None knows quite the world, all are vexed
By impenetrable clouds of various fortune,
Caught upon the stage of time, mankind showing.
Some lights we turn up in our cynic syllables
To show the faltering steps of Everyman.
> JASON

Attitude is all.
> ROBIN

         Ours is disinterest.
We have shown the brutal spectacle of the world,
Evading the true awe of reality,
To plumb down into blood-deep savagery,
But we would throw out scenes of the passional
And weave around them pleasing ideation,
Evoke, and leave the rest to contemplation.
Thus, in our modernistic, small society
Handle chaos, and keep a balance of sanity.
> BERYL

Let us end it then on a round of drinks.
 She passes drinks around.
I propose a toast—
> JASON

         To purity of discourse.
> WENDY

To the larger vantage in the smaller scope.
In times of hurtling egomania
A little touch of modesty is nice.
> GRAYCE

To poetry.
> CHARLIE

    To dialectical maturity.
> BERYL

Let us sum it up and drink to Comedy,
A bobbing freight upon a fashioned sea.
> ROBIN

Disinterested, yet with some love of man.
There is a justice beyond character that is time.

                           CURTAIN

A NOTE ON THE PRODUCTION, *The Poets' Theatre, Cambridge, Massachusetts, May 1952*

To confine a verse play to a naturalistic set is to put a dancer into a tailored suit. The play should be set free to evoke whatever images it will and utilize the theatre's most powerful weapon, the dramatic imagination. Verse, starting an echo of some half-remembered moment in the life of the spectator, will create its own scenery in a way that painted canvas cannot. If we are allowed to listen without distraction, we are caught up in its sound. We are in this room—yet we are not. We are in another place, the image-place, the story-place, until it is finished and we are released.

It was this state of suspended time that we were eager to catch in the Poets' Theatre production of *The Visionary Farms*. We wanted Adam Fahnstock's story to be greater than the party, but to grow out of it, to burn in its midst, and to die out before the eyes of the spellbound guests, who were kept on stage throughout, at times as spectators, at times as critics, and at times becoming so emotionally involved that they felt compelled to *act* the parts. Robin played his own leading man. Wendy and Grayce, acting as a sort of chorus, moved from the shadowy edge of the room into the light to make their comments. Simultaneously, the actors changed the angle of a table, moved a chair or two—whatever was needed to set the next scene, using only what was on hand in Everyman's living room. A cocktail muddler became a wand, a woman's feathered hat the prize rooster, etc. At no time was there a pause in the action, and the curtain was not pulled until the very end. Thus Adam's story was told, as any good story should be, without interruption, and only one "realistic set"—Everyman's living room—was used.

> "What, universal in a little room?
> An everywhere."

Mr. Eberhart's lines had been the key. His others did the rest. The unity of the play was preserved by not allowing it to break up into apparently disconnected scenes.

Like all good plays, *The Visionary Farms* can be produced in many ways, but the play must be kept going, its spell unbroken, and nothing allowed to detract from the verse. For the verse is evocative and powerful and the play strangely moving in the theatre. We were honored to have been permitted to do it.

JEANNE TUFTS, FRANK CASSIDY

Christopher Tunnard and Henry Hope Reed, Jr.

Associate Professor of City Planning in the School of the Fine Arts of Yale University, Christopher Tunnard is the author of GARDENS IN THE MODERN LANDSCAPE (Charles Scribner's Sons), the standard work on contemporary landscape architecture. His second book, THE CITY OF MAN: ITS ARCHITECTURE, PLANNING AND CIVIC ART, will be published by Scribner's in 1953. An assistant in the Graduate Program in City Planning at Yale University, Henry Hope Reed, Jr. has published in the architectural magazine *Perspecta* and elsewhere. *The Temple and the City* is part of a work in progress on the American scene and the aesthetics of environment, in which the physical pattern of the cities and towns is related to American traditions and institutions—economic, religious and governmental.

THE TEMPLE AND THE CITY

Illustrated by John Cohen

(The Temple and the City: Copyright, 1953, by Christopher Tunnard and Henry Hope Reed, Jr.)

TEMPLES OF COMMERCE

Take the skyline of any city in the United States. Above a low line of houses, factories and commercial buildings, a skyscraper, or a cluster of skyscrapers, announces the urban gathering of humanity. If there are exceptions, the dome of a capitol or the pediment of a city hall, they are so few that they serve to underline the vertical element. There is nothing in the shape of the monoliths to reveal their use, ranging from hotels to the offices of great telephone companies. But they have a message: We are a business society.

The United States is not a great nation because of business alone, but business accounts for its spectacular material progress. If the office tower of Waco, Texas, or the Travelers' Building of Hartford, Connecticut, is insufficient evidence, go to the Tribune Tower in Chicago, or better still, the RCA Building in New York, and from its eminence stare at the piles of steel, brick and stone. There is no escaping them here, so overwhelming the number and the variety, a menagerie of shapes and sizes. A thousand monsters, which seem to move and breathe as the noise comes up from the crowded streets below. White plumed monsters in winter as wisps of steam toss in the clear sharp air, lighted monsters at night like giant electric eels, headless monsters when, on occasion, their upper stories disappear in the fog and mist.

What disorder the scene presents from the sidewalk or from the observation tower! There a fifty-story building rises opposite one of ten stories, another looks down on an empty lot, and yet a third stands apart among rows of low houses, stiff as an out-of-season bather in the cold water. On the street below, the same disorder appears in the signs, the shop fronts, their varied uses, the now omnipresent parking lot and gas station. Over there a new front is being placed on an old building; further on an apartment house of twenty stories is being replaced by an office building of thirty, and another is being torn down to save money on taxes. All is change where there is money to be made, for all is business. "Business underlies everything in our national life," Woodrow Wilson once said, and nowhere is it more true than in these cities where American business has created its own work of art, the skyscraper.

There is nothing new in American business society. Its tradition is long and fascinating. The businessman is lost in time, and if we must have evidence of him, it can be found in Ur of the Chaldees, in Tyre and Sidon, along the Silk Route of China, in the great buried cities of the East; for the merchant was to be found wherever there was a city. When they gathered in any number, they reared temples to their gods. The Roman merchants gave the name *Mercury* (from the Latin *merx, mercis* or merchandise) to the messenger of the gods and proclaimed him the deity of business. In New York City he takes an easy stand upon the cornice of the Grand Central Terminal; with his right hand he welcomes the unheeding crowd below to his wonders, while in his left he holds the caduceus with its entwined serpents of prudence, an essential business virtue.

Thanks to this long tradition, the eighteenth-century European businessman came on a stage already cluttered with the actors of another age, feudal and monarchical; *in America he had the stage to himself*. The members of the landed gentry were to disappear from the commercial scene or to be reduced to such minor parts that it was only a question of time before business was to have almost every role. There was, of course, the South and its slave economy, but trade in cotton, after all, came to be controlled by Northern businessmen.

The overwhelming presence of business is emphasized in the plans of American cities. The skyscraper is one symbol, the gridiron plan another. There are parallel streets and right-angled streets in every community. With a few exceptions which serve to confirm the rule, the cities of America have been laid out mercilessly "by the compass," as James Fenimore Cooper observed, and no hill, no lake, no river or other natural obstacle bends the straight line.

Consider the fact that land in the United States has always been available for a price and even for the taking. How difficult it is for the American of today, seated comfortably in his automobile while driving to his home in the suburbs, to understand the excitement caused in Italy by a few peasants occupying fallow land, the property of an absentee marquis? Can he, the owner of his own home, grasp the political events of China, Iran and Egypt which spring from land hunger? *His own land revolution took place three hundred years ago.* If he lacked the money to buy a lot, he would move onto some land held by a proprietor. "To squat" meaning "to settle on uncultivated or unoccupied land without payment of rent" is a wholly American invention. William Penn, the founder of the Pennsylvania Colony, was continually beseeching James Logan, his agent, to provide a return on his vast property. "I say once again, let me have a rent roll, or [I] must sink with gold in my view but not in my power," he wrote in 1704. A quarter of a century later his heirs asked Logan to take steps against the squatters who had already occupied 100,000 acres of Penn-owned land, a revolutionary act occurring fifty years before the Declaration of Independence.

As events in our time have so forcibly brought home, land hunger is no more part of the American than it is of all men, but in the United States the hunger has a different pattern. On the one hand, the desire can only be satisfied by living on the land that is plowed—the countryside is set off in freeholds each with its house and barn—and, on the other, the same land will be sold without hesitation if a better living can be made elsewhere. In some countries, such as France and Italy, the aim is to own and to hold; in the United States it is to own and to speculate. In their desire to keep their land, early settlers would refuse to leave their tracts, at the warning of an Indian raid, to find refuge in a nearby fort; instead they persisted, and at times foolishly, in staying alone in the wilderness. ". . . Neither the interest nor inclinations of the Virginians," wrote an eighteenth-century observer, "induce them to cohabit towns." But, despite the effort that the settler spent to make a home, he would sell out and move on; "pull up stakes" he would say, the stakes marking the bounds of his land. It was true both of the wealthy and of the poor and remains equally true today. With the whole country taken as real estate to be bought and sold, the nation itself has been carved into a giant gridiron by a series of land laws beginning in 1785 and culminating in the famous Homestead Act of 1862. The desire to live on the land was made a condition of ownership in that the government recognized ownership only when a house was built on the claim. The gridiron pattern, dividing the land into quarter-sections of 160 acres each, permitted easy surveying, registration and, inevitably, speculation.

There is, of course, the very size of the country itself. All of nature is big, the rivers, the lakes, the mountain chains, the prairies and the distances. "Chicago," wrote the civic designers Daniel H. Burnham and Edward H. Bennett, "has two dominant features: the expanse of Lake Michigan, which stretches, unbroken by islands or peninsulas, to the horizon; and a corresponding area of land extending north, west, and south without hills or any marked elevation. These two features, each immeasurable by the senses, give the scale. Whatever man undertakes here should be either actually or seemingly without limit." There you have it! Would the skyscrapers have risen in a country with limits? The bigness itself has helped shape the economic pattern as well by creating a market so vast as to rival nature's scale; this market can only be supplied by mass production and mass distribution, two great American phenomena. Interchangeable parts, harvesting machines, the great railroad terminal, the chain store, the inexpensive automobile and its superhighway, all these and other products of what Santayana was the first to call "free co-operation" were not only essential to the economic development of the country but have conditioned the form of man-made America and have produced its giant farms and spreading cities.

TEMPLES TO GOD

It is this business society which constantly invites the comment that "Americans are materialistic" (as if we differed from others in our appreciation of money). It is true that in all the great cities of the world, except in the United States, the temples to God stand higher than the temples to commerce. In Peiping there is the Temple of Heaven, in London the dome of Saint Paul's, and even in Paris the Sacré Coeur of Montmartre looks down on the Eiffel Tower, but here it would seem that the omnipresent office building has taken command. Let no one be misled, as they stand on the top of the RCA Building looking at the city below, into thinking that business so dominates as to exclude other human interests. Let those who believe this look once again, for there, in and about and behind the clustered skyscrapers, are the church steeples. Everywhere they are present, not a few but a host, and in New York City so numerous are they that a whole section, Brooklyn, is known as the "Borough of Churches."

As early as the 1830's such cities as Cincinnati had twenty-four churches, Philadelphia ninety-six and New York itself a hundred, in every instance a church to each thousand of the population. Today, in smaller communities the steeples still shape the skyline, not just one tall one as in a Canadian or a European village, but several, each announcing a different sect.

If we leaf through American history we cannot help seeing how religion has touched events, more especially in its Protestant form. In the fight to free the slaves the churches, beginning with the Quakers, took the first step. Harriet Beecher Stowe, daughter and sister of Congregationalist ministers, wrote *Uncle Tom's Cabin,* which hastened the coming of the Civil War. Then the war itself with its hymn-singing, its fighting preachers, its appeals to God. There was Lee kneeling in prayer before battle, Stonewall Jackson reading the Bible by campfire, Meade discerning God's hand in his victory at Gettysburg, and Sherman's troops marching through a silent Charleston where the streets echoed with "Mine eyes have seen the glory of the coming of the Lord . . . Glory, Glory, Hallelujah!" And there is the extraordinary part that the churches have played in our own time in the struggle over Prohibition, the defeat of which marked a severe blow to the evangelical Protestants. We understand a great deal when we know that in its formative years in the last century Brooklyn was dominated by Congregationalist merchants and their preachers, or realize that the great bankers and industrialists of Pittsburgh are descended from Scotch-Irish Presbyterians, or yet again that the faint worldliness of Baltimore stems from the presence of the primatial see of the Roman Catholic Church.

The cities of America would be quite different without the ornament of the churches, and although they are often screened by the towers of commerce, the variety of this ornament is greater than may at first meet the eye. Much is added to the North End of Boston by the baroque spire of Christ Church where the lantern once burned for Paul Revere. The plainness of Shenandoah, Pennsylvania, is atoned for by the bulbous domes of the Greek Orthodox church rising on the hill. The interior of Peter Harrison's synagogue of Newport is one of America's greatest contributions to eighteenth-century architecture. Impressiveness marks the Episcopal Cathedral on its elevated site in Washington, and luxury the church of John D. Rockefeller on Riverside Drive in New York, denoting a recent and more sophisticated trend in Baptist church building. The three towers of the Roman Catholic Cathedral in New Orleans' Place d'Armes are imposing, where the effect would be dull without this central feature.

Yet these examples of churches which are civic ornaments are few and America's cities and towns, on the whole, have not derived as much physical, or aesthetic, benefit from religion as might be expected from its importance in American life. The reason for this lies in our religious traditions.

If England gave us our free individuality and our free cooperation, as Santayana put it, it also gave us our Protestantism, not the Protestantism of a single state church, but the radical Protestantism where the individual made his own covenant with his God and where he turned to the Bible for his own interpretation of God's Laws without the help of a hierarchy, ceremony, prayerbook, or a magnificently decorated house of worship. It was no gentle Protestantism which first took root here, but the stern religion of the Frenchman John Calvin, first in the seventeenth century with the great migration from eastern England to New England and, later, in the eighteenth, with the migration of the Presbyterians from Northern Ireland to the frontier along the Alleghenies. (It was the former who evolved the clapboard frame house so prevalent today in the countryside, while it was the latter who took the log cabin of the Swedish and German settlers, adapted it to their use, and made it the symbol of the frontier.) When the United States was recognized as a free and independent nation by the Treaty of Paris in 1783, two-thirds of its three million people were Calvinists, being either Congregationalist or Presbyterian. In New England where the Congregationalists were the majority by far, their church remained the official one in three states, Connecticut, New Hampshire and Massachusetts, the only church to be so privileged after the Revolution, and it was not completely divorced from the government of Massachusetts until 1833.

It is hardly surprising that eventually the mass of the people, needing something more emotional and richer in humanity, turned eagerly to the Baptist preachers and Methodist circuit riders with their message of warm love, of a faith where all men stood equal before their God and welcome in His sight, not impotent and helpless, and where salvation was offered to all, as against salvation for the few. The new sects came with the Great Revival of 1800 which spread like a flash flood up and down the frontier and east to the great cities. Baptists and Methodists would hold huge camp meetings which were social gatherings as well as spiritual ones, where men preached around the clock, read the Bible and sang hymns, and where people found temporary release from their harsh lives. By 1830 the Methodists had become the largest denomination in the country, with the Baptists a close second. Thus the main currents of the religious stream were fixed: the Presbyterians and the Congregationalists already making their great contribution in education, which had begun with the founding of Harvard College in 1639, appealing largely to the well-to-do and the professional elements; and the Baptists and the Methodists with their warm evangelism making their great contribution in the shape of friendliness and good works which are still so much a part of the American character.

The stream of American religion is broad and deep, and there are other currents—the Lutherans (chiefly people of German or Swedish descent), the Unitarians who represent Boston's revolt against a too severe Calvinism and who won Harvard College to their faith in 1805, and, above all, the Episcopalians and the Roman Catholics, as American as the rest, but who are set apart because they both acknowledge a great past and are marked by a continuity of tradition. The Roman Catholics can draw at once on the great heritage of Rome, Christian and pagan, and of all the Latin world, to the general exclusion of things English; the Episcopalians on the other hand have, in addition to the world of Rome, that rich English past so superbly symbolized by the Book of Common Prayer which, with the King James Version of the Bible, is one of England's most precious gifts. Where the Roman Catholic Church can boast of its great congregation, the largest in the country, the Protestant Episcopal Church must be content with a restricted flock, and point to its many sons and daughters who have led America in all fields, from politics to the arts.

Despite the fact that both have a larger frame of reference, neither can escape a slight tinge of Calvinism, so much a part of the American heritage. It is stronger in the Roman Catholic than in the Episcopalian; compare an American Roman Catholic church building to one in Rome, and the difference will be seen at once.*

If most of the churches built in America were plain, ignoring the message of Jeremy Taylor that "it is good that we transplant the instruments of fancy into religion: and for this reason musick was brought into Churches, and ornaments, and perfumes, and comely garments, and solemnities, and decent ceremonies, that the busie and lesse discerning fancy being bribed with its proper objects may be instrumental to a more coelestial and spiritual love,"—if so, it is no wonder that the lesser buildings of the towns and cities were commonly without adornment or formal sophistication. The religious influence in America has helped foster our genius for education, for individual liberty and for brotherhood, but in modern times it has

---

* The Roman Catholic Church in the United States—a nation predominantly evangelical Protestant—has inevitably taken on local coloring, although it would be misleading to say, as some maintain, that it has turned to Jansenism, the seventeenth-century heresy resembling Calvinism, which was condemned by Louis XIV of France and by Pope Clement XI in 1713. The Jansenist Abbey of Port Royal in Paris, as Sainte-Beuve reminds us, allowed only the luxury of choir music; Jansenism still has its attraction in French intellectual circles, both Catholic and non-Catholic, which is hardly surprising when it is recalled that Blaise Pascal and Jean Racine were among its defenders.

not yet had its potential effect on our physical surroundings, unlike religion's role in medieval or Renaissance times, or on this continent in the period of Spanish colonization. The American church today is clean and bare, an echo no doubt of John Wesley's dictum that "cleanliness is indeed next to Godliness." Is it not time to couple beauty and Godliness, as Jeremy Taylor advised, and increase the influence of the church on the physical scene?

Temples of Government

If we leave the portals of the church and look once again at the skyline, we may perhaps discern other temples rising beside those to commerce and to God: the temples of the State. We usually think of the American government in a more abstract way: in terms of its Constitution, of its elected representatives, its President, its Congressmen, the state governors and the mayors of cities, as well as the income tax; and we also think of it in terms of the army and navy, of atomic energy, of the great public works. Yet the State in America, more modest than business, less obvious than the churches, has done as much as both of these to shape the scene about us. In the center of Galveston, far removed from the cotton sheds and the factories, a columned building, modeled perhaps after Palladio's Palazzo Chiericati in Vicenza, quietly reminds us of the United States government, for it was once the custom house. Or there is the Subtreasury on Wall Street staring calmly down Broad. Or better still New York's City Hall, by the architects Mangin and McComb, a building of such exquisite proportion and detail that the surrounding skyscrapers stand back from it as if in awe. Then again there are the domes of the state houses, the golden one of Bulfinch rising above Beacon Hill which still defies competition from business towers, the more modest capitol of Alexander Jackson Davis in Raleigh, North Carolina, or Cass Gilbert's in Charleston, West Virginia, with its dome raised on a great stone drum, symbol of the state's presence.

Above all it is the Capitol in Washington which reminds us that the State has been no idle patron of the arts in decorating America. The Founding Fathers, having created monuments of democratic government in the Constitution and the Bill of Rights, were conscious of having achieved their mission in the creation of these instruments and were not afraid to symbolize in stone the message of the Republic; whereas we today eschew symbolism in building a world capital in New York.

The intense pride that Americans once had in government is shown in the history of the Capitol itself. At the outbreak of the Civil War the building was still unfinished, and instead of delaying construction President Lincoln was insistent that it be carried to completion, as symbol of the Union's strength and determination. On December 2, 1863, Thomas Crawford's statue of Freedom (modeled in a Roman studio) was hoisted to the top of the cast-iron dome as thirty-five guns roared out below, to be answered by the boom of the guns from the twelve forts which then surrounded the city.

Dilatory as it may first appear, the State in America, in all its various divisions, stands out even ahead of business as the most steadfast patron of the arts, and that continuing tradition is underlined by the creation of Washington. When Major Pierre Charles L'Enfant first drew up his monumental plan at the behest of George Washington, he saw it as his duty to create a capital worthy of the young Republic. If he suffered the fate of many planners in being forced from his post by ambitious speculators, his work was continued in spirit by Jefferson who, in his passion for architecture, saw the mission which lay before him. It was he who appointed Benjamin Henry Latrobe supervisor of public buildings; it was he who retained the services of Giuseppe Franzoni, an Italian sculptor, to work on the Capitol; it was he who persuaded Congress to appropriate moneys for the improvement of the city and spent a third of it in laying out Pennsylvania Avenue in the manner of a Paris boulevard.

The tradition once begun has never been totally neglected and when the Federal Style had passed and the country was lost in a Romantic mist, an artifact worthy of ancient Rome, the giant obelisk called the Washington Monument (it was begun in 1848 and finished in 1885), was placed near the crossing of the axes of the White House and the Capitol. With each revival of interest in the classical tradition, the capital city has continued to grow and expand; with the Neo-Classic Revival which followed on the Chicago World's Fair in 1893 all of America came to blossom in the manner of the ancients, and it was Washington which guided and set the measure. Again when the classic had all but been forgotten, it was Washington which continued in our time to sponsor tradition in the shape of the National Gallery of Art by the architects John Russell Pope and Eggers & Higgins. This building stands for much that is typical of the United States—a wealthy businessman, Andrew Mellon of Pittsburgh, contributing to the nation under the sponsorship of the State, a believer in private enterprise joining in support of government patronage of the arts.

American business society may worship the new but it never quite forgets the old. It does not hesitate to destroy old or new when the practical sense comes into play. The American sense of what is beautiful or fitting is a paradox, one which can only be understood by knowing the people and their institutions. Matthew Arnold pointed out that "until I went to the United States I had never seen a people with institutions which seemed expressly and thoroughly suited to it," and it is no less true that America reflects in its form the instruments that man has chosen to perform his will.

Government buildings in American cities have taken the form of public palaces, Federal Hall in New York being an early and splendid example. Here in 1789 Washington was inaugurated in a chamber rich with American marble, designed by L'Enfant as his first effort to serve the new nation. It is largely through these public palaces that Americans have expressed their desire for splendor, and the visitor to our cities must go to the state houses, post offices and courthouses to find the mural painting, sculpture and ornament which is missing elsewhere. If it were not for government patronage of the arts, admittedly spasmodic and at times inadequate, American communities would be much further from satisfying the need for symbols of civic and national pride, which the people of a Republic demand no less than kings and popes.

Instead of dismissing American physical creations for their sameness, ugliness and want of order, it is good to look again, as did Matthew Arnold who thereafter found himself treating our "institutions" with increased respect. The American tradition, in giving the physical patterns of the country both shape and variety, is far richer than we realize. As we have seen, the business society has planned communities, the churches have helped to decorate the cities, and the State, although the Federal government does not as yet number a Secretary of the Arts in the President's cabinet, has some tradition of patronage.

The expansion of American cities not only makes us examine our surroundings more closely, it forces us to look into the past to learn what has shaped man-made America and wherein lies our heritage. Beyond the physical problems which have come as a result of increasing urbanization, there is the responsibility thrust on the United States by its position in the world today. It is not mere chauvinism to suggest that world leadership demands a splendid physical setting. And there is a choice of directions for the new buildings, installations and facilities which will inevitably accompany American spiritual and economic maturity. Will they emphasize expediency, provincialism and a negative approach to city planning, or can they be molded into a more noble form? Can American institutions—business, religion and government—be made aware of their responsibility as patrons of civic art? This is possible, when they understand their great traditions, now obscured by the obsession with technology.

Like a child fascinated by a new toy, the American is seduced by the idea of technological advance. Material progress and scientific development are, of course, to be fostered so that we may enjoy their priceless benefits in hygiene, comfort and convenience. It is too easy for Americans, like children, to point to the mass-produced automobiles and television sets, imagining that they are the emblems of a new, bright and shiny culture, forgetting that the machine is only a tool for achieving greater things. Permanent monuments are measured in terms of art and humanity, and as we wander, often quite obliviously, among the temples that have been built in America, it would be well to pause and examine what has been created here. The scene about us, of which the mechanical toys are only a part, has after all something greater and more lasting to offer because here the artist has contributed his priceless gift and has, in his way, brought solace and pleasure to the citizens and sometimes glory and honor to the Republic. We must turn once again to our temples, whether of Commerce, God or Government, and see what the past has given, and where the present fails.

VALSE TRISTE

David Dempsey

Born in Pekin, Illinois, David Dempsey is a graduate of Antioch College and has done graduate work at Yale and Columbia. He has been a journalist most of his working life, on the staff of magazines such as *Time* and *Reader's Digest,* and as a combat correspondent with the U. S. Marine Corps during World War II. Mr. Dempsey has contributed articles and several short stories to national magazines, and from 1949 to 1953 was with *The New York Times Book Review.* He is married, the father of three children, and lives in Rye, New York.

All afternoon Miss Lovely's dancing class was pinning crepe paper along the walls and across the ceiling of the ballroom. It had been easy to disguise the room's ugliness for the Harvest Dance (tepees of corn-stalks, clusters of roasting ears hung in the corners, mounds of pumpkin around the pillars); the Cotillion, in turn, had been cheerfully bathed in gauze that was splashed with giant cardboard Easter eggs, giving the room a synthetic gaiety. But the middle of May had driven the dancers back on a season pregnant with nothing but promises—half-sprung Mayberry buds, filament-thin branches sprouting leaves like feathers that were nervous to every random current of air, and scattered in vases throughout the room, timorously arranged bunches of narcissus: the result was insubstantial; transparent to Miss Lovely's too-critical eye.

She blamed the Committee, which retaliated by looping entrails of creeping myrtle around the punch table; someone put a spray of lilac behind the ear of Stephen A. Douglas, pedestaled at one end of the hall. "Surely, Angela, a little more crepe across the bay window," Miss Lovely commanded and Angela, thin, pretty, seventeen, crisscrossed more bunting between the two fluted pillars framing the bay, which gaped out of the wall like an idiot's mouth.

They knew that she was not as disappointed as she pretended. Miss Lovely had seen too many badly decorated ballrooms made attractive by turning down the lights. Still, she had her fee to earn and, besides, there was the recital. There was no way of dimming the lights for that; mothers had to see their children. Fathers would want some idea of the return on their investment. After all, dancing (Miss Lovely assured parents) improved manners. If not at home, then at least on the dance floor.

The confusion persisted. The "service" arrived—a mixture of cut-glass sherbet cups and two large punchbowls—and was deployed across the table. Someone switched on the lights, pressing a gloomy saffron fog into the late afternoon. Up front, Humbert Wrogman was heard to say, "Old Snooty can go lump it when this is over." He expressed the consensus. A certain prospect attached itself to Miss Lovely's recital and May Dance: all suffering earns a reward, if only its cessation. The evening would be the finish line of a hard race.

Humbert had been put on "chairs." He unfolded dozens with as much clack as his loathing could command. Someone followed him with a box of palm leaf fans, sent from one of the local funeral homes. The rows of chairs reminded Humbert of Sunday School, which he had ceased to attend. In fact, the whole set-up gave him an uncomfortable, itching sensation. Miss Lovely, poised supremely on the piano stool, surveyed the results with a look of professional mistrust. It would do; it would have to do. She piped an "All right—thank you everyone—be back at eight o'clock—" and the Committee retired in disorder.

2

Actually, the Moreland Club, where Miss Lovely functioned, was a men's club. But the "ladies" (as they were always called) had come to command such influence that they no longer were required to enter at the side door, but passed directly to the ballroom by going through the game rooms. Here, tobacco-stained gentlemen at card tables leered at them politely. To the young ladies, on their way to a rehearsal, the fumed-oak paneling, the spittoons, and the gilt-framed paintings of Rembrandt nudes gave off an air of suppressed concupiscence. To their mothers, appearances—more so than the men—were deceiving. The Moreland Club was a decent enough place, even during a Wednesday night smoker.

"You may be sure," people said, "that Miss Lovely would never set foot in it otherwise." But Miss Lovely had done more than set foot in the Moreland; on those agonizing, steam-heated Saturdays in winter when her dancing class held forth; on those four or five "occasions" every year when the "social set" engaged her to manage its dances, she enjoyed court privileges, and the ultimate spoil of conquest—the allegiance of those who thought her insufferable. A social commissar, she stripped the town's social eligibles to an elite corps.

It had been quite a battle. It was one thing to have a ballroom. It was another to turn the Moreland into a dance hall. And that, in a manner of speaking, is what Miss Lovely had done. It was she who proposed the Club for Kathy MacDougal's coming-out party. Up to then such affairs had been held in the home (Miss Lovely frequently officiating). But the kind of party she envisioned for Kathy had been too ambitious even for the MacDougal place. Ian MacDougal was on the board of governors of the Club and when she proposed that he secure the use of the ballroom no one had objected. That had been years ago, and people remembered it only when they stopped to think that Kathy's party had not been the beginning but the end. Kathy—awkward, homely, desperate, with freckles and crooked teeth—had "come out." But Miss Lovely, having got her foot in the club door, had gone on. In the long run, the young ladies of New Linden could thank her.

The story is not quite so simple, of course. Miss Lovely's standing was entirely professional and, therefore, pre-eminent and non-competitive. She prospered because New Linden existed at the rim of the social whirl and she had come from the center: Philadelphia, or some such place. Her size, her mature age (she was sixty or so), her retinue (a chauffeur, who delivered her in a limousine, and Mrs. Monks, the accompanist), her bland and uncontested assumption of power enforced by a genteel Eastern accent and symbolized by an amber, tooth-like pendant which floated on her operatic bosom like an amulet—these were manifestations of authenticity which induced belief.

Yet at the moment, Miss Lovely was disturbed. Wisely, she waited until the Committee had started to leave before disturbing others. It was Humbert whom she impaled with her gaze as she approached the door. Humbert, who knew a reproving glance when he saw one, stopped short. Miss Lovely, still seated, held out a plump, withered hand. Humbert, recognizing this as the friendly (as distinguished from the angry) approach, prepared for the worst. Obligingly, he let his fingers couple themselves under hers. She sighed. Humbert fidgeted.

"Dear boy, you *are* a problem sometimes, aren't you? When I first knew you—a little boy of ten—you were the politest child in the class."

It wasn't true: Miss Lovely knew it, and so did Humbert. He had been shy, and evasively decent, but not polite. Humbert, at bottom, had the bad manners which are the privilege of the children of the well-to-do. He had once brought a poker deck to class, introducing the wicked game to his friends in the cloak room when the lesson was over.

Still, Miss Lovely had a duty, and one does not perform it by making enemies. She was determined to overlook her pupil's less agreeable qualities. "Humbert, I wonder if you are not attaching too much importance to physical appearances," she said, adopting a solicitude quite foreign to her dominating nature. Humbert mumbled something indistinct, and shifted to the other foot.

"I did not intend my classes to be free-for-alls," she went on. "One is always bound by the common sense of one's background. My pupils have been carefully picked, but that doesn't mean that we all have the same—interests. My dear Humbert, I am trying to keep you from making a mistake!"

Humbert, who was surprised to find that his hand was still locked in Miss Lovely's, felt a tightening clutch, as though she were warning him against some imminent physical danger. He backed away, all too aware that she was going to tell him Something For His Own Good. He prepared to resist: there was no doubt in his mind what was coming.

It was at Miss Lovely's that he had met Helen Snickel. Nothing short of a dancing class could have brought him close to her; close enough, at least, to recognize virtues that were suppressed in his own surroundings. Helen, whose father was foreman at the cooperage works, was rather an exception in the class. How she had ever got in was not quite clear; but once admitted, she had quite overwhelmed everybody with her gay, spontaneous ways and, as she grew older, her maturity (Miss Lovely's euphemism for sex). Afterwards, Miss Lovely had screened her girls more carefully, and insisted that the young men wear white cotton gloves. The classes were smaller and the gloves a nuisance, but Miss Lovely's position was secure.

Humbert alone, a very sour young man on the subject of girls, had not been impressed. For two years he had danced with Helen Snickel out of necessity, thanks to Miss Lovely's system of changing partners after every dance. Then one day during the preceding fall—he not quite turned sixteen—he found himself dancing not only with a girl but a female. He parted from her ten minutes later with the only regret he had ever felt at being detached from another human being. In that rhythmic interval Helen Snickel had pressed into his too-couth soul the raw poetry of her being. Nothing like it had ever happened to Humbert before. Later attempts on the part of his parents to demonstrate that other young ladies had charms only confirmed the evidence of his senses.

It was, of course, Humbert's parents and not Humbert that

worried Miss Lovely. Mrs. Wrogman had held her responsible for what she termed Humbert's "foolishness." It was, she declared, "socially awkward" to have him seen with a girl whose father worked in a factory. Miss Lovely understood, even though at heart she disagreed. And to the class, cocooned in the protocol of formal introductions, curtsies, stiff bows from the waist, and a minimum twelve-inch distance between partners, young Wrogman's fall from grace lent a certain fantasy, if not exactly a prospect of better times. "Put some sense into him," Humbert's mother had insisted. "After all, you are the one who makes the rules in this town."

"I make the rules? Yes, if you want to put it that way." Miss Lovely had sighed. "Just the same, I cannot run the young peoples' lives."

"What are rules for?" Mrs. Wrogman had wanted to know. And Miss Lovely, remembering that although she had a reputation, Mrs. Wrogman had influence, dropped the argument. "I will do what I can," she had replied with dignity.

And so, looking at Humbert, who looked at the floor, she came to the point. "Do you mind my speaking frankly? That's an advantage of *not* being your mother, isn't it? They couldn't say to you what I am going to—you wouldn't accept it. And why should you, my dear boy? Mothers are biased."

Miss Lovely let her eyes drift over the top of Humbert's head to where the ceiling fan tried to throttle life into the still air. "Gentility, Humbert. That is what I am trying to say to you. We have all kinds here, and it is better to make friends with those who fit our own way of life."

Humbert, who was no more enlightened than before, and twice as embarrassed, pawed the floor. "What's wrong with her?" he asked.

Momentarily, Miss Lovely was disarmed. "Her? Well, since you bring up the subject, I will answer you. Background. That's the dividing line, Humbert. We stay on our own side. It's like a game—a game in which the sides are marked off by a chalk line. . . and each team goes back to its own place when the game is over. You must look at my little social affairs in that light, Humbert. No matter what we do, we must not forget the chalk line. . ."

For a moment it seemed so logical that Humbert was almost convinced. The only thing that had never occurred to him was that he had been playing a game. He supposed himself in love, and although at sixteen this is a dangerous assumption, it has never been a doubtful one. He raised his head and gently detached his fingers from Miss Lovely's. "I hate girls," he said tonelessly. "I always have. Besides, I didn't want to come to dancing class in the first place."

Miss Lovely was unperturbed. "Who does?" She smiled forgivingly. "Go home now, Humbert. Come back tonight. This will be your first grown-up affair. You are graduating into a grown-up world tonight—your first real dance. The rules of the game hold fast, Humbert. It's not a class after this. No one is going to call you back and make you do the step over. Remember that, won't you?"

Humbert, released at last, fled without speaking. He ran through the arched doorway, under the fanlight of nervous fretwork, and down the dark, curved, carpeted stairway. Miss Lovely purposely kept her eyes on the floor. The line that had been drawn for the grand march stared back at her.

3

Miss Lovely's recital was a yearly event. It assured parents that the awful ordeal of learning had been worth the cost, that it had equipped their children for that other ordeal, the social life of a small town. The recital was followed by the Club dance, to which the oldest of the pupils—the teen-agers— were invited. Although the Club "gave" the dance, the class somehow was expected to make all the arrangements. It was a system that had been followed for years.

By eight o'clock parents were assembling in the lounge downstairs. By 8:15 they had moved upstairs, where they manned the coat room and at 8:30 they advanced bravely into the ballroom. Ten minutes later a dimming of lights settled them in their seats. Miss Lovely suddenly hove in view like the prow of a ship swaying toward them through vibrations of expectancy. It was not so much what she said that enraptured the parents, as the petals of reassurance that dropped from her presence as she passed across the floor. The recital was a personal triumph, the president's report to the stockholders on a successful year, and her welcome mesmerized them against too-critical scrutiny. And so, the spell cast, she retired. The orchestra blared out the opening bars of the grand march and from the coat room advanced the dancers, a little army of white taffeta and blue serge.

One thing about Miss Lovely's recitals—they followed a pattern; you could predict what was coming, and that was a great advantage about the time the heat drove fingers inside shirt collars and sent eyes furtively peering at watches. The grand march, for instance, was succeeded by a dissolving movement in which the dancers somehow swam together, the girls melting like spinning snowdrops against the courteous receptacle of outlatched arms. Out of the melee emerged pairs of dancers anchored by the one-step. They alternated, and the steps changed, and after a time the dancers, like the dances, looked alike—a school of terpsichoreans feeding off the shoals of parental approval.

Throughout the evening, Humbert was aware of two forces: his mother and father, who sat in the third row from the front and bore with fortitude the wonders of the evening; and Helen Snickel, with whom, in the course of changing partners, he danced the waltz. Humbert's feelings were ruptured. With his parents he experienced embarrassment and self-pity. With Helen, there was the more immediate contact of the flesh— more of it, in fact, than he would have chosen, for there was nothing about Humbert that was explicitly sensual. Helen wore an evening gown that bore the unmistakable appearance of having been "made over." Humbert supposed, rightly but without prejudice, that she could not afford one of her own. At any rate, the dress hung poorly, letting her arms dangle angularly and accenting, somehow, all the bony joints of her body. Humbert felt a forest of eyes laughing silently, and was made chivalrous.

After the recital, when the parents, in the communion of the occasion, had partaken of the punch and cookies, and Miss Lovely had given them her benediction, the dance began. The younger children were snatched, so to speak, from the very threshold of the evening, but the older ones, whose evening it was, stayed, waiting for the junior members of the Club. Humbert watched his mother and father depart; they had remained just long enough to satisfy the amenities. Mr. Snickel, who had sat in the next to last row, conspicuous in a suit too tight across the shoulders and hair pomaded flat against a dolomitic skull, did not linger after the final cotillion. Helen was stranded.

The crowd was coming in now; the orchestra—Jack Watson's Rhythm Ramblers—was emitting those vagrant discords that warn dancers that the time is near. Miss Lovely's graduates, huddled at one end of the hall, suddenly found themselves strangers at their own frolic. Miss Lovely had a cure for this; she drove the newcomers into their midst, scattering them like chickens before a terrier with bland impartiality. Up front, a roll on the snare drum was followed by an announcement from Mr. Jack Watson himself that the dance would start with a mixer, couples changing partners with the couple nearest them when the music stopped. A foot tapped four beats and the music exploded into the room, stunning Humbert into near panic. The lights went down and Humbert, starting to leave the floor, collided with a girl in pink organdie and a glinting pearl choker, who interpreted his awkwardness as an invitation. She accepted, and Humbert found himself with a partner.

Her name was Blanche. She was older than Humbert by two or three years, and a stranger. "I don't know *what* happened to Guy," she giggled, "and I don't care. He can just wait his turn."

They danced a few steps and Humbert gave up trying to lead. He had a pretty good idea of what had happened to Guy. Blanche said: "I'm new in town. I hardly know anybody here."

Humbert, deciding that his mother would approve of her, replied in grunts. Blanche, taking this as shyness, chattered on as he tried to maneuver them near Helen. In this he was foiled. Blanche refused to be led. Helen swam into view only to swim out again. When the music did stop it was to dump him callously into the arms of Candace Smith, a fellow pupil, willing to be led, but heavy on her feet. Humbert struggled toward Helen while Miss Lovely watched through the scented mists of the room; nay, she did more than watch—like some gravitational force, she seemed to pull them back.

And then, by one of those turns of luck possible only in the imagination or on the dance floor, Humbert found himself looking past Candace's eyes and into Helen's. The music stopped; he slid across the spangled floor, arranged that Helen's partner should dance with Candace, and thereby laid claim to Helen. The band resumed and Humbert swept his partner away to the strains of "Melancholy Baby."

How say that Humbert, at this moment, felt a new tenderness? How describe the shudder of expectancy that ran through his body like a chilblain, leaving him the frightened victor of his own ambitions? What Humbert experienced was gallantry; innate, unsuspected. Helen was no longer the weaker sex; she was the weaker class. Good breeding, ultimately the downfall of the rich in their struggle with the poor, floated to the surface of his being. With Humbert, a strange experience; something that had been prodded into life by Miss Lovely.

When he spoke it was with an air of triviality. "Say, that was some luck. I didn't see you down this way."

"I'm glad the music stopped," Helen replied. "I couldn't keep up with *him* very long."

"Him" was Tom Demarest, the football captain.

"He dances like an ape," Humbert said. "I hate him."

"Humbert, I want to stay with you. Do you mind? I don't want fellows like Tom Demarest and Si Blake asking me to dance. They think I'm just a kid. I guess I am, too. I'm afraid with them, Humbert. I don't know what to say to them."

"I'm glad you feel that way," Humbert mumbled. "No, I'm not glad. I mean, as long as you do, I'm glad you want to be with me."

From the punchbowl Miss Lovely watched. Well, she had

done her best. Mrs. Wrogman could go hang. Humbert and Helen danced well, she would say that. Isn't that what she was hired to do?

"You'll have to admit, Humbert, that we're kind of different," Helen had said to him once, but under the rustling ceiling of crepe paper their divided worlds were joined. The lights played tricks with her hair. It fell in a shower of gold to her neck, straight down, making her face seem less thin, rounder. She had never seemed as silly as the Morrison Street girls that he had grown up with and now, in some inarticulate way, she needed him. Yet always at a loss when it came to small talk, Humbert tried gallantly to pitch the conversation on a serious plane: his troubles with solid geometry, the Junior Class play (in which he was taking the role of prosecuting attorney), the camp he had attended for the last three years and would probably go back to in the summer, his sister's engagement to a young man she had met at college ... Humbert's talk had a tendency to center on himself. As the evening wore on he assumed a confidential tone. The waltz, probably (Helen thought), the dimming of lights, the muting of the orchestra, until at last Humbert spoke from some lower register of the soul.

"Look here, Snickel," he whispered. "Let's get out."

Surprised, Helen became morally punctilious, as her father had taught her to do when young men made dubious suggestions.

"What d'ya mean, Humbert?"

"Out. Home. Any place," he mumbled secretively.

"The dance isn't over," was not very convincing.

"All I want to do is breathe some air. I mean, it would be nicer with you along. We can put the top down and let the wind blow in our faces."

"Really, Humbert?"

"Why not?"

They danced to a corner of the room, a dark corner where paper streamers shimmied languidly in the draft of an open window. Humbert stepped off the floor, drawing Helen after him, and unnoticed they slipped behind the stag line and into the cloak room. Putting Helen's coat on her, he let an arm cling gallantly to her waist. She looked into his face, laughed, and let him draw her closer.

4

They drove along the river road as far as Murphy's Crossing, where the Prairie City had gone down off a sandbar years before, its half-sunken paddlewheel still marking the grave. Stopping there, Humbert turned off the lights. Frogs croaked in the reeds and the wind riffled the surface of the water. Moon-bent, willow trees clung to the shore.

"It's eerie. . ." Helen said, breaking the silence.

"You scared?"

"Not with you, Humbert." She laughed nervously.

He reached into a side pocket of his coat and brought out a package of cigarettes.

"Humbert Wrogman!"

"Look, Snickel," he said, almost defiantly, "keep this to yourself. If this got back to my old man. . ."

"Oh, I won't say a word, Humbert. But gosh, I didn't know you—"

"Neither does anybody else." He opened the package, drew out a cigarette, and lit it inexpertly. "It's a damn shame when your parents don't understand you. 'Come right home when it's over.' That sort of stuff. They check up, too. That's why I wanted to get out of there early." Humbert puffed viciously at the cigarette. "I was afraid you wouldn't come, Snickel."

"I'm not afraid with you, Humbert," she said and, in truth, she was not. She leaned her head against the leather seat. All that seemed beautiful pressed down at her from the purple sky: the stars, the sad, melancholy night, the moon-pierced clouds. Humbert pressed an arm around her and blew smoke across her face; faint passion, like a tiny flame, licked at the edge of innocence.

And yet—and yet: there was no response. Humbert enclosed her with nothing but his own self-awareness. As trembly as a colt, he faced temptation like a soldier challenged; the clear, frosty voice of his conscience said "Who goes there?" And Humbert went nowhere at all. She hoped that he would kiss her—after all, she had been warned by her father to expect the worst of young men; instead, he lit another cigarette and she sighed with the relief that often accompanies disappointment.

They sat through five of Humbert's cigarettes. Mist, drifting in from the river, glazed the windows of the car. The night condensed all around them, but its dissolving bleakness left them intact. When Humbert finished his cigarette, they started home. The windshield, swiveled into a horizontal position, scooped air into their faces as the car bounced jauntily over the dirt road. Yelling against the wind, Humbert said, "Look, Snickel, I've got an idea. You come back to the house with me. We'll grab something out of the icebox."

"Oh, I couldn't," Helen shouted. "It's late. Dad just wouldn't stand for it."

"He wouldn't know," Humbert shouted. "We'll sneak you in the back way."

When they drove up Morrison Street Humbert was surprised to notice that the downstairs of his house was a blaze of lights. Helen, hardly aware of them, recognized her father's car parked in front. Mr. Snickel, ordinarily a mild enough little man, was pacing anxiously across the front porch. The door was open and Humbert could see the silhouette of his father, clad in pyjamas and dressing gown, standing at the screen. He approached the steps cautiously.

Helen's father turned; his voice leaped out angrily: "Where is she? What have you done with her?"

Mr. Wrogman's voice, heavily censorious, boomed from behind the door. "Do you know what time it is, Humbert?"

"Answer me, you little imp!" screamed Mr. Snickel. "Where is my daughter?"

"In—in the car," Humbert stammered.

"Humbert—Humbert. . ." his mother wailed, somewhere out of sight. "We've all been so worried. . ."

"Well, I'm home," Humbert said. "What's all the fuss?"

"Listen to that, will you?" Mr. Snickel piped. "The nerve of 'im! What d'ya think I've been doing here? Well, are ya going to produce the girl, or have ya got her hidden away?"

But Helen was standing there, and seeing her, Mr. Snickel's wrath momentarily softened. "Are ya all right, daughter? Has he harmed ya? Come here to me."

Helen burst into a flood of embarrassed tears.

Humbert, who had stood his ground at the foot of the steps, strode onto the porch. "I don't know what this is all about. Why don't we all go inside and straighten it out?"

Mr. Wrogman coughed discreetly. "Humbert, I have been inviting Mr. Snickel to come inside where he can be comfortable since 12:30. He insists on walking a corporal's guard on our front porch."

"And why shouldn't I?" Mr. Snickel wheeled about to face the rumpled figure of Humbert's father. "Ain't I half dead with worry? I've told ya my daughter has no business runnin' around with your son and by the same token I've no business in your house. Thank you, I ask no favors."

Humbert, seized with a sudden and terrifying sense of defeat, clapped a hand to his forehead in astonishment, a gesture borrowed conveniently—if quite unconsciously—from the Junior Class play. "Helen—" he began, intending to plead her case, but Mr. Snickel rancorously cut him short.

"Words'll do ya no good, young man. It's the time a night that I'm thinkin' of. Two o'clock! You and your fancy cars running around all over the place. No thank you, we'll have none of it."

Humbert made a final stab at reconciliation. "Won't you just let me explain?"

Mr. Snickel drew himself up full stature. "Not a step beyond that door will I go. Any explainin'—which I doubt—can be done right here. There's such a thing, young man, as stayin' on your own side of the fence. I'm not to be tricked into thinkin' better of ya now. Good night."

Humbert, for a brief, horrifying moment found himself staring at Miss Lovely whose wraith-like figure shimmered into existence before him. Then they were off. "Helen—" Humbert shouted after them, but she followed doggedly at her father's heels and gave no sign that she had heard.

Inside, Mrs. Wrogman lay stretched on the mission sofa, with its bearclaw legs and fringed slipcover. Humbert threw himself into a chair and his father padded over to the mantel, his hands jammed in the pockets of his dressing gown. "Well, that's that," he said.

"That awful man," Mrs. Wrogman moaned. "He got us out of bed—been out there for an hour and a half, and your father and I have had to sit here trying to humor him. Do you see what you've done, Humbert?"

"Did you ever notice the odd shape of his head?" Mr. Wrogman asked of no one in particular. "He kept taking his hat off and putting it back on and I couldn't help notice the way it fitted him—like something hung on a newel post."

Humbert bounded up in a fury. "Do you have to make fun of him? No wonder he hates us." He started for the stairs.

But his mother, half raising herself, called him back. "Humbert, I want you to tell me— Oh, we were worried when you didn't come. That girl—Humbert, you didn't do anything you shouldn't have?"

Humbert stared at her as he had a hundred times when she had accused him of some wrongdoing. Arching her eyebrows in alarm, she pressed him for an answer. "You didn't, did you, Humbert?" He prepared to tell them about the cigarettes. And then, seeing the stricken look that gathered on his mother's face, he hesitated. "Yes, I did," he said, and heard her final comic peal of agony making a man of him.

ALFREDO AND THE ENGINEER

Translated by
Darina Silone

Ignazio Silone

Born in 1900 in a village in the Abruzzi mountains in Central Italy, Ignazio Silone was educated in Jesuit and other Catholic colleges. For a time he was the editor of a Socialist Youth newspaper, then a member of the Italian Communist Party from its foundation in 1920 until his break with it in 1930, so eloquently described in a chapter of THE GOD THAT FAILED (Harper). From then until 1944 he lived in Switzerland, where he wrote FONTAMARA, BREAD AND WINE and other books. From 1944 until 1951 he was active in Italian politics as a member of Parliament. Mr. Silone now lives in Rome where he is at work on another novel and a book of essays. A HANDFUL OF BLACKBERRIES, from which these chapters are taken, is his first novel in ten years. The background is the same as in his other novels, the mountain villages of his native Abruzzi. The period is that of the chaotic years immediately after World War II. The old idols have been cast out and are being replaced by new ones, but the age-old patterns of this rural society remain the same. One of the chief characters in the book is Rocco, a Communist leader in crisis with his conscience. A HANDFUL OF BLACKBERRIES will be published by Harper in 1953.

(Alfredo and the Engineer: Copyright, 1953, by Harper & Brothers.)

"In other words," said the man with the straw hat and the red badge in his buttonhole, "you think I'm a scoundrel. You simply don't trust me."

Bored and weary, the Engineer closed his eyes.

"I know, you distrust me because of my past," the other pursued. "Well, here's my answer: maybe you're right. There's sincerity for you. Now did you ever hear of a scoundrel being sincere, confessing the truth about himself? Perhaps I'm not as much of a scoundrel as you imagine. Hell, can't you say what you're really thinking?"

"No," murmured the Engineer. "I've a splitting headache."

"Bad digestion, maybe," said the straw-hatted man. "Maybe disappointed hopes have turned your stomach. But you can be certain of one thing: if I did make mistakes in the past, it was for love of the People. I sinned out of generosity, so to speak."

"You've been admitted to the Party: what more do you want?" asked the Engineer. "I hear your wife keeps a perpetual candle burning before the statue of St. Anthony."

"They're letting dogs and swine into the Party," said the straw-hatted man. "But what good is my membership card if you persist in treating me like a mangy sheep?"

He hesitated, as though searching for a word, and then added in a new, urgent tone: "Rocco, I need your esteem."

Perhaps the Engineer failed to notice that the other's eyes were full of tears. "My esteem can't get you anywhere," Rocco told him with a yawn. "Do you realize I didn't close an eye all night long?"

The two were seated outside the Café Mazzini (formerly Café of the Empire), at the only table having a large green umbrella to shade it from the sun. The reflection of the umbrella turned the Engineer's natural pallor to a look of sickliness, while the straw hat protected his companion's rubicund glow. Gathered round the other tables were silent groups of peasants, wearing dark clothes for the most part, their hats squarely on their heads and their knapsacks or other bundles clasped on their knees. They sat staring at their glasses, indifferent to the sun and the flies. Some wore tufts of badger bristles in their hatbands to ward off the Evil Eye. Among them was a young woman who held in her arms a baby so soft and tiny that it seemed just out of the egg. Everyone in this little crowd was waiting for the mail bus.

"As I was saying . . . ," pursued the straw-hatted man.

But Rocco was no longer listening to him. Shortly before, a belated traveler had arrived from the railway station, carrying a heavy suitcase on one shoulder. A working man, to judge by his appearance. It was not easy to guess whether he was native or foreign to the place. Although he had inquired at once about the time-table of a certain bus, he had neither said where he wanted to go nor bought a ticket at the counter of the café. After a while Rocco lost sight of him and stood up to take a look around. Where could the man have disappeared to? Meanwhile Filomena had brought the wine. She too wore a red badge, pinned on her bosom.

"For God's sake, don't talk in riddles," said the straw-hatted man as he filled Rocco's glass. "Try to convey your meaning in plain language."

"Well, I have a vague feeling that everything is coming to an end," Rocco found himself saying. "That's all."

"If only you were right," said the straw-hatted man. "But as usual your natural optimism deceives you. Keep this in mind: here, nothing comes to an end—ever. What do you think of the wine?"

"Begging your pardon, Don Rocco, for overhearing," said Filomena in alarm, "but what was it you said is coming to an end?"

"Everything," said Rocco, emptying his glass. "But, I repeat, it's just a feeling I've got."

"When there's an earthquake," said Filomena, "it's always the tradespeople that lose in the long run. Fields, orchards, meadows, what can happen to them? They don't change, that's natural. But do you know what it costs to replace the casks and demijohns and glasses and bottle-stands and all the rest of the broken crockery?"

"You see?" said the straw-hatted man, addressing himself to Rocco. "At most it may be a question of cash. But here nothing comes to an end, ever. Drink, my boy, this is a good little wine for clearing up one's doubts."

The road that stretched on either side of the Café Mazzini encompassed the little town. Parallel to the road, just at that point, lay the wide, stony bed of the stream, now completely dry, with a few shrubs and bushes growing here and there on the higher sand banks. A dazzling sun reverberated from this shadeless expanse of pebbly soil; the air seemed to be frying. The hills on the other bank appeared remote and faded.

Only a small part of this encircling road could be seen from where the Engineer sat with the straw-hatted man. A hundred yards farther on it curved at right angles, in front of the flamboyant baroque portal of the Convent of Santa Chiara. But if you stood on the opposite sidewalk, with your back turned to the riverbed, you saw the whole district that had been destroyed by air-raids two years previously; and beyond the ruins and a crowded agglomeration of shacks, the dark and massive outline of the prison of San Rufino and the graceful dome of the Jesuit college, both miraculously spared by the bombs.

Meanwhile two particularly shabby peasants, an old and a young one, strongly resembling each other—unmistakably father and son—had appeared in front of the café. They stood motionless and silent in the middle of the road and cast imploring glances at the straw-hatted man. He was busy pretending not to see them. The younger peasant also wore a red badge on his lapel.

"What do they want?" murmured Rocco.

"They're waiting for an answer," explained the straw-hatted man in an undertone, without looking in their direction. "From morning to night, at home, in the office, at the café, wherever I happen to be, it's a boring non-stop procession."

"What answer? Do they want to buy an indulgence?"

"Of course not. Surely you know that the poor don't need indulgences. The old day-laborers are looking for work, any kind of work. In building, or transport, as factory-hands, here or in another province, or abroad. The young ones, however, are after jobs as flunkeys; a soft job, they'll tell you, a job that doesn't tire you out. But, let it be said to their credit, there are a few young married men willing to be janitors."

"Why only the married ones?"

"The wife can sweep the stairs. This sort of thing happens after every war, it seems. The aftermath of a war is the worst calamity of all."

At last the old man standing in the middle of the street managed to catch, and for a few moments to hold, the eye of the straw-hatted gentleman. With an affectionate gesture toward his son who was beside him, the old man then asked humbly: "Is there any answer for him, Don Alfredo?"

"Unfortunately, nothing."

"But, begging your pardon, Don Alfredo, may I still hope?"

"Of course, of course, while there's life. . ."

The old man looked at his son with a reassured smile; then, pointing to himself, as though in a humble act of *mea culpa,* and in still lower tones, he added: "Don Alfredo, begging your pardon, what about me? Is there any answer for me?"

"Unfortunately, no, there's nothing for you either."

"But, begging your pardon, Don Alfredo, may I still hope?"

"Of course, of course."

"Thanks to you, Don Alfredo, a thousand thanks for your kind words. Will you pardon us if we come again tomorrow?"

Meanwhile the shade, like a vast canopy of pale purple, had spread to the other tables of the café. Filomena hastened to shut the green umbrella and carry it inside. Just then there rose a warm, light breeze; the town was breathing freely before dusk. A breeze, so light that it passed through the walls, reached the kitchens and entered the remotest sacristies, from which it intermittently wafted smells of green peppers, freshly baked bread and incense.

"Where, at the moment, is your legal residence?" Alfredo asked the Engineer. "The authorities are looking anxiously for you."

"The authorities?" said the Engineer. "Do they want to arrest me?"

"Good Lord, what are you thinking of?" Alfredo protested.

"They want to present you with the certificate and silver medal for valor, for your action against the Roadhouse."

Rocco made a bored grimace. "I've no right to it," he said. "They can give it to Zaccaria. The merit was his."

"If it's not important for you, it's important for the Party," declared Alfredo. "It would be a proof to our opponents that we. . ."

"Who is 'we'?" interrupted the Engineer.

But his tone left Alfredo speechless.

For the last half-hour Filomena had been proclaiming to the clients of the café: "It'll be here any moment, it can't be much longer now." Suddenly an uproarious clatter heralded the arrival of the mail bus. It was a gigantic bus, out of all proportion to the modest dimensions of provincial roads. The peasants sprang to their feet at once, hoisting their belongings on to their shoulders or clutching them under their arms. Resigned to the obligatory scuffle, they thrust themselves at the door of the bus. It was in point of fact already overcrowded with passengers and overloaded with sacks, hampers and suitcases. A tall, thin woman, dressed in black and carrying a large basket on her head, was protesting loudly to the driver, demanding a seat. "I paid to be seated," she said. "And I want to be seated."

"Show me your ticket," said the driver. "Just show me where it's written that you've a right to be seated."

The passengers who already had seats laughed, whereupon the woman became still more resentful and turned her exasperation on them.

"Listen," said an old woman to her through the window, "if you happened to have a seat, wouldn't you laugh yourself? Well, then!"

Alfredo was laughing too.

"What is there to laugh at?" asked Rocco. "This wine is the only thing worthy of respect I've found here so far. Filumé, another bottle."

"I'm laughing because I've got a seat," said Alfredo. "And you're wrong not to laugh, since you've got one too. You're entitled to laugh. But you never did have any sense of solidarity."

Strangely enough, when the bus got under way, not a single passenger seemed to have been left behind. But shortly afterward the man with the big suitcase reappeared in the doorway of the café.

"Didn't you manage to get on?" asked the Engineer.

The man made no reply. Leaning with one shoulder against the door-post, he seemed absorbed in watching a little donkey that stood motionless and indifferent in the middle of the sun-baked and deserted riverbed. What could he be waiting for? It was not easy to guess.

"The bus to San Luca—you were asking for its time-table a while back—" explained the straw-hatted man to the newcomer, "stopped running a good fifteen years ago. There was a time when every village had its own mail coach, but now the Fornace bus serves the whole valley."

"Won't you sit with us?" said the Engineer, smiling at him. "Help us finish this bottle. The wine is still the same."

The man sat down, raised his glass politely saying "Your health," and emptied it. He was about forty years old and sturdily built. His hands were clean and strong but deeply fissured, like those of a mason or stonecutter. The most striking thing about him was his way of looking at people—open and straightforward, yet wary. He showed no sign of embarrassment at finding himself seated with persons of a different class.

"I'll bet that handsome sweater you're wearing wasn't bought in our part of the world," said the straw-hatted man. "You never see that kind here. The suitcase, too."

"Drink," said the Engineer. "The wine at least is still the same."

"Your health," said the newcomer. "Yes, the wine is still the same; but maybe they keep it in demijohns and not in casks. Am I right? The next bottle is on me. *Padrona*, another."

"Later on, if you like, I can take you to San Luca," said the Engineer. "I've got a car, and I'm going that way myself."

Alfredo grew pale. "That means you won't wait for this evening's meeting with the contractor?" he asked. "Are you serious? I don't understand."

Rocco's only reply was to shrug his shoulders, without looking at him.

"I don't understand," repeated Alfredo dejectedly. "Good God, can't you see how important this meeting is? The prestige of the Party is at stake. Three hundred unemployed will be certain of a job for at least two years. The contractor, luckily for us, needs to buy some indulgences because of his past. He said he'd be delighted to meet you, he admires you, he knows everything about you."

"Everything?" Rocco interrupted incredulously.

"Everything," Alfredo assured him bravely.

"Then he knows a lot more than I do myself," Rocco concluded.

Alfredo seemed to be genuinely upset. "You promised you wouldn't let me down this time," he complained. "Don't you understand, we mustn't let any opponents of our Party get the credit for rebuilding the bridge. I've asked some friends to dinner too; there'll be a young lady who's anxious to meet you. She's worth meeting, believe me. She's not a woman, she's a magnolia. Just wait till you see."

The stranger appeared somewhat bewildered by this conversation, whose meaning escaped him, but which incidentally concerned him also. At the first pause, not without embarrassment, he tried to change the subject.

"Are you a native of the valley too?" he asked the Engineer. "May I know which family?"

Rocco smiled and filled the three glasses. "Strange," he said. "Reserved people, as a rule, are not given to curiosity."

The man reddened and excused himself somewhat awkwardly. "It wasn't curiosity," he said.

"All right," conceded the Engineer with a smile. "Reserved people have the right to be on their guard. Well, you guessed it. My birth certificate would have it that I too am a native of this valley."

"As for surnames," said the straw-hatted man, "they still exist. So far, no one seems to have thought of abolishing them. But they don't tell you anything about a person nowadays. They're as antiquated as the stage-coach."

Holding his glass at eye-level and pretending to observe the red color of the wine against the light, the stranger was musing. An intent, weary look came over his face. The Engineer watched him, trying to recall something, unable to take his eyes off him. "Where did I meet him?" he seemed to be wondering. Something important, he felt, was eluding his grasp.

"Do you really mean to drop this evening's meeting?" Alfredo again asked Rocco. "Has it occurred to you what the Party might think?"

Rocco took no further notice of him.

"You needn't bother driving me right into the village," said the stranger to the Engineer. "You can leave me on the main road, at the foot of the hill. As a matter of fact, that would suit me better."

"What about your bag?" asked the straw-hatted man with a smirk. "You're hardly going to climb the mountainside and arrive in the village with that big suitcase on your shoulders?"

The stranger looked at him as though from far off; as though he were deaf. The straw-hatted man blenched under the look and relapsed into silence. But for some time past Filomena, anxious not to lose the thread of the conversation, had been polishing the marble top of the table next to theirs, patiently going over and over the same bit of marble with her duster. Now was her chance.

"A while back, this man asked me to keep his bag for him," she said. "Is there anything wrong? Should I refuse?"

Her look seemed an appeal to Alfredo for advice.

"Pardon me, pardon me," said the latter, suddenly edging backward on his chair. "Nowadays a man has no right to wonder at anything."

"When the bottle is finished, we'll leave," said the Engineer, laughing. "The visitor will get out wherever he pleases, that goes without saying."

Alfredo hastened to make clear his train of thought. He could not bear to be distrusted, to have doubts cast on his discretion and solidarity. The Engineer tried to follow him, but gave up when he realized how disproportionate his effort was. The stranger, on the other hand, paid no heed to him at all; he remained pensive and impassive, watching the Engineer pour the wine.

"Your health," he said with a ceremonious gesture, as he drank the last glass before getting up to go.

Rocco vanished behind the café building, to reappear a moment later at the wheel of a battered jeep bearing numerous scars of repairs and collisions.

"When are you coming back?" Alfredo called after him.

"Maybe tomorrow," he answered from the moving car. "Or maybe in a month."

2

Alfredo removed the straw hat from his head and proceeded to use it as a fan. It had left a red mark on his forehead and temples. He abandoned all effort to hide his disappointment and disgust. Filomena lingered near him, polishing away at the marble table-top. Her brawny forearms were adorned with blue tattooing which depicted the Blessed Virgin with the Holy House of Loreto, and the Blessed Sacrament in the eucharistic form of a chalice surmounted by the Host.

"A man like you, Don Alfredo, has no reason to lose heart," Filomena told him in almost maternal tones. "What the devil, you're out of danger now, you're back in the saddle again."

A strange kind of saddle, however, on a queer bastard horse.

Under the previous regime Alfredo Esposito had for many years filled the important post of municipal tax collector, although his true vocation, as even his friends admitted, was vernacular poetry. It was the Head of the Government in person who had forced him, during a public ceremony, to accept the post then and there, so impressed was the illustrious personage by Alfredo's skill in performing an innocent little experiment which he had devised without any ulterior motive and purely for the sake of entertainment. He had plucked a live hen, swiftly and completely, without provoking the slightest complaint on her part, and indeed to her visible satisfaction. Alfredo accepted the onerous and unexpected appointment, as he put it, "out of abnegation and for the People's sake." Contrary, however, to the apprehensions shared almost universally by the literary critics of the district, his poetic vein did not suffer in the least as a result. Moreover, he gave evidence of surprising practical virtues. In the space of a few years he settled all his own debts and those of his in-laws, paid off various mortgages, and finally built himself a beautiful house with a large garden on a hill overlooking the town. Once his more urgent needs were satisfied there began what was undoubtedly the happiest period of his life. He threw himself heart and soul into works of charity. It was at his instigation that the municipality established open-air camps for rickety children. He was often to be seen in the poorer districts of the town. No needy person appealed to him in vain. The parish priest actually used to call him the Good Samaritan. His next inspiration was to build a grotto with a white statue of the miraculous Lady of Lourdes in the tender green shade of some weeping willows that stood in the center of his garden. This, he would explain, was meant to show that his good fortune had by no means withered his most tender childhood sentiments; it was also to protect his new property against the Evil Eye of the envious. The day His Lordship the Bishop came in person to bless the holy grotto was undoubtedly a solemn date in the life of Collector Esposito. The sherbet served to the guests was prepared by an ice-cream specialist summoned expressly from Sulmona and remained, in that part of the world, an inimitable paragon to be recalled whenever refreshments were discussed.

Collector Esposito could, however, prove himself severe and inflexible when the occasion demanded. Charity was his right, but not his duty. He allowed no one to make claims on him. His refusal of the town messenger's request that the municipality pay for the resoling of his shoes remained memorable as an example of the healthy and rigorous principles which inspired his administration. It was on that occasion, during a public meeting in the biggest hall in town, that the Collector pronounced the motto which went down to posterity as the quintessence of his economic doctrine: "The resoling of shoes," he said, "is a private concern." And since the town messenger had the impertinence to appear barefoot next day in the town hall, he was immediately dismissed for this grave offense to civic decorum. It was of course inevitable that when the regime changed hands, Collector Esposito should run the risk of winning a martyr's crown.

"But now you're back in the saddle again," Filomena repeated to console him.

Back in the saddle? A fool's consolation, that. If it is important to avoid dying, the method of surviving is not any less important. Alfredo continued to fan himself with the straw hat. Now and then he would mop his flushed face and his neck, chest and armpits with a large handkerchief. In the storm that had accompanied the change of government, several of Alfredo's best friends had been killed—martyred without any special merit on their part. But he and others in his situation, without any special demerit, had mysteriously and inexplicably found themselves overnight among the victors. In fact, it was in the house of ex-Collector Esposito that the historic first meeting of the Liberation Committee of the province took place. Among those present was the former town messenger who had been dismissed by Alfredo after the shoe incident, now the representative of an important underground group. Their meeting was simple, significant and touching.

"Now and then I may have been obliged to wear a mask of severity, but it was only to hide my real feelings, which were always on the side of freedom," Alfredo apologized, amid the handshakes and warm congratulations of the bystanders. People's eyes were moist with genuine emotion. It seemed the dawn of a new era.

No one who paused to reflect on this memorable rescue operation was able to find any natural, much less logical explanation for it. The ex-Collector's wife, Donna Matilde, spent several sleepless nights tormented by the suspicion that it might all be a hoax to render doubly cruel the assassination which would make her the Widow of a Martyr and deprive her of the possessions so laboriously accumulated during the period of the Collectorship. But when at last she was persuaded that the new Party had really accepted her husband as one of its leaders, she ran straight to the Jesuit church to light a candle of thanksgiving in front of St. Anthony's statue. When her husband learned of it, he made provision for this dutiful homage to be continued *in perpetuo*. He took the precaution, however, of leaving his wife the task of arranging with the sacristan about the renewal of the candles, the position of the new Party with regard to the Miracle-Worker of Padua not being as yet altogether clear. To symbolize the (for the time being) "irrevocable" nature of the political event taking place in the Villa Esposito, the drawing-room clock was stopped at the precise moment when the historic meeting began. Unfortunately this was to become a constant source of disturbance for the ex-Collector's domestic peace. No public holiday could pass (there were already a number of them, but a host of new ones had lately been added) without long processions of red-badged pilgrims appearing at the gate, wanting to see the historic clock. On being warned, Donna Matilde would hurriedly replace the Persian carpets with pieces of matting and hide the silverware under the beds. Meanwhile Alfredo would run out with open arms and a broad smile to greet the crowd of comrades and slow down their onset with appropriate little speeches.

"What a great honor for my modest abode," he was fond of repeating.

All things considered, he was not so rash as to complain of the fate meted out to him by Providence. But he felt mortified because in the new Party, despite all his pains, he could find no outlet for his two chief natural gifts, conviviality and inventiveness. One well-timed proposal of his had indeed been greatly praised and immediately put into effect: the establishment of an Indulgence Office, as one of the chief organs of the Party, to help rehabilitate capitalists and other important personages compromised by their association with the defunct regime. The office would determine the sum to be paid in each case, taking into account the gravity of the errors committed and the financial resources of the penitent. But Alfredo felt certain that he could fly much higher than this. Finally he became convinced that his bad luck was all due to his having as immediate superior in the Party the Engineer, Rocco De Donatis, in manners an utter porcupine, and for the rest an enigma.

"Don Rocco can't possibly stay away a whole month," said Filomena in an attempt to humor him. "He has duties to the Party, but besides he can't leave that girl all by herself for so long. I mean the one that looks like a plucked chicken—no one can tell me if she's daughter or wife to him, but it seems they're inseparable."

However, the social distance between himself and Filomena made Alfredo disinclined to this sort of familiarity. Being in the same Party does not call for drinking out of the same glass.

"On the other hand, there's never any knowing just how a madman will behave," pursued Filomena.

"Rocco is no madman," Alfredo corrected her. "He's merely absurd. You may not understand, but there's a difference."

"He has the pale, bored look that turns a girl's head nowadays," added Filomena. "Cruel men have that same pale complexion. If you ask me, he'd be capable of murder. Maybe I'm wrong, but it's a feeling I've got."

"What makes you say 'capable of'?" asked Alfredo.

"They tell queer things about him in the Party," added Filomena. "They say that when he goes to bed with a woman he doesn't even bother to say an affectionate word. He gets up, washes and goes away."

"Good God, wouldn't you want him to wash?" Alfredo protested. "Is washing an outrage, in your opinion? You've got a peculiar notion of dialectical materialism. To my way of thinking, what matters in such cases is that he shouldn't forget to pay the agreed fee."

"But I wasn't referring to that sort of female," Filomena retorted in exasperation. "I was referring to his dealings with honest women."

"Honest?" exclaimed Alfredo. "Aha, so you think there's no dishonesty except where money is concerned?"

"Listen, Don Alfredo, I'll go on talking just the way I feel," declared Filomena indignantly. "I haven't been to the Party School and I've neither time nor wish to go there."

"That's bad," Alfredo commented. "Very bad. So you'll never know the poetry of the iron law of wages."

"That's all humbug," said Filomena. "Fine words and nothing else. Work is what the poor folks want. May I ask when they're going to start rebuilding the bridge?"

"The contractor was going to discuss it this very evening with Rocco," explained Alfredo. "But you saw for yourself how that extraordinary individual made himself scarce, for no reason at all."

"So the unemployed are going to lose their chance of a job through that madman's fault?" Filomena began to expostulate. "He'll get an earful from me at the next Party meeting."

Alfredo smiled. He was by no means displeased at having stirred up this little hornet's nest, accidentally as it were. There was a Providence after all.

"Now mind you don't say you learned this from me," Alfredo hastened to warn her. "My situation in the Party is still rather delicate, as you know. As a matter of fact, I don't even think you should be the one to launch the attack at the meeting. One thing leads to another, and Rocco would soon guess your source of information. Do you have any friends in the stonemason's union?"

"Nearly all the top people," Filomena assured him. "My father was a foreman. Don't you remember him from the time your house was being built?"

"That's the girl," said Alfredo with a smile. "Find some way to arouse the stonemasons, get them buzzing. But don't forget. I'm entirely in the dark about the whole affair."

3

With a lightning swerve the jeep had taken the main road along the river and disappeared, roaring at eighty miles an hour, in a thick cloud of smoke.

"Hang on to your seat," Rocco shouted to his companion.

"What the hell is this, a tin can?" said the other.

For a good part of the way neither uttered another word, but there was no trace of embarrassment in their silence. Each was absorbed in his own thoughts. After leaving the town the jeep continued to follow the riverbed for several miles, passing long processions of peasants with their carts and enveloping them in a cloud of dust. The houses along the road were few. Women and children clustered in the doorways, heedless of dust and flies, waiting for the men to return from the fields, and for suppertime. Rocco tore around the curves without slowing down. At one point, however, he was forced to do so in order to cross the riverbed. The old bridge had been blown up during the war and nothing remained of it but the piers. The rudiments of a path had been beaten into the gravel by the daily traffic of vehicles. Beyond the riverbed the road began again on the level between vast expanses of yellow stubble. Tall poplars lined it on both sides. The jeep could resume its wild race. Two *carabinieri* leading a handcuffed prisoner at the edge of the road barely managed to escape being run over. Rocco appeared suddenly to have lost control of the steering-wheel. At the entrance to a village the jeep caught up with the bus and passed it.

Soon they would have to climb. The road was almost deserted. Only at the last houses of the valley did the jeep pass little groups of black-clad women returning on foot from the market with their purchases, like slow and silent processions of ants. Low rows of vines, green with sulphur, crept up the rocky ashen slopes of the hills. Here and there beside some stunted bush, isolated like stray bees, men could be seen busily poking at the earth. Then the road narrowed and grew steeper, with frequent piles of stones at either side and tiny flocks of sheep grazing on its border of parched dusty grass. A big white sheep-dog, his collar bristling with nails, burst out from a hedge and hurled himself at the car.

"In summer there's no danger of wolves," said the Engineer. "Why don't they let those animals go without collars?"

But the man beside him made no reply; in fact, he gave no sign of having heard. His hands folded on his knees, he was gazing impassively at the road. Later, however, he asked:

"Have we far to go yet for the Old Mill?"

"We've passed it already," the Engineer told him. "The road-menders were working there. I had to slow down. Didn't you notice?"

The village of San Luca was not visible from the road on which they were driving. But the whitish smoke of its chimneys could already be seen rising from a gorge in the mountains this side of the Gap.

"I'll stop for a moment at the Roadhouse, below the cheese dairy," said the Engineer. "I need gas."

"That suits me too," said the man at once. "I was just about to say so."

Rocco made it elaborately clear that he did not bother to notice which direction the other took after leaving the car. Three trucks were already lined up near the gasoline pump at the far end of the yard. From the adjacent well a disheveled barefoot woman was drawing water in a bucket held by a long rope. Rocco parked the jeep close to the ruins of the old building and walked toward the tavern. As in some childish game, he played fair and looked straight ahead.

The tavern was a two-storied building, its façade scarred by missiles and blackened by gigantic inscriptions in tar. Those still legible said DOWN WITH TAXES, LONG LIVE THE BLACK MARKET, BIG-WHISKERS IS BOSS HERE. A great pine tree grew close by the door. Its foliage rose higher than the roof, and just then, lit up by the setting sun, it formed a kind of golden dome over the dark house. In a wicker armchair under the tree old Zaccaria, the owner of the tavern, the master of the Roadhouse, sat resting. He was massive, corpulent and ruddy, but he held his head majestically erect, his eyes, as usual, half shut. He still wore overalls, although a pair of crutches propped against the tree within his reach showed that he no longer had the use of his legs. The overalls did not prevent him from displaying a "for valor" ribbon on his chest.

"Zaccaria," asked Rocco in a loud voice, "how is it now at the San Luca Gap? Is it safe at night?"

The old man did not answer. He remained motionless, his eyes still half-closed. It was hard to make out if he was awake or asleep. But a youth in gray jeans, with tools in his hand, came running at once out of the garage.

"Why does your grandfather sleep like a bear?" Rocco asked him. "Never mind, I'm not in a hurry. And the car could do with a washing."

"If you're not in a hurry, wait till I've served the trucks," answered the boy. "Do you want to pass the mountain tonight?"

On the threshold of the tavern Rocco finally yielded to his

curiosity. The time required by discretion had undoubtedly elapsed. He turned round abruptly and looked in all directions. The man had vanished. The Roadhouse looked the same as ever.

THE GEM-LIKE FLAME

Louis Auchincloss

Born and brought up in New York City and Bar Harbor, Louis Auchincloss practiced law in New York for a number of years before deciding to devote full time to writing. His distinguished short stories have appeared in *The Atlantic Monthly, Town & Country, Harper's, The New Yorker* and elsewhere. THE INJUSTICE COLLECTORS, a book of short stories, and SYBIL, a novel, were published by Houghton Mifflin, who are also the publishers of his new novel, A LAW FOR THE LION

When I looked up Clarence McClintock that summer in Venice it was partly out of curiosity and partly out of affection. He had long ceased to be anything but a legend to the rest of our family, the butt of mild jokes and the object of perfunctory sympathy, a lonely, wandering, expatriate figure, personally dignified and prematurely bizarre, rigid in his demeanor and impossibly choosey in his acquaintance. It was universally agreed among our aunts and uncles that he had been an early casualty in the terrible battle that his mother, my ex-aunt Maud, a violent, pleasure-loving woman with a fortune as large as her appetites, had waged over his custody with my sober, Presbyterian uncle John. Yet I had remembered the Clarence of those early years and how, for all the sobriety of demeanor that had so amused our older relatives, there had also been a persistent gentleness of manner that had gone hand in hand with kindness, particularly to younger cousins. Clarence as a boy had been scrupulously fair, invariably just, in his personal dealings with me. The fact that I choose such words may imply that he set himself up as a judge, and there may have been a certain arrogance or at least fatuity in this, but it is the impression of his integrity and not his pretentiousness that lingers. If Clarence was magisterial to my childish eyes, he was also loyal.

When we met at the appointed café on St. Mark's Square I felt more like a nephew than a cousin. Clarence, tall and bonily thin, with small dry lips and a small hooked nose, with thin receding hair and dark, expensive clothes, did not seem a man of only thirty-seven. I did feel, however, that he was glad to see me.

"So at last one of the family comes to Europe!" he exclaimed with a small, shy yet hospitable smile of surprise. "And is writing a novel, too! Let us hope that Venice will do for your fiction what it did for Wagner's music. You're very good to look me up, Peter. No one does any more, you know. No one, that is, but Mother. She cannot, in all decency, quite neglect the sole fruit of her many unions." He smiled bleakly at this. "But give me the news," he continued in a brisker tone. "About all the good aunts and uncles and all the cousins like yourself."

News, however, was the last thing that he seemed to wish to hear. He interrupted me when I started on Aunt Clara's stroke with a sudden rush of reminiscence about the secret gift drawer that she had kept for us as children. When I tried to tell him about Uncle Warren's law suit, he broke in with apostrophes about the nursery rhymes which the old man used to write for us. What obviously intrigued him about me was the fact of our cousinship; it provided him with a needed link to the past which still seemed to occupy so many of his thoughts. His memory was extraordinary. It was almost as if he had spent his early years carefully collecting this series of vivid images which he somehow knew even then were to be his only companions in the self-imposed loneliness which the future held for him. My turning up after so many years must have given him a sense of reassurance, a proof of the facts on which these images were based whose very existence he may have come to doubt.

We dined together the following night and the one after. He helped to get me settled in a hotel that he recommended and which turned out to be just right for my needs. He attached himself to me with all the pertinacity of the very shy when they do not feel rebuffed, and I began, perhaps ungraciously, to see that he might become a problem. For, as far as I could make out, despite the fact that he spent every summer in Venice and had an apartment there, he not only had no friends in the city but no inclination to make any. He was too stiff and too reserved, and his Italian, although accurate, was too halting for native circles. He loved Italy and its monuments, but he would have preferred it unpopulated. Americans abroad, on the other hand, he had even less use for. He divided them into four categories, all equally detestable. There were the diplomats who alarmed him with their polish, the strident tourists who reminded him of the business world in New York that he had found too competitive, the women who had married titles whom he thought pretentious, and finally the artists and writers whom he regarded with a chaste suspicion as people of unorthodox sexual appetite who had come to the sunny land of love in search of a tolerance that was not to be found in the justly censorious places of their origin. And he himself? Clarence McClintock? Why, he had simply come to Italy to admire it and be left alone. The noisiest Italians could be noisy without making demands on him. That was their great virtue. It was as if they had a self-assurance that his fellow Americans lacked which enabled them to pass by the lone observer from across the seas without the compulsion to turn and make him part of them.

On the third night after our meeting I dined out with Italian friends and was a bit discouraged, I confess, on returning to my hotel, to find Clarence waiting for me in the lobby. He seemed upset about something and wanted to talk, so we went over to St. Mark's Square for a *cinzano*. There he told me that he had had a letter from his mother. She was coming to Venice at the end of the following month to attend the fancy dress ball at the Palazzo Loredan.

"You mean she'll fly all the way from New York to go to a ball?" I asked in mild surprise. "All those expensive miles for one party?"

Clarence nodded grimly. "She's even proud of it," he affirmed. "Mother's not afraid to face the absurdity of her own motivations. I'll say that for her."

"But I rather admire that, don't you? I hope I have that kind of spirit when I'm seventy."

There was a disapproving pause while Clarence sipped his *cinzano*.

"Sixty-eight," he corrected me dryly. "You forget, Peter," he continued more severely, "that someone always pays for a woman like Mother. I don't mean financially because, obviously, my grandfather left her very well off. But emotionally. She is quite remorseless in the pursuit of pleasure."

"Oh, come, Clarence, I'm sure you're being hard on her," I protested. "How do you know she isn't really coming over to see you?"

He smiled sourly.

"The Loredan ball is far more important than I," he replied. "Though I won't deny," he conceded, "that seeing me may provide a subsidiary motive for her coming. She knows how I feel about Olympia Loredan and that set of international riff-raff."

"You mean she's coming here to *annoy* you? Don't you think that's going rather far?"

He shrugged his shoulders.

"Not altogether to annoy me, of course not. But it adds the icing to the cake. Oh, she's up to no good. You can be sure of that."

I had to laugh at this.

"Do you honestly think she cares that much?"

Clarence had to pause to think this over.

"We are the two most different people in the world," he said more reflectively, "and we know it. We each know in our heart that the other will never change. Yet we go on as if there was a way, or as if the other must be made to see the way even if he won't take it. In any event," he continued, changing to a brisker, more deliberate tone, as if embarrassed by his reverie, "she will not find me this time. I shall be safely in Rome while the Princess Loredan's friends are debauching the bride of the Adriatic."

"You won't even stay to see your mother?"

"She can meet me, if she cares, in the eternal city. Will you go with me?"

I told him I had to stay in Venice and work, ball or no ball.

"I suppose you might even go to it?" he speculated.

"I might. If I'm asked."

"I see, Peter, that I must not overestimate you," he said regretfully, shaking his head. "You are essentially of that world, aren't you? Yet I wonder how any artist could really prefer to dance and drink with those shallow people than walk in Hadrian's Villa or in the moonlit Colosseum. Mind how you reject me, Peter. Haven't I told you that I burn with a 'hard, gem-like flame?'"

As a matter of fact, he had. He had told me the first night that we had dined together and in that same mocking tone. He had said that most people saw only the "brownstone front" side of his nature, the austere, stiff, conservative side, but that there was another, a truer side, a romantic, loyal, idealistic one. This was what he meant when he quoted Walter Pater, but the disdainful smile that accompanied his phrase made me wonder if any gem-like flame within him had not been smothered or at least isolated so that it burned on invisibly, a candle in a crypt.

"Well, some of us have to do more than burn for a living," I was saying, rather crudely, when looking up I saw Neddy Bane crossing the square alone.

"Why it's Neddy Bane!" I exclaimed.

Clarence looked up too, immediately alarmed at the prospect of a stranger.

"And who, pray, is Neddy Bane?"

"An old friend of mine," I said promptly, feeling for the

first time that he was. "We went to school and college together. Let me ask him over, Clarence. You'll like him."

"Yes, why don't you do that?" he said in a dry, suddenly hostile tone. "But if you'll excuse me," he continued, glancing down at his watch, "I think it's time that I was on my way."

"Now, Clarence, wait. Don't be rude." I put my hand firmly on his arm. "It's not that late."

I turned and waved at Neddy who stared for a moment and then smiled and started toward our table. It was suddenly important to me that Clarence should make this concession. The sight, as he approached us, of Neddy's friendly smile made me feel that the last three evenings had been a lifetime. It was as if I had been locked in a small dark library with the windows closed and Neddy Bane, of all unlikely people, was life beating against the panes.

"Neddy!" I called to him. "How are you, boy? Come on over and drink with us." And as he came up to the table I put my hand on Clarence's shoulder. "Do you remember my cousin, Neddy? Clarence McClintock?"

2

Neddy was my age, about thirty-three, but he was not as tall as Clarence or myself, and this, together with his gay sport coat and thick, brown, curly hair made him seem like a smiling and respectful boy at our table. He had large blue eyes that peered at one with a hesitant, almost timid friendliness, but when they widened with surprise, as they were apt to if one said anything in the least interesting, their blue faded almost into gray, the puffiness above his cheekbones became more evident and he seemed less boyish. He was weak, and he was supposed to be charming, but I have often wondered if his charm was not rather assumed by people who had been told that it was a quality that went with weakness. He had been a stockbroker in New York with an adequate future, married to a perfectly adequate wife, the kind of nice girl of whom it was said that she would bloom with marriage, that even her rather pinched features would separate into better proportions and glow when love had touched her. Conceivably something like this could have happened had another husband been her lot. She wanted only what so many girls wanted, a house in the suburbs in which to bring up her children and a country club whose male members were all doing as well or better than her husband. But Neddy was constitutionally unable to find content in any regular life. He could not even commute. He would get to Grand Central and drink in a bar until he had missed his train and every other reasonable one and had to spend the night with his widowed mother in the city. He was fond of rather dramatic collapses, of simply lying back and doing nothing when he felt pressure, refusing to answer questions or to give explanations, and his poor wife, lacking the maturity or the understanding to be able to cope with him, gave vent to her deep sense of injustice that he was not as other husbands and nagged him until he walked out on her and the children and fled to Europe.

It was like Neddy that he had made no arrangements for divorce or separation or for his own or anyone else's support. All this he left to his mother who, far from rich, sent him a check when she could, at great sacrifice. He professed to be an artist, but he did condescend to take various temporary jobs. He worked for a travel agency, for the French edition of a New York women's magazine, as secretary and guide to a Pittsburgh industrialist. Now, he told Clarence and me, his money had really given out and he was going back to New York.

"Well, it's been fun while it lasted," he said with his disarming smile, raising the drink I had ordered for him, "and I'm never one to regret things as you, Peter, ought to know. Peter has never really approved of me, Mr. McClintock," he continued turning his attention suddenly to Clarence. "Peter is the greatest bourgeois I know. Despite his writing and despite his being over here. Fundamentally, his heart has never left Wall Street."

I glanced at Clarence and noticed to my surprise that he no longer seemed bored.

"But you're quite right, Mr. Bane," he said seriously. "Peter isn't really willing to give himself to the European experience. I'm interested that you see that."

I could hardly help laughing at this unexpected alliance.

"Perhaps it's because I don't burn with a hard, gem-like flame," I retorted. "Do you, Neddy?"

Neddy glanced from me to Clarence and saw from the latter's quick flush whom my reference was aimed at.

"Do I? Of course I do!" he exclaimed. "And I'll bet your cousin here does, too. Every true artist or art lover burns with a hard, gem-like flame." He turned back to Clarence. "Naturally Peter doesn't understand. What would a novelist of manners, bad manners at that, know of the true flame? I can see, Mr. McClintock, that you're a person who cuts deep into things. You have no time for surfaces. It's the only way to be. Oh, I've batted around a lot myself, as Peter here knows; I've wasted time and energy, but none of that's the real me. The real me is a painter, first and last!"

"Is it really?" Clarence asked. "But how sad then that you

have to go back. People who can paint Italy should stay here. It's the only way we can contribute."

"Do you paint yourself, Mr. McClintock?"

"Alas, no. I'm a bit of a scholar, that's all. I hang my head before a real artist."

"But why!" Neddy cried. "The artist and the scholar, weren't they the team of the Renaissance?"

They continued to talk in this vein, Neddy putting himself out more and more to please Clarence. I knew his habit in the past of trying to placate the kind of disapproving figure that Clarence initially must have seemed to him at the expense of familiar and hence less awesome figures like myself. I had never, however, seen him carry it so far. When he talked about painting he deferred with humility to Clarence's amateur yet aggressively old-fashioned judgment and sought his opinion on recent exhibits. When he elicited the fact that Clarence's last monograph, on the art collection of Pius VII, was to be published in *Via Appia*, he praised the discrimination of Princess Vinitelli, its publisher. I knew that he must have heard me describe Clarence in the past as my "rich" cousin, and decided that he was simply after a loan. What really surprised me, though, was Clarence's reaction. At first he glanced at me from time to time while Neddy was talking to see if I shared his interest, but after a couple of rounds of drinks he forgot me entirely and kept his eyes riveted on Neddy. I had noticed on our previous evenings that he had drunk almost nothing, which was evidently because of a light head, for now under the influence of the mild *cinzanos* he became almost as loquacious as Neddy.

"It's wonderful to find someone who really *feels* Italy," he said, looking around at me again, but with a reproachful look. "I had begun to be afraid that the whole world was a Loredan ball."

When I glanced at my watch and saw how late it was and got up to go, Clarence only squinted up at me, his usually sallow features softened with what struck me as an air of rather smug satisfaction and said that he and "Neddy" would sit on a bit and have "one for the road." I left them together, amused at their congeniality, but slightly irritated at being made to feel like an elderly tutor after whose retiring hour the young wards, released, may frisk in the dark of a forbidden city. Really, I said to myself, with a sneer that surprised me, what an ass Clarence can be.

I didn't see either of them again until I ran into Neddy a week later when I was getting my mail at the American Express.

"I thought you were going home," I said.

"Well, no," he said, looking, I thought, slightly embarrassed. "I'm not exactly. Not for a while anyway."

"Where are you staying?"

He hesitated a moment and then stuck his chin forward in a sudden gesture of defiance.

"I'm staying with Clarence."

"With Clarence!" I exclaimed. "In his apartment? Why, I thought nobody ever stayed with Clarence."

"Maybe he never found anyone he wanted to ask," Neddy said in a superior tone.

"But how did it happen?" I asked. "How did you ever pull it off?"

Neddy was like a child in his obvious pleasure at my interest. All his pores opened happily under the reassuring sunshine of curiosity.

"Well, after you left us the other night," he said eagerly, "Clarence and I sat on and had a few more drinks. He became very reminiscent and told me about his mother and how dreadfully she had treated him when he was little. She must have been awful, don't you think, Peter? Except rather wonderful at the same time." He looked at me questioningly, afraid that his speculation was bold. I shrugged my shoulders. "Well, anyway, when I finally got up to go, just when I thought I was saying good-by to him for good, he suddenly seized my arm and blurted out: 'If you really want to stay here and paint, you can, you know. You can set yourself up in my apartment. I'm quite alone.' Don't you think that was marvelous, Peter? From someone who looks just as cold as ice?"

"Marvelous," I agreed drily. "And you accepted, of course?"

"I moved in the very next day! Wouldn't you have?"

"What does that matter?"

I thought over what Neddy had told me, and two days later I called on Clarence at his small, chaste, perfect apartment. He received me alone, as Neddy was out sketching. I noted that the somber living room with its carved wood medieval statues and red damask curtains had already been turned into a studio.

"I suppose you've been wondering," he told me in his cool, formal tone, "whether or not I've taken leave of my senses."

"No, Clarence. I'm just interested, that's all."

"As a cousin or as a novelist?"

"As a friend."

He looked at me suspiciously for a moment and then, nodding his head as if satisfied, proceeded in his own slow, measured pace to give me the story of what had happened. I had the feeling as he went along that his formality concealed a sort of defiance, a smug, rather cocky little satisfaction that he should have captured Neddy. It didn't matter what I thought;

I was simply a person to whom an accounting had to be rendered, a visiting parent at the school where Clarence was headmaster. He admitted, to begin with, that he had been terrified at what his unprecedented impulsiveness might have led him into. Never before, he assured me, had he assumed so much responsibility for a fellow human being. But Neddy, it appeared, had soon set his mind at rest. He had proved as docile and pliable as a well-brought-up child, not only applauding the quiet and orderly routine of Clarence's life, but earnestly adapting it to his own. Clarence had found himself the preceptor of a serious and dedicated art student.

"What Neddy needs," he told me gravely, "happens to be exactly what I can offer: order and discipline. I get him up every morning at eight and send him off with his sketch book. In the afternoons he paints in here." He pointed proudly to an easel in the corner of the living room on which stood an unfinished painting of a canal after the manner of Ziem, colorful and dull. "In the evenings we relax, but in a tempered way. We dine out in a restaurant and drink a bottle of wine. But that's all. Bed by eleven is the rule."

"I see that it's wonderful for Neddy," I said at last. "But what, Clarence, is there in it for you?"

He stared at me for a moment and then shook his head thoughtfully.

"Well, if you don't see that, Peter, what *do* you see? It's what I have always waited for."

When I walked back to my hotel I reflected with some concern on these words of his. I couldn't help feeling a certain responsibility at having been the agent who had brought him and Neddy together. Yet who was I to say that it was a bad thing? I had seen Clarence before he had met Neddy and I had seen him after, and I wondered if I could honestly say that the irritation which I felt at his blind enthusiasm for so fallible a young man was anything more than the irritation that we are apt to feel when an outsider helps one of our family for whom we have given up hope. If such was the case my doubts were the doubts of a dog in the manger.

3

Having established myself on a friendly basis in Clarence's new ménage I was asked there from time to time, but by no means constantly, during the rest of the summer. It was apparent that both Clarence and Neddy were slightly on the defensive with me. The mere fact that I had previously known both of them without losing my head over either may have seemed an implied reproach to the extravagance of their mutual admiration.

When two weeks passed in August without my hearing from either of them, I assumed that Clarence had carried Neddy off to Rome to avoid the pollution of the city by the influx of guests for the Loredan ball. It was with surprise, therefore, that I received a card one morning from Aunt Maud, Clarence's mother, telling me that she had arrived at the Grand Hotel and asking me to come in that afternoon for a drink with her and Clarence and "Clarence's friend."

Aunt Maud Dash, as she now called herself, having resumed her maiden name after the last of her marriages, had done me the dubious honor of singling me out from the other members of her first husband's family on the theory that I was not "stuffy," or at least, as she sometimes qualified it, not quite as stuffy as the rest. There was also, of course, the fact that I was comparatively young, male, unattached, and last but not least, a writer. When I came into her sitting room at the hotel I found her on a chaise longue, her large round figure loosely covered by a blue silk negligee, examining with a careful, almost professional interest, a wide ruff collar that was obviously a part of her ball costume. Her hair was pink, a different shade than when I had last seen her, and her skin, dark and freckled, was heavily powdered. Propped up in her seat she looked as neat and brushed and clean as a big doll sitting in the window of an expensive toy store. There was nothing, however, in the least doll-like about her eyes. They were small and black and roving; they seemed to make fun, in an only half good-hearted fashion, of everything about her, even of her own weight and of the stiff little legs that stuck out before her on the chaise longue and the wheezing, asthmatic note of her breathing.

"Why, Peter," she called to me, "you've got a corduroy coat! We'll make a bohemian out of you yet."

"Maybe it's time I went home."

She turned away now from the ruff collar and examined me more critically.

"Not yet, dear. Wait a bit. You're almost presentable now. I always said there was a chance for you."

"It's what has given me hope."

She snorted.

"Tell me about Clarence," she said abruptly. "I know I can count on you. They say he has a boyfriend."

"Neddy Bane is not exactly a boy," I replied with dignity. "He's my age. As a matter of fact I introduced them. Neddy's wife used to be a friend of mine." I hoped by this to change the direction of her thinking. It was a vain hope.

"Now look here, Peter Westcott, if you think you can put me off with some old wives' tale at my time of life and after all that I've seen——" She stopped as we heard steps in the corridor and then a light, authoritative knock on the door.

"Mother?" I heard Clarence's voice.

"Come in, darling, come in," she called, and the door opened to admit Clarence followed by a rather sheepish-looking Neddy. "How are you, my baby," she continued in a husky voice that seemed to be making fun of him. "Give your old ma a kiss."

Clarence bent down gingerly and touched his cheek to hers, emerging from her embrace with a white powder spot on his face that he immediately, without the slightest effort at concealment, proceeded to rub off with a handkerchief.

"And is this your Mr. Bane?" Aunt Maud continued in the same voice. "What sort of man are you, Mr. Bane? Are you as severe and sober as my Clarry?"

"No, but I try," Neddy answered shyly. "Clarence is my guide and mentor."

Aunt Maud looked shrewdly from one to the other and grunted.

"Are you going to the ball, Mother," Clarence put in quickly, with a bleak glance at the ruff collar, "as the Virgin Queen?"

"Clarry, dear, your *tone*," she reproached him. "But since you ask, child, I am. I've always liked the old girl." She turned suddenly back to Neddy. "Do you believe in the theory that she was really a man, Mr. Bane? Nobody ever saw her, you know, with her clothes off."

Neddy was fingering the red velvet hoopskirts of the costume spread out on the chair beside him.

"Oh, never!" he protested with unexpected animation. "You don't think so, do you?" Then he appealed to her suddenly, with a rather sly little smile that I had not seen before. "You mean she was really a queen?"

Aunt Maud put her head back and roared with laughter.

"But I *like* your friend, Clarry!" she exclaimed. "Can I call him Neddy? I shall anyway," she continued, turning glowingly from Clarence to his friend. "And you, Neddy, must call me Maud." She nodded in satisfaction. "Perhaps you will be my Essex? I have a man's costume, too. It's over there in that box on the chest."

Neddy glanced questioningly at Clarence and then hurried over to the box and took out the red pants and doublet. He stood before the long mirror and held them up in front of him.

"But they fit perfectly!" he exclaimed, and went back again to the box. "Oh, and just look at that sword! Gosh, Mrs. Dash, I mean Maud! Don't you love it, Clarry? Do you think we could go?" He looked anxiously at Clarence.

I didn't have to look at Clarence to know that he would resent Neddy's calling him "Clarry," aping his mother so immediately. He stood there primly, his lips twitching, like a governess who has been overruled by an indulgent parent. Then he turned on Aunt Maud.

"Why must you have an Essex?" he asked sharply. "Would you not do better to search among your own contemporaries for a Leicester? Or even a Burleigh?"

But she simply laughed, this time a high, rather flutey laugh that was just redeemed from silliness by its mockery.

"Because I *want* an Essex!" she said defiantly. "A young, attractive Essex." She winked at me. "Clarence is so absurdly conventional," she continued, more maliciously. "He thinks one should only see people one's own age. As if life were a perennial boarding school. But Neddy doesn't have to be Essex, does he, Peter? He could be one of those pretty pages whom the old queen used to favor, tweaking their ears and pinching their thighs." She threw back her head and gave herself up once more to that laugh. "Or even," she added, gasping, "stifling them half to death in her musky old bosom!"

I could see that Clarence was beside himself. I could only hope that he would not interpret her laugh as I did, as a challenge to compare the relative improprieties of Neddy as an escort for her or Neddy as a companion for him. She picked up the ruff collar now and put it almost coyly around her neck.

"Don't you think it's a good idea, Clarence?" Neddy asked hopefully. "You don't really mind, do you?"

"Mind?" Clarence snapped at him. "Why on earth should I mind? You don't expect me to decide every time you go to a party, do you?"

He got up and walked across the room to the little balcony and, going out, stood by the railing and stared down into the canal. Neddy was at first abashed by his sudden exit, but after I, at Aunt Maud's bidding, had mixed a shaker of martinis from the ample ingredients with which she always traveled, he cheered up again. In a very short time he and Aunt Maud had discovered a series of mutual acquaintances and become positively noisy. I had to leave early and went out on the balcony to say good-by to Clarence. He was still standing there, gloomily watching the line of gondolas arriving at the hotel, bringing more and more guests to the hated ball. He hardly turned when I spoke to him, but simply pointed to the scene below.

"I warned Neddy about this, but he wouldn't believe me," he said. "All hell is breaking loose here."

The very next morning he came alone to see me at my hotel. He looked tired and worn.

"I want to ask a favor of you, Peter," he said gravely.

"A favor, Clarence? How unlike you. But go ahead, I'm delighted."

"It is unlike me," he agreed, frowning. "I am not in the habit of asking favors. I am sure you will be sympathetic when I tell you that I do not find it an easy experience."

I hastened to cut short his embarrassment.

"What can I do for you, Clarence?"

"You know my mother," he began rapidly. "You understand her. She'll listen to you. You can tell her that she mustn't take Neddy to this ball."

"But why mustn't she?"

"Why?" he exclaimed in a suddenly shrill tone. "Good heavens, man, you can't have known Neddy all your life and not see what this will do to him! Just now, of all times, when he's really painting, when for once he's got parties and girls and drinking out of his mind—"

"But one ball, Clarence," I protested.

"One ball!" he almost shouted. "One marihuana! One pipe of opium!"

"But what am I going to tell your mother?"

"Tell her—" He paused and then appeared to give it up. A bitter look came over his face. "Oh, tell her," he went on harshly, "that as long as she's taken everything she could from me all my life, she may as well take Neddy too. But why she has to have her gin-soaked body hurtled in a plane three thousand miles through the ether just to interfere with the only friendship I've ever had—"

"Clarence!"

But he was completely out of control now.

"Why do I ask you, anyway?" he cried. "You like people like her, you even write about them! You think she's admirable, the old tart!"

"All right, Clarence, all right," I said firmly, putting my hands up to stop him. "I'll speak to her, I promise. But calm down, will you?"

He seized my hand in sudden embarrassed gratitude and hurried away without trusting himself to say another word. I shook my head sadly, amazed to have discovered such depths of feeling in him. I had always known that he had disliked his mother; I had not realized that he hated her. She must have seemed, in the isolation that even as a child he had preferred, the very essence of the vulgarity of living and loving as the world lived and loved, the symbol of the Indian giver, because for all her vitality he may have instinctively suspected that she wanted back the one pale spark she had emitted in bearing him. And even now, when she came to his beloved Italy, wasn't it the same thing all over again, didn't she participate of his back, the erectness of his carriage, I had a feeling that there was a process of exorcism going on inside him, a process that was symbolized in his very act of walking away. If his mother liked a circus, the stiff back of his neck seemed to be saying, if Neddy liked it, if the Venetians liked it, if *that* was all they cared about, poor creatures, to be distracted in a distracting world, were they really to be blamed? Was it even reasonable of him, he seemed to ask himself, to assume that Neddy had the patience and devotion to tend the hard gem-like flame that burned within? Should not the true flame-tenders, the people like himself, enjoy in solitude the special compensations of their devotion? I realized suddenly that I had become accessory, irrelevant, and I stopped, calling after him that I was going back for another look at the ball. He barely turned his head to bid me good night as he continued his resolute stride away from the lighted palace and the gondolas that swarmed about it like carp.

ANTHEM FOR FRENCH HORN

M. R. Kadish

A New Yorker by birth, M. R. Kadish holds a Ph.D. from Columbia University, is presently teaching philosophy at Western Reserve University in Cleveland, Ohio. He is the author of the novel POINT OF HONOR (Random House, 1951), and is now at work on a second novel and a series of short stories, of which *Anthem for French Horn* is the first.

Thomas MacIntyre was born in Scranton, Pennsylvania, thirty-two years ago. Although his voice was weak—he never learned to bring his voice up from beneath the level of his throat—his lungs were strong and he loved the power of a full, clear note, very hard to sustain on a French horn. He also wanted his due. He never thought much was due him so he turned it all down, the whole shooting works, toys, girls, dollars, out of a sense of justice, you must understand, without the slightest suspicion of a hard feeling. Nevertheless, he insisted on his due. This is how he got it.

First by saving money at the tire factory.

"Mother," he said one day, pale-eyed and ashen blond, "there's no place for a French horn in Scranton." It wasn't much money, but it permitted him to say this.

excitedly, "but I wonder if you're not really the worst of all bigots. It's amazing to me, Peter, that someone who even pretends to write should be so entirely incapable of visualizing the kind of love I feel for Neddy, a love that I've looked for all my life—ah, but what's the use?"

He broke off and left me, and I stood there thinking of the hopelessness in his face, the hopelessness of ever explaining that even if there was something on which to base his mother's leer, even if her leer was inevitably and forever tied up with every emotional state on his part, still there was a quality in his feeling that was over and above what was called sublimation, a quality that made of it—but what, I asked myself with a sudden shrug of the shoulders, echoing his thought, was the use? I hurried after him, determined that while he was desperate I would not leave him alone.

5

On the night of the ball Clarence and I went for a walk through the crowded streets of Venice. Olympia Loredan had come through with an invitation at the last moment, but I did not feel I could leave him. Besides, I had no costume. In the neighborhood of the Palazzo Loredan wine was being served to the public from huge vats, and in the little squares boys shinnied up and down the greased poles. There was dancing in the streets near the palace, both for the public and for those guests who found it more fun there; ladies in sixteenth-century costumes whirled about in the arms of Venetian boys to the hectic music of strolling players. Standing on a bridge in the area we had a view of the great baroque façade of the palace, lit up by rows of lights attached at the floor levels. In front was a wide platform, covered in red, where the guests were disembarking from gondolas freshly painted in gold or green or yellow and covered with wide silk canopies. Other gondolas glided under the bridge where we were standing, and the laughter of their masked occupants floated up to us. From one in particular we heard a loud and familiar laugh; it came to our ears while the gondola was still under the bridge, and Clarence drew back quickly as it emerged, but not so quickly that he didn't see his mother in her enormous ruff, a small jeweled coronet perched on top of her pink hair, gesticulating with a paste scepter to friends in other gondolas. At her feet in red tights and smiling up at her—well, we did not need to look more closely to see who that was. Clarence turned away from the palace, and I followed him. Obviously he did not wish to be observed, lonely and ridiculous, watching their gaiety from the shadows. We did not talk but as I walked behind him, observing the straightness pressing my own uneasiness at what I might have done to Clarence.

Retribution did not wait long. When I walked through the hotel lobby at noon, on my way out for lunch, I saw Clarence standing at the desk talking to the clerk and then I saw the clerk nod his head and point to me. He turned around as I started over to him, and I saw that he looked pale, almost stunned. His eyes met mine and wandered off in a way that was not like him.

"He's gone," he said as I came up to him. "He's gone to Padua to paint. He said he couldn't paint with me nagging him. He said awful things to me."

"Let's go out, Clarence. Let's take a walk or have lunch or something."

He followed me obediently into the little square on which I lived.

"He said you said terrible things to him," he continued in the same dazed tone. "Terrible things, Peter."

I said nothing.

"Do you think if we both went to Padua," he asked desperately, "and if you apologized and I promised not to nag him any more, he'd come back?"

I shrugged my shoulders.

"You don't think he really might?" he insisted.

"Clarence," I said firmly, turning to him, "for God's sake, let him go. You ought to be congratulating yourself that you're rid of him. You don't know that guy, Clarence. You don't know what he's like. I'm sorry I ever brought you together."

"Sorry!" he exclaimed, coming suddenly to life again. "Sorry! When it's the one thing you've ever done for me! The one thing *anyone's* ever done for me! Don't you know what Neddy is to me, Peter?"

I looked down, embarrassed.

"Perhaps," I muttered. "In a way."

"Perhaps!" he repeated scornfully. "In a way!" We had stopped walking and were facing each other, Clarence again the dominant older cousin of my childhood, simply angrier, that was all. "Well, as a matter of fact it isn't 'perhaps' or 'in a way.' For all your reading, Peter, and for all your parade of tolerance, you're as bad as Mother. You don't want anyone to be happy unless they find their happiness in some noisy normal way. You tremble at the least deviation from your own mean little code or even the appearance of one. That's why you and Mother leer and sneer and pretend I do things with Neddy that Italian boys do with middle-aged male tourists for a few lira!"

"But, Clarence, I never—"

"You pretend to be on the side of the angels," he continued

answered less and less, but Clarence, straining after his attention, had only become more vehement in tone and more fantastic in argument, hoping apparently by the very hyperbole of his speech to instill into his threadbare subject some dash of interest to make him listen. He had exhausted the epithets of his rather chaste vocabulary in withering descriptions of the aging guests and how they would look in their monstrous costumes. He had even tried to shame Neddy by telling him how contemptuously people spoke of impecunious young men who acted as escorts for rich old women and to alarm him by insinuating what attentions his mother, aroused by champagne and late hours, might take it into her head to expect from so junior a companion. He had cut reports out of the paper of the magnificent preparations for the party, insisting on reading them aloud with prefaces such as: "Neddy, listen to this! This really *is* the limit!" And when all else had failed, when he was desperate, he had actually resorted to the argument that the ball was a Communist plot designed to bring discredit on the idle rich of the Western world.

I listened to it with a sick feeling. I could hardly deny that the whole account, even exaggerated, had an unmistakable ring of truth. But in my sudden confrontation with the full extent of Clarence's obsession, I found myself losing my temper at its fatuously smiling cause. Neddy stood before me smugly, relishing each detail of his sorry story, pleased at my obvious dismay, satisfied that I would have to concede to him now that anything Clarence might have done for him was only a token compensation for what he, the long suffering, had had to put up with.

"You're nothing but a God-damn sponge, Neddy Bane!" I exclaimed angrily. "You don't deserve to be considered anything but what you are considered!"

He turned pale.

"And what is that?"

"As Clarence's kept boyfriend!"

He stretched out an arm to me in shocked protest, he opened his mouth to remonstrate, but I turned quickly on my heel and strode away.

I was quite unable to do any writing that morning. I thought how abominably Neddy had treated his wife and children, how shamelessly he had used his old mother, and even went further back to our school days when he had always been careful to curry favor with the strongest clique in the class. I conjured up other and more stinging things that I could have said to him and reminded myself that I had only done my duty. But at heart, all the time, I knew perfectly well that I was only re-

I saw neither Clarence nor Neddy for several days, but one morning as I was picking up my mail I encountered Neddy again at the American Express. He had evidently been waiting for me for he came right over and asked if he could talk to me.

"Why not?" I said, glancing through my envelopes.

"I wonder," he began in a rather embarrassed way, "if you're not doing anything tonight, whether you wouldn't have dinner with Clarence and me. Quite frankly, I think we need a change."

"Why? Are you bored with each other?"

"It's not that exactly. But I'm worried about Clarence. He's got this fetish about my not going to that damn ball."

"Why do you go then?" I asked coldly.

"Why shouldn't I?" he protested. "Who do you think I am, I'd like to know, that Clarence can boss me around?"

"It's not a question of bossing. It's simply a question of doing a very small favor in return for the considerable number you have received."

Neddy smiled uneasily, probably the way he used to smile at his poor wife when she reproached him for spending his evenings in bars. He had almost a genius for evading any unpleasantness in the facts that surrounded him. When I failed to return his smile, however, he rather drew himself up.

"Any small financial aid that I have received from Clarence," he told me with dignity, "will be paid in full when I'm on my feet. It will not be difficult, I assure you. You probably know your cousin well enough to be aware that he doesn't play fast and loose with his money."

The impudence of this quite took me aback.

"Why do you stick around him, then?" I demanded.

"You think it's all one-sided, don't you?" he retorted. "Well, you don't know the half of it. You don't have to listen to his ravings day in and day out. And when I say ravings, I mean ravings!"

"What sort of ravings?"

Neddy proceeded to tell me. I leaned against the counter and puffed gloomily at a cigarette while he unfolded, with the relish of one unjustly accused, the whole sorry picture. For the past five days, apparently, the ball had been the sole subject of their conversation. Whether in the studio while Neddy was trying to paint or during their long dinners in little restaurants, and even on Sunday when they had been lying on the sand at the Lido, Clarence had held forth on the iniquities of Olympia Loredan's friends and their destructive effect upon all who had any serious purpose in life. Neddy, thoroughly bored, had more in the carnival life of the country by attending one crazy ball than he with all his monographs? That, she must have known, was his vulnerable point; that was why she struck at it year after year. It was as if she resented the very existence of what he called the gem-like flame within him and had determined to blow it out.

I telephoned Aunt Maud and invited her to have cocktails with me at Harry's Bar that afternoon. She arrived in high spirits, in a red dress and an enormous red hat, and, as I had known she would, flatly refused my request about Neddy.

"What's wrong, infant?" she asked suggestively. "Do you want to take him to the ball yourself?"

"I'm only thinking of Clarence," I retorted. "This whole thing is bothering him terribly."

"And why should it bother Clarence?"

I noted the glitter in her eyes. It was as if she had been playing bridge with children and had suddenly picked up a slam hand, a waste, to be sure, but a hand that she could still enjoy playing.

"You know perfectly well why, Aunt Maud," I said wearily.

"My dear Peter," she said firmly, "I know a great many things, including what stones do not bear turning over. I have no idea of asking Clarence to explain to me, his mother, what his involvement with this young man is. But I cannot see that borrowing his precious Neddy for a single evening is interfering very much. Must he have Neddy with him every second? Why doesn't he keep him in a harem?"

"You don't understand, Aunt Maud," I tried to explain. "Clarence thinks that Neddy has finally settled down to be a painter and—"

"Nonsense," she interrupted firmly. "It's selfishness, pure and simple, and you know it, Peter. Clarence is simply scared to death that Neddy will find the big world more fun than his cell. Which I should hope he would!"

"Aunt Maud," I said desperately, "*I'll* take you to the ball."

"Thank you very much, Peter, but I haven't asked you. It's all very well for Clarence to go on about my interrupting Neddy's work, but I'll bet he doesn't begrudge him the hours they waste sipping chocolate on the Piazza San Marco while he rants about his poor old mother's wicked life. Oh, I know Clarence, Peter!"

This was a home thrust that I could not honestly deny. And what could I do, in any case, for Clarence with a mother who felt this way about him? When I wrote him that night, for I couldn't bear to face him, I made as light of it as I could. Aunt Maud, I told him, had refused to give up her "hostage."

"Yes, my son," she said, having taken many short courses in Telepathy with the Rosicrucians, thinking, therefore, among the rubber plants of the living room in perfect Concord with son Thomas, and of the same thing, too, a membership in an orchestra, so there! She packed a box lunch for him to eat on the Greyhound bus which he mounted, horn and baggage, the very next day.

On the bus he carved his hoard with a careful budget and, dreaming of the orchestra, fell asleep. On reaching town he went straight to the nearest YMCA, in one hand the clean cardboard suitcase with its frayed edges and in the other the black case containing his power.

Second, he had to approximate his due (he wasn't complaining) by getting a job. This was because tire money didn't last forever. Who wanted to hire a French horn? Nobody, and particularly for the wage it needed because—who wanted even to let a room to a French horn?

Daily at eight the want ad pages rustled their falsehoods to him. To begin with they rustled him into selling vacuum cleaners and sewing machines—a good salesman made a mint. Not Thomas. For two weeks he was a bookkeeper with ink-blots on his hands. For three, the pages turned him into a machinist's helper, but when one day he saw his father's face on a shiny tin can top he trembled and quit. Soon the succession of his metamorphoses and the regulations of the Y diminished not only his cash balance but his skill on the horn. This made him desperate although he was not the man to complain for failures which were your own fault because of you-didn't-have-it-in-you, he could nevertheless grow desperate.

Thomas' horn teacher, first horn at Terminal Hall no less (Thomas had talent, he did), scratched his head. "Ever thought of working as a watchman?" Mr. Benton said and scratched his head again.

Great men think of things without even thinking. Mr. Benton's suggestion gave Thomas his due in the job line. Due was that a man should live by the sweat of his brow but the sweat should at least not get in his eyes or give him chapped lips if he played the horn. At any rate, it wasn't the first watchman's job which had the proper sweat differential. The first job fell through when late at night people going by the warehouse heard the distant call of Thomas' horn within the boarded building and ran for the police. It was the second job.

> Dump head wanted. No exp.
> Night work. GA. 7-0009
> Come and get it.

Thomas came and Thomas got it. Next is third. Third is the city dump at which they burn the rubbish. Last is his due.

Third begins with the jungle because one night the call swept over half an acre of burning, faltered, and dropped with a quantity of smoke upon the jungle near the railroad tracks. The smoke provoked the travelers' eyes to tears, but the new sound made them sit up and take notice. Hey! The new sound, big as a truck, clumsy as a fat man, rich, came clear over the crackle of old uprights, incandescent sofas, spare wood parts, over the spitting lead of tin cans and over the hiss of newspapers and old paper bags.

Two stirred their butts to see what the hell. They marveled: "Sonuvabitch!" across the plain, in and out the billow of the smoke, stumbling here and there, locators of variety in early spring with the huge red mass of the glowing, burning dump to guide them, with the constant glare of the single bulb in the shack on the dump's edge for an azimuth. They knew all about the watchman's shack, all about the dump loaded with warm newspaper, convenient cardboard and every material for impromptu lean-tos spiraling up nightly in the snap of flame, a waste. They had never heard the horn before.

"Some'pin new has been added!"

It lived in the shack. Intermittently it broke from the shack, returned to it, broke out again. Hope lit their eyes. Could it be? It was! Edison in the 100-watt bulb showed it. They'd tracked the big noise down and found it in a watchman. They could hardly believe it, but and how they believed it. Nobody ever saw such lips before in any window: pouting, tender, tentative lips curled so happily over a bit of tubing. The watchman's lips! Close to the glass of the window their mouths sucked together with the mouth inside which never saw, which never heard what with the crackle of burning and the fitful burst of the horn. The knowledge that this was the watchman, they thought they'd go crazy with it, they could hardly keep it down with only two feet of distance between and a pane of dirty glass.

The Limp said thanks for the knowledge. "Le's rip up the dump. Le's tear it up." He grappled with his laughter, he smacked his thighs. "Le's have a party!"

Still, inside, beyond the window, the watchman blew heavy plate glass figures until they cracked down through the middle and crashed down on the heads of the two men on the outside and made them chirrup with delight.

"Le's ask him what he's playin'. Ask him!"

The slow one knew pleasure when he heard it. "Yeah . . ." buttering a thick fat affirmation over a long, long moment.

Should we knock on the door, should we break in the window, should we burn down the shack, should we kick it in, should we go in like gentlemen and ask him? "Illegal entry!" guffawed the Limp. "Jailed onct on illegal entry. Break down the door! The guy's deaf!" They had been knocking on the door. They were calling, "Hey watchman, watcha playin'?"

The door opened slowly, the head of the watchman protruding beyond. "From Till Eulenspiegel, the horn part. You know it?"

The watchman carried a revolver.

As Rimsky-Korsakov said, "The tone of this intrument is soft, poetical and full of beauty. In the lower register it is dark and brilliant, round and full in the upper. The middle notes resemble those of the bassoon and the two instruments blend well together. The horn, therefore, serves as a link between the brass and woodwind. In spite of valves, the horn has but little mobility and would seem to produce its tone in a languid and lazy manner."

These words were written in code; the faint warm flush of Thomas' body, the cipher.

Thomas gave them a job. He didn't intend to, but what could he do?

"Rats," he said, turning to them after he had demonstrated his horn. "Where do you think they come from? You'd think they'd get burned up all of them every night."

You'd think. "Huhh?"

"I said rats. Listen!" The watchman's thin beaked head tilted in the pose of listening: The fires. Wind also. Inside, a quantity of bad breathing. "You can't hear it now. When the rats get burned out they come bumping into the shack, scratching and squealing something awful. You can't hear it now. Some nights it's real ferocious, throws my breathing off.

"Guy who was here before me used to kill 'em with a stick. One after another. They couldn't see anything. I'm too busy. Where do you think they come from?"

"Burn 'em," said the Limp. "Burn 'em with kerosene, the little bastards. Every night ya burn 'em dontcha? Every night!"

But "Mister," said the slow one, the cautious one, the taker-in of situations—"Mister, we could help ya kill 'em!"

"Quick, with no noise," the Limp said, avid. "Sanitary!"

The watchman talked like a sign, a public sign, a talking Post No Bills, No Trespassing: "Intruders are not allowed," he told them. What he have to say that for?

Frowning, the serious one, the slow one turned the problem

on his tongue: "If ya ask us in t'help then we ain't no more intruders. If on'y ya ask us in, mister. Ask us!"

The watchman turned his head. Gravely, he stared through the window, but they wouldn't stop. "Ask us!"

"I don't even have to kill 'em," he said to them. "It's voluntary."

"Ask us! Ask us in!"

Abruptly, but with care, he put down his horn. "I sleep in the day time," he said. "I practice here at night. I'll cook some coffee."

All through spring and into high summer the Limp and the others would follow Thomas around the great pile of junk. The Limp would have a clean white stick and he would make sure his guests had sticks also. Whatever happened to the big, slow one? Thomas asked. He'd gone off some place.

They had a system, a set-up, a pattern saddled on the full, warm nights, called off only on account of rain or when the Limp went away on a business trip. They would walk a large and magic circle about the dump. Thomas' part was to sprinkle kerosene from the can. He had to call "ANYONE IN THERE?" (Better safe than sorry) poking and intervening with his flashlight at the edges of the rubbish because it would be dark before they started. "ANYONE IN THERE?" The question always tickled the Limp. Thomas had to raise it three times before he tossed in the match, and started the fire going which always surprised people how quickly it could girdle the dump before starting inwards, squeezing. Then Thomas would return to his shack to let the Limp and his men take over, and while they danced and poised before the fire he would send out from the cool and empty nothing behind them his sudden horn cry to jump into the crackle and spit of the burning. Sometimes, pausing for a breather, he would see the white sticks leap together in the flamelight, but then he would return to his horn.

Such long nights he had of practice! A time came when Mr. Benton, Benton of the Terminal Hall Orchestra, the French horn, no less, gave up, shook his head from side to side, said he didn't know how Thomas did it and promised that before very long he would arrange an audition with the conductor. (Thomas smiled diffidently and stroked his horn.)

The Limp was a happy man too. "Me and the watchman," the Limp would tell his guests, "we're pals," and laugh until his sides hurt and lead them back from the dump to the shack. "Coffee is bein' served," he'd say with an elaborate gesture.

Gaiety also reigned. Gaiety is the due of cooperation.
One night the Limp saw the watchman at his windowsill

watching for them. "Ya see?" said the Limp calling his guests to witness how and where he stood.

"It's on me boys, it's on me."

The watchman poured his coffee, the watchman filled the cups of his companions. Juggling the cup, oh how the Limp had it tonight. His Adam's apple bobbed with the thrill of possession. The flames noised high, higher than Limp's voice.

"Oh ber-ree-mee . . ."

Everybody, everybody: "On the lone prair-eee . . ." The watchman nodded and beat his spoon upon the iron lid of the stove. "Where the coy-otes howl . . ." He beat his spoon upon the iron lid to put a rhythm upon the singing but gave it up and smiled.

"And the wind moans free . . ."

"Hey boss, whyntcha 'company us? On yer horn. Whyntcha blow it? Whooooooo . . ." mimicked the Limp. "Whoooooooooo." Can you see how he has it, can you see, everybody?

The horn the giggling watchman played together with their voices was a riot, a regular riot, an invention of that smart clever powerful authority, the Limp. "The boss, the boss," he cried, he the Limp, one foot shorter than the other, patting the boss on the shoulder, feeling the holster black and shiny, "Look what a long one the boss got, look what a long one!"

The watchman said, "You should restrain yourself." "Hee hee hee" went the conjoint snicker of the others, a gift he took from them, the Limp did, with his own two hands which fingered the watchman's shoulders.

"Ree-strain yerself, you guys. The boss gonna play us a solo piece." Those were his two hands on the boss's shoulders. Squeeze! "Aintcha?" What was underneath the shirt—bone, only bone? The palms of the Limp's hands itched. The twitching of the shoulders was what made them itch. "Aintcha?"

The Limp would be damned! When the boss wrenched his shoulders away, he'd flung the Limp back so that the Limp almost burned himself on the hot stove. "Don't touch me!" So the Limp's hands were hanging loose with no more shoulders in their grip although they still felt the grip and the shoulders.

"Fer Chris'sakes, boss!" but he was discovering something. He was grinning at the boss and the boss couldn't even look him in the eye! This boss with the bony shoulders! He had agony on his face.

"I don't like to be touched," explained the boss.

"Sure, sure," said the Limp. "I unnerstan." He did, he did. In the center of the room, in dead center, he balanced himself upon his unequal legs, and squirmed to feel the power tickling his thighs and burying itself in his stomach and broadening his mouth into a wide, wide grin. "Sure, boss," he whispered.

And soon, sure enough, Mr. Benton had fixed the date for Thomas' audition: in two weeks, with Dr. Pfeffer the conductor. Now wasn't this wonderful? But that very night, after his helpers left, Thomas went out and saw the little black bodies still spotting the ground. How the burned hair stank! To shovel them up, to throw them into the fire took some time. It wasn't the time. He didn't think they should have left this for him. How lucky he was a patient man.

The next night he said to the Limp, he said to him, "Why don't you throw the things in when you're finished?"

The limping fellow was funny, he never answered on the dot, he was slow. "Huh?" said the limping fellow. So Thomas MacIntyre told him again. "Jeez," said the Limp, "We did throw 'em in, din' we fellers, din' we throw 'em in?" "Yeah, sure," they said. Thomas MacIntyre knew you should never judge a man by his clothes, but these men were not telling the truth.

"I shoveled them in myself after you went home, I myself," he told them.

"Oh," said the Limp, screwing up his mouth the way he always did. He had almost no teeth in his mouth. "Oh, las' night. He means las' night, you guys. Whatsa matter, ya don' unnerstan English?" They were all making fools of themselves laughing. "Las' night, we forgot."

Although anyone could forget, it was wrong to lie about it. Also, it wasn't fair. "Well, did you shovel 'em up when you finished tonight? Did you?" He didn't want to have to do it himself again after they left, he just didn't, so he turned to the window and saw that they hadn't shoveled them.

"We gotta go somewhere tonight, don't we boys? We got no time tonight."

How dare they? "You've got no place at all to go tonight," he told them. He was very emphatic. Maybe it was unkind to use the word, but a bum never had any place to go, that was why he was a bum.

"Look," the Limp was positively snarling at him. "Do ya maybe pay us we gotta do the dirty work fer ya also?" He was red in the face, he was almost spitting. More than likely he'd been drinking. "We kills the little fellers fer ya an' ya want us t'bury 'em also? Fer extra service ya gotta pay. Pay!"

So he had to shovel up the little bodies once again after they had gone.

"Dear Mother," he wrote at the Y with a good sharp pencil,

and stopped for fifteen minutes. The sun shone in. It came through the curtains, through the shades, however he arranged them. He would have to ask the clerk for a less sunny room, so the red light wouldn't get in behind his lids while he slept.

> I have the whole afternoon to myself, so I am writing this letter. Practicing at night is not as good as practicing in the daytime after all, but I am making progress. My health is very good. How are you?
> Mr. Benton is arranging to get me an audition for the orchestra very soon. He is a fine musician, only I am better. I think I will pass the audition. Yes, I will take you to see Terminal Hall when I am a member of the orchestra.

"Your loving son Thomas," he finished and appraised his letter. He'd already told her about the audition, but thought it worth repeating. It was fortunate he had so much on his mind or he really wouldn't know what to do. For the moment the thought of the coming audition stirred in his throat and blinked his eyes but he was too tired for excitement.

The clock said to him one o'clock, that's all. He really should go back to sleep, he really should. He really should shave. He didn't like afternoon movies. He really should hop on one foot ten times around the block, make a face, two faces at the same time, stretch a rubber till it broke if it hollered that's a joke.

He found himself quivering with rage.

They'd all come down from the jungle tonight. The Limp was a fool. What did he want? They were there for the fun.

"ANYONE IN THERE?" That was the watchman.

"Who ya expec'? Santa Claus?" The Limp made as if to pat Santa Claus on the back, but stopped and laughed.

Up went the flame.

"Ya c'n go in now, boss." The Limp was all hopped up. It was funny to watch the boss and his bent head going back into the shack. Old jag-on Limp, he had it made.

He wasn't kidding, either. There were rats by the dozens. They leaped out at the men and the men caught them with the nails in their sticks and flung them back into the fire. That horn! The jungle had never had a night like that. When the hunting was over some of them went back to the jungle but more stayed on with the Limp.

The watchman didn't want to let them in, he only half opened the door, but they crowded in behind the Limp anyway. Sure enough, he held the brass horn under his arm.

The Limp said, "Coffee, boss! Whas' matter, boss, no coffee t'night after we work our nuts off fer ya, boss?"

"Make yerself at home, boys," said the Limp. He had to put up the coffee himself. What did he have on the watchman? They looked at the watchman; they looked at the Limp. They laughed.

"What's funny?" the watchman wanted to know. The Limp knew a touch when he saw one. What do you do with a valuable one like that? Not what the Limp does.

"Show the boys how it works, boss," says the Limp.

"No," says the watchman, frowning and licking his lips.

"All ya gotta do is blow it onct."

"You're making me angry," says the watchman.

They could see the Limp didn't know what to do, so they grinned at the Limp, silently, showing the questions on their bared teeth. Thought you had influence, said the teeth.

"Aaagh," cried the Limp. "Give it t'me an' le' me show 'em!"

So asking no questions and telling no lies the Limp wobbled up to the watchman before the watchman or anyone knew what he was up to and put his hands on the horn, which looks like a lot of plumbing going in circles with a big flare at one end of it and a mouthpiece at the other. The Limp had hold of the flare part. He gave it a little tug.

We're waiting, Limp, said the teeth.

"Let go," said the watchman. "You're smearing it up. Let go!"

Hee hee hee said the teeth to the Limp.

"Gimmee!" screeched the Limp, pulling at the horn with both his hands. Go to it, Limp. Go to it, watchman!

"Let go," said the watchman, pulling. It was sure the Limp wasn't letting go, so the watchman let go all at once, because it was either that or ruin the horn, and the Limp fell back with the horn into the music stand and went crashing and ringing down upon the floor. What do you think of that? Then somebody with a quick foot kicked over the coffee pot.

"Oh, no!" said the watchman scrambling down on his knees to save his horn. "Kee-ryst!" yelled the Limp on his back when the hot coffee got into his pants.

Oh brother oh brother oh brother. Did you ever see anything like it? Look at the watchman feel up his horn down there on his hands and knees. Look at the Limp wave his arms and legs, look at him try to catch hold of something so he could get out of the coffee. They would all die laughing. "I won't stand it!" said the watchman. But don't you think they weren't ready. "I won't!" the watchman was telling them all. They knew you didn't do with a valuable watchman what the Limp did although of course you had every right to enjoy it if the Limp wanted to spend every bit of it he had all at once. For

suddenly the watchman had risen, he was shaking all over—
and tugging at his holster, by God, his holster!

Hey watchman, fer Chris'sakes! The holster held because he
didn't have enough sense to unbutton it, but he was tugging
away just the same, holding the horn under his free arm while
he tugged but the holster was going to give. Hey, let's get outa
here!

"So long, Limp" they shouted, but the god damned door
opened on the inside and they couldn't all get out at once and
they couldn't stop, they were laughing their heads off. They
were digging their elbows into one another while they laughed
and that watchman was going to get his gun out! "So long,
watchman!" At the same time the Limp was crawling crab-like
on his stomach toward them making for the door. Maybe that's
why they were laughing. "Get out!" that watchman yelled, but
they couldn't, the door was jammed, it opened on the inside,
hold everything, watchman! "Get out I tell you!" and then
they were spouting out of the doorway at last falling all over
themselves with the Limp pulling at them to let him by.

"I'll shoot, I'll shoot, I'll shoot."

When they turned around to look there was the Limp
sprawled upon the ground before the shack with the watchman
standing over him but damned if they'd go back because, the
little sonuvabitch, he might shoot any minute! The burning
dump lighted the news up for them on the watchman's face
which didn't have a single expression upon it any more, which
was cold and fixed and full of the red light, and they couldn't
help but stand when the watchman aimed his gun at the Limp.
The watchman's voice came from the empty face so that you
could hear it very clear. The light of the dump was all over
him, although you could hardly see the Limp only his arms
stretched out above him. "What do you want, Limp?" the
watchman was pleading. "What do you want with me?" Then
he lifted his gun high into the air above his head and it looked
for sure as though it would come down upon the Limp's skull
and that would be the end of the Limp, but the Limp let out a
scream and the gun held burning with the dump light while
he screamed. They hadn't thought the Limp had that much
scream in him.

It must have surprised the watchman too, because the gun
hand dropped to his side, which gave the Limp a chance to
scramble to his feet and run. He ran fast for a man with one
leg shorter than the other.

In his room at the Y with the clean white walls and the iron
bedstead and the chair very much like the chair he had in his
room in Scranton, Thomas MacIntyre removed his horn from

its instrument case and fondled it where the dent was which the Limp had made. On Monday, *this* Monday coming, he had an appointment with the conductor. Softly, softly he blew upon his horn, again and again, knowing that still his instrument was soft, poetical and full of beauty. It might not have been.

The Limp waited until the watchman had made the rounds and retired to his shack, then listened to the horn and shivered, remembering the gun, and crept close to the window. He'd been afraid to approach the window before, just looked and dribbled the curses. They had laughed him out of the jungle.

So he'd come home. He'd come and tapped with his finger on the window but the boss didn't hear him. The boss just blew his horn. Behind the Limp the flame raged and the singed rats died in their own time, and the Limp tapped with the nail of his forefinger and smirked through the glass and tapped. He would take the boss up and carry him in his arms to the flame and dump him in, that's what he would do. He would kiss his ass, he would take a stick, and smack! Tap. But the boss horned on. Tap. The boss saw him, but he horned it on.

"Hi boss, 'lo boss, hi boss . . ." pronounced the muscles in his larynx, never his lips. "Hey!" he yelled.

That did it. That got in even through the plate glass window. The Limp sucked in his breath. From the shadow, standing back, in the shadow the boss's shack made when it raised up before the fire, the Limp watched the boss with the light on him. "What do you want?" said the boss.

"I never meant no harm," the Limp said. In his heart the flame went Whoof as when the watchman lit the kerosene and the dump blew up.

"What do you want?" said the boss, stroking the horn. The Limp could see it. He should have taken that horn while he had the chance, and he should have, he should have . . .

"Yeah, but the rat job, the rat job, who's gonna do it if I can't come? Who? Boss, I'll kill 'em fer ya, ya won't hear a thing boss, not a thing."

"I don't care about the rats."

"Every night I'll throw 'em on the fire. Every night before I come in. Huh, boss?" C'mon boss, give it t'me, give it t'me. Let the Limp in. Please. I said please.

"No," said the watchman and the rectangle of light closed out. For a moment the Limp thought the boss was coming after him. He started to run but then he realized the boss had gone inside and left him outside with the horn in his ears and knowing that soon he'd have to get going. Then, every night after the Limp had gone the boss would take his can of kerosene and sprinkle the dump, but the Limp would not be there. Every night the boss would walk round and round with the healthy fat pistol hanging at his waist.

His mouth opened to explain his rage but no sound came. The sound of the horn came into his mouth and took the shout away, so the Limp sought his way back to the jungle and the fire where they would grin at him again because he didn't have it with him, because he'd left it behind with the boss after all. The further he walked from the shack with the electric bulb and the horn the sicker he got, the angrier, until he was almost crying aloud for the boss to come out of his shack and see him, only see him, walking like this on the empty plain between the burning dump and the railroad siding. The size of his indignation tore the Limp's thin chest, amazed him. The boss would have to come to him, it said. The boss would have to save him. Because if the boss saved him, the boss would care for him.

And this time when the Limp opened his mouth he shouted with delight at what he would do to the bastard now, what he would do to him. Later, squatted at the fire with the others and silencing their hoots with his silence, the lines for frown between his eyes went deep and intent and stern above the watery eyes. Every now and then he'd giggle, so they asked him what the hell he had up his sleeve but he wouldn't tell them.

The big one, the cautious one, the one with a sense of fact, he'd been a long way on the rails and in the freight cars, all up and down the old creation and back again. Now he was back again, all ready for another fling with the white sticks, and damned if the Limp bastard wasn't still there and damned if the Limp hadn't crapped up the works. But the Limp had an idea. The Limp grinned at him, told him to take it easy and told him what the idea was. So he went along that night to see how it worked, and it better, it better, because what had he come back for but another fling at the little fellers?

"I'll hide myself," grinned the Limp. "He'll never know it I'll hide myself so perfec'" and his two heels did a sluggish dance.

They had brought along two sticks, white, bare sticks, to be prepared. The big one took along a stick wherever he went, only sometimes he threw it away. He would pick up a stick and take a long, full swing with it and maybe hit something, then look at the stick and wonder how it got into his hands and let the stick drop and go off all up and down the old creation which had nothing whatever new in it. Nothing would ever pry the Limp away from his stick. Would he cry if someone took his stick away from him? The big one was tempted, and leaned over the Limp and put his arm upon his shoulder, and forgot about it because now he was supposed to hide and watch while the Limp did his business.

There were many places to hide here. There were heaps of ashes pocking the plain, there were gullies which could protect one. And, soon, in the moment before the watchman set the flames even the faint green shine around the plain's edge and over far beyond the railroad tracks would have diminished and made any place a place for hiding.

The Limp did his business very cautiously. He chuckled to himself—the big one heard him and fondled the stick he carried—then the Limp had clambered from the gully, no longer waiting with the big one, limping instead, bent over, silent, watching as the man who knew fact watched, the lighted shack. For this was the time when the night watchman took over from the day watchman, and this was the time in which the Limp could move unseen, unheard. Then the door of the shack opened and a great stream of light gushed from the shack, light without end, reaching over the plain and over the dump and losing itself on the other side of the dump where the green band no longer was. But the stream never touched the Limp.

The man who understood the way things were settled back. The day watchman who was coming from the shack now silhouetted himself in the doorway and then the silhouette closed the door and killed itself, which the cautious one thought very funny. This left only the night watchman alone inside, the fellow with the great noisy horn which would soon be sounding off.

A wide grin rode upon the big one's face. Both his hands gripped the stick he carried. By this time the Limp would have reached the dump. Wheezing in his chest, the Limp, that little man, would have clambered up the rubbish pile so that now at this time when the shack door opened again he would be safe as a bug in a rug, in the heart of his idea. It was all very gay and joyous because something was cooking, something was moving, not only the watchman behind the moving searchlight; and soon, so very soon, the big man's stick would rise again and bear down with all the enormous force he felt flooding his muscles, but controlled.

It was funny to see the patch of light moving irregularly to the dump where the Limp was waiting. He moved forward until he was no distance at all from the watchman. He was unseen and unknown, like the Limp perched now in the heart of the dump on tin cans and two by fours, and cartons and shoes and all the great discharge of the city the lights of which never saw the Limp and never saw him but lived in their little holes in the black shapes on the edge of the distance where the city was and never left their holes but stayed there on and on, every night, on and on through all the times he came and went with wrath and caution.

"ANYONE IN THERE?"

Dear boss, dear boss, it's me in the middle of the junk! Thanks boss, I almost got burned up, you saved me boss, we're friends now boss, you'll give it back to me now, huh boss, we're pals like crap an' paper stuck together you and me together boss, in a minute I'll come off the pile boss and you'll take hold of my hand and you'll be forever obliged to me, forever and a day and time and a half for overtime and I'll carry the white stick for you boss, all this in a minute boss but in the meanwhile here's old Limp sittin' on a pile and laughing to himself because he knows what's coming and because, you know boss, he don't want to get off this pile, it's his pile, he wants to sit here watchin' you walk 'round and round the dump sprinklin' your kerosene and never guessing, never guessing what old Limp has ready for you. Dear boss, it's me in the middle of the junk. In a minute you'll hear me! But not yet.

And had the watchman not deserved well at the hands of the conductor that he should be fearful? Had he not put aside all wanton ways? Had he not put aside all wanton ways from the beginning? He was poised on the brink of Monday. Would he not on the seventh day rest in the lap of the conductor while the choir of musicians, priestly in the black tuxedos which were not for one day but for all days and hereafter, cheered and tapped with their bows (but gently) the wood of their instruments? So on the seventh day he would put on the black tuxedo and be as a man come home, the prodigal son, from Egypt and all points West, to take up permanent and legal residence here in the temple of his brethren and wear the many-colored coat though the heathen raged.

How many days to go? And they would come to him, and they would take him upon their broad capacious shoulders. For those who are lowly and modest in every requirement shall be raised up. And he would love them. Oh, yes! Nor would he ever say how strong their grip was and what it did to him and he would forgive them, yea though they had rejected him yea though they had made light of him. Yea, though he walked on the Hill of Gethsemane and in the shadow of the Dump, he would practice patience and foresight and diligence in all his ways, and what did anybody else know about it? Nothing. They passed over his head like the idle wind which understands not. He would be firm. He would stand fast. And they would come unto him.

On Sunday night, all fresh from church, and having transposed with considerable ease from F to E and G, and being ready therefore for all future transposition, the watchman pays the dump its due and notes how soon is Monday, collection day.

"ANYONE IN THERE?"

The watchman had called twice and still the Limp was quiet on his hill of crap, with only one more call to go. For Chris'-sakes, what was wrong with the Limp, the Limp was crazy, how could a man tell what a watchman would do next following a flashlight round a dump? C'mon, Limp, you bastard, watcha waitin' for? Because the watchman has almost finished his circle. Can't you see the flashlight circling?

"ANYONE IN THERE?"

Eeeee, went the cautious one, pounding the earth with his big white stick. Good for the Limp who played it till the end, who did this for the big man!

Limp, the watchman's lightin' a match my God! My God the little bird of light between his fingers!

Was that the Limp? His voice from the center of the dump? "HOLD IT BOSS, IT'S ME!" The cracked and burning voice spattering from the center of the dump? Yes. But look how the bird flew, how it didn't listen! The big one, the cautious feller, he saw the watchman open his hand and let it fly and in all the world of city, dump and stars there was only the flying little bird of light dropping down upon the kerosene, and the cautious one's vast disbelief. Whoosh! went the kerosene lifting up its great red arms and running and hopping and skipping and jumping, quick, double time, one two three around the dump, and roaring!

Watchman, Watchman!

"IT'S ME, BOSS, IT'S ME!" That was the Limp, telling him. But the flare of the flame was rising high and lighting up the boss and hiding the Limp although you could hear him. "IT'S ME, BOSS!" You could hear the Limp stumble among the old tin cans toward the flame where the boss stood. The big one was running there too. He could see the boss just standing there bug-eyed, his face all red and shiny with the flames.

"YA SAVED MY LIFE, BOSS. WHAT THE HELL YA DOING?"

The big one, the cautious one, had the boss by the arms now. He was shaking the boss and listening to the sound of the flames and of the Limp running around inside the burning dump, scampering around, striking out with his long white stick—you could see the stick rising over the flames. So he turned from the boss and started hitting at the flames also, but it did no good. So he watched the boss while he hit at the flames with his heart shouting and attentive to the Limp's wail in the heart of his idea, when there, there on the face of the boss the tears streamed, he saw them, tear after tear streaming down the face of the boss and the cautious one found himself laughing at the top of his lungs, but striking at the flames. How big the flames were, anyway, how the wind made a wall of them! He came and stood beside the boss and stared into the flame and listened to the howling of the Limp, to the thrashing of his stick forced backward, always backward, slowly, to the very center of the dump.

Then he heard it. The boss heard it, too. It came from the heart of the burning dump, there was no mistaking it. The boss raised his empty arms to it and very gently shook his head from side to side. "BLOW YER LOUSY HORN, BOSS, BLOW!" What could the boss do? "QUICK!" The boss just didn't have his horn with him!

The rats were running from the fire.

"I don't have it with me," said the boss to the cautious one, the quiet one, imploring him. "Honest!" showing his empty hands.

SCREAM! went the Limp, SCREAM!

"Quiet, Limp," yelled back the boss. "You must be quiet!"

When it was quiet, when the boss turned to look at the companion at his side with inquiry in his eyes, with all the questions watchmen ever raise and he himself had ever raised, when the man who knew the score could feel the questions of the boss reaching in to him—but all they said was How'd it happen? What happened? How do you figure it, Bud?—the slow one, the cautious one, the man who knew the score could only shake his head from side to side, smile in a way, put his arm around the boss's shoulders.

Last was Thomas MacIntyre's due. This he found in Terminal Hall. There on Monday he blew such notes for the conductor as he was sure the conductor had never heard before, full notes, clear notes, round notes calling loudly through the perpetual flame.

"He's a little too emotional," he overheard the conductor say to Mr. Benton, the best French horn in the Terminal Orchestra (yet knowing he was better, that no man would ever play the horn as he would, no man). "What's he cry for when he plays? How does he do it? But I suppose we can use him."

Thomas was able to give up the dump. His tears stopped. He sat full fledged, a member of the orchestra.

Edith Sitwell

From

THE ROAD
TO THEBES

Doctor Edith Sitwell, eldest of
the three famous Sitwells, grew
up at Renishaw Hall, which
has been in the Sitwell family
for over 600 years. She has written a novel and books of biography, essays, and criticism,
but is best known as a poet.
More than a dozen collec-
tions of her poems have appeared in book form. CANTICLE
OF THE ROSE, published here
by Vanguard, is the most
recent, though another volume
is promised within the year. She
has given dramatic readings
from her own poetry
on both sides of the Atlantic.

II INTERLUDE

After the intolerable weight of tyrant suns
(Caesars with masks of gold) wave after wave the early
                                                     evening
Comes with the sound of sea and siren cave
To continents and cities after the long heat—

And echoes in buried cities—the azoic azure
Calls to the sphinxes of the silence and unburied sapphires
Staring across the lion-breasted sands in the great deserts,

And to the azoic heart (where Time, that Medusa, reigns,
                                          turns all to stone)—
To the orange-flower, the oragious hair of youth that cool
                                          airs lift—the orb.
And the golden nodding nursing nurse that we call Eve

And evening, sighed, "The first and final Adam—he who is
                                   one with the immense Ceres
And all day broke the gold body of the giantess as in love

And he who forsook her for that other giantess,
The city, the vast continent of stone

Are homeward-going."
                        Soon night falls like fire, yet vine-dark.
                        In the cities
The girls with breasts like points of sun in the vine-dark night
And gowns the colour of the thunder's reverberations
Among the forests, seek a love in which to sink like the sea.

What do the seraphs and sapphires of air among the branches
Hear, as the voices pass? "Your hair is ringed as the tendrils
Of the first plantations of the Vine after the Flood!"

"The vines of the Sun? Or the vines of Darkness? and of all
                                      damnations—
The vines of Medusa's serpents?" "Ah, your kiss is the light of
                        the planets, burning among the leaves!"
                      No, it was Lucifer,

Son of the Morning. Then it changed to the Prince of the Air,
                                    —the brightness
That rules in Hell. Grown cold! I am Medusa! And my other
Name is Time!

            Come to my lips, the long horizon—
Cold with the serpents' buried wisdom that has known the azoic
Continents the secrets and night-haunted jewels of the
                                      catafalques!

Come! I will seal your eyes that they no more shall weep,
No more behold another. Once, at your grief,
The sea o'erfraught would swell, and the unsought diamonds

Rise with your tears.
                   Now you shall faithless be
To the flesh of orange-blossom and of arbutus honey-hearted,
Seeing my lips cold as the unburied sapphires in the desert air
Approach your own—
The one horizon—the azoic continent of night and stone.

III THE NIGHT WIND

O heart, great equinox of the Sun of Night
Where life and death are equal—Lion, or Sphinx—
What can you tell of Darkness

To the vast continent of hungry stone
Long as the lips of Medusa, our horizon?

Heart (Lion or Sphinx) what can you tell the city
Of breasts like Egypt where no lightning shines,
Because of their great heat? This is the hour the night-wind
Asks those born in Hell concerning their foredoom.

Now in the streets great airs the colour of the vines
Drift to the noctuas, veiled women, to the faceless ones, the
                                        nameless ones—
To Lot's wife staring across the desert of her life.

Those airs of sapphire drift from violet vines—
Elixirs and saps of sapphire beloved of Saturn
And planets of violet dew from vine-branches

Fall on the lips of fashionable women
The abominable Koretto and Metro (cities buried
Under the sands of the Dead Sea: Adama and Gomorrah,
                                                Segor),
And cool the cheeks where the long fires of all Hell are dyed;

Drifting to women like great vines:—(what was the first
                                    plantation since the Flood?
The vines of Grief?
The first sin of the new world, and the last
Of the ancient civilisation? You, the night-wind,
What was the first plantation since the Flood?)

And to old Maenads of the city, where the far-off music
Dying in public gardens wraps their flesh—
That vast immundity from which the Flood receded,
Their hearts, those rocks from which no Moses could strike
                                                    tears

With a little comfort, they, awhile forgetting
The mobilisation of the world's filth, the garrets, garners
Of Nothingness, and the sparse fires' infrequent garnets,
The ragpicker's great reign, their empty mouths like Chaos
                                                    ruined,

Speak for a moment with their other lives:

"Who is it knocks at that tomb, my heart? Is it the grave-digger,
The final Adam? There was one knocked so:
He would not know me now. For all Time's filth, the dress
I stole from the habitations of the Dead,
Hides me—a body cold as the wind-blown vines,
And the sad sapphire bone shrunk by Time's fires

To this small apeish thing."
                            "Ah, what was I inferior to Death,
That you should be untrue? Now kindly Age,
My one companion, holds me close, so I
Forget your kiss. The fires in my heart are gone.
And yet as if they had melted into rain

The heart itself, my tears
Are faithful yet."
                    "Is there another language of the Dead?
Is that why those for whom we long, return
No more? For the small words of love they say—

How should we hear them through the Babel-clamour?
They make no sound:
All the great movements of the world pass with no noise;
The golden boys,
The great Spring, turn to dust as to a lover—
The heart breaks with no sound."

"And in the day, the empire of hatred and of hunger,
Even the Dog pities us. 'I would be destitute as Man,
So cast from me my faithfulness, my one possession.
All day my throat must multiply its thunder
To the triple violence of Cerberus
To proclaim your misery and mine. Why should the Beast and Reptile
Be imprisoned in their small empire of aggression—
The claw, fang, sting, the twining, the embrace?
Has Man no more than this? Does not the lover say to lover,
Is that your kiss?

It is more cold than the python, the shining one, the viper,
Its venom is perfidy, outshining all the stars.' "

Then where the suns of Night seek in the rock for unborn sapphires
And cornflowers like blue flames or water-drops from wells of blue fire
Deep as the heart of Man, from which to build the Day,

I went upon my road to Thebes from Athens, Death from Birth,
And to my heart, that last dark Night in which the long Styx weeps its woe,
Held close the world, my wound.

Notes: "Interlude"—Verse 6, lines 4 and 5, "with breasts like points of sun," and "gowns the colour of the thunder's reverberations" are adaptations of lines from André Breton's "un homme et une femme touts blancs," Verse 11, line 3, from Milton. "The Night-Wind"—last verse, last line, is an adaptation of a line by Dylan Thomas, "the world's my wound, God's Mary in her grief."

Sacheverell Sitwell

MRS. H. OR A LADY FROM BABEL

Art critic as well as poet, Sacheverell Sitwell is the younger brother of Doctor Edith Sitwell and Sir Osbert. He is a graduate of Eton and Oxford, and the author of works that have appeared almost annually since 1924, among them EGLANTINE AND OTHER POEMS, DOCTOR DONNE AND GARGANTUA, and THE HUNTERS AND THE HUNTED, published here by Macmillan. He is married and has two sons.

"Sprechen sie Deutsch? Parlez-vous Français?
Parlate Italiano? Dearest Child!"

Mrs. H. would float the words
As jewels from her sunshade,
Which to my infant eyes
Seemed as the fountain of all frankincense.
Beneath the twittering shadow
She leaned out, looking in my eyes,
Her body perfectly enmeshed
Beneath the clinging scales of gold,
And all her landau
Filled with the falling jewels—
The melting of the million bells
Set ringing when the wind breathes
And the blue spaces of the sky
Are filled with shaking leaves—
Divine wisdom as a freehold gift
From black gloved hands—
The feast of untold tongues!

On a bridge one evening
From behind the nearest house
The sunset air came suddenly alive with sound,
The throbbing from a mandoline fell forth
As the long lines of water when a boat floats by.
This ended, she was asked for coppers
In Italian.
"Coachman, drive on!
Mes meilleurs sentiments, à maman,
Mes meilleurs . . ."

PACKING A PHOTOGRAPH FROM FIRENZE

William H. Matchett

Currently a graduate student at Harvard University, and on the staff of The Poets' Theatre, William H. Matchett lives in Cambridge, Massachusetts. Born in Chicago in 1923, he was educated at Westtown School and Swarthmore College. His work has appeared in *Harper's, The New Yorker* and *Furioso*, and in 1952 he was awarded the first prize in the *Furioso* poetry contest.

1

This house that has been our home has been condemned
To be demolished as part of a master plan
That calls for enlarging the institution next door.
Overnight, on the torn, raw ground, they will graft a new,
Of course modern, stainless, leakproof research
Laboratory, with interphone system and guards.
Here, where the staircase creaks and the furnace complains,
Where brown fingers have clutched the plaster through countless rains,
Steel and concrete will shield the tempered air.
Here, where the ashtrays have spilled the warm ends of thought
While the coffee grew cold, none being afraid to speak,
Where we have lain locked through long nights and were loath to arise
On grey winter mornings when chickadees came to the window,
In sound-proof cells on registered pads
The approved will doodle death with indelible ink.

2

The artery sings in the wrist, *time passes, time passes;*
Youth, though it swings with the cadence, is deaf to the song,
Which is its horror, poignancy and salvation.
Michelangelo's David, firm, with the poised repose
Of a hidden lion, drawn by the will of the blood,
Sling in hand, muses of greater Goliaths.
If this were the boy portrayed, not the image given
To life in the lifeless stone, if this were the flesh
That now is the dust of ageless mutations of dust,
The flesh, defiant, perplexed, ashamedly lonely,

Then in the depth of the chest, in the ribs' cave,
Would lurk, unperceived, the treacherous final plague,
The twisted limb, the sagging physique, the intense
And fussy attention to each misbeat of the pulse.
But the stone that stands transcends the David that died,
Though he died a king. Is it better to make an end
Than to face the interminable pains and the diminutions?
Perhaps it is progress, this pure research into killing;
The suddenly dead avoid their slow decay.

3

I hear the mouse in the laundry and know that fall
Has arrived to drive him in again; on the lawn
The last of the leaves are collecting in drifts at the base
Of the purple beech. One straggling chrysanthemum
Dips and drips bronze-gold on the crusted earth.
This clear, suspended moment before the frost
Is the time for turning the compost and mulching the rose,
Spreading the wholesome corruption that feeds
Through the probable winter to the impossible spring.
But let it pass. Why enrich the soil
That will never produce? A jungle of structural steel,
Though rooted firmly in humus as black as war,
Is no less barren. A buried seed that is warmed
By a basement floor will unwrap the tallow coil
From its pallid core and, seeking the sun, will rot.
So it comes to an end, breaking the usual cycle;
The frame is ravaged behind the evicted soul.

4

The affections, ever conservative, cling to the forms
Worn smoothest by custom, resisting even improvement,
Content, when pressed, with the shreds of a wretched past.
E pur si muove. I would not wish to be
The hierophant proscribing Galileo.
Yet truth is not false because the affections agree.
This is not science, this furious drive for extinction,
The spurious promise of power perverts cognition
While the single-minded pursuit of enslavable facts
Neglects the very ravines where the victims lie strangled.
I must affirm this ill-proportioned house
And the earth around it, even the mouse and the staircase.
All change is not progress, nor is all age decline.
There is more to be drawn from the line of the silvered limbs
Of the purple beech, more from the silvered line
Of David's limbs, more from the intercourse

Of hearts, fertile minds, dirty fingers and growing things
Than from all the sterilized data of destruction.

*   *   *

But the time has arrived for removing all we can save
In an echoing search through painfully naked rooms
Where stark, dark wallpaper celebrates each missing picture,
Revealing the silent advance of ceaseless change.
We have been warned. We clasp our belongings. We flee.
Yet slowly, inexorably, the future pursues
With the final knowledge of all that we shall lose:
In the fall of this house all houses stand condemned.

Spencer Brown

CANDLEMAS

NEAR A PARKWAY

A graduate of Harvard University, Spencer Brown now teaches at the Fieldston School and has served on the faculties of the Taft and Loomis Schools. His work has appeared in *Partisan Review, Classical Journal, Commentary* and *The New Yorker*. Born in Hartford, Connecticut, he now lives in New York.

The shadowing woodchuck dives below
After one fable-frightened peep,
And morning will March in at last.
With bull in barn and snake asleep
And poison ivy sheathed in snow,
The countryside is safe to all
Not old enough to fear a fall:
Nothing more menacing than ice
And thin powder where troops of mice
Last night trod a paw-pointed breed
Of trapezoids in search of seed.
No house, no hunter keeps policed
The hills where any potent beast
Flees me unarmed a mile at least:
For over pathless slopes and ridges,
With moving scales and bracelet bridges,

A split gray serpent-sentry glances;
And hours hence, opening its eye,
The guardian city dusk-beset
Will glare under the edge of sky
And muster from a silhouette
Where tree sways and sapling dances
A buried legion with bent lances.
   Yet there a turquoise tint behind
Recalls unwanted to my mind
The glow that once, from a hurt cat's paw
Under fluoroscope, I saw
In brittle spider-tracery
Of bones through green transparent fur.
   Today is double purification,
From childbirth, for annunciation.
Making ready for life to stir,
Persephone-Aphrodite-Mary
Renews her brief virginity
By bathing in blue February
Pools of shadow and streams of sky.
It is not coming life I fear,
Nor maiden landscape safe and drear;
It is a twinkling menace high
Above, behind those trees, below
The farther ridge, that without reason
Profanes the sacrament of snow
And Nunc Dimittis of the season:
   As if from the corner of my eye
I saw white-parka'd figures crawl;
As if, beyond the frozen wall
Of un-twig-broken silence round,
I heard the stutter and crack and clank
Of hidden enemy gun and tank;
As if, before remotest sound
Could pierce the miles of muffling air,
Over the bastion city there
I saw a great white blast of sky;
As if when, pulse in unison,
My love and I lie safe in bed,
The skull glowed through her saucy head,
Within her loins the skeleton.

Alexander Trocchi

HE TASTED HISTORY WITH A YELLOW TOOTH

Twenty-seven-year-old Alexander Trocchi was born in Glasgow and now lives in Paris, where he is the editor of the literary quarterly *Merlin*. His work has been published in *Botteghe Oscure*.

The long tusktooth of his nether jaw
cast a yellow shadow
broke through the thin bone of history
loosing tides,
"My personal Ides"
he said, wrote at night
red ink
on cheap paper
his big quick letters (always for the greater glory of God)
round as nuts or girlbreasts
a terrible child's message to a world at war.

Eggs again.
My aunt laid an egg once
all smooth and creamy
you wanted to stroke it as you want to stroke a woman
but she was ashamed of it
and took it away from me
I think she buried it in the garden—
anyway, there's a patch of violets there
ten yards from the stair
that goes to the loft where my uncle kept the saddles
and they bleed each spring,
in spring there is a bleeding.

He's a bit of a Jesuit
his brain full of bits of history
which he chews over with his yellow tooth,
a strange Balkan name
an Icelandic god,
Did you know that somewhere in Africa
a woman walks naked to her wedding?

I tell you there is no use talking about the "Renaissance"
it was a falling off
a *ruining* of towers (you know the derivation?)
Late? I suppose it is. Not want tea?
—I wonder when a woman will walk naked to me?

FIRST SONG

Galway Kinnell

Director of the Liberal Arts Programs at University College, University of Chicago, Galway Kinnell was born in Pawtucket, Rhode Island, and was educated at Princeton University and the University of Rochester. He is a contributor to the forthcoming NEW POEMS BY AMERICAN POETS, edited by Rolfe Humphries (Ballantine Books).

Then it was dusk in Illinois, the small boy
After an afternoon of carting dung
Hung on the rail fence, a sapped thing
Weary to crying. Dark was growing tall
And he began to hear the pond frogs all
Calling upon his ear with what seemed their joy.

Soon their sound was pleasant for a boy
Listening in the smoky dusk and the nightfall
Of Illinois, and then from the field two small
Boys came bearing cornstalk violins
And rubbed three cornstalk bows with resins,
And they set fiddling with them as with joy.

It was now fine music the frogs and the boys
Did in the towering Illinois twilight make
And into dark in spite of a right arm's ache
A boy's hunched body loved out of a stalk
The first song of his happiness, and the song woke
His heart to the darkness and into the sadness of joy.

Patrick Boland

TRIALS
OF A POET

The son of a former Detroit Tiger pitcher, Patrick Boland is a native and still a resident of Detroit. He graduated from the University of Michigan, where he won an Avery Hopwood award in 1949. His poetry has appeared in *Flair* and elsewhere.

And is it true: you understand this stuff
You write yourself, but do not understand—
If one may cite the poem by Winston Clough—
The brightness of this people and this land?
    It is, and is not, I am sane enough.

And is it true: whenas you read those rough
Rhapsodists of her stockyards and her prairies,
You still maintained an absolutist tough
Contempt for most of your contemporaries?
    It is, and is not, I am sane enough.

And is it true: although intolerant of
Yiddish, American, and Esperanto,
You then embarked for Europe in a huff
To praise its tongues in canto after canto?
    It is, and is not, I am sane enough.

And is it true: you did affect to love
No symbol of the state where you were born—
The large potato, the majestic bluff—
But did prefer that fairyland forlorn?
    It is, and is not, I am sane enough.

And is it true: you did abuse, sir, a
Free system which insured your daily bread;
Nor hesitate to call it USURA
For which innumerable bankers bled?
    It is, and is not, I am sane enough.

It being true: no man would rise above
Our laws, whether in Provence or Cathay;
No man would ever play at madman's buff
Who is not—Is that all you have to say?
    It is, and is not, I am sane enough.

Note: The last line of each stanza is the first line of an early poem by Ezra Pound entitled "Sub Mare."

Howard Moss

VENICE

The author of two books of verse, THE WOUND AND THE WEATHER (Reynal and Hitchcock), and a new volume to be published by Charles Scribner's Sons, Howard Moss was born in New York City. A member of the editorial staff of *The New Yorker*, his work has appeared in *The Kenyon Review*, *Poetry*, and elsewhere.

Its wingéd lion stands up straight to hide
The source of pain: the reign of the unnatural.
One cannot tell how really false the real is.
One cannot tell how real the really false is.
Seen in one light, we apprehend the Beautiful:
The thinnest minarets of lattice lacework
Tangibly recovered from the hardest natural
Elements command our endless homage:
One doorway makes our human lives seem trivial.
In yet another light, a scabrous limb of Venus,
Dangling in rank water, rots to golden bone—
The swank and stink of the imagination
Beautifully gone bad. Its waterways re-weave
The only city that has seen itself
Reflected in the mirror of its very eye,
Made-up, each century, in vain for views
No one can now remember. How the painters lie,
Taken altogether in their fabrication!
Even the Adriatic, static in its green,
Evokes no known sea. From the campanile,
One sees, face down, a short, ceramic fish
Glittering its red-tiled scales below.
Exquisite emphases and subtle losses
Make up its tide. For power, four bronze horses,
Brought from Byzantium, outpace the sun.
Dwindling to our shadows in outside salons,
Where orchestras of afternoon rehearse our evening,
We sound the very history of fear we felt
Through all the shorter histories of fear we feel.
Is it true, we think, our sorry otherness
Is to fall in love with beasts whose beauty ruins us?
Those beasts are everywhere, though Venice says
Lions to be golden must be painted gold.

Sydney Goodsir Smith

CREDO

A leading Scots poet of the younger generation, Sydney Goodsir Smith, who writes in Lallans, has published several volumes of poetry in England and in Scotland, including UNDER THE EILDON TREE and SO LATE INTO THE NIGHT. In this country his work has appeared in NEW BRITISH POETS (New Directions).

Celebrate the seasons
Haud efter veritie   (Pursue
Find your equilibrium
And tell what happened ye.

Syne lay doun in a hole   (Then
Be the worms' victual
The tyke has had his day
And this is all.

Accept the praise
Put by the blame
Bard, sing on
In the goddess' name

Neer seek her out
Hers be the advance
But name thy bruckle barque   (fragile
Bonne Esperance.

Gey aft she'll gie   (Very often
Ye stanes for breid
But whiles her gift
Is life frae deid.

What mair is there ye wish?
Luve's memorie dwynes, the prufe   (dwindles, declines
Is there for ye that watch
The hevins muve.

Celebrate the seasons
And the Muse that rules
Aa truth is dream but this   (All
Aa dreamers fules.

Luve is the infant treason
O' the saikless saul   (innocent soul
Luve is the black dirk
Sheath't i the hert of all.

Hert can nocht live athout
This traitor's skaith (wound
Ye can dee a thousand nichts
And neer ken daith.

Luve was the first was struck
By the goddess mune
The luve she gied she took (gave
—The tides aye rin.

Celebrate the seasons
And the hours that pass
She that rocks the tides
Rocks ye at last.

Byron Vazakas

SKATING AT VERSAILLES

Author of TRANSFIGURED NIGHT, a volume of verse published by Macmillan, Byron Vazakas has contributed to literary magazines in this country for the past twelve years, and to half a dozen anthologies. Born in New York City, Mr. Vazakas now lives in Cambridge, Massachusetts.

Watteau congeals. Vistas recoil. This park, thank God, shall never end, nor should it! Pain jells. The tragic spells the iced macabre. As lakes by cold are marbled, anguish stills. Air wisps. Fear flakes. And the fountains freeze the terror's cancered porcelain. Look back, December, five o'clock, to schizoid gardens, past and safe. Be there. Fool pain. Escape. Watch time, six-sided, skitter through. Where elegance airs loneliness, ice mirrors it. The lake whips out. A skater rings a figure eight. Woods glint. Snow tufts the tree-spiked violet. All legs, lean, slow, now right now left, a skate is lifted and a skate comes down. Haze helps. Mist blues the personal. The skater smiles. Rococo as gilt pediments, his breath frosts up. Deft, on one leg outstretched, he turns. His cap, a beaver coronet, his body belted, slim and young, he eyes perspectives, rich and dark. They're his. The chalked pavilions shelter him. Like time, before and after time, he clocks the landscape, safe as self. See, he is skating farther off, a fiddled figure dipping swirls. Last daylight sparks the glassy boughs. He pivots, dims. He did it! lake by lake, farther and farther ... Nothing can touch him. Nothing can reach him now ...

John Ashbery

HE

Born in 1927 in Rochester, New York, John Ashbery was educated at Harvard and Columbia University, and now lives in New York City. His poetry has appeared in *Partisan Review*, *Furioso* and *New Directions*, and in 1952 he was one of the winners of the Y.M.H.A. Poetry Center Introductions contest in New York. Mr. Ashbery recently issued a privately printed pamphlet of his work, which includes the poem "He."

(He: Copyright, 1953, by John Ashbery.)

He cuts down the lakes so they appear straight.
He smiles at his feet in their tired mules.
He turns up the music much louder.
He takes down the vaseline from the pantry shelf.

He is the capricious smile behind the colored bottles.
He eats not lest the poor want some.
He breathes of attitudes the piney altitudes.
He indeed is the White Cliffs of Dover.

He knows that his neck is frozen.
He snorts in the vale of dim wolves.
He writes to say, "If ever you visit this island
He'll grow you back to your childhood.

"He is the liar behind the hedge.
He grew one morning out of candor.
He is his own consolation prize.
He has had his eye on you from the beginning."

He hears the weak cut down with a smile.
He waltzes tragically on the spitting housetops.
He is never near. What you need
He cancels with the air of one making a salad.

He is always the last to know.
He is strength you once said was your bonnet.
He has appeared in "Carmen."
He is after us. If you decide

He is important, it will get you nowhere.
He is the source of much bitter reflection.
He used to be pretty for a rat.
He is now over-proud of his Etruscan appearance.

He walks in his sleep into your life.
He is worth knowing only for the children
He has reared as savages in Utah.
He helps his mother take in the clothesline.

He is unforgettable as a shooting star.
He is known as Liverlips.
He will tell you he has had a bad time of it.
He will try to pretend his pressagent is a temptress.

He looks terrible on the stairs.
He cuts himself on what he eats.
He was last seen flying to New York.
He was handing out cards which read:

"He wears a question in his left eye.
He dislikes the police but will associate with them.
He will demand something not on the menu.
He is invisible to the eyes of beauty and culture.

"He prevented the murder of Mistinguette in Mexico.
He has a knack for abortions. If you see
He is following you, forget him immediately:
He is dangerous even though asleep and unarmed."

Harry Duncan

MONODIES

Since 1938 Harry Duncan has been associated with the Cummington School of the Arts in Cummington, Massachusetts, during the summers. For a time he was connected with the now suspended Cummington Press as editor and printer. Born in Keokuk, Iowa, he was educated at Grinnell College in Iowa and Duke University, Durham, North Carolina. His verse has been published in literary magazines here and abroad. "Monodies" first appeared in *Botteghe Oscure*.

> Thy lines ar now a murmeringe to her eares
> Like to a fallinge streame which passinge sloe
> Is wovnt to nurrishe sleap, and quietnes . . .
> —*The Ocean to Cynthia*

Only a strenuous ghost
Remains for me to lay:
Her lanky corpse is compost

Tempering teeming clay
No farmer may plow or sow,
Settled in town to stay.

As sure as a man can know
That part will bear less touch
Of death being dead now

Than ever alive, much
Less. What if grubs have nursed
At wasted breasts and such?

My old maid was there first:
Her skull that had worked through
Before its pith dispersed

And backbone still askew
From the sarcoma's guile
Are rigid residue.

The undertaker-smile
Had glossed these data out
That term I stood in the pale

With the rest and thought the spot,
Railway-tracks, hemlocks,
And water-tower, ought,

With its quarrelling squirrels and flocks
Of starlings, to be all right
As a plot to lay her box.

But I got no sleep that night
In the Albany Y.M.C.A.;
Street noises and street light

Dunned my insomnia
Until she spoke to me,
Clear as the young day

Woke, loud as a fly:
"My unquiet friend, I am
Surcease, success, set free.
But you are left my tomb."

II

At home in Cummington
Whose rude hills mock the sea,
A skeleton of stone,

The antique cemetery
(Its washed-out monuments
Piled stubs no tides defray,

Their legends long since
Unread, discredited),
For all the hoard it stints

Cannot invest the dead;
Yet here, adjoining, where
Your whole estate and stead

Await apparent heir,
All places and memories
I move among for fair

As tortuous worm that tries
The abandoned body and
Worries its old disease

Or as witch-obsessed wand
Constrained relentlessly
To blind veins underground,

Which no shift can allay
Till the gorged heart will slake
And drain itself dry,

Drilled on a wooden spike
Fast to its furthest floor.
How shall I drive my stake?

You had lately told me: "Our
Evil must be lived out
That the soul ascend pure."

My eyes heavy in debt
Are drying, mistress, drying
With dust drifted about

The empty house and lying
Unminded and all save
Your death alone denying.
Water wells in the grave.

III

Knowledge that we withhold
Will, by act of will
Thrown over and untolled,

Never become nil,
But change, rise again,
And spell wordless evil.

Underwater, men
Cannot hear the sound
Of the sea so close, then

In their own blood are drowned
And silence washed ashore.
Thoreau on the beach found

Flesh to be bloodless where
Remnant rag and wound,
Pearl feet, matted hair,

Eyes estopped with sand,
Had been embalmed at sea
And laid out on the strand.

And had you gone to die
Against a margin you
Knew uses crossed, the high

Tide might have had you too.
Once walking on Cape Cod
Below the shrill sea-mew,

I heard and understood
The eternal surf-knell
Resounds the same as the blood

Controlled in a narrow canal,
Borne on the winding ear
From the whorl of a Unicorn shell;

And tolls on that swept shore,
Requited siren, sleep
Steady, senseless, sheer,

As from a solvent keep
The sea only returns
The sea, unsounded deep
For whom a cold child mourns.

Herbert Morris

SUNS

Born in New York City in 1928, Herbert Morris is a graduate of Brooklyn College, and also attended New York University. Drafted into the Army in 1950, he was released from service late in 1952. He has appeared in *The Beloit Poetry Journal, The Sewanee Review, Accent, Poetry,* and elsewhere.

I

These eddies tell, in years, their constancy
and force among the piles sunken in sand
where you were bathing then and had your hand
held to these planks to wait the coming sea
waves (open you were for all the foam and crash).
These eddies tell, in sand, what years, what light
filtering flickering faltering has been,
shifting your slight remaining traces in
the silt. I am a child seeing the height
of surf advancing, fearing that it will smash
terribly what you were here: if only the pier
would resist, as we, the shatter and the quaking shocks,
and the shells be calm, and all the great mossed rocks
not move where you stepped among them,
    and the suns not sear.

II

Supper by candles in the little room
full to the leaves and foliage past the screens
and with the sun (as all the light careens
to gold) to golden us and bronze, to loom
our fabric of the dusk-tint and the hiss
muffled and surfing down the swirling shore.

We were in sea nets and our food was air,
the light fixing itself about our hair
as something finding its known place to pour
and give itself deeply. And only this:

that we would move, as we moved then, into
the other rooms from where we were to know
what night was, and what dark, and softly go
(after the cards and coffee) into blue.

III

Only the trembling waters in the sun's
light was this room, a marble table top

cool and pink-veined, a porcelain basin white
with morning, lingering with the smell of light
and soap you used (not even years could stop
the odor and the cool, not even stuns
of day and darkness, salt and sea), and the
creaking floor-boards and the closet's musk
(no rounds of season, rain, sun, dusk
could weather, and no smashing of the sea).

Light will unfold like petals and the walls
will crumble with the ceiling's flickered bloom
as the day largens: it is Victor's room,
and waters seep, a sun starts, a gull calls.

IV

A Sunday, and the flowering linden trees
crowding the air with all their redolence,
the nuns, in white and grey (the clouds like tents
with purple tops), passing in twos to teas
on campus, dappled in sunlight. After he moved
from the train platform dark in the engine's smoke,
and singular, they sat in some glade grooved
with green and shadow, gold, tree-bark, and spoke
softly within the rings of wavering heat.
A Sunday, and he walked with Helen through
the gardens with their fountains and their neat
autumnal paths and arbors. Soon the blue
enclosing, deepening, paths deserted, and
dark of a railway station, darkness, land.

V

The seas ran and the nights extended far,
sweeping untouching hands and the great wells
of rooms we were and, entered out from, are.
France, Germany, names through an engine's bells
from a window on a darkened train,
the Belgian mud, and the great nights of rain
packing the sunken soil where you were steeped.

Victor, the seas still spill, and all these nights
have come up with a great smoke and suffused
the bogs and tracts of marshland and the heights
above the lowland forests with their bruised
and terrible tree remains. All deeply here
is ashen (but we hold), with nothing that can veer
the darkness of the suns where you are deeped.

Dylan Thomas

FOUR LOST SOULS

The first section of Dylan Thomas' novel-in-progress, ADVENTURES IN THE SKIN TRADE, so delighted readers of the second *New World Writing* that the next chapter is now presented here. Dylan Thomas, who lives in Carmarthenshire, Wales, with his wife and three children, is best known as a poet. THE COLLECTED POETRY OF DYLAN THOMAS, 1934-1953, was published here in the spring of 1953 by New Directions. Three other volumes have also appeared in the United States— SELECTED WRITINGS, IN COUNTRY SLEEP and THE PORTRAIT OF THE ARTIST AS A YOUNG DOG. His poetry readings have also attracted devoted attention. *Four Lost Souls* continues the London adventures of Samuel Bennet, who, when last seen, had fallen to sleep in Mrs. Dacey's bathtub, from which he then had been lifted by his new friends—Mr. Allingham and George Ring.

(Four Lost Souls: Copyright, 1953, by Dylan Thomas.)

He sank into the ragged green water for the second time and, rising naked with seaweed and a woman under each arm and a mouthful of broken shells, he saw the whole of his dead life standing trembling before him, indestructible and unsinkable, on the brandy-brown waves. It looked like a hallstand.

He opened his mouth to speak, but a warm wave rushed in.

"Tea," said Mrs. Dacey. "Tea with plenty of sugar every five minutes. That's what I always gave him and it didn't do a bit of good."

"Not too much worcester, George, don't bury the egg."

"I won't," Samuel said.

"Oh, listen to the birds. It's been such a short night for the birds, Polly."

"Listen to the birds," he said clearly, and a burning drink drowned his tongue.

"They've laid an egg," Mr. Allingham said.

"Try some Coca Cola, Donald. It can't do any harm, he's had tea and a prairie oyster and angostura and Oxo and everything."

"I used to pour the tea down by the pint," Mrs. Dacey said affectionately, "and up it came, lump sugar and all."

"He doesn't want a Coca Cola. Give him a drop of your hair oil. I knew a man who used to squeeze bootblacking through a veil."

"You know everybody piggish. He's trying to sit up, the poor darling."

Samuel wrestled into the dry world and looked around a room in it, at Mrs. Dacey, now miraculously divided into one long woman, folding her black silk arms in the doorway, at George Ring arching his smile and hair toward the rusty taps, at Mr. Allingham resigned above him.

"Polly's gone," he said.

It was then that he understood why the three persons in the bathroom were so tall and far. I am on the floor, looking up, he said to himself. But the others were listening.

"You're naked too," Mr. Allingham said, "under the blanket."

"Here's a nice wet sponge." George Ring dabbed and smoothed. "Keep it on your forehead. There, like that. That better?"

"Eau de cologne is for outside the body," said Mrs. Dacey without disapproval, "and I'll give our Polly such a clip. I'll clip her on the earhole every time she opens her mouth."

Mr. Allingham nodded. "Whisky I can understand," he said. "But eau de cologne! You put that on handkerchieves. You don't put whisky on handkerchieves." He looked down at Samuel. "I don't."

"No, mustn't suck the sponge, Sam."

"I suppose he thinks red biddy's like bread and milk," Mr. Allingham said.

They gathered his clothes from the side of the bath and hurriedly dressed him. And not until he was dressed and upright, shivering along the landing to the dark stairs, did he try to speak again. George Ring and Mr. Allingham held his arms and guided him toward the top of that winding grave. Mrs. Dacey, the one mourner, followed with a rustle of silk.

"It was the brandy from the medicine cupboard," he said, and down they went into the coarse, earthlike silence of the stairs.

"Give me furniture polish," Mr. Allingham said. "Crack.

Mind your head. Especially when I'm out of sorts in the bath."

The darkness was settling like more dirt and dust over the silent shop. Someone had hung up a sign, "Closed," on the inside of the window, not facing the street. "Meths is finicky," Mr. Allingham said.

They sat Samuel down on a chair behind the counter and he heard Mrs. Dacey, still on the stairs, calling for Polly up into the dark, dirty other floors and caves of the drunken house. But Polly did not answer.

She would be in her locked bedroom now, crying for Sam gone, at her window staring out onto the colorless, slowly disappearing street and the tall houses down at heel; or depicting, in the kitchen, the agony of a woman in childbirth, writhing and howling round the crowded sink; or being glad at a damp corner of the landing.

"Silly goose," said George Ring, sitting long-legged on the table and smiling at Samuel with a ferocious coyness. "You might have been drowned. Drowned," he said again, looking slyly up from under the spider line of his eyebrows.

"Lucky you left the door open," Mr. Allingham said. He lit a cigarette and looked at the match until it burned his finger. "I suppose," he said, his finger in his mouth.

"Our maid at home always said 'drowned,'" said George Ring.

"But I saw Polly lock the door. She put the key down her dress." Samuel spoke with difficulty from behind the uncertain counter. The words came out in a rush, then reversed and were lost, tumbling among the sour bushes under his tongue. "She put it down her dress," he said, and paused at the end of each word to untie the next. Now the shop was almost entirely dark.

"And chimbley. You know, for chimney. Well, my dear, the door was open when we went up. No key, no Polly."

"Just a boy in the bath," Mr. Allingham said. "Do you often get like that, Sam? The water was up to your chin."

"And the dirt!"

"It wasn't my dirt. Someone had been in the bath before. It was cold," Samuel said.

"Yes, yes." Samuel could see Mr. Allingham's head nodding. "That alters the situation, doesn't it? Dear God," he said, "you should have gone in with your clothes on like everybody else."

"Polly's gone," said Mrs. Dacey. She appeared out of nowhere in the wall and stood behind the counter at Samuel's side. Her rustling dress brushed against his hands, and he drew them sharply back. I touched a funeral, he said to the dazed boy in his chair. Her corpse-cold hand fell against his cheek, chilling him out of a moment's sleep. The coffin has walked upright into my sitting bed.

"Oooh," he said aloud.

"Still cold, baby?" Mrs. Dacey bent down, creaking like a door, and mothered him about the hair and mouth.

There had been little light all day, even at dawn and noon, mostly the close, false light of bedroom and restaurant. All day he had sat in small, dark places, bathroom and traveling lavatory, a jungle of furniture, a stuffed shop where no one called except these voices saying:

"You looked so defenseless, Sam, lying there all cold and white."

"Where was Moses when the light went out, Mrs. Dacey?"

"Like one of those cherubs in the Italian Primitives, only with a bottle on your finger, of course."

"In the dark. Like this."

"What did our Polly do to you, the little tart?" Mrs. Dacey said in her tidy, lady's voice.

Mr. Allingham stood up. "I'm not listening. Don't you say a word, Sam, even if you could. No explanations. There he was, gassed in the bath, at half past four in the afternoon. I can stand so much."

"I want to go out," Samuel said.

"Out the back?"

"Out."

Out of the blind, stripping hole in a wall, aviary and menagerie, cold water shop, into the streets without locks. I don't want to sleep with Polly in a drawer. I don't want to lie in a cellar with a wet woman, drinking polish. London is happening everywhere, let me out, let me go. Mrs. Dacey is all cold fingers.

"Out then. It's six o'clock. Can you walk, son?"

"I can walk okay, it's my head."

Mrs. Dacey, unseen, stroked his hair. Nobody can see, he said silently, but Mrs. Susan Dacey, licensed to sell tobacco, is stroking my hair with her lizards; and he gave a cry.

"I've got no sympathy," said Mr. Allingham. "Are you coming, Sue?"

"Depends where you're going."

"Taking the air down the Edgware Road. He's got to see around, hasn't he? You don't come up from the provinces to drink eau de cologne in the bath."

They all went out, and Mrs. Dacey locked the shop.

It was raining heavily.

2

"Fun!" George Ring said.

They walked out of Sewell Street into Praed Street arm-in-arm.

"I'm a fool for the rain." He shook his clinging curls and danced a few steps on the pavement.

"My new brown overcoat's in the bathroom," Samuel said, and Mrs. Dacey covered him with her umbrella.

"Go on, you're not the sort that puts a coat on in the rain, are you? Stop dancing, George."

But George Ring danced down the pavement in the flying rain and pulled the others with him; unwillingly they broke into a dancing run under the lampposts' drizzle of light, Mrs. Dacey, black as a deacon, jumping high over the puddles with a rustle and creak, Mr. Allingham, on the outside, stamping and dodging along the gutter, Samuel gliding light and dizzy with his feet hardly touching the ground.

"Look out. People," cried Mr. Allingham, and dragged them, still dancing, out onto the slippery street. Caught in a circle of headlights and chased by horns they stamped and scampered onto the pavement again, clinging fast to each other, their faces glistening, cold and wet.

"Where's the fire, George? Go easy, boy, go easy." But Mr. Allingham, one foot in the gutter, was hopping along like a rabbit and tugging at George Ring's arm to make him dance faster. "It's all Sam's fault," he said as he hopped, and his voice was high and loud like a boy's in the rain.

Look at London flying by me, buses and glowworms, umbrellas and lampposts, cigarettes and eyes under the watery doorways, I am dancing with three strangers down Edgware Road in the rain, cried Samuel to the gliding boy around him. Light and without will as a suit of feathers, he held onto their arms, and the umbrella rode above them like a bird.

Cold and unsmiling, Mrs. Dacey skipped by his side, seeing nothing through her misted glasses.

And George Ring sang as he bounced, with his drenched hair rising and falling in level waves, "Here we go gathering nuts and may, Donald and Mrs. Dacey and George and Sam."

When they stopped, outside the Antelope, Mr. Allingham leaned against the wall and coughed until he cried. All the time he coughed he never removed his cigarette.

"I haven't run for forty years," he said, his shoulders shaking, and his handkerchief like a flag to his mouth. He led them into the Saloon Bar where three young women sat with their shoes off in front of the electric log fire.

"Three whiskies. What's yours, Sam? Nice drop of Kiwi?"

"He'll have whisky, too," Mrs. Dacey said. "See, he's got his color back."

"Kiwi's bootpolish," one of the young women whispered, and she bent, giggling, over the grate. Her big toe came out of a hole in her stocking, suddenly, like a cold inquisitive nose, and she giggled again.

This was a bar in London. Dear Peggy, Samuel wrote with his finger on the counter, I am drinking in a bar called the Antelope in Edgware Road with a furniture dealer, the proprietoress of a tea-shop, three young women and George Ring. I have put these facts down clearly because the scent I drank in the bath is still troublesome and people will not keep still. I am quite well but I do not know for how long.

"What're you doing, Sam? Looks like you're drawing. I've got a proper graveyard in my chest, haven't I? Cough, cough," Mr. Allingham said, angrily between each cough.

"It wasn't the cough that carried him off," the young woman said. Her whole plump body was giggling.

Everything is very trivial, Samuel wrote. Mr. Allingham is drunk on one whisky. All his face goes pale except his mark.

"Here we are," Mr. Allingham said, "four lost souls. What a place to put a man in."

"The Antelope's charming," said George Ring. "There's some real hunting prints in the private bar." He smiled at Sam and moved his long, blunt fingers rapidly along the counter as though he were playing a piano. "I'm all rhythm. It's like a kind of current in me."

"I mean the world. This is only a little tiny bit in it. This is all right, it's got regular hours; you can draw the curtains, you know what to expect here. But look at the world. You and your currents," Mr. Allingham said.

"No, really it's rippling out of me." George Ring tap-danced with one foot and made a rhythmical, kissing noise with his tongue against the roof of his mouth.

"What a place to drop a man in. In the middle of streets and houses and traffic and people."

The young woman wagged her finger at her toe. "You be still." Her friends were giggling now, covering their faces and peeping out at Mr. Allingham between their fingers, telling each other to go on, saying "hotcha" and "hi de ho" and "Minnie the Moocher's Wedding Day" as George Ring tapped one narrow, yellow buckskin shoe and strummed on the counter. They rolled their eyes and said, "Swing it, sister," then hissed again into a giggle.

"I've been nibbling away for fifty years now," Mr. Allingham said, "and look at me. Look at me." He took off his hat.

"There's hair," whispered the young woman with the hole in her stocking.

His hair was the color of ferrets and thin on the crown; it stopped growing at the temples but came out again from the ears. His hat had made a deep, white wrinkle on his forehead.

"Here we are nibbling away all day and night, Mrs. Dacey. Nibble nibble." His brown teeth came over his lip. "No sense, no order, no nothing, we're all mad and nasty. Look at Sam there. There's a nice harmless boy, curly hair and big eyes and all. What's he do? Look at his bloody bottle."

"No language," said the woman behind the bar. She looked like a duchess, riding, rising and sinking slowly as she spoke, as though to the movements of a horse.

"Tantivy," Samuel said, and blushed as Mr. Allingham pointed a stained finger.

"That's right. Always the right word in the right place. Tantivy! I told you, people are all mad in the world. They don't know where they're going, they don't know why they're where they are, all they want is love and beer and sleep."

"I wouldn't say no to the first," said Mrs. Dacey. "Don't pay any attention to him," she said to the woman behind the counter, "he's a philosopher."

"Calling everybody nasty," said the woman, rising. "There's people live in glass houses." Over the hurdle she goes, thought Samuel idly, and she sank again onto the hidden saddle. She must do miles in a night, he said to his empty glass.

"People think about all kinds of other things." George Ring looked at the ceiling for a vision. "Music," he said, "and dancing." He ran his fingers along the air and danced on his toes.

"Sex," said Mr. Allingham.

"Sex, sex, sex, it's always sex with you, Donald. You must be repressed or something."

"Sex," whispered the young woman by the fire.

"Sex is all right," Mrs. Dacey said. "You leave sex alone."

"Of course I'm repressed. I've been repressed for fifty years."

"You leave sex out of it." The woman behind the counter rose in a gallop. "And religion," she said.

Over she goes, clean as a whistle, over the hedge and the waterjump.

Samuel took a pound out of his wallet and pointed to the whisky on the shelf. He could not trust himself yet to speak to the riding woman with the stuffed, enormous bosom and two long milk-white loaves for arms. His throat was still on fire; the heat of the room blazed up his nostrils into his head, and all the words at the tip of his tongue caught like petrol and gorse; he saw three young women flickering by the metal logs, and his three new friends thundered and gestured before him with the terrible exaggeration of people of flesh and blood moving like dramatic prisoners on a screen, doomed forever to enact their pettiness in a magnified exhibition.

He said to himself: Mrs. Antelope, pouring the whisky as though it were four insults, believes that sex is a bed. The act of love is an act of the bed itself; the springs cry "Tumble" and over she goes, horse and all. I can see her lying like a log on a bed, listening with hate and disgust to the masterly voice of the dented sheets.

He felt old and all-knowing and unsteady. His immediate wisdom weighed so heavily that he clutched at the edge of the counter and raised one arm, like a man trapped in the sea, to signal his sinking.

"You may," Mrs. Dacey said, and the room giggled like a girl.

Now I know, thought Samuel beneath his load, as he struggled to the surface, what is meant by a pillar of the church. Long, cold Mrs. Dacey could prop Bethesda on the remote top of her carved head and freeze with her eyes the beetle-black sinners where they scraped below her. Her joke boomed in the roof.

"You've dropped a fiver, Sam." Mr. Allingham picked up a piece of paper and held it out on the sun-stained palm of his hand.

"It's Lucille Harris's address," Samuel said.

"Why don't you give her a ring? The phone's on the stairs, up there." George Ring pointed. "Outside the Ladies."

Samuel parted a curtain and mounted.

"*Outside* the Ladies," a voice said from the sinking room.

He read the instructions above the telephone, put in two pennies, dialed, and said, "Miss Harris? I'm a friend of Austin's.

"I am a friend of nobody's. I am detached," he whispered into the buzzing receiver. "I am Lopo the outlaw, loping through the night, companion of owls and murderers. Tu wit tu woo," he said aloud into the mouthpiece.

She did not answer, and he shuffled down the stairs, swung open the curtain, and entered the bright bar with a loping stride.

The three young women had gone. He looked at the grate to see if their shoes were still there, but they had gone too. People leave nothing.

"She must have been out," he said.

"We heard," said Mr. Allingham. "We heard you talking to her owl." He raised his glass and stared at it, standing sadly and savagely in the middle of the room like a man with oblivion in his hand. Then he made his choice, and drank.

"We're going places," he said. "We're taking a taxi and Sam is going to pay for it. We're going to the West End to look for Lucille."

"I knew she was a kind of Holy Grail," George Ring said when they were all in the darkness of the taxi rattling through the rain.

Samuel felt Mrs. Dacey's hand on his knee.

"Four knights at arms, it's terribly exciting. We'll call at the Gayspot first, then the Cheerioh, then the Neptune."

"Four lost souls."

The hand ached on along the thigh, five dry fishes dying on a cloth.

"Marble Arch," Mr. Allingham said. "This is where the fairies come out in the moon."

And the hurrying crowd in the rain might have had no flesh or blood.

"Park Lane."

The crowd slid past the bonnet and the windows, mixed their faces with no features and their liquid bodies under a sudden blaze, or vanished into the streaming light of a tall door that led into the bowels of rich night London where all the women wore pearls and pricked their arms with needles.

A car backfired.

"Hear the champagne corks?"

Mr. Allingham is listening to my head, Samuel thought as he drew away from the fingers in the corner.

"Piccadilly. Come on Allingham's tour. That's the Ritz. Stop for a kipper, Sam?"

The Ritz is closed forever. All the waiters would be bellowing behind their hands. Gustave, Gustave, cried a man in an opera hat, he is using the wrong fork. He is wearing a tie with elastic at the back. And a woman in evening dress cut so low he could see her navel with a diamond in it leaned over his table and pulled his bow tie out and let it fly back again to his throat.

"The filthy rich," he said. My place is among the beggars and the outlaws. With power and violence Samuel Bennet destroys the whole artifice of society in his latest novel, *In the Bowels*.

"Piccadilly Circus. Center of the world. See the man picking his nose under the lamppost? That's the Prime Minister."

The Gayspot was like a coal cellar with a bar at one end, and several coalmen were dancing with their sacks. Samuel, at the door, swaying between Mrs. Dacey and George Ring, felt his thigh, still frightened. He did not dare look down at it in case even the outside of the trouserleg bore the inexcusable imprint of his terror in the taxi.

"It's cosmopolitan," George Ring whispered. "Look at the nigger."

Samuel rubbed the night out of his eyes and saw the black men dancing with their women, twirling them among the green cane chairs, between the fruit machine and the Russian billiard table. Some of the women were white, and smoked as they danced. They pussed and spied around the room, unaware of their dancing, feeling the arms around them as though around the bodies of different women: their eyes were for the strangers entering, they went through the hot movements of the dance like women in the act of love, looking over men's shoulders at their own remote and unconniving faces in a looking-glass. The men were all teeth and bottom, flashers and shakers, with little waists and wide shoulders, in doublebreasted pinstripe and sleek, licked shoes, all ageless and unwrinkled, waiting for the fleshpot, proud and silent and friendly and hungry—jerking round the smoking cellar under the center of the world to the music of a drum and a piano played by two pale white cross boys whose lips were always moving.

As George Ring weaved Samuel through the dancers to the bar they passed a machine and Samuel put in a penny for a lemon. Out came one and sixpence.

"Who's going to win the Derby, Sam?" said Mr. Allingham, behind them.

"Isn't he a lucky poet?" George Ring said.

Mrs. Dacey, in half a minute, had found a partner as tall as herself and was dancing through the smoke like a chapel. He had powdered his face to hide a scar from the corner of his eye to his chin.

"Mrs. Dacey's dancing with a razorman," Samuel said.

This was a breath and a scar of the London he had come to catch. Look at the knickerless women enamoring from the cane tables, waiting in the fumes for the country cousins to stagger in, all savings and haywisps, or the rosy-cheeked old men with buttonholes whose wives at home were as lively as bags of sprouts. And the dancing cannibal-mouthed black razor kings shaking their women's breasts and blood to the stutter of the drums, snakily tailored in the shabby sweat-smelling jungle under the wet pavement. And a crimped boy danced like a girl, and the two girls serving were as harsh as men.

Mr. Allingham bought four white wines. "Go on. He did it on a pintable. You could bring your Auntie here, couldn't you, Monica?" he said to the girl with the bow tie pouring their drinks.

"Not my Auntie," Samuel said. Auntie Morgan Pont-Neath-Vaughan in her elastic-sided boots. "She doesn't drink," he said.

"Show Monica your bottle. He's got a bottle on his finger."

Samuel dug his hand deep in his jacket pocket. "She doesn't want to see an old bottle." His chest began to tickle as he spoke, and he slipped two fingers of his right hand between the buttons of his shirt on to his bare flesh. "No vest," he said in surprise, but the girl had turned away.

"It's a Sunday School," Mr. Allingham said. "Tasted your wine yet, Sam? This horse's unfit to work. A regular little bun dance. You could bring the vicar's wife in here."

Mrs. Cotmore-Richards, four foot one and a squeak in her stockinged trotters.

"A regular little vestry," Mr. Allingham said. "See that woman dancing? The one who fell in the flour bin. She's a bank manager's niece."

The woman with the dead white face smiled as she passed them in the arms of a padded boy.

"Hullo, Ikey."

"Hullo, Lola. She's pretendin', see. Thinks she's Starr Faithfull."

"Is she a prostitute, Mr. Allingham?"

"She's a manicurist, Sammy. How's your cuticles? Don't you believe everything you see, especially after it's dark. This is all pretending. Look at Casanova there with the old girls. The last time he touched a woman he had a dummy in his mouth."

Samuel turned around. George Ring whinnied in a corner with several women. Their voices shrilled and rasped through the cross noise of the drums.

"Lucy got a beating the last time I see her," said a woman with false teeth and a bald fur. "He said he was a chemist."

"Lucille," George Ring said, impatiently shaking his curls. "Lucille Harris."

"With a clothesbrush. He had it in a little bag."

"There's a chemist," said a woman wearing a picture hat.

"He doesn't mean Lucy Wakefield," another woman said.

"Lucy Wakefield's in the Feathers with a man from Crouch End," said the bank manager's niece, dancing past. The boy who danced with her was smiling with his eyes closed.

"Perhaps he got a leather belt in his little bag," said the woman with the fur.

"It's all the same in a hundred years," said the woman in the picture hat. She went down to her white wine, widening her legs like an old mule at a pool, and came up gasping. "They put hair oil in it."

This was all wrong. They spoke like the women who wore men's caps and carried fishfrails full of empties in the Jug and Bottle of the Compasses at home.

"Keeps away the dandruff."

He did not expect that the nightclub women under the pavement should sing and twang like sirens or lure off his buttons with their dangerous, fringed violet eyes. London is not under the bedclothes where all the company is grand and vile by a flick of the cinema eye, and the warm linen doors are always open. But these women with the shabby faces and the comedians' tongues, squatting and squabbling over their mother's ruin, might have lurched in from Llanelly on a football night, on the arms of short men with leeks. The women at the tables, whom he had seen as enamoring shapes when he first came in dazed from the night, were dull as sisters, red-eyed and thick in the head with colds; they would sneeze when you kissed them or hiccup and say Manners in the dark traps of the hotel bedrooms.

"Good as gold," he said to Mr. Allingham. "I thought you said this was a low place, like a speakeasy."

"Speak easy yourself. They don't like being called low down here." Mr. Allingham leant close, speaking from the side of his mouth. "They're too low for that. It's a regular little hellhole," he whispered. "It's just warming up. They take their clothes off soon and do the hula hula; you'll like that."

"Nobody knows Lucille," George Ring said. "Are you sure she isn't Lucy? There's a lovely Lucy."

"No, Lucille."

" 'She dwells beside the springs of Dove.' I think I like Wordsworth better than Walter de la Mare sometimes. Do you know 'Tintern Abbey'?"

Mrs. Dacey appeared at Samuel's shoulder. "Doesn't baby dance?" He shuddered at the cold touch of her hand on his neck. Not here. Not now. That terrible impersonal Bethesda rape of the fingers. He remembered that she had carried her umbrella even while she danced.

"I got a sister in Tintern," said a man behind them.

"Tintern Abbey." George Ring pouted and did not turn round.

"Not in the Abbey, she's a waitress."

"We were talking about a poem."

"She's not a bloody nun," the man said.

The music stopped, but the two boys on the little platform still moved their hands and lips, beating out the dance in silence.

Mr. Allingham raised his fist. "Say that again and I'll knock you down."

"I'll blow you down," the man said. He puffed up his cheeks, and blew. His breath smelt of cloves.

"Now, now." Mrs. Dacey leveled her umbrella.

"People shouldn't go around insulting nuns then," Mr. Allingham said as the ferrule tapped his waistcoat.

"I'll blow you down," the man said. "I never insulted any nun. I've never spoken to a nun."

"Now, now." The umbrella drove for his eyes, and he ducked.

"You blow again," said Mrs. Dacey politely, "I'll push it up your snout and open it."

"Don't you loathe violence," George Ring said. "I've always been a terrible pacifist. One drop of blood and I feel slimy all over. Shall we dance?"

He put his arm round Samuel's waist and danced him away from the bar. The band began again though none of the couples had stopped dancing.

"But we're two men," Samuel said. "Is this a waltz?"

"They never play waltzes here, it's just self-expression. Look, there's two other men dancing."

"I thought they were girls."

"My friend thought you were a couple of girls," George Ring said in a loud voice as they danced past them. Samuel looked at the floor, trying to follow the movements of George Ring's feet. One, two, three, turn around, tap.

One of the young men squealed, "Come up and see my Aga Cooker."

One, two, three, swirl and tap.

"What sort of a girl is Polly Dacey, really? Is she mad?"

I'm like thistledown, thought Samuel. Swirl about and swirl again, on the toes now, shake those hips.

"Not so heavy, Sam. You're like a little Jumbo. When she went to school she used to post mice in the pillarbox and they ate up all the letters. And she used to do things to boys in the scullery. I can't tell you. You could hear them screaming all over the house."

But Samuel was not listening any more. He circled and stumbled to a rhythm of his own among the flying legs, dipped and retreated, hopped on one leg and spun, his hair falling over his eyes and his bottle swinging. He clung to George

Ring's shoulder and zig-zagged away from him, then bounced up close again.

"Don't swing the bottle. Don't swing it. Look out. Sam. Sam."

Samuel's arm flew back and a small woman went down. She grabbed at his legs and he brought George Ring with him. Another man fell, catching fast to his partner's skirt. A long rip and she tumbled among them, her legs in the air, her head in a heave of bellies and arms.

Samuel lay still. His mouth pressed on the curls at the nape of the neck of the woman who had fallen first. He put out his tongue.

"Get off my head, you've got keys in your pocket."

"Oh, my leg!"

"That's right. Easy does it. Upsadaisy."

"Someone's licking me," cried the woman at the bottom.

Then the two girls from behind the bar were standing over them, slapping and kicking, pulling them up by the hair.

"It was that one's fault. He crowned her with a bottle. I saw him," said the bank manager's niece.

"Where'd he get the bottle from, Lola?"

The girl with the bow tie dragged Samuel up by the collar and pointed to his left hand. He tried to slip it in his pocket but a hand like a black boxing glove closed over the bottle. A large black face bent down and stared into his. He saw only the whites of the eyes and the teeth.

I don't want a cut on my face. Don't cut my lips open. They only use razors in stories. Don't let him have read any stories.

"Now, now," said Mrs. Dacey's voice. The black face jerked back as she thrust out her opened umbrella, and Samuel's hand was free.

"Throw him out, Monica."

"He was dancing like a monkey, throw him out."

"If you throw him out you can throw me out too," Mr. Allingham said from the bar. He raised his fists.

Two men walked over to him.

"Mind my glasses." He did not wear any.

They opened the door and threw him up the steps.

"Bloody nun," a voice shouted.

"Now you."

"And the old girl. Look out for her brolly, Dodie."

Samuel fell on the area step below Mr. Allingham, and Mrs. Dacey came flying after with her umbrella held high.

It was still raining heavily.

4

"Just a passing call," said Mr. Allingham. As though he were sitting indoors at a window, he put out his hand to feel the rain. Shoes slopped past on the pavement above his head. Wet trousers and stockings almost touched the brim of his hat. "Just in and out," he said. "Where's George?"

I've been bounced, Samuel thought.

"It reminds me of my old man." Mrs. Dacey's face was hidden under the umbrella, as though in a private, accompanying thunder cloud. "In and out, in and out. Just one look at him, and out he went like clockwork."

Oh, the Gayspot? Can't go there, old man. Samuel winked seriously in the dark. Oh, carrying a cargo. Swinging a bottle around. One look at me, out I went.

"He used to carry a little book with all the places he couldn't go to and he went to them every Saturday."

Fool, fool, fool, Samuel said to himself.

The steps were suddenly lit up as the door opened for George Ring. He came out carefully and tidily, to a rush of music and voices that faded at once with the vanishing of the smoky light, and stood on Mrs. Dacey's step, his mane of curls golden against the fanlight, a god or a half-horse emerging from the underworld into the common rain.

"They're awfully cross," he said. "Mrs. Cavanagh ripped her skirt and she didn't have anything on underneath. My dear, it's like Ancient Rome down there and now she's wearing a man's trousers and he's got legs exactly like a spider's. All black and hairy. Why are you sitting in the rain?"

"It's safe," Mr. Allingham said. "It's nice and safe in the rain. It's nice and rational sitting on the steps in the rain. You can't knock a woman down with a bottle here. See the stars? That's Arcturus. That's the Great Bear. That's Sirius, see, the green one. I won't show you where Venus is. There's some people can't enjoy themselves unless they're knocking women down and licking them on the floor. They think the evening's wasted unless they've done that. I wish I was home. I wish I was lying in bed by the ceiling. I wish I was lying under the chairs like Rosie."

"Who started to fight, anyway? Let's go round the corner to the Cheerioh."

"That was ethical."

They climbed up the street, George Ring first, then Mr. Allingham, then Samuel and Mrs. Dacey. She tucked his arm in hers.

"Don't you worry. You hold onto me. Cold? You're shivering."

"It'll be Cheerioh all right."

The Cheerioh was a bad blaze, an old hole of lights. In the dark, open a cupboard full of cast-off clothes moving in a wind from nowhere, the smell of mothballs and damp furs, and find a lamp lit, candles burning, a gramophone playing.

"No dancing for you," Mr. Allingham said. "You need space. You want the Crystal Palace."

Mrs. Dacey still held Samuel by the arm. "You're safe with me. I've taken a fancy," she said. "Once I take a fancy I never let go."

"And never trust a woman who can't get up." Mr. Allingham pointed to a woman sitting in a chair by the Speedboat pintable. "She's trying to get up all the time." The woman made a sudden movement of her shoulders. "No, no, legs first."

"This used to be the cowshed," George Ring said, "and there was real straw on the floor."

Mrs. Dacey never lets go. Samuel saw the fancy shining behind her glasses, and in her hard mousetrap mouth. Her cold hand hooked him. If he struggled and ran she would catch him in a corner and open her umbrella inside his nose.

"And real cows," Mr. Allingham said.

The men and women drinking and dancing looked like the older brothers and sisters of the drinkers and dancers in the club round the corner, but no one was black. There were deep green faces, dipped in a sea dye, with painted cockles for mouths and lichenous hair, sealed on the cheeks; red and purple, slategray, tide-marked, ratbrown and stickily whitewashed, with violet-inked eyes or lips the color of Stilton; pink chopped, pink lidded, pink as the belly of a newborn monkey, nicotine yellow with mustard flecked eyes, rust scraping through the bleach, black hairs axlegreased down among the peroxide; squashed fly stubbles, saltcellared necks thick with pepper powder; carrotheads, yolkheads, blackheads, heads bald as sweetbreads.

"All white people here," Samuel said.

"The salt of the earth," Mr. Allingham said. "The foul salt of the earth. Drunk as a pig. Ever seen a pig drunk? Ever seen a monkey dancing like a man? Look at that king of the animals. See him? The one who's eaten his lips. That one smiling. That one having his honeymoon on her feet."

John Lee Weldon

SERMON

Born in Birmingham, Alabama, John Lee Weldon now lives in New York City. He studied at City College in New York and has worked as an employment clerk, an actor, and as a typist for *The New York Times*. *Sermon* is from Mr. Weldon's first novel, THE NAKED HEART, which Farrar, Straus & Young are publishing in the spring of 1953.

(Sermon: Copyright, 1953, by John Lee Weldon.)

Everybody please git settled now, be quiet, listen, listen to me: my heart aches, bleeds, cause O, sinners, I tell you this now once and for all if you don't accept Him, accept Christ Jesus your Lord and Saviour, if you don't accept Him, take Him in your hearts, take Him, let Him come in, let Him, He will if you jist let Him, give Him a chance, sinners, I tell you if you don't you're goin down down down into that bottomless pit, pit of fire; and O how my heart weeps for you, it's wringin wet with tears and you'll be boilin in your own tears—think of it, lost souls, think of it, boilin in your own tears; and O, yeah, yeah, I know, I know, yeah, you think you git hot out there in your fields whilst plowin, specially round noontime when the sun's its hottest, but, sinners, listen, let me tell you, I am tellin you, you don't need to be told, you should already know, you should, but I'm tellin you anyway—that sweaty heat of the fields aint nothin, it's pleasant, you'll be wishin you had it back, it'd be refreshin compared with that awful awful awful, I tell you, sinners, AWFUL fire of hell, seven times, not once, not twice, not three times, NO! God, no, not four, five, six, but! listen, I'm tellin you, SEVEN! times hotter than natural fire, your next home, sinners, that's where you're gonna spend eternity, not jist a short little visit, not jist a week-end trip, sinners, but O, merciful God! eternity eternity eternity; and do you know, sinners, do you know how long eternity is, do you, I ask you, do you know how long eternity is—well, I'll tell you, and God's listenin at me —He knows I'm tellin you the truth, He hears every word I say, yeah, shore He does, and He even knows what I'm gonna say fore I say it myself and O praise His name, praise the name of Jehovah God, He knows what I'm gonna say fore I even know what I'm gonna say—I tell you this, sinners, better listen to what I say, better take heed, jist listen to this: eternity aint got no end, that's how long it is—it jist goes on and on and on and O Lord God! there aint no stopping it and O I tell you, sinners, I pity you, I pity you, I weep for you, my tears sometimes feels like they're made of blood, that's how much I pity you, that's how my heart goes out to you, you what aint got the love of the Lord in your hearts and souls—O! you wicked, wicked sinners, you evil doers of iniquity, you folks what has laid in sin, gived up your precious temple to the lust of the flesh, the evil lust of the flesh, the heat of the flesh, the passion, well, it's gonna git cooked in hell, roasted like a wienie on a hickory stick over a camp fire and you'll curl up and your flesh will bulge out and pop open in places jist like a wienie does when you keep it over the fire for too long and you'll be thinkin down there that you've been over the fire too long but the devil aint gonna pull you outta the fire, no sir, no sir, sinners, he's gonna poke you in jist a little more and you'll burn to a crisp and keep burning and he—the devil, I'm talkin bout, your next landlord, the next un you'll be sharecroppin for without gittin your share of the goods—the devil will run git a bucket of water to throw on you and you see em comin with it and you open your scorchin lips to git a little drop of it and you think with your heart poundin like a Lord-knows-what that you're gonna git a little relief, but do you? NO! pore sinner, no, no, that water aint well-water, it aint spring-water, it's FIRE-WATER, that's what it is, yeah, I tell you Satan got that bucket of water from the LAKE OF FIRE and throwed it on you, yeah, and you jist keep on a-groanin and a-yellin and a-screamin, but listen here, listen, don't nobody hear you, not a soul—you know why —I'll tell you why: the devil's laughin so loud atcha can't nobody hear you, not even the blessed Lord God in heaven can hear you, No sir, no! not even God hisself, cause you know why—cause you turned your back on Him in this world, He turns His back on you in that other world, and you know jist as well as I do that that's only right, cause iffen you don't listen to Him, why, I'm askin you, why should He listen to you—an eye for an eye and a tooth for a tooth, right—shore, I'm right, and you know it, you know you'll be gitten jist what you deserve: the boilin pot, the lake of fire, your future home, and there aint gonna be, let me tell you this, evil-doers, there aint gonna be no sweet sign crocheted by your sweet ole Maw or painted in school by your little sister on a piece of cardboard, readin "Home Sweet Home," cause it aint gonna feel so sweet down there, no sir, and you aint gonna hear nobody a-tall singin that mighty good song "Keep the Home Fires Burnin," cause that's a different kind of fire down there, that's a fire you'll be wishin year in and year out that'd go out, but your wickedness will be jist like pine logs throwed on a open fire, you and you and you, sinners, and other sinners all over the world now and since time begun will be down there feedin that fire with your own wickedness, yes sir, yes sir, you'll be jist like knotted pine logs in a fire yourself but you won't burn up and away into ashes and you won't melt away, you'll feel like you will, but you won't—you'll jist keep on and on burnin, burnin on and on all through eternity, and O how you git tired of it! how you'll git tired of it! O yeah, yeah, you adulterers and adulteresses, you what's throwed yourself into that infamous act of fornication, into the lewdness of the flesh, you scarlet women—and let me tell you this: there's scarlet men amongst you, yes sir, there is and I don't know why folks when they talk bout scarlet women forgits to talk bout the scarlet men, cause the world's full of em, and hell's gonna be packed with both scarlet men and scarlet women, and I'll tell you this: you'll be seein so many naked bodies in hell—your clothes is gonna burn slap off jist as soon as the gates of hell open up for you and you'll be naked as a jay-bird, naked as the day you was born, and you'll be regrettin the day your ole sweet Maw brought you into such a world where you thought by the time you was twelve or fourteen you could strip-off and jump in sin with jist anybody who was willin to strip-off and jump in sin with you—O, yeah, yeah, there'll be so many pantin, writhin naked bodies in hell you'll git sick and tired of the sight of flesh and you'll wish you could close your eyes to it all, to all the naked pain, and see nothin a-tall but if you don't close your eyes to sin in this world, you won't be able to close em in the next world, cause you'll git your eyelids burned off and you can't close your eyes iffen you aint got no eyelids, O, yeah, yeah, you'll try to roll your eyeballs into the back of your head but the devil aint gonna let you do that, he aint gonna be easy on you—your eyeballs'll be stuck wide open with jellied flesh, seein it all, seein all the others sufferin like yourself and maybe you'll see one naked body touch another naked body, maybe jist by accident or maybe jist to try to comfort an ole friend, but you won't see no naked bodies lovin-up to each other down there, cause when flesh touches flesh there'll be a powerful explosion that'll throw you a hundred thousand mile—yeah, I said a hundred thousand mile, cause hell is a big place—it's gotta be to take care of all you sinners—yeah, it'll smoke up and explode and throw you all that way away from that body you touched, and you'll regret the evil ways of your earthly flesh that helped make hell your home; and you'll weep and the flesh of your cheeks will break out in great whelps and blisters where the hot tears roll down, yeah, yeah, yeah, you'll weep, you'll moan, you'll sob, and you'll try to pray, but you'll find out you don't know how to pray—iffen you don't learn to pray in this world, how you gonna expect to learn to pray in hell, how, huh, how, sinner, HOW! well, now then, there aint gonna be nobody down there to help you pray and you jist won't never learn how down there, but here, here you can, cause this here world of ours is jist a schoolin ground where we learn how to either go to heaven or go to hell, and, brothers and sisters, you all know we got plenties of folks to help learn us how to git to hell, but, listen, listen close to me, yeah, praise the blessed Lamb of God, we got a few down here on this ole wicked earth what can learn us and show us how to git to heaven, how to git up there with all the saints in gloryland, yeah, yeah, there's a few who don't wanta go up there all by theirself—they want you and you and everybody to repent and go long up there with em, and, listen, sinner, listen, I'm proud, I'm pleased, I'm honored to tell you that I'm one what's been chose by the King of Kings, the Lord Highest, to lead you the way, to say follow me, little children, follow me, and that's what I'm a-sayin, that's what I been a-tellin you all this while, not to follow the ways of the world, not to follow the ways of the devil down into hellfire and brimstone, but follow this servant of the Lord Jesus up those silver steps to the golden gates of heaven, leave your evil ways behind you, stop thinkin below your belt and start doin a little thinkin above your belt, and listen, boys and girls, and you older folks, too, listen, you know why that lewd part of your body is below your belt, you know why it's where it is, do you, well, listen, I'll tell you: it's where it is cause it's pointin down toward HELL! it's facin HELL! yeah, I know, I know you menfolks sometimes thinks it's a-pointin toward heaven, you sometimes feel like you're in heaven, but you aint, it aint even then pointin toward heaven, cause when you turn over it's pointin toward hell agin, and I tell you you better watch how you turn over, cause one of these days or one of these evil nights you liable to turn over and roll right straight down into hell and find yourself hotter'n you ever thought you'd be, you pore wicked, wicked, misled soul, pore lost sinner, pore misdirected flesh, I beg you, I plead with you, I cry out in agony to you to give up that way of yours, cause you're diggin your way down to hell jist as fast as a bolt of lightnin digs its way cross the clouds of the sky and once the devil sticks his fork into you you're gonna feel like it's a bolt of lightnin struck you and you're gonna be rememberin what I said to you up here on this earth on this blessed night of our Lord Jesus Saviour, and you're gonna wish you had of took heed, and, if you don't take heed now, the devil's gonna take you, YOU, you pore lost sinner, when your time comes; and, yeah, I know, shore, shore, I know you got your belly full and you feel healthy as a young pig, but pigs have to go to the slaughter and meet their end and you've gotta meet your end some day, some way, and it's gonna be too late to repent then, yeah, too late to meet Jesus but jist on time to meet the devil—the devil aint gonna run off and leave you, the devil aint gonna keep you waitin, no sir, he'll be right there at the gates of hell waitin to grab you, but, when he grabs you, you young maidens what's lost your maidenheads, he ain't gonna love you up, he aint gonna stroke your pretty hair like some young rascal might of done here on this wicked land, no, he aint gonna tell you how pretty you are, no sir, but what's he gonna do—I'll tell you: he's gonna take you by your pretty curls and sling you into the boilin lake of fire and you'll have a slab of brimstone for your lover, and that young swine, whoever he was what took that precious, short-lived jewel from you, he aint gonna rescue you in your distress, cause he's gonna be in enough distress of his own and he jist aint gonna find time to slip way from it like he slipped way from his Paw's farm to help you out none—no, cause he's gonna be a-wallowin and a-squirmin in that same lake of fire and his evil tongue what said to you what you thought was pretty love-words is gonna be changed into a serpent and that tree of life of his what he should of used for nothin but bringin babies into this world is gonna be changed into another serpent, and, iffen you happen to git a glance of him down there, you ain't gonna wanta be loved with it none, and I don't blame you a-tall, but that's the way hell is.

THE INDIAN INTELLIGENTSIA AND THE WESTERN WORLD

Hamdi Bey

A member of the editorial staff of *The Times of India,* in Calcutta, Hamdi Bey was born at Chapra, Bihar, India. He writes that he "went through a university curriculum, at Patna, which made him feel more at home in the English language (and yet not fully at home) than in Hindi, his mother tongue. That was rather unfortunate, for till India became independent in 1947, writing in English by Indians was suspect. To Englishmen it seemed to bristle with 'babuisms.' To fellow Indians any literary effort in a foreign language seemed unpatriotic and a social waste."

Mr. Bey's short stories have appeared in most Indian journals in English. The present article is his first publication outside his own country.

If tradition and interested support are necessary to the health of an intelligentsia, then conditions in India today are at once famishing and challenging. Both India and the Western world face an uncertain future, largely ideological.

In India tradition is not always apparent because of the two violent breaks in the country's cultural history. The glorious epoch of classical Sanskrit literature had already ended when the Moslems came to rule over India and imposed Persian as the language of the elite. During that period and the succeeding era when Urdu evolved as the primary Indo-Moslem language, the intelligentsia could not reasonably look back to the works of Kalidasa as models, because the sentiment of Urdu literature was largely in conflict with that of Sanskrit. Urdu was closer to Persian, but the hedonism of the walled garden in the desert was not true to the life in bountiful India with its months of rain, its luxuriant verdure and deep forests. The Urdu intelligentsia—which contained many Hindus, too—continued to live in the spiritual refuge of a walled garden of its own making and the walls were opaque not only to the life outside the wall, but to the earlier literary tradition. Those who wrote in Hindi or *Brajabhasa,* as it was then called, were more attuned to tradition and to life and had contacts with both. But the Moslem courts were lukewarm in their patronage of such writers—several of whom were Moslems—because there was a latent rebelliousness in the Hindi literature of those days, and it lived on its own consuming passions, in a romantic world, without achieving classic grandeur. Medieval or postmedieval Hindi, therefore, has little to offer as tradition.

The second unconformity cut deeper through the crust of Indian cultural continuity. During British rule the number of people knowing English was much larger than that of those knowing Persian during the period of the Moslems. When the English language became current in India, about 1818, Persian as a literary medium declined sharply throughout the continent extending from Dacca in the extreme east of India to Teheran in the extreme west of Persia, and finally died out.

More important, the English literature with which Indians became acquainted in the nineteenth century was living and contemporaneous, a product of the European rationalism of that century, and was, therefore, much advanced in its social, ethical and ideological content over both the ancient Sanskrit and the medieval Persian. Between the last two the gap was small; the classical period of Sanskrit had coincided with incipient feudalism, while that of Persian had as its background the relatively mature feudalism—which did not reach a climax in Asia as in Europe, despite a longer period of growth—to which Islam had succumbed. The strongest note of the Persian literature which came to India was monotheism, which the Indian intelligentsia adopted.

But the strongest notes of English literature were disturbingly powerful. The Indian intelligentsia had the experience of living in feudal conditions but escaping from them in the writings of Milton and, later, those of Shelley. By 1850 English had become the language of the country and was the medium of instruction in over 300 secondary schools, one in each district of roughly 4,000 square miles. New ethical, political and social ideas were absorbed and India experienced something approaching a renaissance. During the latter half of the nineteenth century the Indian elite came to treat English as its own language and there was considerable literary production. But the study of English also led to the desire for representative government. When the English suppressed that desire, an essentially democratic attitude was perverted into a narrow nationalism and eventually a certain coldness toward the English language. This led to revivalism, which had an objective basis in the desire to recover neglected values from the cultural debris of a civilization extending back five thousand years.

In the nineteenth century educated Indians believed in the superiority of the Western way of life. Two wars and the decline of Europe have shaken that belief. The severest critics of the West, however, do not sincerely believe that the glory of the Indian life of early times can be revived. Therefore, during the last 30 years a considerable minority of educated Indians has come to look upon Russia as affording an alternative to the West. Many such people are also convinced that Communism represents an advance over the Western democratic civilization.

The Indian educated class is led by its creative section—the writers and scientists—and it in turn leads the rest of the population. According to some observers, Indians educated in the English language today constitute the "ruling class," but are in the process of handing over their power and influence to uneducated workers and peasants. The uneducated classes are prone to follow either the extreme Right, represented by revivalist Hindu orthodoxy, or the extreme Left. The present Congress regime, the remnants of a liberal movement which came into being as the result of English education, is the Center. Like most middle-of-the-road parties it suffers from instability and is liable to being coerced into making concessions to the extremes of Left and Right alternately.

The political problems of India are co-extensive with the problems of the country's intelligentsia. The Congress Party and the democratic, liberal, educated people have a very emaciated tradition to support them, if by tradition is meant only what is local. Actually, they have the whole body of thought from Plato down to the present as their tradition if they would only claim it. But that amounts to merging themselves with a universal tradition, a development not wholly reconcilable with nationalism. The 62 years of struggle against British rule have bred pathological conditions and the Indian Congressman is in the habit of denying the liberal Western tradition, not realizing that in so doing he is singing the swan song of his own party.

The creative intellectual is also continually engaged in the effort to deny his universal tradition, as represented by post-Renaissance European thought, art and literature. Tagore, strictly Western in his thought, sought a tradition to justify his work in Kabir, a poet-saint of Moslem times in whom India came closest to contemporary European thought. Iqbal denied his debt to Europe and looked to Jami (Persian) and Bharthrehari (Sanskrit) as sources of inspiration—an influence which his really good poetry never sustained. In painting and sculpture there were overt revivals, but they did not last and modern Indian art is largely universal in its spirit.

In science there could not reasonably be any revivalism, and the Indian scientist never suffered the schizophrenia of the writer or the artist. Indian achievements in science have, therefore, been more substantial, but the future of the scientist in

India is threatened by changes in educational policy and the status of the English language.

In the interests of informing the vast populace and making democracy effective, the medium of instruction and the language of administrative communication have to be the language spoken in a locality. India has approximately ten regional languages. In over six states Hindi is the spoken language, is understood in all towns, and has become therefore, inevitably, the interstate language of democratic India. Such a development can only be at the expense of English. An initial decline in educational standards (which may well last 30 years or more) is sure to occur; the study of science will suffer especially and the vigor of democratic thought will languish. The elite which has built up modern India is sacrificing itself in the interests of the multitude, whose potential for good is yet unknown, but about whose capacity for evil there is much valid foreboding, for this multitude has inclinations toward either revivalism or Communism.

We are viewing the end of an epoch—that of nearly a century of general education in English. If the transition had come earlier the situation would not have been fraught with so much danger. Today, however, India is in danger of withdrawing itself from the universalism of the English-speaking world—of which it was virtually a member until now—with disasters threatening the position of her elite, the way of her thought, and the future of democracy in her territories and elsewhere.

In the coming years the small popular support that exists in India will go only to those writing in the Indian languages and writing down to the level of the newly literate readers in those languages. In a society where the writer or the artist finds it difficult to live, even the smallest support or patronage assumes importance. In the last four years, Communist patronage of the arts has become a strong factor. Indian fiction is being translated and published in East European languages. Indian music put down in staff notation is being sent to Moscow and other Communist capitals. The Communist Party of India which arranges for such patronage to the artists is, thereby, able to win their allegiance.

This state of affairs is a result not only of poor support of the arts within the country, but also of the absence of local tradition. The artistic tradition in India, having suffered the shock of two conquests, is very thin, and because of its poverty the national standards of evaluation are poor, too. Foreign opinion counts for much; even Tagore gained acceptance in India only after he had won the Nobel prize.

The desire for foreign recognition is more than an admission of low standards at home; on the positive side it is an index of an objective stirring toward universalism, a desire to rise from the status of a provincial culture to fuller participation in a world culture. Few Indian thinkers can avoid noticing the fact that Indian writing, painting and sculpture in the eleventh century approximated the European standards of that time. Since then the gap has widened.

And they cannot forget that, although India was in contact with universal trends during Moslem and British rule, it still retained a provincial culture. The Moslems who transmitted the torch of Greek and ancient Sanskrit learning to Europe failed to illumine India with it. Avicenna, one of the leaders of Moslem learning, and a contributor to the development of Renaissance thought, though born close to the Indo-Persian border, traveled West instead of East.

Indian isolation might well have been lessened if the works of Toru Dutt and others writing in English in the last century had been better received by snobbish Victorians who seemed to detect the color of the skin of the authors in their writings. Even in the field of science, which was less afflicted by prejudice, J. C. Bose had to overcome handicaps which were largely racial. Events would have taken a different turn had Britain given representative government to India in the early part of this century.

The past can only be rectified in the future. The problem today is whether India will be helped to share the universal democratic Western culture, allowed to lapse into provincialism, or snubbed into seeking international contacts elsewhere. Of course, what happens depends too on the quality of the work of Indian writers, artists and scientists. It is, however, also true that Indians can be encouraged by the assurance that the days of Western exclusiveness are over and that their work will not be wrongly evaluated either through a patronizing attitude or through a refusal to see its merits. The assurance amounts to tentatively conceding to India a full place in the postwar universal culture and not making a special category of her present civilization—the living India.

Gene Baro

BEREAVEMENT

Curator of the Collection of Creative Writings at the University of Florida in Gainesville, Gene Baro has published verse, stories and criticism in a variety of periodicals. Born in New York, Mr. Baro was educated in Florida. He dedicates his story to William G. Carleton.

He liked to sit this way: the pen poised lightly in his right hand, his chin supported in the palm of his left, all of him leaning slightly forward in his chair, his weight balanced against the long rosewood desk. Before him was the neat pile of chaste white paper, which, toward the end of the afternoon, he would begin to cover with his fine, meticulous writing. He liked to sit this way, an hour past his frugal lunch—a coddled egg perhaps, a bit of toast, sometimes in the summer a bowl of cold soup, some fresh greens from the garden—with the words forming and re-forming themselves, with his thoughts opening themselves to him—as he said—like flowers, leaf and petal, petal by petal opening. It was his custom now never to hurry, instead to give himself up entirely to the flowering of his own mind—a hothouse, he had called it in an essay, bearing in any season, cultivated, and yet without any forced blooms. If his flowers were larger than nature's, even more perfect and beautiful, it was because he did not challenge the natural order, or presume to generalize it, but sought only its laws that pertained to his own, his individual order of being, his timeless fertility, as it were.

The essay, published a number of years ago in a small but distinguished literary quarterly, reprinted first in England, later in Italy, had been possibly somewhat obscure. Nevertheless, it had been one of those pieces that had served to initiate and justify Canning's fame, for it had provided in those hectic days of international disorder and social emphasis an affirmation of personality, of those qualities of individuality that were being trampled in the charge of events. And, shortly, it became apparent to many cultured readers that Canning blended temperament with a classical intelligence, that he had, so to speak, the best of two worlds, that his aloofness, his icy clarity and crystalline insight—though some said his coldness—were passionately in the service of the best human traditions, those we were fighting to save. It was certainly to the credit of many of our distinguished editors and critics—indeed of all of our literate population, if not of our society itself—that a writer like Canning, whose subjectivity was so objective, could have come to prominence during the terrible time that he did.

Canning cared little for fame, except to take a mental pleasure in it. One might say, as he pointed out, that fame centered his existence more completely in the creative, but would this not have been the inevitable development of his writing at all, of his thought? His whole life became directed toward his realization in literature, and he was organized, mentally, emotionally, physically, and environmentally, to resist those vicissitudes of fame of which so many great writers have complained. Sitting at his desk of an afternoon, his eye would sometimes stray along the shelves that flanked the old stone fireplace, and he might smile to recognize his own volumes, in many fine and limited editions from the most tasteful presses, set out in the company of exalted names. In fact, he had already been called "a living classic," and his hours in his study were devoted to that somnolent and fervid abstraction that resulted in his writing at about five.

Everything else that Canning did was in preparation, in anticipation, of those two hours when his words were ready to be set down. His routine was inflexible, that is, he had found his proper means for creation, his natural order, was, in truth, like a flower, whose whole dreaming life is for that wide hour in the sun. Canning did this or that, as was needful to him; he did and waited, in a timeless suspension; and every afternoon, he worked. The distractions of fame, appointments, lectures, dinners, the grand confusions of city life, travel, were too time-bound, he said, for an art that drew its strength from the mystery of self and from an eternal sense of the self's fragility.

Time is his great subject, and those slim volumes, for which the public came to wait more impatiently than he, play a thousand exquisite variations upon that tortured theme. From those pages, Canning emerges like a sphinx, utterly solid and serene; and his riddles, delivered in the form of gracefully modulated aphorisms and mocking paradoxes, strike to the meaning of these frantic days. "Canning releases us into the eternal," a poet said at a public lecture, and though he said it with some bitterness, the audience felt it was true.

That Canning began his serious literary career late in life is said by some to account for the immediate maturity of his work. Perhaps a man ought not to write until he has had time to reflect, but Canning himself has said somewhere that a writer is soonest best through print. At least, he was of the best, at once. There is no record of his having written creatively before his forty-sixth year. When he was in his late twenties, he wrote a volume of commentary on Keats, and this book has been recommended for its enthusiasm and style. Some years later, when he was already teaching English at Asher College in Maine, Canning produced two articles concerned with Wordsworth's "Michael," and recently certain critics have discovered that these essays have an ironic intention. But it was not until the year that he was awarded an associate professorship, the year that he had the serious illness necessitating his missing a full semester's work, that he began the series of papers by which his importance was established.

The heart attack that interrupted his teaching was preceded by a month of the most uncertain health, by a depression so pervasive that Canning asked his superiors to relieve him temporarily of a share of his classwork. Two doctors concurred; he must have more rest, for a while, at least; and the department chairman, Dr. Griggs, considerately excused Canning from most of his duties. He continued teaching only the Early Romantics course and the Wordsworth seminar, for these were his specialties. But he was advised by his doctors even to put aside an article on Wordsworth's Lucy poems, at which he was working. "If you must work, write something light. Amuse yourself," old Dr. Maxwell told him kindly, for he knew that the Wordsworth paper was to have been read at the spring meeting of the English Association.

The result was that Canning, going home to his bachelor apartment before noon instead of at four, and not having to stir outdoors from Friday until Monday, read Landor, Horace, Catullus and Ovid, and produced the three brilliant essays that first brought him to the attention of the readers of the best "little" magazines. But his heart gave way: it was only when he was brought home from the hospital for his long convalescence that he found himself to be a "new literary figure." Not only were two of his essays boldly in print, but stacked neatly beside the magazines were more than a dozen letters from admiring readers. Several of these were requests from editors for some of his work, and one was from Case and Sons, who were to be his publishers.

Lying in his narrow bed day after day, a bed that faced not the window but the wall, that overlooked not the splendid maples of College Row but a maple chest of drawers, the top set out precisely with his toilet articles and medicines, Canning took time to ponder. He had few visitors, for he had made few friends. A scattering of colleagues and students came round to mumble their regrets. He looked at their faces, alive and rosy with the cold, and met their self-deprecatory smiles shyly. He did not permit himself any mild jokes at the expense of his health, but he was not so well either as to complain when his landlady, Mrs. Ferguson, brought him his soup not quite hot.

If he read, it was the Greek and Latin classical writers, whom it might technically be said he had rediscovered in the weeks before his attack. Actually, a difficult student had insisted on doing a Landor paper, rejecting, with uncommon insight, the subject of Pantisocracy. Thus, Canning had stumbled backward to the classical world, which was truly his own, as he was to prove. And when he puzzled over Lucretius, with the aid of a borrowed dictionary, he found that he had lost all sense of duty to Wordsworth.

Sometimes he took his pulse, but not often, for it accelerated after a moment. He thought of his father, who had been a country doctor, and of his mother, who had died of a heart attack while his father had been gone on a long obstetrical call. Life and death consumed his attention, while he realized that he had never cared much for people. The slow silence of the days gave him a pleasure that colored his regret, and he became aware again of his body, much out of sight and mind in that severe Maine climate.

When Mrs. Ferguson asked him, as she did boldly one afternoon, why he had never married, Canning replied quite simply that there had been nobody much to marry at Asher, or at Coles before it. The flesh had taken care of itself one way or another; his conscience had belonged to English Romanticism rather than to New England; and one did not marry the librarian, Miss Singleton, who had been his mistress of sorts for eleven years, a thin, blanched woman, now in California, who had been fond of saying to him in husky tones, "You are just like Byron, except that your hair is straight." He had always thought how Byron's valet had put the poet's hair in curl papers, but he had never told Miss Singleton.

In fact, Canning was good-looking: not handsome, but with a pleasant, wide brow and abundant chestnut hair. His mouth was his mother's, full and sensual, and he had the doctor's straight but fleshy nose that favored a trifle the left. As a young man, he had been impressive, if rather late in coming to physical maturity, and he sometimes wondered whether it had been more his looks than his mind that had led Dr. Scudder, his faculty advisor at Coles, to exclaim, "But you must study the Romantics, my boy. Shelley, Keats, Byron. You simply must. You will fit perfectly!" This cryptic enthusiasm, and the fact that he was then familiar with no more than Scott's novels, on which his mother had fed, directed Canning through college and into graduate work. Laboring at Wordsworth—Professor Morgan did not quite share Dr. Scudder's tastes—Canning had come to believe in the rightness of a certain melancholy.

Thinking of the essays that had come to him recently without benefit of research, he reflected also upon Dr. Griggs's disapproval and upon his own tired—and he now felt—somewhat hysterical rejoinder. In the course of one of the head professor's visits, the character of which was set by his having refused to remove so much as his gloves, standing at the foot of the bed, red-faced, and muffled in his outdoor clothing, Griggs had remarked, less than benignly, "Canning, if you were too ill to teach, you were surely wasting your strength writing that stuff." A copy of one of the quarterlies lay on the bed, and he regarded it sullenly, picked it up in a gloved hand and dropped it.

Then Canning said, "I have had a fine response, you know. Very many letters." More than one might expect from the English Association, he thought. "And I have been asked to do a book of that kind of thing," he continued. "Literature. And I have agreed to do it."

But he hadn't, though, of course, it came increasingly to his mind. These afternoons, when Mrs. Ferguson had gone with the lunch things, having repeated all the physicians' warnings of the morning, and when Canning was entirely still and alone, lying back with his eyes closed, unthinking, really, the words would at length begin to shape themselves in his mind. Often he said them aloud, his cheek turned against the pillow, so that he could hear a resonant voice in his skull; or he spoke his words toward a lithograph of Carlyle, a legacy from a former tenant, but this picture, hanging between the two frosty windows, itself offered a cold and glassy stare to his irresolution.

When at last Canning took up a pen and held a new notebook against his drawn-up knees, he was betrayed by the trembling of his hand. The words that matched so perfectly in his mind became disordered as they met the paper. If the letters could not be made decisive, what of the meaning? He felt now that art was an accident, a conspiracy of irrelevances, that the circumstances of creation lay hidden in the obvious, small satisfactions opening the way even to the work of genius. Robbed of the possibility of neatness, of the sense of himself, as it were, in the carefully shaped letters he had commanded for so many years, he was unwilling to go on. His new-found career as a literary man ended as he sank deeper into the pillows moist with his effort.

Yet, so great are the powers of irrelevance that Canning's resolve was doubled the next day, though he waited patiently. However, it was with pure irritation that he responded to Mrs. Ferguson's knock at three in the afternoon, an hour at which his illness had accustomed him to solitude. Nor was it with anything less than dread that he heard a Miss Wheeler had come to visit him. Suddenly, he felt very ill indeed, ill and ill-used; he could not recall a Miss Wheeler, and if it had not been for his conviction that she was already at his door, standing silently beside Mrs. Ferguson on the soft hallway carpet—as she was—he would have asked that she be sent away. But his book had left him in that moment, his ego vanishing as delicately as it had come, and he laid aside the pen, just taken up, and faced the doorway with a weary smile.

Miss Wheeler disclosed herself with timidity, however, with a timidity that was extinguished by the force of her full stature. A tall girl, dressed in a bright red woolen coat, hatless, with rich, flowing yellow hair, a complexion all white and pink, she stood clutching a beribboned package in her mittened hands. Canning recognized her, but he did not know her. "Miss Wheeler?" he said, in a voice weaker than necessary.

At this, she approached the bed. She seemed suddenly older, as if time and his memory had warped her image; and she stood regarding him now with such a wide gaze of sympathy that he was determined to resent it. "Should I have come?" she then asked, and the question rang hollowly in his mind.

"I'm afraid . . ." he began, but he had identified her. "Weren't you in school at Asher four or five years ago?" She nodded. "But no student of mine?"

"No," she confessed, "I was to have taken your Romantics, but I left. It was my father. He was taken gravely ill." She stopped, alarmed. "Oh, I'm so sorry!" she cried.

"No, it's I who am sorry," Canning assured her.

She then told him of her father's lingering illness, of years mingling hope and anxiety. She pulled a chair to the bedside, placed her package on the floor, drew off her mittens. Her father was dead since Christmas, and she had come back to school.

"But why have you come *here?*" he wanted to ask her, but there was no need.

"I have read you!" she cried out, clasping her hands.

"Oh," he sighed, relieved that it had not been the English Romantics.

There followed a conversation that exhausted Canning as it exhilarated Miss Wheeler. She took on the color of her woolen coat, and he faded to his sheets' whiteness. "You have genius! You must go on!" she had told him fervently, and under the ardor of her bright gaze, Canning had confessed his desire, his determination, to write a book. Still, he contrived to sound irresolute; his voice had become querulous with the recital of his difficulties. It seemed to him that a chill was enveloping his staggering heart: that heart might be a child lost in a local blizzard, as Miss Wheeler might represent the sentimental dénouement, the sudden right turn taken in the storm, a light in a window, hearth and home, mother-love. Speaking out of his conception of wretchedness, he had wanted to be warmed by her, Dr. Griggs and his own fragility having given him a shiver, and he had been warmed. She had told him that she would come every afternoon to take his dictation. "Use me!" she had cried, and he had accepted with a willingness that surprised him, overpowered perhaps by her indelicacy, which left no room either for convention or failure. And to write a book was, of course, unconventional. At the last, she had leaned toward him and plucking his hands from the coverlet had kissed them. Presenting him with the beribboned package, she had backed to the door, calling loudly, "Dear Professor Canning, it is for you. I can't wait for tomorrow! Have courage!"

Whether this last advice was addressed to him, he had no way of knowing, for she had gone. He lay in a twilight stupor, then, and when Mrs. Ferguson had brought his supper, he had possessed himself to agree with her that Miss Wheeler was a nice young woman. Idly, he had undone her package. It was a book, Gide's *Fruits of the Earth*. Canning had never heard of it.

Thus began what Canning was later to call so gallantly their "collaboration." Every afternoon, through the last months of Canning's convalescence, Miss Wheeler appeared with a thick, black copybook. In all weathers, she followed his light lunch as regularly as his yellow capsule, and it is in her favor that she was even less demanding of his attention and—let it be said— far more salubrious. The excitement of their first meeting gave way to a strict decorum; she scarcely spoke unless he addressed her; and it seemed she merged with the chair by his bedside. The copybook was held in her lap; her pen was ready; her eyes were downcast.

For his part, Canning pursued his own thoughts, and he knew that she must sometimes think him napping. Now and then, he opened his eyes, and if, at long intervals, he would find her gaze upon him, it was always she who seemed disconcerted by this naked contact. So the afternoons would wear themselves away in shared patience, with Canning speaking at last the words that rose as far as his lips. There were never any corrections to be made. What was uttered was final, despite the quizzical scratchings of her pen. But the pen revealed its own nature, and Miss Wheeler said nothing. Often Canning wondered how she was able to suppress her enthusiasm, or whatever, but on the whole he was grateful for her silence and for the simple warm squeeze of the hand she gave him at parting.

Inevitably, they were drawn closer by the familiarities they denied themselves, so that at last they were most discreetly James and Catherine. Occasionally, she stayed later and he felt better, and one evening, when she had taken the soup from Mrs. Ferguson's reluctant hands, and when the door had closed upon the retreating figure of that lady, Catherine Wheeler had whispered, "But this soup is so cold!" After that, she asserted the rights of his own small and unused kitchen, and it was not long before she herself was preparing his lunch and supper, now painfully hot, Mrs. Ferguson having been relegated somehow to the meager breakfasts. True, Catherine did manage the groceries with a minimum of bustle, and she had an eye to order that Canning could approve. Also, she undertook to keep a strict account of her purchases, an area of life where Mrs. Ferguson surrendered to vagueness. It was possible for Canning to be sufficiently concerned with himself.

When he was able to get up and move about, their life changed very little. The book had been begun in bed, and it was appropriate to finish it there. His recovery was not allowed to interfere. And except for his sitting a few hours in the morning by the window, enjoying the spring sunlight and one volume or another of Bergson's that Catherine had loaned him, their routine of work continued to dominate them. She squeezed his hand more often now, perhaps, but his book was very good indeed.

The writing of the last page coincided with the first day of warm weather, but the following day brought a spring storm and the doctors' final warning. Canning would never be much better, was well enough to resume an almost normal life, but must always be careful, careful, careful. He had grown to like the care, so that his muted recovery did not sour for him Catherine's lyrical reading of the completed manuscript. On that gloomy afternoon, she might have been the first vivid robin of spring. With the publishers' song of praises a few weeks later, their whole confined world broke into blossom.

It was with amazement that he learned from her during their first walk together across the campus, he, shrunken inside his clothes, she, seeming to burst hers with sheer vigorous joy, that she had resigned from school the day she had assumed his book. It had never occurred to him to question the freedom of her afternoons. Dismay possessed him, for he now felt bound to her devotion, whereas he would have preferred graciously and with a deferred sense of obligation to have offered his own. But she assured him that her sacrifice was not one. She had money from her father, she said, and Canning noticed for the first time her evidently expensive clothes. That nothing was more important than his art, she continued to tell him through the remainder of their walk; and, indeed, she followed him to the shore that summer, where he had gone to rest before resuming his teaching in the fall, and daily delivered this garland of dedication to his genius.

Before September, they had begun a second book, so that upon his return to the campus Canning's lectures were informed by an incisive energy unknown to them earlier. He found he was no longer able to approach "literature" with the diffidence of an academician, for he had become a practicing writer, whose interest in the "masters" was directed to an examination of the nature of the writing craft. Students who had come to be told what was "beautiful" were asked instead to theorize concerning the functions and uses of language, and their jaws dropped at the same time that their eyes were held to the speaker. Some of them discovered why they thought and felt as they did, with a delight or anguish that best suited their capabilities, but from this Canning was securely apart. His words were of and for his own essence. He was exploring the dimensions of a mind he had long taken for granted.

His first book was published in November and was received with such a fanfare as permanently blighted the by no means pleasant expression of Dr. Griggs. It was as if he had withered under the noisy discussions of Canning. "Your book seems to be extraordinary," was all he could manage, adding the foolish hope that Canning would do a Wordsworth paper for the English Association. Canning hardly replied, however, hurrying off to meet Catherine Wheeler, who, a week before and a few moments after having received from his hands "the first copy," inscribed with an apt quotation from Gide's *Fruits of the Earth*, had consented to marry him.

"I will not try to give you more than you can bear," she had told him, somewhat in his own style.

"We could not be more to each other," he had replied, but his smile of happiness was not ambiguous.

Two kinds of work, equally demanding, if not equally rewarding, and a marriage, however delicately sensible, with a much younger woman were bound to break Canning's health. "First things first," Catherine told him, simply, if tritely, and thus they reached the complex accord that they would live for Canning's art, the deliberate art, disguised in idleness, beyond which lay the illusion of health, though they did not mention it. His dizziness and palpitations were not, for that matter, the tokens of love.

At mid-year, to the astonishment, relief, and chagrin of Dr. Griggs, Canning resigned from the faculty and prepared to follow Catherine north. She went first to prepare for her husband-to-be the house she had inherited from her father. She was in haste, and having arranged to meet Canning in

Portland, she married him there in a ceremony that fit the schedule of their trains. Nor was there need for a honeymoon, but only for the comforts of home. Miss Wheeler's ardors were refined to the duties and dignities of Mrs. Canning. The brief, passionate interlude between bereavement and refulfillment was at once forgotten.

They entered then the aura of that fine old house, not quite a mansion, to which in time Canning was to lend his own atmosphere. The deep colonial brick, the high-ceilinged rooms with their carved moldings and marble mantels, the furniture, chastely graceful or heavy and enduring as stone, the wide lawns and gardens, the half-exhausted orchard and the half-wild wood bespoke the devotion of many dead generations. There were signs of wakening, and even an old sundial had been polished. The huge beds creaked softly; the shutters swung easily.

Not far away was the town, small, white, prim, and introspective. And the sea, perhaps a hundred yards beyond the south stone fence, swept the gardens with its sound. Open and shut, this world gave a thousand entrances and exits to the mind, and yet was as safe and discreet as Canning's sensibilities, here tested already by favorite rooms and by that first dreamless night in the dead father's bed, where, after a second heart attack, Canning was to finish his second book.

Their lives moved forward almost imperceptibly, flowed with the sluggish, familiar currents of that quiet house, the wash of the world, like the wash of the sea, beyond their fences. A world lay within a world, and there was yet another world within, a womb within a womb, the mind carried softly at the center, cradled in its own fluids. And through these many membranes life filtered inward, like light through the fine lawn curtains, and their lives stirred outward, like Catherine's music of an evening at the old piano that trembled the china, shook loose the faded petals of yesterday's cut flowers, and breathed out into the nighttime garden.

Canning had soon mingled the rhythm of the house with his own silence and contemplation, with the slow flowering of his own words that was like the house awakening gradually to its own routine. Waking late, he lay still in the huge bed, hearing at last the faint clatter of his breakfast being carried upstairs. Catherine did not stay a moment, and when he had cleaned himself, and had finished his roll and coffee set out on a small table by the window, he took up a volume of Horace or Vergil, and sat or lay reading till noon. Lunch was at one precisely, and precisely groomed Canning descended the stair. Afterward, they talked for an hour in a downstairs parlor, or, if the weather were fine, they walked among the flower beds or to the sea.

Always, then, it was he who spoke most, commenting, perhaps, upon something he had read, examining it and turning it this way and that. Catherine listened, smiled, asked a question, nodded, walked with him to his study door.

Usually, there was a fire in the grate, playing its light upon the bookshelves and the velvet-covered chairs; but in the rare hot days, the French windows behind the desk were open, the fine lawn curtains fluttering in the mild sea breeze. As he stepped into this room, Canning felt that he had entered the ultimate dimension of his being. Like an act of pure love was his moving toward his desk, his sitting in his chair, his lifting of his pen. His eyes delicately closed, and he felt his flesh hushed and flickering; he waited, timeless, and grew. And he was watching himself, watching the exquisite combat of his nerves, the excitement of waiting, the awareness of emotion calling limitless images out of his own depths. If he had needed to know Egypt, he would have known it; and what passed was not the afternoon but his own quality.

He knew very well what he wanted to write, but what he would write out of this desire interested him supremely. The decision was at the heart of his unfolding, and when the pen met the paper in his resolve, at about five, he was created anew. There was no slough, but seed and flower, seed again.

After supper, he read to Catherine what he had written, superbly potent in her smile. Later, she would take away the pages and type them. Now, she would go over with him the letters he had received that day, the ones she had selected for his attention. There were usually many of them, requests, entreaties, praises, arguments. He was famous, and she sat, as of old, with a notebook on her knees, to take his replies. And because he could afford to be generous with his correspondents, he guarded himself carefully. These hours at the end of the day delighted them both; these were an exercise in wit they both could perfectly share. She was the bright student of his heart, and he the courtier to her laughing favor.

Sometimes he wondered what her life was apart from the immediate demand of his presence. Though he could appreciate her satisfactions, he could not explain them. Her youth and vigor confounded him, moving, as they did, in his own quiet channel. She loved him for some secret part of herself, he concluded, and while it did not rankle him, he was sensible of a solitude in her own nature that was beyond his reach. She was unobtrusive and good-humored, exceptionally sensitive to his needs, and he could not place her. The joy she took in his fame was, he felt, another matter.

"Ought we to have a child?" Canning asked her, the third year of their marriage. He had had a period of good health that yet did not permit him more than the usual small share of her company.

"Here?" she had replied. She recalled to him that they neither traveled nor entertained, except for the few literary visitors, who followed too swiftly upon their letters, and of whom Canning seemed at once to weary. "Think of the unwelcome reminders," she said.

Still, he thought her too much alone. "What do you mean?" he insisted. But she remained vague, and he had felt obliged to love her too often and, it seemed to him, not too well. Their stillborn son was buried the following spring; nevertheless, Canning was allayed.

He came to regard their relationship as the most comfortable of mysteries. Catherine attended him in illness and in health, and he lavished upon her the exquisite flowers of his art. These were only for her, he sometimes thought, remembering her child's delight in a new volume that her womanly maturity had helped to make possible. But paradox did not oppress him; he was accustomed to stating what might be true, and often was, but without himself too much questioning it. The world's crookedness came to him in balanced prose.

The summer Canning reached his fifty-seventh birthday, he was at the zenith of his powers. His reputation, already international and beyond most critical question, was soon to be crowned with the glowing work that proved the co-existence of the classical world with our own. Several chapters had been published in the leading literary quarterlies, but no one could have anticipated from them the dark and agonized Epilogue, in which the writer doubts the whole validity of art and the life of the imagination.

"I have been interrupted by time," Canning wrote, and that summer he had been interrupted, sitting at his desk as he liked, his pen poised, his chin resting upon the palm of his left hand; the words forming had been drawn out of him late one golden afternoon by the sound of voices in the garden. Catherine had gone to town, and he sat still, almost trembling, in the shadow of the curtains. His words had fled from his mind, but others replaced them, the words, it seemed, of a young girl who stood beside the flower beds.

"They are so beautiful!" the voice cried, "Do you suppose he grows them himself?"

An unreasoning anger swept Canning, and a man's voice, flat and passionless, replied. "What difference does it make?"

"All the difference," she said. "Aren't you a writer? Don't you know? Don't you feel?"

Canning rose and stepped from behind the curtains. He saw them beside the narcissus, a girl, perhaps just past twenty, slight and very fair, and a boy, only a few years older, it might be, tall and thick, with dark, curly hair.

"They are grown by my wife," Canning said.

They whirled to face his careful smile, the boy coloring deeply, the girl uttering a high startled cry. Then she came toward Canning, her arms outstretched. "Oh, Canning! You are Canning!" she exclaimed, her face transfigured with pleasure. "We didn't know you would be here, never imagined it!"

"This is my home," Canning replied sententiously. Noting her beauty, he became unsure of his irritation. He was moved to take her hands, but as she stopped before him, she dropped them. Her hair was flaxen, her eyes green; her small mouth quivered, but she seemed now unable to speak. Canning hardly assisted her. "If you did not expect to find me here, why did you come? And what is more, why should you come?" He pursued her. "Yes, I *am* Canning." The question of her identity was set between them.

The boy came forward. "Our car is in town, being fixed." He paused and was aware of his insufficiency. "We're on a trip around New England, Mr. Canning, and as long as we were here, and the car being fixed, Carol thought she wanted to see your house. That is, she wanted very much to see it."

"Yes," the girl cried. "I didn't dream you'd be here, I don't know why. And now you're angry!" He was, but she continued, taking the only course that could assuage him, telling him her name and the boy's, speaking her admiration and speaking it, too, in every gesture. Canning was a dream come true; Carol and Len were both writers, trying to be writers, anyway; Canning was so admired, so loved. Did he remember her? Canning did not, and he thought only that she and the boy were not married, as he had supposed they were. Traveling together? With distaste, he concluded that they were bohemians, and he assumed the nobility of his essays.

"How should I know you?" he asked politely. There was now no edge to his curiosity.

She laughed with confusion. "I wrote to you last year. We were starting a magazine—*Rival*." She indicated the boy. "We asked for a contribution, but said we couldn't pay. There was no reason for you to remember us, really."

"It is simply that I had no contribution to make, and I have what is truly a burden of mail. You may imagine it." That he had compromised himself into the merest intimation of apology annoyed him; and yet he was blowing hot and cold, so to speak; but there was no time to define his dignity, for the boy was addressing him, between smiles.

"You certainly could have helped us, you know. Not that we blame you. We wrote all the important people, and only a few of you came through. I told Carol not to expect much. Famous people have to make their way, maybe more than most. What is an unknown name on a letter? And I told Carol that even if you read the few poems she's published, or a dozen of my short stories, it wouldn't make much difference. You probably wouldn't have liked them, their not being your sort of thing. It wouldn't really be the money, or anything like that."

"No, surely not the money," Canning said impatiently.

"Well, in a way, you're the old tradition," Len continued. He frowned: the measure of sincerity, Canning thought. "You're such a great writer, you've influenced us all right, but that doesn't mean we imitate you, or that you'd recognize *us*. Writers used to talk about three-dimensional character. Well, you've shown how ideas are three-dimensional, shown how they have a life of their own, without needing time or people. As a matter of fact, you've shown that keeping alive is just a state of mind. Hasn't your coldness been a sort of symbol—an ironic conception of the self directed outward? You've really set the limits of the personal, telling us how to make out when life seems impossible, just too much. I've really wanted to ask you, because I feel that basically you don't believe in life, what men make out of life."

"Len," Carol said, but he went on. He pointed a finger at Canning.

"But don't you think that action is really the answer? If we use your basic attitudes, detachment and cynicism and all that, couldn't we go on from there to strip away the dead wood? Maybe that's where we differ, and I think I speak for a whole lot of young writers. We saw the war. You showed us the falseness of life and what the possibilities of the individual imagination are, but what is the self? Men die; it's society that goes on, whatever happens, the race, the mass. Shouldn't we use ourselves up for the future? Maybe time doesn't exist, but it does in the practical world. Why can't we make time and action real? Really, there's never *enough* time, you see. Whatever happens to a man."

His young voice went on, beating above the inexorable echo of the surf. Carol had taken his arm; his dark head nodded above Canning, who noted the movements of the thin, pale lips.

"In regard to the self," the girl said, interrupting. But Canning had turned away, and he saw in a moment of dizziness Catherine coming through the open garden gate. She cast an enormous shadow in the failing light.

"Catherine! Catherine!" he called, and as she hurried forward then, he said in a hoarse, urgent voice to the young people, now dumb with astonishment, "Forgive me." And he walked around the corner of the house, quickly.

At the far end, beside the doorway of the screened porch, he stopped. His throat ached, as if he had strained it in calling. He said his name aloud, "Canning." He tried to think of the magazine, *Rival,* but he could not remember it. "Canning," he said again; and then he went inside, wandering slowly through the downstairs rooms between the porch and his study. At the study door, he stopped once again, listening, but there was nothing to hear. Inside were the words, his, lost, the whole afternoon lost and empty, empty and lost, a loss. Quietly, he entered.

Beyond his desk were the French windows, still open, and he could see that Catherine had taken up his position in the garden, standing between the strangers and the house. They were telling her of the conversation, it seemed, and then Canning could hear them quite plainly.

"It was thrilling," the girl said.

"Really fine," said Len," he really belongs to the world."

"He's mine," Catherine said, and there was a pause.

"Will he come back, do you think?" the girl asked. "Can we say good-by? We would like to thank him."

"I will tell him," said Catherine.

"If we offended him. I wonder if we offended him," the girl said.

"We didn't really mean to intrude, you know, but Carol just wanted so much to look at the house. We didn't think you'd mind."

"I think perhaps you reminded him he is dying," Catherine said. "Let me walk with you to the gate."

"Oh," the boy began, as they moved off, asking some questions, but Canning could not hear that Catherine replied. He went to the desk and gathered his papers. It was almost dark, and he could not see very well what he had written. Then, he sat at the desk and took up his pen; he did not turn on his lamp; he sat quite still, but Catherine did not come to him; and after a while, he put the pen down and laid his head and arms upon the desk; he closed his eyes and wondered if he would cry, but he did not.

Robert Pinget

MAHU OR THE MATTER

Translated by
Lionel Abel

A persistent traveler, Robert Pinget has visited England, Belgium, France, Spain, Switzerland, Yugoslavia, Italy, Corsica and Israel. He took his degree in law in Geneva, where he was born in 1920. He went to Paris in 1946 to enter the Beaux Arts school of painting, and in 1950 had his first show. A collection of tales and a scenario were published in Paris in 1951, and MAHU OR THE MATTER appeared in 1952, its limpid and poetic prose attracting particular attention among the younger French writers. These rapid monologues and fragments of narrative from MAHU are, according to one French critic, "like so many drops of acid falling on reality. To dissolve it? Or to dissolve what is unreal, leaving only the essential? But what is the essential? It is for you to discover."

THE FIGS

I just had to be up and doing. You can see that. Fall to, they told me, constantly. I would hear them, all of them, getting up at six-thirty, to go to the office. My fourteen brothers. At six-twenty-five, the one with the alarm clock would wake up, and go to wake the others. I would hear him, rapping quickly, oh very quickly, on all the doors; it was as if the same door were being rapped on for a long time. We lived in a hotel.

He skipped my door. But I was awakened at a quarter after six each day. I wondered whether someone wasn't going to wake me up like the others, saying to me suddenly: "The office!" Beside me was my chair with my things on it. At six-twenty I reached out from under my blanket, and put my hand on my pants. What if someone did come to wake me? I should find an office. I should say: "Mr. Office Manager, look here, someone woke me at six-thirty. I am at your service." There are offices everywhere. One cannot take a step, not where we live, not a step in the street without finding offices, without finding people going to an office, and offices looking for people.

Six-twenty-five. I hear the alarm which awakens my brother.

Six-thirty. Trrrrrr. He has skipped my door. I can draw back my hand. I hear the others getting up, the faucets working in the washroom, running water hot and cold, gas on all floors, please do not wipe razor blades on the towels, breakfast served in your room, the management is not responsible for theft of articles not left at the desk.

Long ago there was, as I recall, an immense clatter in the corridor at ten minutes to seven. This was their period of apprenticeship. They must have been twenty years old. They liked clatter. Almost always someone shouted at my door: "Mahu, are you sleeping, good-for-nothing?" My mother forbade anyone to open my door. She said that no one should wake me up, that no one should speak to me of the office, she forbade the clatter. Bit by bit with the years the clatter subsided, they no longer asked if I were sleeping, good-for-nothing, they let me take my arms from under the covers and wait for someone to wake me, perhaps. This took how many years? They must be about thirty years old.

Ten minutes to seven. The faucets stop running. The windows open. The keys turn in the doors. Since we were twenty-five our doors have been locked. The steps glide in the corridor. The hall door shuts. But this time it is no longer the same.

"So, Mahu! you are sleeping, good-for-nothing?"

"What is it? Who is it?"

"It's me, Frédy."

"Which one, Frédy?"

"The twelfth. Open."

I get up. I open. Frédy has a beard. There is a handkerchief in his breast pocket. He is beginning to lose his hair. He resembles our father who is in heaven, may your name be blessed, may your. . . . I have to sit down on the bed. I am trembling.

"What's wrong with you, Mahu?"

"Oh, it's nothing. I'm not used to this."

"Do you want a glass of water? Do you want tea? Do you want an aspirin?"

"No, it's nothing. Tell me about the office."

He sits on the armchair:

"Exactly, I came for that. Don't say anything to Mama. Look, they need a clerk in the office. I thought of you. All that time—you must have been bored stiff. Do you agree?"

"Yes, sure! Thanks, Frédy. I'll get dressed."

"You'd better hurry. It is five minutes to seven."

I, who knew all the noises by heart, all that time, the faucets that opened, running hot and cold water, now did everything wrong. I opened the window, I cut the towel with my razor, I turned on the gas on all floors, I put my trousers on last. Frédy laughed. He told me: "You have a baby's ass. Hurry, it's a quarter past seven." And I was on my way. But I remember that just before closing the door, just before, I caught a glimpse of my photo, not meaning to. A snapshot of figs I photographed one summer at Fantoine. One summer on vacation. I felt . . . there, exactly as when one smokes the first morning cigarette. That makes one empty. I almost fell down. Frédy said to me: "Is something still wrong?" I told him: "Nothing, it's the figs."

Now I'm a clerk at Juan Simon's. I no longer go to our place. I sleep in the warehouse. I have found a spot where the rain doesn't reach. I have an old bedstead. I have tacked my snapshot of figs on a board facing me. At night, a pal comes to sleep there. He sleeps beside me on the ground on blankets with the tarpaulin of the Simon's old truck over him. This way he does not get wet when it rains. He is a model at the Beaux-Arts. He is a Hungarian, or something like that. He tells me he loves me. When he says this too often I tell him he bores me, and that makes him cry. I give him some of the honey mama brings me from time to time. She is afraid that I don't get enough to eat at Juan's; it is old honey which she kept in reserve during the war for the guests at the hotel. It is crystallized. But I do not wish for my old room. That awakening of the others every morning was fierce. . . . Now I get up when Traiko does, we wash our hands and faces at the pump in the court. He goes off for a coffee in a different place each morning. They offer him coffee free of charge. I, I take out my pot of honey, eat some, and put it back under my bed. And I play the clerk.

Bitty-Crap is the daughter of Juan Simon. She is eleven years old. On her way to school she generally arrives at the store at the same time as I. She shows me drawings of hers and sums wrongly added, I think. I don't dare correct them for her because I don't remember whether the result should be written above or below the column. When I write it above, the sum is different from when I write it below. Juan gives me parcels which I carry to the post office or to the warehouses or to the stations. I know how to use the big scale. I know how to fill in the carbon paper forms with sender, receiver, weight, character of the merchandise. I write all that down.

One day I found myself at ten o'clock before the school of Bitty-Crap. It was during recess. She saw me in front of the gate. She called me. She called her little friends and introduced me: "Mahu-the-Screw." I wanted to slap her, but there was the gate. A nasty kid.

LATIRAIL TRAVELS

I have a horror of trips, thought Latirail. One prepares in anxiety, one goes off in a fever, one returns with the blues, and I don't get *that* out of it.

If I take another trip, it will be because of Ninette. She wants to broaden herself, as she puts it. I myself find her no less limited than before. On the contrary. I let her keep her illusions. One day, of course, she will be rid of the mania, yes, it is a mania, but right now each day there is a discussion about our next trip. Rather, I let her talk. I just make remarks like: "Do you think we'll have the time?" or "Won't it cost too much?" simply to make it look as if I were participating, but these discussions bore me to such a point. . . . She understands this, she calls me Tightwad when she makes projects, but she keeps on making them. She claims that this keeps me out of my slippers, that if she were not there I would be the worst of all dopes. I let her talk. We leave. . . . .

I grant that if I show such good will toward Ninette it is also because of a prediction made by a fortune teller. She foretold many voyages for me. I can't go against that, can I? It gives me a chance to find out if the prediction was right. But no wonder I have misgivings: didn't she prophesy many trips?

So we go off. Immediately I am hot for it. This seems contradictory, but that is the way it is, I take on the fever of my wife, or rather it is I who have her fever. As for her, she comes to life again. She has a wonderful time. My fever mounts constantly, I see nothing, I can't even think, I am sick as a dog and there is Ninette relaxed and sprawling beside me. It is just hell. Simply to recover a little, I write letters to acquaintances. At the bottom of the page I always add this notation: "Please return this letter to my home," and on my return I find a package of letters which I reread and correct. Thus I waste much time. And it is so boring. . . . Finally I tie them together and note on the package: "Trip to X, Trip to Y." I want to cry when I see the new pile beside the old ones. My piles of travels. They are on the top shelf of the library, yellowing.

When will Ninette get rid of her mania? I said that traveling is no longer profitable to her, she has lost her judgment because of her will to broaden and unfetter herself. She makes acquaintances; they become our friends because we knew them during some trip; the more miles they total up, the better they are. She invites them, we *tutoyer* them, this makes them still more friendly, and I just don't know what to say to them. Ninette makes scenes afterwards because I didn't slap them on the back, because I was as bored looking as a dead rat. I take it on the chin. It is travel that forms young people, but good God, how slowly Ninette ages! Just the same I try to profit from all this, I talk to anybody at all in the hotels, on the roads, in the stations. The first character with whom I take a drink speaks to me of his women; the first woman who sells me a newspaper tells me about her married life. Such is human contact, says Ninette.

THE HOUSE

Went to visit a mill with Latirail and Ninette. It was Saturday, it was winter. Latirail came to look for me, he had accomplished nothing, he couldn't even work any more, he said. So we went to look over a cold abandoned mill which had just been acquired by some wealthy people. They were not there. The caretaker lives nearby, and his wife showed us around nicely. She said to us: "They want to spend the holidays here before the work begins, you see how dilapidated the place is, they want to install a stove in this room for a while, this little stove here, as you see, is much too small; I said to them: 'Take my kitchen range, I expect to have another for my daughter's betrothal, I hope to have this new kitchen range in a few days.' That way, they would have more heat. This is my second daughter. The first was married at the beginning of the war, I don't have to do anything more for this younger daughter, after all she is eighteen years old, and is in no hurry to get married. But René lives with us, and that will make it more proper. This is a dump. When I came here a month ago, that's what I thought it was, but the owner said to me: 'You'll see how wonderful the place will be in summer.' But already my husband had discovered that the water of the millrace seeps through there, they'll have to dig and reinforce the concrete, the repairs aren't nearly done yet. Would you like some cider? I have a very fine cider, and as for my vinegar, do you know cider vinegar? It's the best."

Ninette asked her for a quart of vinegar. We savored its highly-spiced odor; there was a twig of rosemary in the bottle. While the others drank cider, I pursued my examination of the mill; there were rotting stairs and beams; I prowled about. I thought of Negroes, I am always thinking of Negroes and how their magic is probably what we call the blues or the jitters, but they dance and conjure away the blows of fate, whereas we, we are sad and visit rotten mills.

What a curious custom for the rich to own several houses; they make repairs in the blues of the others, who abandoned the house with its leaking walls.

There was a red flower in a field; I went to look at it: a

curly red cabbage in full bloom, I picked it to make a bouquet. The sky became red-cabbage pink, a great walnut tree above the mill, and in the thicket, trees with mistletoe.

The caretaker's wife said they had gone to pick mistletoe to decorate the holiday table; she had told them where to get a goose, they would roast it in the fireplace, the goose was still waddling. When she went out to fetch the vinegar, Ninette asked us: "But is she French? She makes mistakes in French." Latirail replied: "Who knows whether the mistakes are not ours?" As for me, I looked at my red cabbage. I have no vase for it. I shall have to give it to Ninette. I thought of houses that shut you in, I can no longer inhabit my shed, hardly can I recognize it, it often happens that I mistake another for it, and go to sleep elsewhere. Could I come to some agreement with the caretaker's wife or with the new owner? I might have a contract to rid your trees of mistletoe, Madame, and in exchange, let me have a room, please.

I cannot learn magic, what sort of figure would I cut? It is not for me. I shall find a substitute; now that I have a room, I shall invite all the Negroes, we shall form a zone against the blues, and the rich will no longer need to buy ruins.

A Child Draws

A child draws. They talk about it. The story goes from ear to ear. If I get it, that's the end. No more ears, then. I hear a buzzing, but I keep my mouth shut. I do. The story may go around the world, but nobody shall know it. In vain is a secret told in low tones, you take all possible care, and it is out.

A child draws. He puts windows in a landscape. The windows have no house. The child stays at the window a long while, he opens the curtains, he looks out, he draws trees, these very branches, these branches indeed, he scribbles above the trunk with green, he scribbles circles, these make leaves, he makes a lot of trees. A full page.

But this window he is at, this window which looks out, this window set down—this window is an eye. The trees are in the eye, they are green, they are in the fingers, they are on the page. And the eye roving past so many trees is no longer at the window. It crosses over, it comes to rest, it attaches itself to the trunk, it clambers among the leaves, it is no longer at school, it is everywhere. Many eyes. They observe the window from afar, and remark: "Here is a window before us, let's fill the page with it."

Now the child draws no more. The teacher walks by. She sees the drawing, she leans down. She sees these windows without a house. She is surprised. She glances at the child. He is blushing. He is homely. He is silly. No one knew what to do with him at the other schools; they had him draw. It's he who changes the water in the fish bowls, he takes the fish in his hands.

The teacher leans down, down, there are window-fasteners on the windows, there are curtains, then she glances at the window, she doesn't see any trees. She sits beside the blushing child and notes something in his eye, something that moves. The child no longer can meet her gaze. She asks him: "Have you finished drawing?" The child says yes. The teacher takes the page. When the time is up the children leave.

The teacher feels the cold. She puts on her heavy winter coat, but she is still cold; she puts the drawing in her bag, she goes home. She is very sick, and gets into bed. She reaches for her bag. She opens it. She takes the drawing. She pins it on the wall with a thumb-tack. She sees the drawing crooked because she cannot lift her head from the pillow.

The child, too, has gone home. The doctor comes to see him. His mother tells him: "Take off your shirt, the doctor will give you an injection." He takes his shirt off, the doctor gives him the shot, the child doesn't say ouch, but puts on his shirt again.

But whatever moved in the child's eye leaves it and returns to the window. It moves like a dandelion seed. It is surely a seed. You breathe and whiff, it is off. It is almost too light. It perches no matter where. You often see the seeds catch where they light. They don't find the ground. You can say they are of no use, those. They are beat from the start. They end on the broom.

When the child returned to school he told the teacher: "You know, teacher, yesterday I was injected for my glands."

The teacher rested her hand on the child's head, she looked out through the window, she saw lots of trees with roving eyes and returned the page marked "Excellent."

What I am told I keep to myself. So much the worse for those who tattle. So much the worse for their secret. From ear to ear. That helps no one.

The Chick of the Curtains

She says: "We bike-race fans," dipping into her gravy, emptying her glass on the counter, tasting her gravy again; she wipes her hands on her apron and embraces a customer who has come into the place. Just a bistro like any other, but how attractive is the proprietress, with her belly, her cared-for hair, at her stove near the door, her son is a bike-rider, a bike-rider she is in love with, that's clear, she knows it, she says it, and

I am revealing nothing, it is public knowledge. "We, the bike fans, yes, Madame, look at his picture, he won the race." Between a beefsteak and a salad she untacks the snapshot from the wall; let us wipe our hands, yes, do, that's him, he won, he's good-looking, isn't he?

She is the bike-rider, for she wins the races, she says "we, the fans," the *we* of love. Who could say better?

What strange letters I write you! Alas, what can I do? I'm short of breath, there is my accent, I was born thus, what do you expect? If commas are missing, if there are too many, this is because of my country, because of my childhood. How boring is all that I remember! At first it seems like Proust, but really, it is tosh. Tosh, I swear! And you can't cut it short. It carries you back.

I'm thinking of this because a pal came to see me just a minute ago, and very proudly announced: "Now I have curtains in my place." So naturally, I am reminded of the past, another child who is telephoning, using the curtain-cord, it has a metal ball at the end, I am four years old, I am at the telephone: "Hello, Grandma. You know something? I have a chick." It is the very same speech. "I have curtains." Do you see any difference? Very proud he is, and no longer a youth, neither am I, and that's what we say and what we think! Talk about adults!

Rather than not get letters, I think you prefer to overlook the style, or to tap with your foot whenever I exaggerate. That's it, tap with your foot, you'll have the tone exactly.

Lucinda C. Collins

THE CONQUEST

superata tellus,
sidera donat

A graduate of Chatham Hall School in Virginia, Lucinda C. Collins was born in Philadelphia and now lives in Bucks County. "The Conquest" is her first published poem.

With too much ease and grace the poet wrote those words.
If in the outstretched palm, a rock, a piece of glass,
And lump of melted wax, might with our breath alone
Become a church, the world is easy won.
That prince who understood the songs of every bird
When holding in his hand a certain blade of grass
Was, when he stooped to pick it, blinded in both eyes.
And man, to whom is promised brilliance of the stars,
While stretching up to grasp them must leave his body
Unprotected on the earth.

THE ANATOMY LESSON

Evan S. Connell, Jr.

A native of Kansas City, Missouri, and a graduate of the University of Kansas, Evan S. Connell, Jr. has studied painting, sculpture and writing at Stanford and Columbia. During World War II he served as a Navy pilot. His short stories have appeared in *Flair, Tomorrow,* and elsewhere, and he has twice been honored by inclusion in the O. Henry Awards Prize Story volumes. *The Anatomy Lesson* is a chapter from Mr. Connell's first novel, which he is now completing in Paris, and for which he was awarded a Eugene Saxton Fellowship.

(The Anatomy Lesson: Copyright, 1953, by Evan S. Connell, Jr.)

North Fayer Hall stood on the final and lowest hill of the university, a little askew from the other buildings as if it were ashamed of its shabbiness and had turned partly away. Its windowsills were pocked by cigarette burns and the doors of its green tin lockers had been pried open for so many years that few of them would lock any more; the creaking floors were streaked and spattered with drops of paint, dust lay upon the skylights, and because the ventilating system could not carry off so many fumes it seemed forever drenched in turpentine. Mercifully the little building was hidden each afternoon by the shadows of its huge, ivy-jacketed companions.

Just inside the front door was the office and studio of Professor A. B. Gidney, head of the art department, who taught ceramics, bookbinding, fashion design and lettering. Professor Gidney's door was always open even when he was teaching class somewhere else in the building, and in his studio were teacups and cookies and a hot plate which the students were free to use whenever they pleased. There was also a record player and a soft maple cabinet containing albums of operettas and waltzes: every afternoon punctually at five the music started.

Behind his office were the student ateliers, each with twenty or thirty short-legged chairs placed in a semicircle around the model's platform, and at the extreme rear of the building next to the fire escape, and reached by a dim corridor which multiplied every footstep, stood the studio of the other instructor.

This final studio was shaped like an up-ended coffin. In the rafters which surrounded its skylight spiders were forever weaving, and because the window had not been opened in years the air was as stale as that of an attic, always cold in December and always close in July. The window as a matter of fact could not even be seen because of the magazines and newspapers heaped atop a huge, iron-bound trunk with a gibbous lid. In one corner of the room a board rack held rows of somber oil paintings, each nearly the same: marshes in the center of which one hooded figure was standing with head bowed. The first few strokes of another such painting rested on an easel in the center of the room, and around this easel a space had been cleared, but the material that was banked against the walls and rose all the way to the ceiling threatened to engulf it at any moment. There were gilt picture frames, some as large as a door, there were crocks and pails half filled with coagulated liquids, cartons, milk bottles, splintered crates covered with layers of dust and tobacco crumbs, rolls of linen canvas with rectangles ripped out, jugs of varnish and turpentine lined up on an army cot with a broken leg, brushes, rags, tubes, apple cores, wrappers of chocolate bars, Brazil nuts, toothpicks, and pictures everywhere—glued on the walls or on boxes or, it seemed, on whatever was closest: pictures of madonnas, airplanes, zebras, rapiers, gargoyles, schooners, adobe pueblos, and a host of others. There seemed to be no plan or preference: a solarized print of a turkey feather had been stuck to the trunk so that it half obliterated a sepia print of the Bosporus. The glue pot itself could be traced by its smell to a cobwebbed corner where, because it had cracked and was leaking, it sat on a piece of wrapping paper. On this paper was an inscription, printed at one time in red conté but now almost invisible. Beneath the glue and ashes the letters read:

> *I am here,*
> *I have traversed the Tomb,*
> *I behold thee,*
> *Thou who art strong!*

Here and there on the floor lay bits of what looked like chalk but which were the remains of a little plaster cast of Michelangelo's *Bound Slave*. The fragments suggested that the statuette had not fallen but had been thrown to the floor. Also scattered about were phonograph records; most of them looked as if someone had bitten them. Several rested on the collar of a shaggy overcoat which in turn was draped over a stepladder. The phonograph itself lay on its side, the crank jutting up like the skeleton of a bird's wing and the splintered megaphone protruding from beneath one corner of a mattress like some great ear. In the middle of the night when the university campus was totally deserted there would occasionally come from the rear of North Fayer Hall the muffled sound of plain-song or Gregorian chant, to which was sometimes added for a few bars a resonant bass voice in absolute harmony, that of the instructor whose name was printed in gold on the studio door, a door that was always locked: ANDREV ANDRAUKOV, DRAWING & PAINTING.

Nothing interested Andraukov except paint. Each thing he saw or heard or touched, whether it writhed like a sensuous woman or lay cold as an empty jug, did not live for him until he, by his own hand, had given it life. Wherever he happened to be, in a class or outside, he paced back and forth like a tiger, and when with hands laced into a knot at the tail of his sack-like tweed coat and his huge, bony head bowed as if in prayer he stalked the corridors of North Fayer Hall, or the streets of Davenport below the university, he created a silence. Always he walked with his head bowed, and so far had his slanting eyes retreated into their sockets that few people had met his gaze. His teeth were as yellow-and-brown as his leathery skin and it seemed as if flesh was too much of a luxury for his bones to endure.

It was his habit to start each drawing class in the still life room, a damp, chill studio with shelf upon shelf of plaster and bronze casts. He always took his students there the first morning; they stood about uncertainly, their young faces rosy from the September air, clean pencils and papers and new drawing boards clutched in their arms.

"Here," he would say, unrolling a long, cold finger. "Rome. Egypt. Greece. Renaissance. You will copy."

The students looked at him, a haggard old man whose head by daylight could be no more than a skull in a leather bag, and one by one they settled themselves before a statue. Around and around behind them went Andrev Andraukov, taking from awkward fingers the pencils or sticks of charcoal, drawing with incredible delicacy tiny explanatory sketches in a corner of the paper. When he leaned down to inspect the drawings of the girls they stiffened and held their breath fearing he might somehow contaminate them. To them he might have been the Genghis Khan. Slowly and with a kind of infinite patience he wandered from one to another, shaking his head, trying to explain, never taking from his mouth the stub of a brown cigarette which protruded from his drooping and streaked mustache like an unfortunate tooth. The moment he heard the chimes which ended each class he halted his explanation even though in the middle of a sentence and without a single word or another look he went out. The sound of his footsteps echoing in the corridor ended with what seemed like the closing of a hundred distant doors.

When he saw that his students were losing interest in the plasters and so could gain nothing more, he took them into the life atelier. On the walls of this room were tacked reproductions of masterful paintings. Helter-skelter stood drawing boards and student paintings, and on a platform rested an electric heater and a stool. Here, in this studio, he commenced his instruction of the living human body: on the blackboard he drew diagrams and explained for several days, as best he could through the net of language, how it was that men and women functioned. Then he got his students a model. Each morning one would arrive carrying a little satchel in which there was a robe or a cloak to wear during the rest periods and sometimes an apple or cigarettes or even a book.

Generally the models did as others had done for three thousand years before them, so there faced the class each morning a noble though somewhat shopworn pose. With earnest faces the students copied, bending down close to their paper the better to draw each eyelash and mole, their fingers clutching the charcoal as if they were engraving poetry on the head of a pin, and one after another they discovered that if charcoal was rubbed it would shine. In two days every drawing gleamed like the top of a candy box. All the while their instructor, a cigarette fixed in his smelly mustache, paced the back of the room or walked up and down the corridor.

Although the students did not know it, he was waiting. Year after year as students flowed by him this old man watched and waited; he waited for the one who might be able to understand what it meant to be an artist, one student, born with the instinct of compassion, who could learn, who would renounce temporal life for the sake of billions yet unborn, just one who cared less for himself than for others. But there were good foods to eat, dear friends to chat with and pretty girls to be seduced, so many fascinating things to be done and discussed, thus Andrev Andraukov could only watch and wait.

It was as if a little play never ended, wherein, to his eternal question: *Is it not important?*, the young people answered, *Yes! Yes! There must be one who cares!* And he asked: *Will it be you, then?* But they replied, *Ah, no! Not me! Someone else. You see, I have so awfully many things to do . . .*

One November morning the members of Andraukov's class found lettered on the blackboard in his square hand, TODAY: ANATOMY. As a result they did not open their lockers but sat in a semicircle facing the model stand and waited. Andraukov hurried in several minutes late; beside him walked a strange model who went behind the Japanese screen in the corner and began to undress.

Indicating a six-foot plaster man, stripped of skin and flesh, Andraukov asked two of the students to lift it onto the model stand. Next he pointed to the wooden cabinet where a skeleton dangled by a bolt through its skull, and said, "Mr. Bones." Two more students carried the rattling skeleton onto the stand. There was a half-smoked cigarette clamped in the jaws. Andraukov patiently removed it, as he had removed hundreds of others.

"Now," he said, "Miss Novak, please."

His model walked out from behind the screen and stepped onto the platform where she stood between the skeleton and the cut-away. She was a huge peasant girl with tubular limbs and coarse red hair that hung down her back like a rug. Between her great breasts was the tattoo of a ship. Her Slavic eyes were expressionless.

Andraukov took up a position behind the semicircle of students. From one of his coat pockets—which was more of a pouch—he brought up a crooked brown cigarette. After he had held two matches under it the cigarette began to sputter, flame, and finally emit blasts of terra-cotta smoke. Now Andraukov was ready to begin the lecture; he walked a few steps in each direction and then blew from his nostrils such a cloud that he nearly hid himself.

"Well," he began, "here is girl. Young woman. Who does not agree?" He walked out of the smoke, looked around, and then walked back into it. "Good. We progress. On street I look at woman first the head, then down, so we will do here. Who can tell what is the shape of human head? Mr. Sprinkle will tell us."

Sprinkle stood up and fingered his lower lip while he thought. Finally he answered that the human head was shaped like a ball.

"So? Miss Vitale will tell us."

Alice Vitale said it looked like an egg.

"Miss Novak, please to turn around. We will see back of head."

The model gathered her hair and lifted it until the class could see her neck and the base of the skull.

"Mr. Bondon, now, please."

Michael Bondon had begun to grow sideburns, and because his father was very rich he was not afraid to cross his legs and shrug.

Andraukov watched him for several seconds and then without expression continued, "Ball. Egg. Who is correct?" He explained that from the front the human head does resemble an egg and from the rear a ball or a melon, but, he cautioned, the artist must not look at what he sees so much as at what he cannot see, and holding up one hand he demonstrated that the students, seeing his palm with their eyes, must also see his knuckles with their minds. He said that the artist must see around corners and through walls, even as he must see behind smiles, behind looks of pain.

"For to what use you shall employ knowledge?" he asked, walking to the window and gazing out at the slopes covered with wet snow. "For what you shall be artist? To draw such as all the world can see? Pussycat? Nice bouquet of lily? Little boy in sailor suit? Then bring to this class a camera. No! Not to this class. Go elsewhere." He looked out the window again at the soggy clouds which were settling on the university buildings, and then with his cigarette pinched between thumb and forefinger as if it were alive and about to jump, he walked slowly across the room where he stopped with his back to the students. "You people, you wish to be artist. Why? That a stranger on the street will call you by name? You would be famous? You would have money? Or is it you have looked at your schedule and said, 'Ah, this is hard! I need now something easy. Yes, I will take drawing.'"

He turned around, looked at the faces of the men, his gaze resting on each for a number of seconds. "You have thought, 'I will take drawing because in studio will be pretty girl without dress!' So? This is reason? Or perhaps in this room—in this room perhaps now there sits young man who in this world discovers injustice. He would be conscience of the world. Mr. Dillon will now stand up. Mr. Dillon, you would draw picture which is to say: 'Behold! Injustice!'? You would do that?"

"No, sir," Dillon murmured.

"You will not be conscience of the world?"

"No, sir."

"If not you," Andraukov asked, gazing at the boy, "then who?" He carefully licked the underside of his mustache and pushed the cigarette deeper into his mouth. His knuckles were yellow and hard as stone. From the town of Davenport the sound of automobile horns came faintly up to the university hills; but for these noises and the creak of the instructor's shoes the life studio was quiet.

Andraukov walked to the stand where he flattened his thumb against the neck of the cut-away. "Sterno-mastoid. Favorite muscle. Favorite muscle of art student." He asked his model to look at the skeleton and as she turned her head the sterno-mastoid stretched like a rope between ear and collarbone.

"*Beatrice d'Este,* how many know this painting, painting by

Leonardo da Vinci? Three? Three hands? Disgrace! Now I tell you: In *Beatrice* is no sterno-mastoid. And why? Leonardo da Vinci is painting young woman, is not painting tackle of football team." He looked down on the faces turned attentively toward him and did not think they understood, but he did not know how to phrase it any more clearly. He decided to tell a joke. With a piece of green chalk he sketched on the blackboard a grotesque profile. He peered at it and shouted: "Young man after my daughter: Look like this! No, no—" He had confused the grammar. "Would have daughter, such young man like this." The class did not know what he was doing.

Andraukov felt he should explain his joke. He pulled on his mustache for a while and tried again but there was still only a confused tittering. He decided to continue with the lecture. Having become a trifle warm he unbuttoned his vest and hooked both thumbs in the pockets.

"Well, below head is neck. Below neck is breast. You are afraid of this word. Why? This is God's word. Why everybody —all the young girls say 'bust'? Bust is for firecracker. Not for woman. No! Everybody—class entire together—now say correct word."

He listened to the class uneasily repeat the word and he nodded with satisfaction. "So! Not to be 'bust' again. I do not like that word. For drawing: art student draw like balloon. This is wrong. Not balloon, but is bag to rest on rib cage. Is part of body like ear is part of head, like peanut butter of sandwich, not to be alone. Who does not understand? Who has question?" No hands were raised.

Andraukov asked his model to face him with her heels together, legs straight, and hands at her sides. He stared. He was pleased with the way she stood.

"Class. Class, consider Miss Novak, fine model, head high. Is good to be proud of body. Yes. This is true!" He struck himself with a stony fist. "No scent on earth is so putrid as shame. Good students, do not fear to be proud." He paused to meditate. "Well, on rib who can tell status of breast? Nobody? There is nobody to speak? There is fear?" He looked around. "Ah! Brave student. Mr. Zahn will speak. Mr. Zahn stands to tell instructor of breast. Good. Speak." With head bowed he prepared to listen, but almost immediately held up one hand: "No, no! I would know direction. I would know angle. Yes, angle. On breast does nipple look ahead like nose on face?"

Logan Zahn was a thin, heavily bearded young man who sat in corners whenever possible. He was older than the other students and wore glasses so thick that his eyes seemed to bulge. There were rumors that he was writing a book about something.

"No," he answered in a surprisingly high voice.
"The nipple, it will look down, perhaps?"
"No."
"Then where?"
"Up."
"And?"
"Out."
"Good!"

Zahn and the model looked at each other, both expressionless.

"You will tell instructor amount of angle. The left breast now, to where it is looking?"

"At the print of Cézanne's apples on the wall."

"And the right?"

Logan Zahn was not afraid. He pointed out the window. "At the Episcopal church."

Andraukov looked at the model and then toward the church. "That is correct." He tugged from his vest a heavy watch and studied it, pursing his lips. Why, he asked, tucking away the watch, why was it that men wished to touch women? To allow time for his question to penetrate he folded his arms across his chest and began wandering about the studio. He picked a bit of chalk off the floor, he opened a window an inch, he stroked a dusty bronze on a shelf, he went back to close the window, and when at last he felt that every student should have been able to consider his question and speak of it properly he invited answers. Nobody volunteered.

"I will tell you," he said. "No, I will not tell you. Mr. Van Antwerp will stand."

Van Antwerp, who was the university's wrestling champion, scratched his scalp and grinned. Andraukov's face did not move.

Van Antwerp grinned some more. "They're fat," he said.

"Man is not fat? Yes, but different. Well, on woman where it is most thick?"

Van Antwerp began to stand on his other foot. He blushed and sniggered. The class was silent. For a few moments Andraukov stood with eyes closed and head cocked to one side as if listening to something beyond the range of other ears, but abruptly he strode across the room to Van Antwerp's green tin locker and wrenched it open.

"These material, it belong to you? Take it now. You will not return! Who else now—who else—" But not being able to phrase what he wished to say he stood facing a shelf while Van Antwerp collected his things and left, slamming the door. Andraukov looked over his shoulder at the students. He turned all the way around and the color began to come back into his face.

"We speak of shape. Shape, yes. Is caused by many things. There is fat, placed by God, to protect child of womb. There is pelvic structure—so broad!" His bony hands gripped an imaginary pelvis. "There is short leg, spinal curve so deep. There is, too, the stance of woman. All these things, these things are not of man. You will not draw man and on him put balloons, lipstick, hair, and so to say: 'Here is woman!' No! That will be so wrong."

He continued that woman was like the turtle, born to lie in the sun and sometimes to be turned over. Woman, he told them, was passive. She was not to smoke tobacco, to swear, to talk to man, to dance with man, to love like a drunken sailor; she was to brush her hair and wait. As he thought about the matter Andrev Andraukov stalked back and forth cutting the layers of smoke left by his cigarette.

"Trouser! Crop hair! Drink beer! For ten thousand years woman is correct: gentle, quiet, fat. Now?" He paused to stare at the floor, then lifting his head, said, "Well, today is good model. Consider limbs: not little to break in pieces but big and round like statue of Egyptian goddess, like statue in concrete, like *Girl Holding Fruit* of Clodion. This piece, how many know? This Clodion?" He looked over the class and seeing only two hands pinched the bridge of his nose in a sudden, curious gesture and closed his eyes. He instructed them all to go to the library that afternoon and find a picture of the statue. Around the studio he wandered like a starved and shabby friar, the cuffs of his fraying trousers dusting the paint-stained boards and the poor coat dangling from the knobs of his shoulders. The laces of his shoes had been broken and knotted many times, the heels worn round. He stopped in a corner beside a cast of *St. George* by Donatello and passed his fingertips across the face as if he was making love to it. He licked the drooping corner hairs of his mustache. He swung his Mongol head toward the class.

"You do not know Clodion! You do not know Signorelli, Perugino, Hokusai, Holbein! You do not even know Da Vinci, not even Cranach or Dürer! How, then, how I can teach you? Osmosis? You will look inside my head? Each day you sit before the model to draw. I watch. There is ugly model, I see on your face nothing. Not pity, not revolt, not wonder. Nothing. There is beautiful model, like today. I see nothing. Not greed, not sadness, not even fever. Students, have you love? Have you hate? Or these things are words to you? As the artist feels so does he draw. I look at you, I do not need to look at the drawing."

There was no sound but the footsteps of the old instructor. Dust motes whirled about him as he walked through a bar of winter sunlight.

"Good students, why you have come to me? You do not know what is crucifixion, the requiem, transfiguration. You do not even know the simple ecstasy. These things I cannot teach. No. I teach the hand. No man can teach the heart." Holding up his own hand for them all to see he went on, "This is not the home of the artist. Raphael does not live here." Tapping himself on the chest he said, "The home of Raphael is here."

The little sunlight faded so that all the sky was mushroom gray with dirty wet strings hanging down. A wind rose, rattling the windows. The studio's one radiator began to knock and send up jets of steam. Andraukov snapped on the lights. He walked toward the motionless Slavic woman, his eyes going up and down her body as he approached.

"Who can find for instructor, sartorius?"

A girl went to the plaster cast and spiraled one finger down its thigh.

"Now on the model."

She touched the crest of the hip and inside the knee.

"What Miss Grodsky does not say is, ilium to tibia. But is all right because she tries. She will learn."

He asked if anybody knew why the muscle was named sartorius, but nobody knew; he told them it came from the word "sartor" which meant tailor, and that this muscle must be used in order to sit cross-legged as years ago the tailors used to sit. He asked for the patella and his student laid one finger on the model's kneecap but did not know what the word meant. It meant a little pan, he said, as he drew its outline on the model's skin with a stick of charcoal. He asked next for the scapula; she hesitated and then touched the collarbone. He shook his head, saying, "Not clavicle, not the key." She guessed at the ankle and he shook his head again, placing her finger behind the model's shoulder. There with charcoal he outlined the scapula, saying as he finished it, "So! And Miss Grodsky can sit down. Mr. Zahn will find for instructor, pectoralis major."

Logan Zahn got up again and pointed.

Andraukov said, "Miss Novak does not bite." He watched as Zahn placed a fingertip outside and then inside her breast. "Correct. Easy question." With charcoal he drew the pectoralis on her skin. "Now for instructor, gluteus medius." He watched Zahn touch the side of her hip.

"Gastrocnemius."

He patted the calf of her leg.

"Masseter."

He touched her jaw.

Andraukov looked at him intently. "You are medical student?"

"No."

"Find for me—find pectoralis minor."

With his hands Zahn indicated that it lay deeper in the body.

"So. Where you have learn what you know?"

"Library," Zahn answered in his squeaky voice.

"I have told you to study anatomy in library?"

"No."

"But you have gone?"

"Yes."

Andraukov's nostrils dilated and he blew a cloud of smoke dark enough to have come from a ship; he stood in the middle of it, nearly hidden. When he emerged he began to speak of the differences between men and women: placing both hands on the model's forehead he stretched the skin above her drugged eyes until the class saw how smooth the skull appeared, and for comparison he pointed to the ridge of bone like that of an ape's on the bleached skeleton. He pointed to the angle of the model's jawbone and next to the more acute angle on the skeleton. Below the pit of her neck he drew an outline of the sternum and compared it to the skeleton's longer, straighter bone. He said that the woman's neck seemed longer because the clavicle was shorter, thus narrowing the shoulders, that the elbow looked higher because the female humerus was short, that the reason one could not judge the height of seated women was because they possessed great variations in the length of the leg, that female buttocks were of greater diameter than male because of protective fat and because the sacrum assumes a greater angle. He turned the skeleton about on its gallows and placed his model in the same position. He drew the sacrum on her skin, and the vertebrae rising above it. She arched her back so that he could lay his hand on the sloping shelf. Why, he asked, why was it thus? And he answered himself, saying that the spine of man was straighter. Then for what reason did the spine of woman curve? For what reason did the pelvis tilt? Who would explain to him?

But again he answered himself. "Cushion!" A cushion for the foetus. From a cupboard he brought a length of straight wire and stabbed it at the floor: the wire twanged and vibrated from the shock, but after he had bent it into an *S* the wire bounced. He flung it into a corner and walked back and forth rubbing his hands as he lectured. The belly protrudes because there resides the viscera of the human body. Fashion magazines do not know about viscera, they print pictures of young girls who cannot eat because they have no stomach, who cannot walk because they have no maximus, who seem to stand on broken ankles. Although paper was flat the students must draw as if it were round; they must draw not in two dimensions but in three. A good artist could draw in three dimensions, a master could draw in four.

He stopped to consider the attentive looks on their faces and asked who understood, but did not wait for an answer. He spoke of how Rembrandt painted a young woman looking out an open window and said to them that she did not live three hundred years ago, no, she was more than one young woman, she was all, from the first who had lived on earth to the one yet unborn who would be the final. He told them that some afternoon they would glance up by chance and see her; then they would know the meaning of Time—what it could destroy, what it could not. But for today, he said, his voice subsiding, three dimensions would be enough. From his baggy vest he extracted a silver thimble. He held it between two fingers.

"For belly, three dimensions. It is not, like paper, flat. So navel is not black dot. It is deep. It is the eye of God. You are going to see." Bending down he pushed the thimble steadily into the model's navel.

Every little noise in the studio ceased. There was no movement. It seemed an evil spell had been thrown by the thimble which retreated and advanced toward the students in brief, glittering arcs.

Andraukov licked his yellow mustache. "Good students, you will forget again?"

The class was still paralyzed. Waves of shock swept back and forth across the room; with the elongated senses of the mystic Andraukov caught them.

"Good students," he said simply. "Listen. Now I speak. You have come to me not to play. You have come to learn. I will teach. You will learn. Good students, each time in history that people have shame, each time in history that people hide from what they are, then in that age there is no meaning to life. There is imitation. Nothing more. There is nothing from which the little generation can learn. There is no weapon for the son to take from the hands of his father to conquer the forces of darkness and so to bring greatness to the people of earth."

Andrev Andraukov put the thimble back in his vest pocket. The thin soles of his pointed, paint-spattered shoes flapped on the boards as he walked to the cast of St. George and stood for a time gazing absently beyond it.

Suddenly he asked, "Will you like to hear a story?" and immediately began telling it.

Eleven years ago he had taught another drawing class much like their own where the students drew stiff, smudgy pictures of Greek warriors and made spaghetti of Michelangelo's muscles.

But they, too, had worked hard, it had been a good class, and so one day he brought them into the life studio and gave them a woman. He left them alone that first morning and when he returned at noon they lined their drawing boards up against the wall and waited for his criticism.

In regard to the first drawing he observed that the head looked as big as a watermelon and he explained that the human head was nearly the same length as the foot; immediately the class members discovered they had drawn the feet too small. The hand, he told them, demonstrating, would more than cover the face; the class laughed at the tiny hands on all the drawings. How could they have made such mistakes! Well, they would learn.

At the second piece of work he stood facing them with hands at his sides and in a few moments the class discovered what he was doing: they had not drawn the arms long enough. He explained the various uses of the human arm, suggesting that if they would learn to speak truly of function then their drawings would be correct. He looked at their faces and saw the struggle to comprehend. It was a good class.

The next drawing was a tiny thing but when he bent down to peer at it he discovered streaks which were meant to be veins in the back of the model's hand. He held out his own hand with its great veins of red and green twine.

"These are important?" he asked them, and as he lifted his hand high in the air the class watched the veins recede.

So one by one he criticized those first works. When he came to the final drawing he found the figure had been covered by a bathing suit. He thought it was a joke. He turned to the class with a puzzled smile, but seeing their faces he knew it was not a joke.

"Who has drawn this?" he asked. No hand was raised. He returned to the first drawing and asked its owner to leave the studio; he stopped at the second drawing and asked its owner to leave. One by one the students walked out and finally he was left with two drawings but only one student.

"Miss Hugasian," he said, "you draw this morning two pictures?"

She pointed to the first.

"Well, then, this final drawing?"

Her eyes were brilliant with fright but he was patient and at last she said it had been done by Patricia Bettencourt.

"Miss Bettencourt? She is here today?" Then he left the studio and walked up and down the corridor opening each door until finally in the still life room, seated between the casts of *Night* and *Day* with a handkerchief held over her face he saw Patricia Bettencourt. Looking down on her he wondered.

She did not move.

"You are ill?" he asked, bringing a bench close to her and sitting down. "For me today you make very nice drawing, but the bathing suit—"

Andraukov paused in telling the story of Patricia Bettencourt, but he did not stop pacing so the eyes of the students swung steadily back and forth. Once again the only sounds in the atelier were the creak of his shoes and the knocking radiator. From time to time the electric heater on the model's platform hummed faintly. Rain trickled down the windowpanes and finding cracks in the ancient putty seeped and dripped to the floor where puddles were spreading. Before continuing with the story he walked to the door and opened it.

"Miss Bettencourt speaks: 'I did not know model was to be—' This sentence she cannot finish because she weeps. I finish for her. I ask, '—nude?' she does not answer. Shadow like shroud drops on cast of Michelangelo."

Andraukov tasted his mustache and nodded to himself. He walked to the window where he stood with his back to the class; they could see only the thin hair on his skull and his yellow fingers tied into a knot at the tail of his coat.

"Good pupils, the artist is not 'nice.' No, that cannot be. He shall hear at times the voice of God, at times the shriek of each dwarf in the heart and in the soul, and shall obey those voices. But the voice of his fellow man? No. That cannot be. I think he who would create prepares his cross. Yes! It is so. But at his feet no Magdalen. Who, then, shall accuse: 'You are evil!'? 'You are sublime!'? There is no one to speak these words. Miss Bettencourt is in this room? Go now. I do not wish to see your face."

The door to the corridor stood open. Andraukov remained at the window with his back to the students.

"Then I will teach you. I teach of the human body and of the human soul. Now you are young, as once even I was. Even as yours were my nostrils large. Now you shall learn what is the scent of life, and with fingers to touch, with ears to listen. Each fruit you shall taste, of honey and grape, and one day persimmon. I, too, have kissed the hot mouth of life, have shattered the night with cries, have won through such magic millions of years. You will listen now! God is just. He gives you birth. He gives you death. He bids you to look, to learn, and so to live."

The chimes of the university chapel had begun to toll. Wrapping his fingers once again into a knot at the tail of his coat Andrev Andraukov walked out the door. The anatomy lesson was over.

Jay Leyda

MISS EMILY'S MAGGIE

Born in Detroit, Jay Leyda grew up in Dayton, Ohio, now lives in California. He is the author of THE MELVILLE LOG (Harcourt, Brace) and editor of THE PORTABLE MELVILLE (Viking). During the past two years, Mr. Leyda has collected the materials for another documentary biography, applying the method of THE MELVILLE LOG to THE YEARS AND HOURS OF EMILY DICKINSON. *Miss Emily's Maggie* is a fragment from this work-in-progress.

(Miss Emily's Maggie: Copyright, 1953, by Jay Leyda.)

To watch Emily Dickinson sitting in Amherst amid the shades of fading Puritanism has been, too often, the narrow critical frame for examining the contents of her surprising poems and equally surprising life. The other evasion—to pretend that she was totally isolated from *all* surroundings and to examine nothing in her life but its abundant creativity—leaves one just as far from a comprehension of the breathing artist. All these fractional truths and cramping legends tend to hold the fullness of her work and her life out of our reach. It is my belief that the total reality of Emily Dickinson's circumstances and relationships (as far as these can be reconstructed) is the best of all levers to pry off accumulated speculation and romancing in order that we may see what sort of woman it was who wrote those poems. If the result seems contradictory and unsatisfactory and impossibly complex, so much the truer.

To manipulate the larger scale of reference, the tinier scale of the immediate, the intimate, even the trivial offers itself as lubrication. Minutiae can give movement to every sensible generalization about her life, and no analyst of the poems can ignore that life, whether or not he writes of it. To the biographer too sure of what is "unimportant," to the scorner of the momentary, the transiently trivial, Dickinson offers her own formulation—"Forever is composed of Nows."

One of the several harmfully false aspects of the "Emily legend" is that she lived and worked alone. The more one looks into the reality of the matter, the larger grows her circle of friends, acquaintances, correspondents—the more continuous her exchange with other minds and other temperaments. She was ingenious enough to reduce the number of outside pressures to suit the work she was determined to do, but there was a point beyond which she could not and would not go in her social housecleaning. Amherst society bounced off the tight little body of Dickinsons, but there was one Dickinson bent on absorbing every ray of light beamed from any direction—even from within the two Dickinson houses. Everyone who established any degree of contact with the poet writing there requires investigation. The people who worked for the family, for example—should they do no more than slide along the backdrop of this drama, carrying their dish and pitchfork?

There was no real fall from the close cluster of the Dickinson family until Austin's marriage. The family had known sickness, and death outside and on the edges, but Emily Dickinson was 25 before anyone's departure actually changed the family structure. When Austin married Susan Gilbert, the new family thus installed in the newly built house next door made both division and increase in the Dickinson colony on Main Street, now poised above both the center of Amherst to the west and the Irish settlement to the east, down over the new railroad tracks. It had taken Edward Dickinson's sharp dealing and blustering to buy back the Main Street brick house sold fifteen years before, in 1840, to settle the debts of his father's estate. But Edward managed; and the easier life of those past fifteen years in the frame house on Pleasant Street was changed to something more rigid and formal. He had officially retired from the pursuit of political office, and now occupied the position of Amherst's elder statesman. The growing influence of Amherst College added to its Treasurer's social responsibilities; when Massachusetts' governors attended Amherst commencements, they stayed at the Dickinsons, and Wednesday tea at Hon. Edward Dickinson's during Commencement Week became a rite that would alter only with Edward's death.

This all meant more work—the house was larger and Mrs. Dickinson was older. When she had last lived in this house she had had three young children, and employed all the Delias and Catherines and Jameses who made housekeeping possible. But when the Dickinsons had moved to Pleasant Street, the children spent much of the daytime at school, and Mrs. Dickinson got along with less "help"—the girls gradually assuming some of the chores. Both sisters disliked these chores, though Emily's introduction to bread-making at the age of 14 does not seem so dreadful:

> Mother thinks me not able to confine myself to school this term. She had rather I would exercise, & I can assure you I get plenty of that article by staying at home. I am going to learn to make bread to-morrow. So you may imagine me with my sleeves rolled up, mixing flour, milk, saleratus, etc., with a deal of grace . . . I think I could keep house very comfortably if I knew how to cook.

By 1850 she did know how to cook, but the girls were learning resistance, or their mother was weakening, for Edward inserted in the newspaper a somewhat agonized

WANTED.
To hire a girl or woman who is capable of doing the entire work of a small family.

There were no satisfactory applicants—perhaps the Irish girls who sought "constant employment" had not yet arrived in Amherst. With Lavinia away at school and her mother ill, Emily's view of housework grows dim indeed, while washing the noon dishes in the "sink-room," or preparing three meals a day. There is plenty of reasonable self-pity in her letter to Abiah Root even though it is guarded with humor:

> I am yet the Queen of the court, if regalia be dust, and dirt —have three loyal subjects, whom I'd rather relieve from service—Mother is still an invalid, tho' a partially restored one—Father and Austin still clamor for food, and I, like a martyr am feeding them. Wouldn't you love to see me in these bonds of great despair, looking around my kitchen, and praying for kind deliverance, and declaring by "Omai's beard" I never was in such a plight? *My* kitchen I think I called it, God forbid that it was, or ever shall be my own—God keep me from what they call *households*, except that bright one of "faith"!

Her talent for baking, at least, was carried to the brick house in 1855, and she played the roles of prize-winner (75c) and judge in successive Cattle Shows—Division of Rye and Indian Bread. Perhaps because her father demanded that she be the sole author of all his bread, these talents were not displayed so publicly thereafter. Never a "waited-upon" girl, Emily must have been the most relieved member of the household when they acquired their first steady maid.

Irish-born Margaret O'Brien may have joined the Dickinsons on Pleasant Street, but she was a fixture of the brick house —just Emily's age when they moved there—and recognized her own power inside those walls. In early October Margaret would object "to furnace heat on account of bone decrepitudes, so I dwell in my bonnet and suffer comfortably," Emily once reported. When away from home, Emily sent back soothing messages to Margaret, but showed no especial affection for her, and when Margaret married and left in 1865, Emily wrote to her friend, Mrs. Holland:

> Besides wiping dishes for Margaret, I wash them now, while she becomes Mrs. Lawler, vicarious papa to four previous babes. Must she not be an adequate bride?
>
> I winced at her loss, because I was in the habit of her, and even a new rolling-pin has an embarrassing element, but to all except anguish the mind soon adjusts.

It was some time before Margaret was permanently replaced; meanwhile a succession of trial maids passed through the house—the Dickinsons were not comfortable employers. And there were other jobs to be done for the Main Street house: Horace Church, in control of orchard and meadow, was pure Yankee to judge by the recording of his ripe speech ("Squire, ef the Frost is the Lord's Will, I don't popose to stan in the way of it") that Emily sent to Mrs. Holland at the time of his death. There was also a procession of seamstresses—professionally quiet and always changing, because, as one of them said, "The Dickinsons didn't like strangers . . . Outsiders weren't welcome there."

One entire family was semi-attached to the house. Richard and Ann Mathews were immigrants from England who lived behind the Pleasant Street house, and whose sons and daughters fell victim to the diseases of poverty nearly as fast as they came. Our poet's interest in birth and death could have been trained in the Mathews shack—during her lifetime sixteen Mathews children were born, and nine died. The Mathews boys who survived headed the large and fluid corps of Miss Emily's messengers, which included Johnnie Beston, the Kelley boys, and many others. But Pat Mathews (baptized Francis Joseph) had a knack for trouble that must have especially endeared him to Miss Emily:

> *Accident.*—A horse became unmanageable in the street on Tuesday evening about 10 o'clock, near Dea. Mack's, in consequence of the music of the band employed by the serenaders, and plunged in among a parcel of boys, throwing down the son [Pat] of Mr. Richard Matthews,—a boy about 8 years of age, and cutting a gash in the back of his head five or six inches in length. The wound was dressed by Dr. Smith . . . The same boy came very near being killed at the depot only a few days since.

From this date Emily's letters to her brother, then at Harvard

Law School, and to his fiancée, visiting her family in Geneva, New York, report regularly on Pat's condition. The death of another Mathews child, Harriet, brought a bleak November letter to the Hollands:

> I cant stay any longer in a world of death. Austin is ill of fever. I buried my garden last week—our man, Dick, lost a little girl through the scarlet fever. I thought perhaps that *you* were dead . . . Ah! dainty—dainty Death! Ah! democratic Death! Grasping the proudest zinnia from my purple garden,—then deep to his bosom calling the serf's child!
>
> Say, is he everywhere? Where shall I hide my things? Who is alive?

When her uncle, Loring Norcross, died, she sent his daughters sympathy from everyone she saw, including Dick and Ann:

> Even Dick's wife, simple dame, with a kitchen full, and the grave besides, of little ragged ones, wants to know "more about" you, and follows Mother to the door, who has called with bundle.
>
> Dick says, in his wise way, he "shall always be interested in them young ladies." One little young lady of his own, you know, is in Paradise. That makes him tenderer-minded.

Nineteenth-century journalists thought that Ireland would be emptied, deserted, so steady was the stream of Irish to America. What awaited them here bore so little resemblance to paradise that it is hard to realize that famine and rent laws could have produced a hell by comparison with the alien terrors of American cities and villages. In a city the new arrivals had a fighting chance, but those who left the crowded coastal cities for the inland towns of New England in the 1850s found the same poverty of opportunity that there confronted the Jew, the Negro, and those Chinese imported by a North Adams shoe manufacturer who had heard hopefully that Chinese eat very little. As a group the immigrant Irish had even fewer freedoms than American women.

Every fence was employed to isolate the Irishman from the community; his religion, of course, made an excellent barrier in the tightly buttoned Congregationalist villages of western Massachusetts; the only political parties that offered him any pride were the enemies of the dominant Whigs; if he had a taste for irony, he would have appreciated that the whole English repertoire of Celtiphobiac humor and contempt had been imported for development in the American press—with such an advanced newspaper as the *Springfield Daily Republican* being jocular about any local Irish tragedy, or with such a civilized magazine as *Scribner's Monthly*, even as late as the '70s, supporting its shabby Irish anecdotes with threatening editorials.

A symptom of the social level to which the Irish community was confined in Amherst is the cavalier treatment of the "alien" Irish names in its press and town records. One family was variously reported and recorded as Scanlan, Scanlin, Scanel, Scanelly, etc., though it seems to have been always clear that their name was Scannell. It was Dennis Scannell who came to work in the barns and gardens of both Dickinson houses at some time in the mid-1870s. The death from typhoid of his wife Mary in 1876 produced a not unreasonable crisis in his affairs that the Dickinsons helped him to weather. That something was going wrong appeared more than a year after that death when Emily Dickinson sent a half-warning, half-laughing message to her nephew:

> Dennis was happy yesterday, and it made him graceful—
> I saw him waltzing with the Cow, and suspected his status, but he afterward started for your House in a frame that was unmistakable—
>
> You told me he hadn't tasted Liquor since his Wife's decease—then she must have been living at six o'clock last Evening—
>
> I fear for the rectitude of the Barn—

A Christmas later the Scannell difficulties worsened, this time rating local newspaper attention:

> Jerry Scanlan, a lad of 14 summers, who has suddenly disappeared from home once or twice and then returned several days after, wandered away a few days ago and his father, Dennis, was summoned to Springfield, yesterday . . . This morning's *Republican* states that Mr. Burt refused to give the boy up to his father after investigating the case . . .

Miss Dickinson's comment on this, in a letter to Mrs. Holland:

> A Little Boy ran away from Amherst a few Days ago, and when asked where he was going, replied, "Vermont or Asia." . . . My pathetic Crusoe—

But things were somehow worked out—perhaps "arranged" by the passionate, influential Austin—for Dennis stayed to die in the service of "the other house"—with unusual death-bed attentions from Austin, and an obituary-testimonial written by Susan for the town's paper.

Another Irish family watched by Emily was to lose a daughter—and Emily wrote to her Norcross cousins of the death of Margaret Kelley, in 1872:

LEYDA / Miss Emily's Maggie

Little Irish Maggie went to sleep this morning at six o'clock, just the time Grandpa rises, and will rest in the grass at Northampton to-morrow. She has had a hard sickness, but her awkward little life is saved and gallant now. Our Maggie is helping her mother put her in the cradle.

By this time "our Maggie" knew that she was in the Dickinson house to stay. It was almost four years before the gap in the household, left by Margaret O'Brien's marriage, was filled, and the young woman who came in March 1869 was to be the pillar of the home and a blessing to Miss Emily and Miss Vinnie. Margaret Maher was more than cook and maid to the Dickinson sisters; for both she was a protective bulwark—keeping intrusion from the poet, and pain from the poet's sister. Emily Dickinson's letters show a more active function for Maggie, too—a fount of stubbornness and decision and invincible belief. Her healthy presence made her as vital to the skeptic poet as any member of "the peculiar race" of Dickinsons. Yet Maggie Maher first entered the house for a brief time, while waiting for a better job, and was most reluctant to stay.

Past 20, she was well equipped for independence: with her sister and brothers she had made the journey from Parish Kilusty in Tipperary. The boys may have come to Amherst to help build the railroad that was begun with so much jubilation and mouth-watering commercial prospects in 1852. When settled, Maggie, perhaps alone, returned to Ireland to bring their father and mother to the new Amherst home. The older daughter Mary soon married an earlier Irish arrival, Thomas Kelley, and when her parents died and her brothers departed, home meant the Kelley house to Maggie. But the Maher family was intact when the youngster Maggie took her first job, working for the Boltwoods.

Against the considerable odds of time and chance Maggie's letters to Mrs. Clarinda Boltwood have been preserved, and in them we can hear her actual intonation, not only because their Irish accent is recorded phonetically, but the very flow of her straight, dignified speech, is directly attached to her warm heart—"youre letter this wet evening was a grate treete to me for I watched for it very eagrly" and "I eather dreaming or thinking of you I dont know what the reason" and "youre letter of Monday came to me last night I was glad to see youre hand Writting on the out side and to read what it caintain on insoid . . ."

When the younger Boltwoods left Amherst for Hartford, Maggie Maher took other work, though always with the hope of rejoining her beloved family:

You spoke of I going to work to youre mother with anny when I get true with my one work But I dont care where a weeks wages go I shant charge it you you nede not fere . . . I dont wish to go to Work untill I here whether you go or not then I will try to get a plase

She did get to Hartford, but a few months later—in June 1868—a double tragedy brought her back to Amherst and kept her there:

(June 4)
My letter will give you a grate surpris But it is hard for me My dear Father is so bad that We dont expect he to live only a few days so that you see that My Joy is turned to griefe Father only New me I am glad that his reasons to Now me and that I am here [to] take care of him as poor sister is Worn out from Care it is Write that I should care My parants as there is now other thing that I can do for them

Her father died and within the week:

(June 16)
This is a World of trouble our trouble was Never so much as it is at preasant. My dear Brother Thomas [Kelley] was almost killed last saterday at 4 o clock he still lives But we dont know how long he may My dear sister what will she do the father of seven children the lord may comfort her . . .
he fell 30 feet from a building . . . I dont know whether it is day or night sence I left hartford

(June 25)
Brother is a little more comfortabler than he have been sence he was hurt docter Dole tends him 2 a day his arm was not set yet but it will on sunday next with gods help we cant tell how it is going to be yet all say that it got to be cut of[f] . . . the dath of dear father lies in a cloud of sadness on me and I can't get over it he died in my armes and I never can forget it I must hope he is better of[f] . . . But how nice it would be to have all friends lay down and die so that we would not have to suffer the loss of those that gone

Maggie stayed in Amherst, near her broken family; among her several employers was Edward Dickinson. The senior Boltwoods, still living in Amherst, were irritated to find their Maggie committed, even temporarily, to the Dickinsons—there was a scene, reported by Maggie to the junior Boltwoods in Hartford:

LEYDA / Miss Emily's Maggie

(1869, March 2)

... I waited all this time to tell you when I would go to california No, that if nothing dont happen to me I will go the first of May ... I will lave my plase the first of April to get ready My oldest Brother will meet me in Panama ... I was not in to father Boltwood sence I went to see you only once and then no one spoke to me father went true the kitchen But he did not spak to me ... the reason a I was told the[y] have to me is when I left Mrs. tolcott they came down after me to go to work there But I could not go for I was ingaged to Mr. Dickenson 2 weeks before ... I dont want to disapoint any person or Brake my word if i be Poor and working for my living I will alway try to do rite ...

She has no eagerness to stay with the Dickinsons:

... I like it very well But it is not my home my home is with you I am as strange here as if I came here to work yester

Vinnie's cats, with whom Emily was always at war, were getting on Maggie's nerves, too. But she was finding it harder to leave the Dickinsons than she had guessed. The California plan had to be forgotten—and Mr Dickinson had to have his way.

(March 24)

We have so many cats to take care of that I would like to have some help But for I ntend to lave very sone I would be very cross to them But I will keep my temper for a nother while I am always very patient ... Brother tommy wrote to me last week and told me not come out there for there is to much sickness there he have the eagy very bad

(April 6)

... I have tried every way to go to hartford to live this summer but I must stay here for the sumer I tried to get a girl for them But the[y] would not take any one that I would get it is what Mr Dicksom said he would Pay me as much more wages soner then let me go so that I have desided to stay for the Preasent I went to Pa[l]mer the day that Mr. Boltwood was up here to get the girl that worket for them before me and she would come But the[y] would not take her ... But there [is] one thing sure I will do as I like when I will get a chance without giving much notice all that is in the house is very fond of me and dose every thing for my comfort in fact the[y] are to kind to there help the only reason that I dislike is that

I am lonsom in Amherst . . . last night that I settled with
Mr. D if I would lave Now and go to you it would caus
them to be very angry with us all so we will wait for a
nother time the[y] get very excited when you write to
me for fere that [I] will go to you   there is one grate trouble that I have not half enough of work so that I must play
with the cats to Plase Miss Vinny you know how I love
cats

For Mr. Dickinson to threaten "to be very angry with us all"
affected more than Maggie's income. Her niece Margaret was
serving in "the other house," and, too, no vulnerable person in
Amherst wished to excite Mr. D's anger. The Boltwoods were
already receding into a pink past:

(November 2)
I think you for youre kind offer and also hope you will
plas excuse me for not writting to you before   it was not
the reason that I did not love you for I always love you
and Mr B and the Boys and you alwas was a kind mother
to me so kind that I fere that I Never could Pay you for
youre care and interest in me . . . youre offer to me is
what I wold like to do But I cant lave Sister Mary this
winter for she needs me for comfort . . .

But Maggie had found her place in life and history; Clarinda
Boltwood had lost a good maid—Emily Dickinson had found
a priceless ally. A letter written this same month to Cousin
Louise Norcross shows us that she was beginning to guess the
value of Margaret Maher (Tim is the new coachman, and
Dick the horse):

Tim is washing Dick's feet, and talking to him now and
then in an intimate way. Poor fellow, how he warmed
when I gave him your message! The red reached clear to
his beard, he was so gratified; and Maggie stood as still
for hers as a puss for patting. The hearts of these poor
people lie so unconcealed you bare them with a smile.

There is a family photograph of this time that tells us more
about Maggie. In the center sits her handsome, one-armed
brother-in-law, Tom Kelley; on his left is his daughter Margaret, then working for Austin and Susan; and on his right
stands the pleasantly sturdy figure of Maggie—wide mouth,
inquiring eyes; both Margarets are wearing identically styled
dresses, perhaps giving the occasion for the group photograph.

The outwardly placid life of the Dickinson family was about
to explode in a series of crises from which it would never fully
recover—unless the transmutation of tragedy into poetry can
be called "recovery." Edward Dickinson's brief return to legislative life, for the railroad's sake, was unwise: the heat of

argument and of Boston brought apoplexy and sudden death. His wife's dependent life was shattered, and on the first anniversary of his death she was paralyzed with a stroke. The lives of the two daughters and Maggie now revolved around a half-lifeless center that demanded their time and attention. In the confusion something was allowed to happen to one of the family's dependents that Edward's children may never have forgiven themselves: Dick Mathews was admitted to the Alms House, where he died ten days later.

The community of Amherst was aware that the brick house on Main Street housed the most dangerous type of alien— a poet. And Emily Dickinson must have sensed the taboos placed around her, so sensitive was she to the atmospheres and dramas of the village. Though we would call her an "insider," to the town she was an "outsider"; and they were willing to believe any gossip or "revelations" about the Dickinson sisters: madness was one of the gentler accusations. How often Emily must have looked at Maggie as a fellow exile—for community snobbery was directed as much against the "lower class" Irish as against the "upper class" Dickinsons, especially that queer writing woman! There is a wistful poem written in that house about Paradise, ending:

> Maybe Eden aint so lonesome
> As New England used to be!

In 1880 there was a scene that Emily Dickinson had to report to the son of her recently dead friend, Samuel Bowles:

> Our friend your Father was so beautifully and intimately recalled Today that it seemed impossible he had experienced the secret of Death—
>
> A servant who had been with us a long time and had often opened the Door for him, asked me how to spell "Genius," yesterday— I told her and she said no more—
>
> Today, she asked me what "Genius" meant? I told her none had known—
>
> She said she read in a Catholic Paper that Mr. Bowles was "the Genius of Hampshire," and thought it might be that past Gentleman . . .
>
> I congratulate you upon his immortality, which is a constant stimulus to my Household . . .

As a personality seal for the letter, she asked the "servant"— Maggie—to address the envelope, a typically half-hidden Dickinsonian gesture. When, later in the year, Maggie was ill with typhoid fever at the Kelley house, "Her Grieved Mistress" sent another typical gesture—few dared to be playful with the very ill.

> The missing Maggie is much mourned, and I am going out for "black" to the nearest store.
>
> All are very naughty, and I am naughtiest of all.
>
> The pussies dine on sherry now, and humming-bird cutlets.
>
> The invalid hen took dinner with me, but a hen like Dr T[aylor]'s horse soon drove her away. I am very busy picking up stems and stamens as the hollyhocks leave their clothes around.
>
> What shall I send my weary Maggie? Pillows or fresh brooks?

She knew when not to be playful, too. In the following year she wrote to her Norcross cousins:

> Maggie's brother is killed in the mines, and Maggie wants to die, but Death goes far around to those that want to see him. If the little cousins would give her a note—she does not know I ask it—I think it would help her begin, that bleeding beginning that every mourner knows.

Emily Dickinson seemed never to tire of defining Maggie's virtues and qualities, for herself as well as for her friends. To Mrs. Holland she wrote, "Maggie, good and noisy, the North Wind of the Family, but Sweets without a Salt would at last cloy—" and she sympathizes with the Norcross sisters in their new Cambridge quarters: "I am glad the housekeeping is kinder; it is a prickly art. Maggie is with us still, warm and wild and mighty . . ."

"With us still"—Maggie seemed *always* there—to give emergency treatment when it was inconvenient to summon Dr. Fish —to feed Austin an early breakfast when his own household couldn't be bothered—to help out "at the other house" in a crisis—to ease Vinnie away from the door when an arousing enemy called—to slip clandestine letters under the door of Emily's bedroom (Emily aimed to make all her correspondence so private that it all became slightly clandestine)—to take Emily's excuses, in the forms of clover, rose or jasmine, to the door when an uninvited visitor knocked. The friends of the house knew Maggie as well as did the house's antagonists: when Christmas packages were sent to the Dickinson sisters, something for Maggie was packed, too.

The instructions left by Emily Dickinson for her funeral sound like the directions for a pageant of her allegiances. Following her father she was also to avoid the hearse, with its mock solemnity; he had been borne to the graveyard by the professors and successes of Amherst; she asked to be carried by the six Irishmen she had known. Led by Thomas Kelley of the single strong arm, Dennis Scannell, Stephen Sullivan, Patrick Ward, Daniel Moynihan and Dennis Cashman carried Emily Dickinson to the place she still occupies. When Edward Dickinson was buried, the town had closed in his honor, but his daughter's plan was quieter: she asked to be carried out the back door, around through the garden, through the opened barn from front to back, and then through the grassy fields to the family plot, always in sight of the house.

When Emily Dickinson's poems found an audience, and a photograph of her was needed, Maggie offered a daguerreotype that the family (including the sitter) had disliked and discarded. Without her love we would not have the only photographic image of a great poet.

There is a letter that Margaret Maher wrote in 1891, five years after the poet's death:

Vinnia has not being very well this last few weeks . . . to tell the truth of it she is not strong, and cant get a long with things that she have no write to be troubled with   it will always be so as far as I see   all are well around here   But a few are happy . . .

We have 5 cats 2 in the house and 3 in the Barren all well and good apetited so far . . .

YOUR SERVENT

Miss, Emely.'s and Vinnia's

Maggie

[All but one of Margaret Maher's letters quoted are in the Burton Historical Collection of the Detroit Public Library, which has permitted their use here; Maggie's concluding letter, and the letter from Mrs. Eastman, are owned by Harvard College Library. The several already published letters are used with the permission of Millicent Todd Bingham, for THE LETTERS OF EMILY DICKINSON, edited by Mabel Loomis Todd (1931), and the permission of Harvard University Press, publishers of EMILY DICKINSON'S LETTERS TO DR. AND MRS. JOSIAH GILBERT HOLLAND, edited by Theodora Van Wagenen Ward (1951); the lines from "What is Paradise? Who live there?" are quoted from BOLTS OF MELODY, edited by Mabel Loomis Todd and Millicent Todd Bingham (Harper & Brothers, 1945); the incident of the daguerreotype is mentioned in ANCESTORS' BROCADES p. 224) by Millicent Todd Bingham (Harper & Bros., 1945).]

ALEX'S FUN: WELL BOILED

A GAME OF FANCY

R. S. Niedelman

Twenty-two-year-old R. S. Niedelman was born in New York City. He is a graduate of Queens College, New York, where he edited the literary magazine and won the first Annual John Golden Award for Creative Writing. He is presently at work on a novel.

The room was softly silent and warm, from the in-the-wall radiator. Alex reached for a candy, swallowed it quickly, then took another. At first, three days ago, he had let the candies linger on his tongue because he didn't believe the man. He didn't believe he could have all the candy he wanted. He just didn't believe it, even when the man showed him the ribboned boxes in the cabinet. Now he tasted his tongue and knew the promise was real and cherry.

He had been playing jump rope with Sue and Judy only they weren't fair, so he walked away and threw a stone. Then the man came over and said My, he threw just like a big league baseball pitcher, so Alex took a deep breath and smiled. The man started to talk about so many things that Alex became bored and told him he had to go home for supper. The man said if he would go with him he could have anything he wanted and Alex said No, he had to go eat. The man placed his palm on Alex's shoulder and bent down.

—I'll tell you what else I'll do if you come with me. If you come with me, I'll boil you in a nice pot of water.

Alex laughed and liked the man, who was friendly and funny to say such a thing. The man took him to his car and then to his house, where Alex had all he could eat, including two boxes of candy in the evening. The next day, he woke up and saw the man standing next to him.

—What's your name?

—Mr. Bomprey. Call me Mr. B or Harold if you like.

Alex laughed again. So many funny things were happening, but he felt he should go home and tell his mother where he had been. Mr. Bomprey was ruffled when he heard this suggestion; he sat down on the side of the bed and told Alex that if he stayed with him, he'd give him a bath at night, a nice warm bath. Alex was used to taking his own baths, and he told this to his friend, who answered that it was much more fun if someone else gave you the bath. Alex thought about it for a moment, then said yes, he would stay.

—That's a smart boy. See you tonight.

—But where are you going?

—I'm going to work. Don't worry. My mother will take care of you.

He left; five minutes later, a heavy woman with one earring came into the bedroom, told him get-up, get-up, go-wash, go-wash, through there, like a parrot. He washed and dressed, finding his clothes on the hamper in the bathroom. When he re-entered the room, the woman was sitting on a high black stool, throwing darts at a target which she had placed at the head of the bed.

—So you think it's funny, do you?

—I'm sorry if I laughed. I never saw anyone doing *that* before.

—There are lots of things you haven't seen. Want to try a shot?

—If you'd let me.

—Here, take a dart. No, don't stand there. You have to sit right where I'm sitting.

—Don't get up. I can throw it from here.

—I have to get up. It's a rule of the game and we've got to follow rules. Now, sit here on the stool.

Alex sat down and threw the dart. They played at the game all morning, except for a few minutes when Mrs. B went downstairs to get him breakfast. Each time he hit the target she placed a candy between his lips; by mid-morning he had become quite expert. After lunch, which he ate while sitting on the high stool, he was taken to the kitchen, where Mrs. B taught him to bake cookies. The molds had animal shapes; he blocked out mostly turtles, his favorite. He ate the cookies while they were still warm (you could do *any*thing here) and got a stomach ache. Mrs. B took him to her bedroom where she rubbed his stomach till the pain disappeared. At six, Harold came home with a gallon of ice cream, which they ate for supper. Afterwards, Mrs. B knitted, while Harold read the paper and did the crossword puzzle. Alex became bored.

—I think I'd better go home now.

Harold put aside the paper and came over to him.

—Don't you remember what I promised you this morning?

Alex looked down at his body.

—You mean the bath? I guess I don't need a bath. I'm clean.

—This isn't a bath to get clean. It's a different kind.

—Well, if you'll let me call my mother.

—Go ahead.

There was no answer, and Alex decided the call could wait until the following day. Harold told his mother to get the bath ready. After the preparations were made, Harold tested the heat of the water, then called Alex, who came into the bathroom wearing one of Harold's pajama tops.

—Look at you now!

—I guess I do look sort of funny.

They both laughed, and Harold began to slip the top over Alex's head. He did this very slowly, and the material tickled Alex's body. The water was pleasantly warm; Alex let it play around him and then he reached for the wash cloth.

—Alex, you just lie back, and let me do all the work. There, how does *this* feel?

The bath taught Alex a new kind of funny, a strange, unheard-of funny. The next morning he had no intention of calling his mother to tell her of his whereabouts.

After Harold left, Mrs. B had a new game for Alex and it was played with the telephone. She took a large and worn phonebook from the shelf underneath the foyer table, and told Alex to thumb through it and point to a name at random. His finger found Remsen A. Mrs., 336 Hayvy Av. Mrs. B picked up the receiver and called a florist, ordering a dozen American beauty roses for Mrs. Remsen. Then she told Alex to get her Harold's evening paper; when he gave it to her, she proceeded to call various stores that had advertised, ordering for Mrs. Remsen percale pillow cases, two brassieres and a set of living room furniture, all to be sent C.O.D. A Mrs. Grale, W., would receive, within the next few days, twelve hollow-stemmed beer glasses and a "douche for comfort, three ninety-eight." Alex danced around the phone during the calls, and was greatly disappointed when Mrs. B suggested it was time for lunch. After they had eaten (there were some leftover cookies, which Alex devoured) he wanted to return to the morning's game. Mrs. B said they had to wait for the men to deliver a special surprise for him. While waiting, the two sat at the window, each holding a small magnet with which they pretended to draw all the passers-by into the house. In mid-afternoon, the doorbell rang. Alex ran to answer it and found two men in coveralls standing before a large crate which looked as though it could not possibly fit through the door.

—It's here, oh, I thought it would never get here. It's a surprise for our little Alex.

—I don't know what the hell it is, lady, but it weighs a ton.

—You mean you don't know what's in there?

—No, the boss wouldn't tell us.

—Well, maybe it's just as well. If he had wanted you to know, he would have told you. Please bring it in.

—I don't know if we can get it through the door.

—Oh, I'm sure you can. Harold wouldn't have had it shipped if he knew it wouldn't fit.

The men brought it in, and asked where she wanted it set down. Mrs. B said it would be fine if they left it right in the living room, yes, right there, in the center, and thank you, good-by. Alex could hardly contain himself; he asked a thousand questions about the crate's contents.

—You'll have to wait till Harold comes home before you can see what's in it. I'm sure you never saw anything like it before.

Harold came home promptly at six.

—I'm glad to see they brought it. Well, little man, you're going to see the surprise of your life. Just wait.

Harold went over to the crate with a crowbar, and began a slow struggle to remove the nails. The sides came off, revealing a round object at least four feet in height which was wrapped in various hues of tissue paper. Before Harold slipped the tissue off, he told Alex to turn around and not look until he was told. As Alex heard the last of the crinkly paper fall to the floor, he whirled around.

—What *is* it?

—Well, what does it look like?

—It looks like a big pot, I guess.

—That's just what it is, an urn. A big urn.

—But what's it for?

—Don't you remember my promise the first time we met? Don't tell me you've forgotten already?

—No, no, I don't think I've forgotten.

—You have. I know you have. Mother, can't you see he has?

—Dreadful!

—Now I remember. You said you were going to boil me and I laughed. Sure I remember. Don't look so sad, Harold; I remember.

—That's good. Come, let's have a closer look at it.

—What's that, underneath?

—That's an oven; it heats the water. You see, we fill the top with water, light the bottom and the water boils.

Alex walked closer to the urn, and touched it tentatively with his finger. Opening the door to the bottom part, he noticed it lined with coils.

—Is it electric?

—Yes, it's very modern. We plug it in the wall and boomp, it lights up. It's very modern.

—Will the water be very hot; will it burn?

—Don't be silly. Did I burn you last night? No, of course not. Would you like your bath in here tonight, instead of in the tub?

—No, I don't think so. I think I'd rather have it in the tub.

—That's a smart boy, isn't he Harold. Saves special things for special occasions.

—Do you think I could call my mother now? I think I better tell her about all this.

—Of course you can. Go ahead.

Alex told the operator the number and waited for three rings before he heard the receiver lifted.

—It's me, Mom. Yes, it's really me. Well, what's the matter, why don't you say something? Say something! Sure I'm all right, why shouldn't I be. I'm here, that's where I am. I don't know the address, but it's here. Yes, I'm okay, why do you keep asking? It's very nice, I'm having a good time and it's much better than anything else. I'm with Mr. Bomprey. Yes, Bomprey. His mother, too, Mrs. Bomprey. How do I know if he has a father? Oh, no, he's not a kid. He's a man, he's a man. I don't know; I guess I'll be home whenever I want. I like it here. I told you, I don't *know* the address. Okay, I'll ask him.

—He says it's 69 Under Avenue and that you'll never find it, so I guess you better not look. Hello? Hello? Mom! Aunt Jean? What happened to Mom? Oh, all right, I'll wait. Yes, I'm all right, Jean. They treat me like an adult. I do all the things an adult does. They talk to me like I was big and I do all the things they do. I eat ice cream for supper and cookies for lunch. You'd love it here because they'd give you the same thing. And they're going to boil me in a big pot. Harold gave me a bath like I never had. Listen, tell Mom to stop carrying on, I can hear her all the way over here, and she doesn't care what I do anyway. I'll be home soon.

Alex replaced the receiver, and Harold told his mother to get the bath ready. Alex said it was early, but Harold told him the sooner we got up the sooner the fun starts. Alex remembered the newness of the night before, and he ran to his room to slip on the oversized pajamas. They had been in the bathroom an hour and a half when Mrs. B came in and said they had had enough fun for one night. Harold told her to get the hell out of the room.

Alex slept well and late, until ten-thirty, the latest he had ever slept. Before he had gone to sleep, Harold told him that he was going to be boiled tomorrow, which was today. Alex hoped to dream about it; instead, he dreamed of his mother and how she cried because he was lost to her. But she didn't cry real tears, just glass ones, and he was vaguely disappointed. He had been up less than ten minutes when the door to his room opened and Mrs. B walked in with a breakfast tray, heaped with chocolates, cakes, soda and popcorn. He reached for a handful of the popcorn.

—We mustn't be too greedy, must we? That's child's play, you know.

—Child's play?

—That's what I said.

—But this is what you and Harold eat; I see you eat all this.

—Oh, that's what we eat when we're with you. We never eat that when we're alone.

—No, I *know* this is what adults eat. Adults always eat what they want, and they'd want to eat this. My Aunt Jean says she could live on just candy and cake.

—Go ahead then. Eat it. You might as well, I suppose.

After the last bit of soda had been swallowed, he picked out the small pieces of popcorn stuck between his teeth and then got up to dress. Lying on the chair next to the bed was a clean starched shirt, a bright four-in-hand, gray flannel trousers and a tweed jacket.

—What are those?

—They're for you. You want to be an adult, so you might as well wear what they wear. Go ahead, put them on.

Alex felt very uncomfortable in his new clothes, and for an hour he struggled under the tightness of the new collar. Mrs. B didn't teach him anything, or play with him very much; she went around the house dusting and putting things in order, always reminding him that this was a day of no usual standing. It was so important that Harold was going to be home in the afternoon to make final preparations. Alex sat in the softly silent room, tasting the cherry center and looking forward to Harold's return.

Harold came home at three.

—Come with me to the room, Alex. I want to get a few things ready.

—What room?

—The room where we're going to boil you. Come on, let's go.

—Maybe I'd better call home.

—Go ahead, if you like, but you're going to miss out on a lot of fun. That's it, come along. And Mother, when the men come, tell them to bring the urn upstairs to the room. And don't forget to cover it up again.

The attic was very stuffy. Harold took a key from his pocket and opened a door to the left.

—Wait out here till I get the light on.

The room disappointed Alex. It was just any attic room, full of all sorts of junk and trunks that he had in his own home.

—Don't be disappointed. We all have rooms like this, I know. But it's not the room that counts, it's what you do with it.

—What's that?

—The tapestry? That was my father. My mother embroidered him. She was very good at embroidering, but she gave it up when he died. Now don't be frightened; he won't bite.

—But he's so ugly. He scares me.

—He wasn't really that bad-looking. I'll cover him up if you'd like.

Harold threw an old sheet over the tapestry.

—I think I hear the men coming.

The delivery men brought in the urn, placed it down and wiped their foreheads.

—What is that thing?

—I know it must be pretty frustrating to carry it around and not know what's in it. Thanks for bringing it up.

—Do they work for you?

—Yes, they do. Now, go to your room and get undressed, go ahead. Just throw the robe over you.

—I don't have one.

—Yes you do. There's one on your bed. Hurry back.

After Alex left, Harold and Mrs. B filled the urn with water. When it was filled almost to the top, Harold plugged in the socket; Alex returned as the water was coming to a slow boil.

—Go out now, Mother. I want to speak to Alex.

Alex stood in the doorway, a bright red robe flung over his shoulders. Harold beckoned him enter, and the boy edged his way into the room.

—Don't be afraid. This will be a lot of fun, you'll see.

—Will it hurt?

—I don't think so. If it does, it will hurt only for a while.

—I don't know if I want to go into it.

—Well of course you do. Haven't you liked the baths I've been giving you?

—Yes, I've liked them.

—Well, this one will be better than all of them. And once you're through with it, you'll be altogether different. Now, come on, take off your robe.

Alex handed the robe to Harold.

—Why are you looking at me like that?

—Just looking. Come on, I'll give you a hand.

—Can I touch the water with my toe first?

—If you want to be a sissy you can.

Harold stepped onto the chair placed next to the urn.

—Now, stand up here next to me, Alex, and close your eyes. It will be over before you know it.

Alex closed his eyes as Harold called his mother back into the room. He felt Harold's hands under his armpits as he was lifted from the chair.

—Please, Harold, I don't want to go, please.

—Sorry, Alex, it's too late now.

As his body touched the water he screamed, and then he screamed louder. His eyes would not open as he thrashed about, and his cries grew longer and more intense. Over the din he heard Harold:

—Listen to him scream, Mother. And to think, this is only the beginning.

CUTLERY

The house looked like a party and Alex was happy, even though he knew the cakes, meats and wines were for the baby and not for him. The night before, he lay awake in his bed, hearing his mother's slippered feet paddle across the cool linoleum in the kitchen, making final preparations with the caterer they had hired. He fell asleep in the warm odors of simmering meats and perfumed fish.

But now he was confused. His parents told him that the party was a morning party, and he had never heard of that before. Parties were for two o'clock and you ring the bell and give the present. This certainly was something special.

—Don't touch anything yet.

—I'm just looking.

The dining room buffet was covered with their best doilies. In the center was the whisky decanter, and on each end was a bottle of shimmering red wine, surrounded with cut-glass goblets. Everything looked delicious and Alex could hardly wait for the people to come.

—How is Richard going to know the party is for him, Daddy?

—Oh, he'll know.

—How can he? He's too little.

—Well, maybe we'll tell him about it sometime. Then he'll know.

His father walked away to rearrange the candies on the small bridge table in the corner. Alex sucked the juice from a fish ball, then chewed the firm flesh. He followed his father.

—Will we get any presents?

—The baby will.

—Still, maybe they'll bring me something, because I'm his brother.

He started to whistle.

—Alex, not now. You'll wake him up.

—Isn't he going to get up for his party?

—He'll get up but not now.

The doorbell rang, and within fifteen minutes the room became crowded with relatives he had not seen or remembered and with neighbors whom he saw everyday. There was Aunt Rita from Newark, Grandpa from two blocks away, Cousin Harriet who lived alone in Greenwich Village, Uncle Mansfield, the out-of-town college teacher who was divorced. They all pinched his cheek (Cousin Harriet asked him if he wanted wine), and told him how big he'd gotten.

—What a big boy. Almost a man.

This part was nice. This was the nicest part of meeting relatives. They told you how big you were getting. But then they left you and spoke to each other about business, travel, *their* children and about relatives who weren't present. Alex took another fish ball, and he heard Harriet speaking to Uncle Mansfield about a New Bohemia and of a writer with a foreign name. She reached for a fish ball which he was going to take originally, but he felt it was too large and impolite.

—I hate to come to these cutting things. Can't they give the child something so he doesn't feel it?

—I guess not. Otherwise they would.

—But to just cut into him like that. It's medieval, I tell you.

Mansfield saw Alex listening, and he started to speak of the writer with the foreign name. But Alex had heard. The fish ball felt stuck in his throat. He went over to his father who was pouring a drink for a neighbor.

—What is it, Alex?

—I want to ask you something.

—Go ahead. Ask me.

—I want to ask you alone.

—All right. Come on.

He put his arm around Alex and led him to the foyer.

—Now, what is it?

—What are they going to do to the baby?

—Do?

—I mean, do they do something to him?

—Well, there's a little ceremony, that's all. We had the same thing for you. Who told you they do something?

Alex was going to tell him he had heard Harriet speaking,

but before he could, his father left him and walked over to a short, stout man who had just come in. The man had a short beard, white and sort of yellow; Alex had seen him once before in the synagogue, praying very loud. In his hand he carried a small bag, like a doctor. But a doctor's bag didn't jingle. The man nodded to Alex's father and walked directly into the kitchen. He heard his mother answer yes, the water was boiling. Alex went to his father's side.

—Why is the water boiling?
—Alex, why don't you go talk with Aunt Rita or somebody? You haven't seen her in so long.
—Why is the water boiling?
—Because it's part of the ceremony, that's all.
—What's in the bag?
—Instruments.
—What kind?
—Look, Alex, all the man does is hold the instruments over the baby's head and say a prayer. That's all. He says a prayer, the baby is blessed and that's all there's to it. Now, go speak to Aunt Rita.

The man in the kitchen asked if everyone was there so they could begin, and his mother said yes. Then the doorbell rang, and the rabbi, with thick glasses and a mustache, was in the room, shaking hands and saying here I am unofficially, just as a friend, how are you? The rabbi called Alex old-timer. His father had taken him to the synagogue just three times and each time he was there, the rabbi called him old-timer and when is the old-timer going to start Sunday School? Only he would never start, he would never go, they could tear him to pieces and he would never go. Not to the smelly building, the old men blowing noses, meaningless mumblings on hard seats, ladies sitting in a separate section, closed windows, standing up and sitting down, Amens when you have to say Amen, black hats so God can't see your dark thoughts. They could tear him to pieces, he would never go.

Suddenly, the talking and chewing sounds stopped, and the room settled in a quiet hush. Alex glanced into the kitchen, where he saw the man in black reach into his bag and remove a long, slender knife. He slid his finger along the blade and dropped it into the boiling water. Putting his hands behind his back, he hummed and waited. Alex pushed past Harriet, who had her back to the kitchen, and ran to his room. As he closed the door, he saw his grandfather carrying the squirming baby on a small, blue pillow toward the kitchen.

Alex stood with his back to his door, then went to the window. It wasn't full autumn yet. The leaves had begun to fall from the trees, but slowly and with little determination. He swam back to the summer just passed, to the day when the sun was cool lemon yellow, flat, pasted and lonely against the pale blue sky. He had been watching the slow, sideward drift of a sailboat in the channel when his mother called.

—Alex. Didn't you hear me?
—No, I guess I didn't.
—Come help me down to the beach.

He walked behind her, head down, hoping no one knew she was his mother. The few scattered people on the beach stared at her, and it was because she was swollen and bloated. He stepped on a sharp pebble and wanted to cry out but she would ask him what happened and then everyone would surely know about them. He hopped silently on his right foot until they reached her beach chair.

—Alex, help me sit down.

He held her arm as she sank heavily into the chair. The chair had been new in July; now it was shabby and ripping at the seams. Alex cherished a secret dream that it would be stolen from the locker one night. He was thankful that the locker boy always had it on the beach before they came down. His mother put her legs on the foot rest and moaned.

—What's the matter?
—He kicked me. He's been kicking me all day.
—Does it hurt?
—Of course it hurts. Would I moan if it didn't hurt?
—Did I ever kick you?
—All babies kick. You kicked too.

He looked closely at her stomach. She had once been perfect and not swollen, but now the bathing suit, with its flaming flamingoes and green palms, strained against her midsection.

—I can't see him kicking.
—Well, if you touch my stomach you can feel it. Go ahead. Put your hand there.
—No, no. I don't want to. Can I go play by the rocks?
—I don't want you to go into the water yet.
—I won't go in. I'll just stay near the shore.
—Stay where I can see you.

The sand was getting warmer, and Alex liked the feel of it slipping between his toes. He skitted in and out of the stiff umbrellas and leaped over casual blankets. The beach was settling itself under more people now, and he smiled happily. No one would know who he was, not even his name. If they asked him, he could say he was a pearl diver by trade who was some day going to swim the ocean. They would rub him in oil, not the kind of oil that lady was rubbing on her arms, but real thick oil, a warm grease. He wouldn't feel the water under all that. He would kiss his parents good-by and his baby brother or sister, and maybe they'd want to come alongside in a boat but he wouldn't let them. He'd go to Portugal, to the street he had seen in *World Geography* that was paved with glistening stones. Some were brighter even than the ones he had found this summer. He'd have to take some of his along, as a gift, and they'd put them right in the center, the exact center, of the street.

—Alex, hello, you little dreamer.
—Oh, hello, Mrs. Shale.
—How's mama today?
—She's fine.
—Soon you're going to be a big brother to somebody.
—I know.
—Do you want a brother or sister?
—I don't care.
—Oh, you must care. Now, tell me, which do you want?
—I said I don't care.

Mrs. Shale shifted in her seat.
—Where's mama sitting?
—Over there.

Alex continued toward the rocks, hearing Mrs. Shale say to the woman next to her that he was a darling child. The tide had not come in yet, and small crabs darted in and out of the puddles at the base of the barnacled rocks. He climbed the one shaped like the bow of an ancient ship and reached over the side for a crab. He lifted one around its middle and watched it struggle to free itself. Then he threw it as far as he could, the soft shell making hardly a sound as it hit a rock and slid slowly out of sight.

Now, Richard was an autumn baby; he had come two weeks ago, on a Friday. His mother said I think it's coming and was taken to the hospital. While she was gone, he lived with Jean, who treated him very nicely. She never became angry, even when he poked Bubi, her parrot, with the handle of a backscratcher. Bubi knew only one word, stop, and she would never say it unless really annoyed, but Jean said her Bubi didn't even know what the word meant. Alex was not really fond of the bird, and he had several unpleasant dreams in which Bubi grew to huge and revenging proportions.

Jean took him to the park every day, and Alex spent most of the time in the reptile house, watching the turtles so still and in their shells. Jean said why don't you watch the monkeys, but he liked the turtles and stayed with them. Jean let him eat a great deal of popcorn and called him her own little boy. The night before he was to go home, she took him in her arms and cried. It was hard to understand, but he let her hold him to her.

The first thing he did when he returned home was rush into his mother's room to see if it was gone, and it was. The huge lump was gone; she was wonderfully flat and straight under the blanket. He kissed her and asked if she were all right. He wanted to see the baby, and she told him he was still in the hospital because he was premature, he came a little early and would be home in a day or two. The baby came into the apartment in blue blankets and silken pillows, bringing with him a fresh and delightful odor. He could see him once a day, only he never really saw him because he was all covered up. He heard him though; he heard him cry and he heard his mother mumble angrily as she changed his diapers.

—We're going to put the baby in your room, Alex. Will you watch him at night, like a good brother?

His desk was taken out, his bed moved and the baby was firmly installed in the rearranged room. At night, he would tiptoe to the crib and watch the child breathe, looking pretty and something soft to touch. Then the baby would scream and his mother would rush in to pick up the red, squirming bundle. Alex would rush into his bed and pretend to sleep.

There was a knock on the door and he heard his father.

—Alex, what's the matter with you? Why did you run in here like this?

—Nothing.

—Alex, I want you out of there. Unlock the door.

—I'm not going to. Go away.

—Did you hear what I said?

—Go cut up the baby. That's what you're doing. Go cut him up.

—Are you crazy?

—Oh go away and let me alone.

He stood next to the crib, holding onto the bars, waiting for the baby to scream as the knife dug into him. There was another knock on the door.

—Alex, it's Uncle Mansfield. We want to bring the baby in here. Will you open the door?

—No; he's cut to pieces and I don't want to see him.

—Who told you that?

—I just know, that's all.

—If I promised to explain what happened, would you let me in?

Alex went to the door.

—Do you promise?

—I promise. There, that's a good fellow. Ah, this is what I like. A real boy's room.

—Tell me what they did to him.

Mansfield walked to Alex's bed and sat down.

—Come. Sit next to me. That's it. Now, Alex, in our religion when a young boy is just a few days old, we hold a little ceremony for—

—What's the knife for?

—Well, we cut a little piece of skin. . .

Alex crossed and recrossed his legs as he heard what had happened. He felt the pain start in his groin and speed through his entire body, trying to force its way through the back of his head. The knife was white hot silver, ready to strike. If he kept his eyes closed and fists clenched, maybe it would go away. But it didn't. And he saw the pool of blood, dripping from the knife, form at his feet. At first, it was a small, pale pool; then it grew larger and darker, covering the floor with itself. It had no escape, and, like a rising tide, it began to fill the room. It was seeping into his shoes, covering his ankles, then his legs. It was up to his chest and he couldn't move. Mansfield, covered only to the waist, continued talking, and Alex knew the voice would continue even after he drowned. The warm blood slapped against the back of his neck, close to his ears.

—And that's all it is, son. Just a little ceremony. Now will you let us bring him back in?

Alex jumped up from the bed and ran into the bathroom. He stood over the sink, retching but unable to throw up. His parents explained to everyone that he never carried on like this before and Harriet said that's how they get sometimes, just leave him alone, he'll get over it. The apartment became quiet, and Alex knew everyone had gone. His father spoke to him through the door.

—Alex, will you please come out of there?

—I won't. I'm not coming out till you take him out of my room.

There was a hasty conversation on the other side; then Alex heard the crib being moved. His father spoke to him again.

—Now will you come out?

—No. You'll hit me.

—I promise not to hit you. Do I ever hit you?

Alex said he would be out in a minute. Before he unlocked the door, he looked at his very private parts and prayed that not too much had been cut away.

His father was holding him roughly and shouting in his ear.

—Answer me! Where were you?

That night, after spending an aimless day in his room with

his parents not talking to him (he told himself over and over he would never look at the baby again), the baby's cries seemed loud, so loud they cut through the wall and curled under the blanket with Alex, biting him each time he closed his eyes in search of sleep. He kicked at the pain when it was at his feet, only to have it slide up to his shoulders, taking little nips out of him as it moved along. And if he slapped his shoulders, to rid himself of the pain, it would sink into the small of his back, where it pierced his spine and ate his stomach. Finally, the cold steel settled at the base of his groin, and no tossing or turning would get it to move elsewhere.

Alex jumped out of bed in a cold and unusual sweat. The yellow light from the street lamp played on his blanket, changing its rust to a pale orange. And underneath, Alex was sure he saw something move among the folds. But when he touched the blanket, with one finger at first and then in the full grasp of his hand, he felt nothing more than the itchy wool. Yet he knew the pain must still be there, for the baby's cries continued. Suddenly, the blanket stopped moving, and the pain walked with Alex as he stepped from the cold floor onto the scatter rug, as he sat with his legs curled under him in the chair next to the window, as he walked, then hopped, then walked again into the shelter of the darker corners of the room.

Not turning on the light, he found his clothes in the dark and slipped into them as quickly as he could. Holding his shoes and jacket, he opened the door to his room. The small light in the foyer was burning and he was afraid he would be seen as he slipped past the door to his parents' room. He was certain that he hadn't taken a breath until he found himself on the steps of the two-family house. Putting on the rest of his clothes, he looked behind him, then ran out through the gate. He hurried past the other houses on the block, crossed two empty lots and headed toward the beach.

But he had forgotten that the entrance to the beach would be boarded this time of year. He sat on the cold pavement and listened to the silence. The pain had disappeared and it was safe to sit here all night and decide what to do. Only it was cold. He turned to look at the row of lockers facing the street. The bright summer paint had peeled off and the wood was black and rotted. He thought he saw a ball lying on the ground near the end of the row, and he ran closer. Yes, it was a ball, a baby's ball because it had a face painted on it, but still a ball, something to hold and play with. He kneeled down and reached under the chicken wire to get it. Then there was a stale and bitter smell next to him, and a voice that came from cotton and broken glass.

—Looking for something, sonny?

The man rocked back and forth, his heavy arm on Alex's shoulder.

—I was just reaching—
—Spying on me! That's what!
—No. I was—
—Sure you were. You were spying! Well, come on. Come inside with me. I'll show you around. I'll show you the sights.

Alex lashed out with all his strength, and began to run.

—Don't try to run. I'll get . . . I'll get you . . . get you . . . get . . .

The voice followed him through the empty streets, racing on telephone wires, on the white lines dividing the tar roads, whining out of darkened windows, rolling from rooftops and falling behind him, through the gate, up the stairs and into the apartment. He didn't remember his father grabbing him and leading him roughly into the living room, nor did he really hear his father's questions.

—For the last time, where were you?
—I went out. I just went out.
—Alex, I never did this before, but I'm going to now.

His father's heavy hand was on his stomach, the strong fingers undoing the belt buckle. He felt his trousers being pulled below his hips, and he was flipped over the hassock. Then the belt came down.

—You've been. . .
But the pain
—acting like. . .
was good and sharp
—a spoiled brat. . .
and real.
—lately. Now, get into your bed or I'll give you some more.

Alex crawled into bed, and remained there, feverish, for two days.

SLEEPING, WARMLY

Alex practiced ignoring his brother for nearly two months. He spent most of his afternoons in the schoolyard and if it rained, he sat in the warm wooded library staring at the crowded shelves. When his parents (they hardly spoke to him at all) asked him why do you stay in your room at night he said because I have to do homework. Actually, he had been leaving his books in his desk at school, and, once safely in his room, he played chinese checkers or monopoly with himself. He tried to be very fair, but he favored the purple marker, and when it lost a game, he would become disappointed and return the board to the cabinet.

Once, when he had misplaced his favorite marker, he decided to be all four people at once. He moved around the board, rolling the dice for the red, blue, green and orange colors. After a while, most of the property was distributed, and several monopolies, with houses and hotels on them, were formed. He became excited; then, he realized he was not at all certain who he wanted to win, who he was for. He was all four players, *that* was sure. But who was *he*? It was orange's turn to roll the dice; instead, Alex swept everything on the board to the floor.

Alex found that he could no longer concentrate in school, and he knew his next report would show his nineties had dropped to seventies and even to unsatisfactory in some cases.

—Alex, would you spell laughter for us?

The class turning to look at him.

—Alex, pay attention. I asked you to spell laughter for us. Now, stand up and spell it.

Squirming in the aisle, fumbling, irritated tap of the teacher's fingernails on the top of her desk, vindictive giggles as the bright boy of the class wiggled on a pin, relief in the warmth of his seat. And the closing remark I don't know what's come over you lately as he studied the carvings on his desk. He had begun to dig into his desk with a miniature screw driver he brought from home. To soften the wood, he would spit on his finger and then rub the saliva over a small section. Taking the screw driver from his pocket, he would carve his initials and his name with precise determination. He traced the grooves with his pencil, watching the crooked lines of his name take on the glow of shining coal.

There were other things you could do in school, too, like watch the trees outside the window and could a big wind blow them over. They could fall in, right into the room, on top of them and crush them. Ambulances would come, white, sleek and rushing. And maybe the Red Cross to bring food to the workers clearing up the pieces of wood and bodies.

Pleasant things, like the painting period, the once-a-week painting period in water colors, when he used the brightest colors.

—But Alex, did you ever *see* a purple tree?

—Sometimes.

Hanging the pictures above the blackboard, where everyone could see his first because the others were pale pinks and drab green. And *he* had purple trees.

Then, quite suddenly, the world changed. Walking home from the schoolyard, in a light slow snowfall, Alex saw his Aunt Jean walking toward him. Her coat was partly open and when she got close, he saw that she had been crying.

She took him in her arms and pressed his head against the wet of her coat.

—What's the matter?

—I was coming to get you. You have to come to my house tonight.

—Why? What's the matter?

—The baby's sick.

—Then why can't I go home?

—Alex, please, baby. No questions. I'll tell you later.

Only she didn't tell him anything except that the baby was in the hospital and she spoke on the phone in the evening telling people yes, that's right, very sick, oh, you can't imagine. Alex went to sleep and he knew he hadn't slept long when he felt Jean's hand on his shoulder shaking him and telling him to get up, Grandpa's here and we have to go to the hospital. Jean's eyes were swollen and his grandfather was standing near the door holding his hat and saying come, Alex, we have to hurry.

He dressed quickly and felt unreal so late at night. The taxi his grandfather had taken was waiting for them. No one said anything on the way and occasionally his grandfather would pat him on the knee. Going up in the elevator, Alex expected his stomach to fall, but it wasn't that kind of elevator like in the department stores. They got off on the eighth floor and his father was sitting on a bench. His grandfather went over to him.

—Where is she?

—With the baby.

He had never seen his father look like this, so white and sick. And like he was sweating. Jean started to cry and his grandfather put his arm around her. She spoke to his father.

—She shouldn't stay in there with him.

—You know how it is. She wants to.

—But it won't help.

—She wants to. She says it's her fault.

His father said she felt the baby was dying because she didn't want him in the first place, that she had cursed him for not being more careful, she cursed her pregnancy, now she cursed herself and was sitting by the baby's bed crying my baby, honey, I love you, get well, I love you, oh, my baby.

—Can't the doctor tell her not to carry on?

She won't listen to him. She just looks at him under the oxygen tent and cries.

Alex ran to his father and held him around the waist. His father held him, then took him by the shoulders and said crying won't help, you've got to try and be a man now. But he couldn't stop and Jean tried to wipe his face with a tissue.

—Now, dry your eyes like a good boy.

His father moved away from him and lit a cigarette, then came back.

—Alex, come here, by the bench. I want to talk to you.

His grandfather was sitting on a gray leather chair, still holding his hat by the brim, staring at his shiny black shoes.

—Alex, you want to be a big boy, don't you?

—Yes.

He shivered slightly. Everything was gray and cold.

—Mommy wants you to do her a big favor. That's why we brought you here.

He saw his grandfather get up and walk to Jean, who was looking out of the window as though nothing was on the other side. And he heard the old man say that maybe they shouldn't have brought him. But Jean said that's what his mother wanted. Now, his father leaned forward.

—She wants you to see the baby, to go in and look at him.

Alex hardly remembered what happened next. There was a funny feeling in his stomach, and he thought he was going to get sick. His father stood up and led him to the door marked 802 in gold, he remembered the gold. But when they told him to go in, to just open the door and go in, he couldn't. He wanted to run, to run down the long hall and never stop. But he could not move; softly, he sank to the floor on his knees, please, I can't go in. His father turned away from him and said take him out of here and I'm disgusted with you. Jean led him to the chill night, taxi fumes and the warmth of her apartment.

He undressed and tried to sleep, but he heard the cry of the baby in every inch of the room, and the pains came back only this time worse than ever. They did not go away until Jean took him into her bed and promised him that everything would be all right, but even then he twitched and cried out often in his sleep. And he had the kind of dream where he knew he was dreaming but couldn't wake up. His brother was being eaten on thin slices of bread by everyone at a big party. Cousin Harriet said the meat was the tastiest she had ever eaten. Alex wanted to tell her that the meat was his brother all cut up and chopped fine, but his teeth melted and stuck together so he couldn't open his mouth. He mumbled and they all laughed.

The next morning was not all right. Instead of hearing Jean in the kitchen when he woke up, he saw a strange woman bend over the radiator and turn on the heat. She was dressed in a shabby housedress and looked as though she had no bones, only fat.

—I'm Mrs. Glass from next door. Your aunt's by the hospital.

She stood with her hands on her huge hips, staring at him and clucking her tongue. The belt of the house coat barely went around her middle, and the ends met in a tight little bow that looked as though it would snap open any minute.

—Such a shame. So young he was.

Alex knew, and felt numb.

—Can I go home?

She answered as though she had not heard him.

—It's Friday.

—Can I go home?

—It's Friday, so they have to rush. They can't keep him, not for a day even, to look at him.

Then she had him in her arms, tears streaming down her puffed cheeks, and she was telling him of my Joey, who died from sunstroke and they had to bury him on the day he died. Alex pushed away from her.

—When can I go home?

—Later. There's plenty time for going home.

—What time?

—About two. I'll take you home. Now I'll get you breakfast.

She dried her eyes and went out of the room. Alex struggled with a large armchair, pushing and pulling it in front of the window. Legs under him, he watched the passers-by and he was angry with himself because he could *think* about his brother dead but could not *feel* about him. Mrs. Glass brought him breakfast on a tray. He spent the rest of the morning and the early part of the afternoon at the window; unable to feel anything about his brother, he tried to forget him.

At two-thirty, Jean returned. She looked very sick and he heard her say to Mrs. Glass that she cried so much she couldn't any more. She told Alex to get dressed. When they left, she thanked Mrs. Glass who said what else are neighbors for if not to help. In the taxi, on the way home, his aunt tried to have him rest his head on her shoulder, but he pulled away from her and stared at his reflection on the other side of the window.

He heard the sounds of heavy sobbing as he went up the stairs to the apartment, and he was frightened. Someone opened the door, and the circle of people around his mother moved away. She had him in her arms and her tears became cold as they touched his face.

—Alex my baby my little boy it was my fault and you didn't see him you could have last night daddy told me you were sick how quiet he was and now he's gone you're all that's left it's like I killed him myself.

And all the people said no, Belle, you mustn't say that.

—It's true like I killed him myself if you could have seen

him I would have been so happy, so happy in a little box I could have held in my arms put in the ground gone he never did anything just a baby like I killed him.

His cousin Harriet came over and told her Belle, get up, please, it's not good for you. His mother's sobbing softened; she held him closely and rocked back and forth. Then, slowly, she stood up and wiped her eyes with a wet handkerchief. Looking up at her, Alex saw an expression on her face that he had never seen before. It was as though all the blood from under the skin had drained away, leaving a hard, white dough behind. Her voice cut through the murmuring of the room.

—Nobody has to tell me. Nobody has to say a word. You weren't sick last night. You didn't come because you didn't want to come. You could have seen him, but you didn't want to. And I will remember that till my dying day.

She ended in a glare of silence and sank back into the chair. Alex looked toward his father who was staring aimlessly at the tips of his shoes. Alex turned, and walked from the living room. As soon as he crossed the doorsill, there was a rush of voices and the high sobbing of his mother. He thought his feet would sink into the carpet as he walked toward his bedroom. Passing his parents' room, he saw the crib in its corner, the blanket hanging between the bars. He went in, closed the door and undressed. Quietly, he climbed over the side and laid the blanket on his shoulders. His eyes closed, and he slept, warmly.

A GAME OF FANCY, FACTIFIED

—Come on, Alex. Get up. Rise and shine,

Alex tried to pull the blanket over his head.

—Now, then, how was it? Come, come, don't turn over. You can't go back again. It's over. Get up.

There was a hand on his shoulder, rolling him back and forth, chanting come, come, no more sleep, come on, up we go.

Then, fully awake, he saw Harold standing next to him.

—Well, my boy, how was it?

—I guess it was all right.

—I can see you don't even remember. You'll clear up, in a minute or two. I'll just open the blinds meanwhile.

The glare of full morning came into the room and Alex recalled the bath of the night before (was it the night before?).

—Oh, sure I remember. I remember what happened, but I don't feel anything.

—That's okay. Now get dressed and come downstairs.

—Where's your mother?

—She's gone now. Come on. No more questions.

Harold left the room, closing the door behind him. There, on a chair next to the bed, were the clothes Alex had worn when he first met Harold. Putting them on, he tried to think of what happened in the urn (where was it now?) but he was interrupted by a call to hurry up downstairs. Tucking his shirt into his trousers, he went down the stairs two at a time. Harold was sitting alone in the living room, his legs stretched in front of him on a hassock.

—Well, Alex, you don't look much different.

—Should I?

—I thought you might. In fact, I was almost sure you would. But it doesn't make much difference. After all, it's not the looks that count.

Harold removed his legs from the hassock and patted it.

—Come, sit here.

—I think I'd rather stand.

—Okay. You can stand. Now, then, before I introduce you to someone special, tell me all about it.

—About what?

—About the bath. What else would I mean?

—Oh. Well, I don't really know what happened except that the water was very hot.

—But what did you think about?

Alex rubbed his chin with his thumb.

—You certainly must remember something!

Alex was about to answer that he really didn't when the doorbell rang. Harold got up and told him he would be right back. Alex sat on the sofa, and heard a conversation in murmurs between two people. Harold returned to the room, with a very tall and beautiful woman walking behind him.

—Alex, I want you to meet Miss Sink.

Alex stood up.

—How do you do, Miss Sink?

—Fine. Pleased to meet you.

Miss Sink had a high voice through the nose and she said meet you like me-tyoo. She spoke funny for such a beautiful lady, and he almost giggled. Harold turned to leave.

—Now, go ahead. You two get acquainted. I'll be upstairs.

Miss Sink walked to the sofa and sat down.

—Won't you join me? That's it, sit right there. Now, where shall we begin?

—Begin?

—I know. You tell me all about what happened last night, everything you thought of.

—I don't think I remember anything.

—That's impossible. How could you forget?

—I just did, I guess.
—Maybe if I give you a hint, you'll remember. Let's see now. You must've dreamed about girls. They all do. That's it. You close your eyes and think. It'll come back.

Alex closed his eyes, but all he saw were bright spots.
—I remember monopoly.
—Monopoly!

He was insulted by her tone.
—Yes, monopoly. I *like* monopoly.
—Well, of all things to remember. Is that all you can think of?
—I'm trying. Why are you asking me all these questions? I don't even know you.
—Well, I like that!

Indignantly, she crossed her arms on her chest. Then she leaned forward and spoke to him quietly.
—Listen, kid, I won't ask you any more questions but one if you promise not to tell *him!*

And she pointed up.
—It's not that I don't want to do my job right, but I'm in kind of a hurry today and we won't lose anything by getting rid of the preliminaries.

She moved toward him, wrapping him in her arms.
—Now, go ahead.
—Go ahead what?
—Look sonny, I don't have all day. Now, go ahead.
—Listen, Miss Sink, will you please get your arms away from me. Let me go.

He thought she was going to hit him, but she just rushed from the room, calling to Harold as loud as she could. He came downstairs and asked what was the matter.
—What kind of kid is that? He wouldn't come near me.

She grabbed her coat from the rack in the foyer and slammed out the front door. Harold looked after her for a moment, then went to Alex.
—Didn't you like Miss Sink?
—I don't know. What did she want me to do?
—Don't you know?
—No. Nobody told me.
—Tell me, Alex, do you recall if your dreams last night were pleasant or unpleasant?
—I think unpleasant.
—And tell me one thing more. Didn't you want to kiss Miss Sink?
—Kiss her? Why should I want to do that?

Harold walked from the room and returned with Alex's jacket.

—You'll have to go.
—Go? Why?
—You'll just have to. Something went wrong.
—But I don't understand. Please, Harold, you were my friend. We played games, and—

Harold was standing at the door.

—I'm sorry, Alex. Really I am. There's nothing I can do.
—But where will I go? I don't even know where I am.
—Here's a dime. You can call home and tell them to pick you up.

Harold watched him as he walked from the house and turned the corner. Then he went to the sofa where Alex and Miss Sink had been sitting, and tried to think. But he did not know what to think about. Alex found a candy store several blocks away. He sat in the phone booth for a long time before calling home.

CONSUELO

Translated by
Adrienne Foulke

Alberto Moravia

One of the best known of contemporary Italian novelists, Alberto Moravia grew up in Rome under the shadow of personal illness and the oppression of Fascism. Of his novels, the following have appeared in the United States: WHEEL OF FORTUNE, THE WOMAN OF ROME, TWO ADOLESCENTS, THE CONFORMIST, CONJUGAL LOVE and THE FANCY DRESS PARTY. His American publisher, Farrar, Straus & Young, has just reissued THE TIME OF INDIFFERENCE (April 1953), and will follow it in the fall with a collection of short stories.

The day was hot and rainy and as soon as Sergio was out of the house, he realized his mistake. He had put on a heavy winter suit when, given the almost tropical weather, he should have worn a light one. Furthermore, he was weighed down by a double-breasted winter overcoat, so that in effect he had not one but two topcoats over chest and stomach. Finally, he was wearing a woolen undershirt, wool socks on his feet and a wool scarf around his neck. In one hand he carried his umbrella, in the other, his gloves.

He had taken only a few steps when he began to feel caparisoned like a medieval horse.

It was, he thought, the fault of those damned black clouds churning in the sky; and his mother's fault, too, for while he was dressing she had come to beg him, for heaven's sake, to dress warmly. For a moment he thought of going back to put on lighter clothing but immediately decided against it. He lived on the top floor, the elevator was not working, and to climb the stairs with all those clothes on would have been too much of an effort. Nevertheless, the further he walked along the crowded street, the greater his discomfort from the heat and the weight became and the worse his temper. What's more, it was now raining, a fine rain, not enough to justify his raising his umbrella but enough to dampen the pavements and make them slippery underfoot. The rain only intensified the suffocating heat; when he reached the end of the street, he realized that he was wringing wet.

He had gone out for a walk but he saw that, with all those clothes on, the exercise was not producing its usual restful effect; on the contrary, in the debilitating heat which enveloped him from head to foot, he viewed with a jaundiced eye only the city's meanest and ugliest aspects. As if for the first time, he saw the shop windows revealed in all their vulgarity, crowded with things which seemed to him useless; the dim, rotting poverty of the alleyways littered with rubbish, and the watchful shadows of cats; the unbecoming dresses of the women; the shabbiness of the men's clothes; the sweaty, unctuous, loose look of the faces which constantly issued from the shadows of the street, advanced toward him, and disappeared. The whole city which ordinarily he loved so much now seemed to him an enormous heap of refuse in which, piled together in confusion, were rotting and decaying men and things that in another place and under other conditions would have preserved their freshness and wholeness.

Meanwhile, evening was coming on rapidly. Feeling distraught, he stopped in front of a tobacconist's window and looked, hardly seeing, at the pipes and packs of cards. What most annoyed him at that moment were his wool socks; he tried moving his toes inside his shoes and they felt limp, as if they were about to melt like candles. Then someone coming out of the shop bumped into him and he looked up and recognized Luciano, whom he had known for years.

He had never cared greatly for Luciano, an old school friend, and in the last ten years he had seen him perhaps once or twice a year. But for all his lack of interest in him and, indeed, his active desire to avoid him, he had never been able to break off their senseless and sporadic relationship. In reality

Sergio recognized in Luciano the personification of a part of himself which he hated and would willingly have done away with, if he could.

The two men resembled each other slightly in appearance: both short, dark, fine-featured, careful in their dress. But Luciano's face bore the marks of dissipation while Sergio's had a gentle, rather melancholy expression. Luciano was pale, almost gray in the face, his thinning hair receded from a high forehead, his eyes were clouded. Sergio's face was fresh, his hair thick and shining, and his glance lively. Both came, as they say, of good families. But while Sergio lived with his parents and worked as a lawyer in his father's law office, Luciano had left home and lived in furnished rooms, did not work, and spent his time with chorus girls, professional gamblers and playboys. Sergio found this world as distasteful as he found the person of his old schoolmate. But through some kind of incomprehensible fascination, Luciano's revolting world and Luciano himself attracted him, and he could not escape his friend the few times they met. On those occasions they spent the evening or the night together, dining in a restaurant and going on to other places. The next morning Sergio would feel humiliated by the memory of the evening spent in such shoddy company and swore to himself he would not do it again.

Sergio's first movement now, on seeing Luciano, was to turn away. But his friend had already seen him and stopped. They shook hands and went off down the street together. Luciano had bought cigarettes and offered them to Sergio. The latter would have liked to refuse but he accepted.

"How are you?" asked Luciano after a moment.

"I'm well," said Sergio dryly.

"Everyone well at home?"

"Yes, they're all well."

"And are you still practicing?"

"Yes, I am."

Luciano seemed in a bad humor; Sergio suspected that he had noticed his earlier move to avoid him. He wanted to be polite and he thought of asking in turn for news of some person dear to his friend. But since he did not know his family, he could find nothing better than to inquire after Luciano's mistress or rather, the latest mistress he had seen him with about six months ago. As he seemed to remember her, she was young, not unattractive although, like all Luciano's women, vulgar. But beyond this hazy impression of her youth, good figure and vulgarity, he simply could not remember what she was like or who she was. The name Albina, remotely imprinted on his memory, seemed unlikely to him. Nevertheless, he hazarded: "And how is Albina?"

Luciano stopped to relight his cigarette which had gone out. In the glow of the lighter's tiny flame, Sergio saw that his question had had a distinct effect, although one difficult to define. Luciano's coldness was too studied to be genuine. "Ah, Albina ... you remember her, eh?" he said in a sarcastic tone. "Perhaps you will be pleased to know that today we have definitely broken off with each other."

"Why pleased?" asked Sergio, astonished.

The other man went on: "Albina is a ..." and here he used a word which made Sergio wince (he could not stand ugly words, especially in reference to women), "and so I told her to get out... You like the idea, don't you?"

"I don't like it," said Sergio, embarrassed. "On the contrary, I'm sorry..."

Luciano stopped and looked him up and down with a sardonic expression: "Come now, what a fine specimen you are ... You're sorry, eh? ... Say that again!"

"Yes, I am sorry..."

"You also have some nerve."

"But I..."

"You want Albina, and how you do! ... And now you're glad she isn't living with me any more." Luciano was silent for a moment, apparently savoring the bitterness of these words. Then he added scornfully: "A fine friend you are. But all friends are alike when it comes to women ... they all try to crawl into the other man's bed."

Sergio was stupefied. He did not remember that he had paid any particular attention to Albina, the two or three times he had seen her with Luciano, nor could he remember that she had ever paid any attention to him. He said, a little nervously: "But I assure you that I..."

His friend interrupted him: "Do you suppose I wasn't watching you that day we went to the races and had supper together later? I'm not exactly blind ... And for that matter, it's perfectly natural."

"But really, that day..."

"This," said Luciano, stopping before a small doorway in a dirty street, "is Albina's house. I had to come to return these gloves ... but it's better if you do it. Go on up ... give her the gloves," and he put a pair of soiled gloves in Sergio's hand. "Go on, tell her I'm through. Naturally the succession is open, get to work on it. She'll be very pleased... That's what she wants."

"But my dear fellow, I..."

"What are you waiting for? Come on, come on ... she's on the top floor." Roughly Luciano gave him a push, forcing him through the door. "Go along now. You're pretty pleased, eh, I've saved you the trouble of looking for her address . . . I brought you right to her doorstep, no less. But you won't want me to undress her for you, will you?"

"But Luciano . . ."

The other was not listening to him. "We're all set, then . . . Treat her well, take her out to supper, don't be stingy and . . . good luck." With a wave of the hand, he bid Sergio good-by and disappeared.

Left to himself, Sergio felt himself sweating more than ever. To the heat had now been added the unpleasant sensation of a false situation. What was happening to him was almost incredible; however, it was not the improbability which annoyed him but Luciano's attitude, and his own. The improbability could be explained either by the fact that Luciano had conceived this jealousy of him for no reason or that Albina had made use of him to make her lover jealous. What gave him food for thought was, on one hand, his friend's tranquil scorn, as if it had been obvious that he would scheme to supplant him in Albina's graces and, on the other hand, his own sudden inclination to accept the traitor's role which had been pinned on him. Sergio had a dignified albeit formal idea of himself. Now the temptation which Luciano's equivocation aroused made him doubt himself. "It's clear," he thought. "I need only give up going to see Albina and go home, and Luciano will be convinced he made a mistake." But he noticed that meanwhile, almost in spite of himself, he had taken one or two steps into the hallway of the house. It was an old house and dirty, the hallway was dark, a damp musty smell filled the air; and yet, inexplicably, that decay, that filth, that dankness, that obscurity attracted and disturbed him. His heart had begun to beat more quickly and his breath almost failed him. "I will deliver the gloves and go away," he decided, walking finally toward the end of the hallway.

Feeling both oppressed and eager, he ran up three flights of stairs, knocked on a little door which seemed in the uncertain light to be smeared with pitch. A big-boned, disheveled woman in an apron came to open it, a child in one arm and a pair of bellows in her hand. On hearing Albina's name, she pointed wordlessly with the bellows to a door at the end of the hallway. His hat in one hand, his umbrella in the other, and feeling more encumbered than ever, Sergio crossed a bare little anteroom, walked to the end of the hallway and knocked on the door.

A woman's voice told him to come in. He pushed the door open and found himself in a tiny, narrow room which seemed simply a prolongation of the hall. Lined up against one wall were a small wardrobe, a sofa covered with worn red cloth and a little table and chair; there was barely room to move between them and the opposite wall. At the end of the room in front of a closed window stood an old dressing table with faded skirts and soiled ribbons; there, before the mirror, sat Albina. Her young, fleshy hips overflowed the stool on which she was seated; she wore a pale green slip and was brushing her hair, her head tilted to one side and her bare arm raised to pull the brush through her hair. She said calmly: "Is that you, Luciano?"

Sergio thought: "I'll just give her the gloves and go." He answered, embarrassed: "No, it's I, Sergio."

Albina whirled about with an almost convulsive movement of her entire body, the whites of her eyes widening and her full, brown breast straining under the lace of her slip. Sergio walked toward her: "Perhaps you do not remember me," he began, endeavoring to achieve a courteous and distant tone, "and you must be surprised to see me instead of Luciano. I am sorry but I am the bearer of bad news. . . Luciano asked me, a short while ago, to tell you that he will not be coming and, in fact, that he does not want to see you again. He asked me to give you these gloves." He laid the gloves on the dressing table.

He expected the woman to comment in some fashion on Luciano's behavior. But Albina was silent, looking at him curiously. He returned her look and noted, almost with regret, that she was really a beautiful girl and that he found her attractive; her small head with round, black eyes, aquiline nose and delicate mouth, had all the grace of the head of a bird; but her throat was strong, her shoulders well-rounded and her bosom firm, and her skin was warm and brown. With her faded green slip and the soft, dark down of her unshaven armpits, Albina had about her an air of slovenliness if not of downright uncleanliness. But even this, he realized, did not displease him. Confused, and almost in spite of himself, he stammered: "If you like, and if you have nothing better to do, we could have dinner together."

He regretted this invitation immediately and hoped that the woman would refuse. At last Albina said slowly: "Luciano is a liar . . . I'm the one who never wants to hear of him again. But that's no reason for you to crow. Do you suppose I don't see through this?"

Albina, too, like Luciano, was convinced that he was paying court to her. Irritated, he replied: "Believe it or not, I only came to bring you the gloves."

"And to invite me to dinner?" finished Albina in a suggestive voice. "Well, where shall we go?"

So she accepted. Sergio could not help feeling pleased. "Wherever you like."

"Let's go to Paolone's," the woman said. "The food is good."

She picked up the brush and began to brush her hair again with those energetic strokes. "Why don't you sit down? What are you standing there for, are you nailed to the floor?"

Sergio sat down awkwardly on the sofa, uncomfortable in his heavy clothes. Now the adventure with Albina was becoming identified in his mind with the wild desire to get out of his clothes. He thought if only he could undress in that little unheated room, and it seemed to him that it would give him more pleasure to undress than to possess Albina. Unfortunately, that longed-for moment was still some time off. "And so," said Albina, without looking at him, "you're glad that Luciano and I are through."

"I!" stammered Sergio. "Truly . . ."

"It didn't seem possible to you," Albina continued. "I can just see it . . . Luciano had no sooner told you that everything was over between us, when you rushed right up here all excited, thinking this was the right moment . . . Isn't that so?"

"I swear you're wrong," said Sergio with some emphasis. However, he was no longer so sure. Was it true that the woman was wrong?

"What did you think? That I hadn't noticed?"

"What?"

"The last time we saw each other with Luciano—in that restaurant—you never stopped for a minute playing footie-footie under the table . . . You practically ruined my shoe. You're quite a guy, aren't you?"

This time Sergio was silent for a long moment. At last it was a question of a precise fact: he had, it seems, pressed this woman's foot with amorous intentions. He remembered, it is true, having gone with Luciano and Albina to a restaurant; he even remembered that Luciano and Albina had sat opposite him on the bench against the wall. But he was absolutely sure that he had not touched Albina's foot intentionally. Perhaps, without meaning to, he had bumped against it under the table. More likely, as he had thought before, Albina had invented the whole story to make Luciano jealous. Heartened by this examination, he said slowly: "Look, you must be wrong. I could never have thought of touching your foot . . . it's something I would never do in any case. Perhaps you are confusing me with someone else."

"Isn't he sweet," the woman sneered. "No, I'm not confusing you with anyone else; I never make a mistake in things of this kind."

"She's impossibly crude," thought Sergio, offended. But he

sensed that this vulgarity, so appropriate to the place and the person, did not displease him. He tried to strike a debonair, libertine note: "Well, since it matters so much to you, let's say I did play footie-footie with you. What then?"

Albina laid the brush down; her hair, all combed and smooth, floated like a veil over her shoulders. She turned toward him: "Come here."

Sergio was upset. He rose and took a step toward her. The woman insisted: "I told you to come here."

Sergio took another step. "And now," she said lightly, the way one speaks to dogs, "down."

"What do you mean?"

"Down."

Sergio bent his knees inside the heavy folds of his overcoat until his face was level with that of the seated woman. She lifted her round, strong arm and passing one hand behind his neck, she began: "Not that I don't like you . . . no . . . in fact. I like you very much . . ."

"What shall I do?" thought Sergio. He brought his face close to Albina's as if to kiss her. She pushed him away immediately. "No . . . no . . . now be good . . . I said I like you but that isn't a good reason . . . naughty boy." She laughed brazenly, revealing small, white teeth, and she struck him on the chest, a strong, hard, peasant's blow. Sergio lost his balance and fell back on the floor.

Furious with himself, he got up again. He realized that by admitting he had played with Albina's foot and by having tried to kiss her, he had put Luciano definitely in the right. And what's more, to no avail. Annoyed, he demanded: "After all, do you like me or don't you?"

Albina replied: "You didn't let me finish . . . I like you, yes, but it's no good, I'm not for you. I belong to Luciano."

This last she said with the stupid, partisan faithfulness, thought Sergio, of the lower-class woman who never questions her lover even if he betrays or physically mistreats her. He could not help saying: "But Luciano doesn't want to have anything more to do with you."

"That doesn't matter. I belong to Luciano. . . And then, you are Luciano's friend and you shouldn't try to take his woman away from him. What you're doing isn't nice."

She shook her head with an air of disapproval and rose from the dressing table. Standing in flat-heeled slippers, she seemed too broad in the hips for her height. She went over to a hanger, unpinned a pair of stockings which were drying there and examined them doubtfully. The stockings she was wearing were heavily darned with visible mends that looked more like patches. She fastened the stockings to the hanger again and went to the closet. Stultified and bathed in sweat, Sergio drew near her and put his arm around her waist. She paid no attention to him and opening the closet, took out the one article of clothing it contained: a ratty little brown suit. She stepped into the skirt and handed him the jacket. "Help me put this on?"

Sergio took the garment and as Albina turned in his arms to slip into it, he kissed her on the throat. He sensed the rich smoothness of her skin and the animal scent which emanated from her hair. She made a gesture as if to brush away a fly: "Ugh, aren't you stubborn!"

She buttoned the jacket which was too tight around the waist so that her hips and breast seemed to explode above and below. She went to a corner, took off her slippers, and hopping from one foot to the other, slipped on a pair of ragged shoes. Then she said: "Let's go."

Sergio picked up his umbrella and hat and followed her with an acute sense of boredom and irritation. The heavy-set, disheveled woman with the baby on her arm came to the kitchen door. "If Signor Luciano comes," said Albina, "have him wait in my room."

They went out and began to walk side by side down the dark and narrow stairs. As they walked, their thighs touched and Albina said with a laugh that seemed offensive to Sergio: "Having yourself a little feel, are you?"

"To hell with you," he thought. But his arm, as if moved by an independent will, rose and encircled Albina's waist. Without saying a word, in the dark she gave him a hard shove with her hip that almost made him fall. Sergio understood and released her.

Outside it was raining and even hotter than before. Albina said to him: "Put up your umbrella." He obeyed and in an almost affectionate gesture Albina took his arm. They walked along together.

"What do you think of Luciano?" she asked him suddenly.

Without thinking, Sergio replied: "I think he's a good-for-nothing and will probably come to a bad end."

She said calmly: "You're on the wrong track . . . I've told you so already. You'll never get me to love you by saying bad things about Luciano."

Irritated, Sergio replied: "I think much worse of him than that. I said only the smallest part of what I think."

"And you want to pass yourself off as his friend."

"But I'm no friend of Luciano," said Sergio violently. "Will you please get that through your head? I scarcely know him."

"Maybe . . . but he says that you're good friends."

"We went to school together, that's all. I could never be friends with a man like Luciano."

"Why not?"

Suddenly Sergio's nostrils flared in anger: "Because Luciano's a shady character and I am not."

"Maybe," she repeated stubbornly, "maybe Luciano is a shady character, as you call him . . . but he trusts you and here you are, trying to get his woman away from him. These are the facts."

"But what's that got to do with it? Anybody could ask you to go out with him."

"Yes, but you're different . . . you and Luciano are friends."

There was nothing to be gained by going on like this. Dripping with sweat and furious, Sergio was silent. "I should ditch her here and now," he thought. But the pressure of Albina's arm, the brush of her rounded hip were enough to make him change his mind. They entered a dark square which was being torn up. The violet neon signs were reflected on mounds of trampled mud and here and there red lanterns warned of deep, water-filled holes. "Wait for me here," said Albina. "I want to stop by general delivery for a minute."

She went into the post office and Sergio waited by the door. It was still raining and in the glare of the headlights the rain looked dense and fine, as if pulverized. People were going in and out of the post office, among them many decent, modest women, and then many others, like Albina. "This is the moment to leave," he thought; he walked away slowly along a scaffolding. But halfway down the street he remembered he had to post a letter and went back. As he was putting the letter in the box, he felt someone touch his arm. "Let's go," said Albina.

She was turning a letter over and over in her hand. Then, without opening it, she put it in her pocket. Sergio asked: "Aren't you going to read it?"

"It's from my husband. I have plenty of time."

"From your husband?"

"Yes," she replied, "I'm married, didn't you know? He's an actor in Goretti's road company. Poor fellow, he's always, always, on the move somewhere and he always writes to me . . . I worked with him for a while—I sang and he accompanied me on the guitar—then I got tired of it. You had to go to such awful little country towns and I wanted to be in Rome." Meanwhile they had left the square and were walking along a wide, muddy street without any sidewalk and jammed with a double row of pushcarts.

Albina was in no hurry to go to dinner. One by one she

looked in all the carts, even the one with the second-hand books, and the one with the razor blades. Sergio could not help but think that she really was the little bit player who leaves her furnished room at nightfall and comes out to enjoy the drama of the streets. But not even the searing light of the acetylene lamps seemed to dull her animal appeal; at most, it emphasized the pallor of her cheeks and the yellow circles of fatigue under her black eyes. In front of a haberdashery shop which had a long rain-soaked banner over the door with enormous letters, "Rock Bottom Prices," she stopped and went in purposefully, saying: "Let's go in. I want to buy Luciano a tie."

Sergio followed her, miffed by this tenacious fidelity. The shop was small and in great disorder; not only had prices been knocked down but the merchandise seemed to have been tumbled all over the counters. The clerk offered for Albina's inspection a rack of dreadful neckties and Albina chose with care the ugliest, inquiring of Sergio: "Isn't this one really stunning?"

"Very pretty."

"Is it for the gentleman?" asked the salesman. "It's just right for the gentleman." Albina searched uneasily in her purse. "I'll pay for it for you," said Sergio, impelled by some vindictive punctiliousness.

When they were outside, Albina said to Sergio: "Thanks . . . but now don't go telling Luciano that you paid for it."

"What do you take me for?"

They resumed their inspection of the shop windows. Albina stopped a long time in front of a shoe shop and then said: "Since you ruined one pair of shoes for me by playing games under the table, you should buy me a new pair." The tone was facetious but not too much so; Albina, the little gold-digger, hoped to promote a pair of shoes. Sergio hesitated a moment and then he decided to buy Albina the shoes. Having bought them, he would still have enough money for dinner but not enough for the usual fee for the night. He thought, however, that Albina would be satisfied with the shoes. She was looking at him hopefully. He said slowly: "How can Luciano, who loves you so much, let you go around in such broken shoes?"

"I don't want anything from Luciano."

"I guess you're the one who buys his shoes. Is that it?"

Albina preferred not to answer and Sergio decided that, as he had always suspected, Luciano had few scruples about taking money from his women. After a moment, he said: "Well, let's go buy those shoes."

Albina must have given up the idea for she turned to

him now with startled, happy surprise. "You really mean it?"

"Certainly I mean it."

They entered the shop. Albina was beside herself with delight, and showed it by strutting up and down, her heavy hips well in evidence in the mirrors which punctuated the rows of stacked shoe boxes. She sat down and thrust her trim and shapely foot at a young, talkative salesman. Among the many pairs of shoes that the salesman offered her, Sergio was surprised to see her choose a heavy sport shoe in light colored leather with a thick sole of rubber the color of lemons. "But wouldn't it be wiser to choose a black pair suitable for town?" Sergio ventured.

Albina answered: "If you play footie-footie under the table again, you won't spoil these." It was a joke in which she tried clumsily to express her gratitude. But Sergio blushed because the salesman was looking at him and grinning.

Outside the shop, Albina kissed him impulsively on the cheek, saying: "Thanks a lot." Sergio replied irritably: "You kissed me on the cheek as if I were your father."

"Luciano's the only one I kiss on the mouth."

Albina, happy, proud and poverty-stricken, was almost touching as she walked along in her too bright, too stout shoes, her brown skirt drawn tight over her heavy hips, the parcel of her old shoes under her arm, and Sergio did not mind her reply, thinking that even if nothing came of it, he had done a good deed. Albina went directly to a little hole in the wall nearby where old shoes were repaired "while you wait." She detailed lengthily to the shoemaker, among his piles of broken and dusty shoes, just what had to be done. Then she bought a tin of polish for the new shoes and left.

They walked on from one sordid block to the next, street by street, alley by alley. Suddenly Sergio looked about him to find the colored glass door of a brothel on his right, on his left a public urinal and, a little further on, the entrance to a *trattoria*. Underfoot the usual dirty, shiny tiles strewn with cabbage cores, hungry, marauding cats around them. Three men came out of the bordello laughing and talking loudly and headed for the urinal.

Sergio was about to say "nice neighborhood," but had no chance when Albina, stopping at the entrance to the *trattoria*, announced: "Here we are."

And in fact the glass doors of the exit bore the legend in ox-blood script:

Paolone
Roman Specialties
Castelli Wines

Albina pushed the door open and went in. Sergio closed his

umbrella and in disgust followed her into the hot, smoky atmosphere of the place. The *trattoria* consisted of a string of tiny rooms. In the first, a little larger than the others, there was a big center table heaped with several pyramids of oranges and bunches of finocchio. Against one wall stood a heavy ice box of natural wood surmounted by an imposing pair of antlers. It was a *trattoria* without pretensions, as one could easily grasp from the frequent cry of "Half portion" which echoed from one room to the next.

Sergio noticed that all the clients were somehow rather like Albina and Luciano; the women young, for the most part heavily painted and poorly dressed, the men dissipated, drained and favoring sharp clothes. Albina went slowly from room to room, frequently greeted by one of the unprepossessing clients, and she seemed to be looking for someone or something. Having walked to the very last room of the *trattoria,* she nodded to Sergio as if to say: "I've found it."

Sergio reached the entrance to the last room and looked in. He saw a tiny room, almost a cell, with only two tables in it. One was empty and Albina was about to sit down at it. Luciano and a woman were seated at the other.

"So that was it," he thought. Luciano did not seem surprised and said, "Hello, Sergio," quietly. Sergio went to Albina's table and bending over her, said: "Let's leave . . . Luciano's here."

"What a discovery!" she snapped. She lowered her head and pretended to be lost in the menu.

"Let's go to the Splendide," Sergio suggested, thinking that the luxury of the place might induce the woman to go with him.

She raised her head and stared at him with feigned amazement: "But why? . . . We're so comfortable here."

There was nothing for it but to sit down. Sergio took off his overcoat and placed it, together with his hat and umbrella, on a chair. The two tables faced each other and the four of them could not help staring at each other. Albina and he were seated on a bench running along one wall, while Luciano and his companion were seated on the bench running along the opposite wall. A curtain hung in the doorway to the room only heightened the sense of being enclosed and crowded together.

Now Sergio realized that he was no more than a pawn in Albina's game of jealousy, and who could know how long the game had been going on. Yet, looking at Albina, he was aware of hoping that between the two opponents, he might be the lucky third who wins out and that, on whatever grounds, he would fall heir to Albina. "I am a fool," he thought scornfully.

He was hotter than ever despite having taken off his overcoat; the air in the *trattoria,* heavy with smoke and the smell of cooking, was stifling. Once more, in this heat, his adventure with Albina appealed to him as a quick and pleasant way to take off his wool socks, tear off his heavy clothes and be naked in the cool air of some dreary furnished room.

Meanwhile Albina had called the waiter and was ordering what seemed to Sergio, whose tastes were always very sober, a gargantuan meal: antipasto, spaghetti, roast kid with baked potatoes. She would decide, she added, about dessert later. He could not help but admire this bouncing appetite which even jealousy had not managed to curb. "Are you hungry, Signorina Albina?" he asked, turning toward her.

She replied aggressively: "Yes, I'm hungry, all right . . . But stop acting like a fool, don't be so formal."

It was really hard to be seated facing one another like this and not stare. After having sought in vain to avoid the eyes of the couple opposite, Sergio decided he might as well look at them openly. Luciano had turned about on his bench and now presented his profile. But the woman sat squarely facing them. She was an unusual-looking woman who aroused Sergio's momentary curiosity. Her hair was coal black and her long, bony face had a coppery yellow cast. Her black eyes were large and brilliant but somehow unfocused and as expressionless as two stones. Her long, high-bridged nose with its wide-flaring nostrils and her disdainful, drooping mouth gave her a virile air. She appeared to be tall, with broad shoulders and prominent breasts tightly bound by the black silk of her décolleté dress. The two things that struck him most about that face were its coppery color and its savage, immobile expression. Beside this woman Luciano seemed spent and fragile while Albina looked quite delicately feminine.

Sergio jumped when Albina interrupted these observations with a quick poke in his ribs. "Know who she is?" she said in her normal tone of voice so that Luciano must have heard her. "She's a Mexican who's singing at the New Theater. Do you think she's attractive?"

"No," said Sergio, lowering his voice.

"Now isn't that the truth, she's downright ugly. She's a redskin. Sitting down like that she looks tall, but when she gets up you'll see . . . it's as if she sunk into the ground. A piece of her legs is missing, it looks like."

"Why are you talking so loud?"

"Oh, she can't understand," Albina replied, shrugging her shoulders. "She only understands Spanish. She's got a man's name, Consuelo."

"That's not a man's name but a woman's . . . it means Consolation."

"Well, Luciano is certainly consoling himself since I ditched him," Albina said spitefully.

Sergio looked once more at the couple seated opposite and noticed that they seldom spoke. The Mexican was eating calmly and Luciano spoke to her briefly from time to time, helping himself with gestures: "Do you want a drink? . . . How is it, do you like it? . . . Have some bread?" The waiter brought the spaghetti and Albina who, despite her jealousy, had already eaten her way through a plate of salami, immediately twirled a great forkful into a compact mass and carried it to her mouth, without once taking her eyes off the Mexican. The woman asked Luciano to refill her wine glass and then drank, nodding a sentimental greeting to her companion over the rim of the glass in a serious, almost ritualistic gesture. Luciano replied by taking the glass from her hand and then drinking, placing his lips where hers had been.

"Just look what an ass he can make of himself," Albina muttered furiously, with her mouth full of spaghetti. All the same, she did not give up emptying her plate and when she was finished, cleaned up the last of the sauce with a big piece of bread. "Later on, we'll go to my house," she said loudly, pushing the empty plate away.

Sergio realized that she was talking only to be heard and was probably not too aware of what she was saying. He could not keep from commenting: "But you didn't want me before."

"Well, I've changed my mind," said Albina loudly, "and anyhow, I've always thought you were attractive . . . more so than Luciano."

"There's no need to yell so about it."

"You're no bum like he is . . . you're a gentleman. Anybody can see that."

Luciano reached for the Mexican's hand and she gave it to him gently. He carried her hand to his lips, watching her through half-closed eyes, and then he bit it. The Mexican smiled, revealing white, sharp teeth, wolf's teeth, Sergio thought. Luciano kissed her hand where he had bitten it. Albina told Sergio with sudden affection: "You know what? I bought you a tie . . . Now we'll put it on."

Sergio was dumbfounded in the face of this improvisation. "But I . . ." he began.

"Come on, don't be stupid. You're not ashamed, are you?"

Albina took the package from her handbag and unfolded the tie with vindictive pride. Sergio thought it served him right for having been delighted at the crudity of the tie destined for Luciano. Not only was he going to have to wear this hideous silk concoction in Luciano's stead but he had had to pay for it. Albina, giggling, turned up his shirt collar, undid the tie he was wearing and slipped the new tie around his neck, tying it in a big, loose knot. "My, how becoming," she said, leaning back to admire her handiwork. Sergio tightened the knot and said: "At least give me back the old one."

Luciano put an arm about the Mexican's waist, laughing and joking with her in a whisper. The Mexican defended herself mildly, replying with some quip in a warm, slightly hoarse voice. Impetuously Luciano threw himself on the Mexican and gave her a long kiss on the throat. The woman sat quietly, her eyes wide, while Luciano sucked at her neck just below the ear. Then, as he withdrew, she shook herself slightly and straightened her hair, just as a hen fluffs her feathers after she has been mounted by the cock. The waiter arrived with the roast kid for Albina and with a second plate for Luciano's table. Albina asked him: "Is this for Signor Luciano?"

"Yes."

"Just a moment." Albina took the pepper shaker, a little terra-cotta chicken with holes in his head, unscrewed the head and quickly dumped the pepper on to Luciano's plate. The dish held a slice of meat in the small metal pan in which it had been fried. The waiter was appalled: "What on earth are you doing?"

"Don't you worry about it . . . I'll be responsible." Sergio, too, was startled. Albina began to eat her kid, her eyes fixed on Luciano. The latter, who had not seen this by-play, calmly cut himself a bite of meat and carried it to his lips. Albina stifled a laugh, poking Sergio hard in the ribs again with her elbow. "Now we'll have a scene. He's so fussy about his food."

But Luciano made no scene. After the first bite, he put his fork down quietly, drank half a glass of wine and lighted a cigarette. "God knows, he must be burning up inside," Albina whispered, "but he's so damn proud, he'd die before he'd show it."

A blond youngster, hatless and wearing a torn jacket, wandered in with a wicker suitcase in his hand. He opened the suitcase and without a word began to set out a batch of colored plaster statuettes. The Mexican, to tell the truth, showed no great desire to have one but Luciano forced her to accept a white and black poodle. Sergio suddenly felt Albina's hand groping for his under the table. She took it in hers and then said loudly: "Oh, aren't you in a hurry, though! At least wait till we get home." Sergio blushed and instinctively tried to draw his hand away. But Albina held on tightly and cried: "Let me go, will you?" Whereupon she threw herself against Sergio and still holding his hand tightly, pretended to struggle with him. Sergio decided that this time at least he'd get some fun out of the game and tried to encircle Albina's waist with his arm. But the girl pushed him away. Luciano audibly asked the Mexican: "Would you care for fruit or maybe a sweet?"

"Sweet."

"I want one, too," said Albina, furiously angry. In a few moments the waiter brought the two women their sweet. Luciano and Sergio had ordered fruit. The sweet was filled with cream and the Mexican ate a part of hers, dousing her cigarette butt in what was left. Albina lowered her head greedily and devoured every speck of hers, then, patting her stomach, she sighed with satisfaction: "Oh God . . . I ate too much!" She leaned back on the bench and tried to open the zipper of her skirt. But the garment was too tight to let the zipper slide smoothly. "Take a look, will you?" she asked Sergio. "See if you can unzip me." Sergio leaned over, took the tab of the zipper and lowered it. Immediately Albina's firm young stomach popped forward with the outline of the navel clearly marked beneath the thin green silk of her slip. Luciano asked the Mexican: "Coffee?"

Albina was now sitting with half her belly out of her skirt. On one side, through a rip in the seam of her slip, her bare hip with the smooth fold sloping inward at the groin was exposed, brown and warm. Two vagrant musicians wandered in, a man and a woman. The man was small, old and thin, with a long face. He wore a black coat that reached nearly to his heels and a cyclist's cap tilted rakishly over one ear. The woman, about fifty and also dressed in black, was tall and imposing, with a cold, sad face. They took their instruments out of their cases and started to strum an old song. Albina said loudly: "That Mexican over there . . . She shouldn't be singing in a theater, she ought to have to go around like these two do, asking for handouts. If you knew how flat she sings . . ."

Sergio asked absently: "Does she sing in Spanish?"

"Of course. Didn't I tell you she doesn't know anything but Spanish?"

The two musicians had finished their song and Luciano called them over. They drew near the table. The old man took off his cap. Luciano talked with them a moment and then turned to speak to the Mexican. She protested but then gave in. Standing before Luciano's table, the two players raised their instruments and began a well-known Spanish song. The Mexican, still seated and staring into space with her dark eyes fixed wide, waited motionless for the right moment. Then she began to sing. Her voice was rough, warm, richly sensual. In the upper register her tones had a savage quality and, in the lower, a sadness, so that with the abrupt rise and fall of the melody the song seemed like a furious argument. Sergio was at first amazed, then admiring and finally, despite himself, deeply moved. Perhaps it was this disastrous evening, he thought, or perhaps a momentary impulse of his nature which had been too long absorbed in pedestrian, impersonal concerns. The Mexican watched the players as she sang and every so often made a gesture of approval or an indication to play more loudly. A few other clients had gathered in the doorway and were listening in silence. Luciano seemed unaware of the beauty of the song and went on smoking with an air of being at once unimpressed and embarrassed; obviously he had wanted the Mexican to sing only to fan the flame of Albina's jealousy. The Mexican stopped singing and sat still, her eyes on nothing, her hands folded in her lap. The spectators in the doorway applauded warmly. Luciano applauded, too, but with condescension; he did not trouble to remove the cigarette drooping from a corner of his mouth. Sergio clapped his hands with genuine enthusiasm. Albina, with a street urchin's gesture, put two fingers in her mouth and whistled.

The long, sharp whistle brought total silence. The Mexican woman looked at Albina as if she noticed her for the first time, then she got up and walked toward Sergio's table. He could not help but admit that Albina was right about her height: she was short, remarkably short, although her shoulders were broad and powerful. The Mexican woman planted herself in front of Albina and vomited forth an incomprehensible torrent of Spanish. Although her speech was violent, her eyes and face were immobile. Albina cried: "I don't understand a damn word and I don't give a damn . . . when you're at the theater, you can whistle down an actor, can't you? Well, I have a perfect right to whistle all I like." The Mexican picked up Sergio's full glass and threw the wine in Albina's face.

A scene of utter confusion followed. Albina, her face and neck streaming with wine, had gotten to her feet and was struggling to hurl herself on the Mexican. She was held back by Sergio who had grabbed her arm, and by her open skirt which started to fall off her as she stood up. "Redskin," she screamed. "Redskin! Let me go . . . I'll scratch her eyes out!" Luciano sat imperturbably smoking with ostentatious indifference. Slowly the Mexican had returned to her table and stood, quiet and dignified, staring at Albina. A few intrepid souls had entered the little room, others stared from the threshold, all asking what was going on. At last, Luciano called the waiter, paid his check and with a nod to the Mexican, left the room with her.

The waiters and musicians went off about their business. Albina sat gasping and began to wipe the wine from her face with her napkin. Some wine had dripped down on her belly and her slip, glued to her body, revealed its full, girlish rotundity. Sergio said: "I told you it would have been better not to stay here."

He was amazed to see that Albina's rage had quite disappeared. She asked: "Do you like me?"

"Yes," said Sergio, disturbed.

"Would you like to make love to me?"

"Of course."

"Well then, don't think about anything else and don't worry about anything else."

At this point Sergio was sure that Albina would spend the night with him, if only to revenge herself on Luciano. The little room was empty and from the one next door no one could see them. He drew Albina to him, as if to kiss her. This time she allowed herself to be embraced and at the end, as if suddenly aroused, she passionately returned his kiss. She stank of wine, not unpleasantly but in an ingenuous, disarming way. They drew apart and Albina, tugging on her zipper, said: "Let's go, shall we?"

Sergio paid and they left. It was no longer raining and in the flat, empty air, the black sidewalks shone under the headlights. But it was hotter than ever and again Sergio thought with longing of the moment when he could undress in Albina's room. She was walking apart from him, as if she were alone, her hands in her pockets, her face lowered and thoughtful. The new shoes with their thick soles made her seem more stumpy and tiny than ever. Sergio said: "Shouldn't we stop for coffee first?"

She drew near him and with a forced gesture put her arm around his waist. "No, let's go home . . . you're going to stay all night with me?"

Her voice was sad and full of tears. Sergio put his arm around her and answered: "Of course I will."

"Let's sleep together and tomorrow morning," she concluded, her voice pleading with him, "you can stay in bed as long as you want—you can sleep till noon, if you like."

Passing street after street, alley after alley, with their arms entwined, at length they reached Albina's house and began to climb the stairs. At the first landing, Sergio kissed her on the neck. Albina said not a word.

They reached the little black entrance to the flat. Albina opened the door with her key and went ahead down the corridor. Sergio followed her, hampered as usual by his overcoat and umbrella. Albina opened the door and said: "Well . . . and what are you doing here?"

Her voice was joyful. Sergio looked in and saw first the Mexican sitting glumly on the couch and then Luciano, seated at the dressing table and facing the door. Luciano had assumed a cheaply conventional pose, his smile was insolent and mocking, and he dangled his cigarette loosely between his fingers. Sergio thought he remembered a similar scene in some film he had seen. He said to himself, annoyed: "Here we are," and they entered the room.

Albina went directly to Luciano and stood near him, one hand on his shoulder, as if defying Sergio and the Mexican. Luciano, like a bad film actor, took a long pull on his cigarette, exhaled a cloud of smoke and then said with affected languor: "Fine, fine, that's just fine. So I was right all along . . . you just couldn't wait . . . Quite a friend you turned out to be."

Sergio felt himself blushing. Not so much because he had been caught out as because he felt himself at a disadvantage before a man he despised. He thought that the ill wind had blown some good, however, since he could now break once and for all with Luciano. He said, trying to be emphatic: "First of all, I am not your friend . . ."

"And then what?" said Luciano, theatrically.

"And then," Sergio went on, "Albina is not your wife . . . she is free to go out with whom she pleases. She told me to come back with her and I did."

"Is this true?" Luciano asked, turning toward the girl.

Everything was happening just as in a Grade B film. Albina retorted violently: "It's not true. He's a real liar. He kept insisting . . . I didn't want him to . . . He forced himself on me . . ." She had taken Luciano's hand and was frantically kissing it, on his palm and on the back of the hand.

"A liar, on top of everything else . . ." Luciano sighed.

"Oh, go to hell," Sergio shouted with real feeling.

The Mexican rose from the couch, drew close to Sergio and, putting a hand on his shoulder, said something that Sergio did not understand but interpreted as "Let it go . . . you'd better just leave." He shook her off and added angrily: "It's understood that we're finished, you and I. If we ever meet again, I forbid you to speak to me."

"*Vamos*," said the Mexican, trying to draw him toward the door. Unexpectedly conciliatory, Luciano replied: "Don't lose your temper . . . There's nothing wrong, we'll still be friends. It's only natural that you found Albina attractive. But you can go with Consuelo now . . . I talked to her about you, she's interested in you. Consuelo, you two go on, both of you. Go to bed." He gestured expressively with one hand. But the Mexican shrugged and answered him in a cutting, scornful voice, as if to let him understand that she was not taking any advice from him, she would make up her own mind. Luciano began to laugh and Albina, now sure of having what she wanted, dropped his hand and went over to the dressing table to take off her dress. The Mexican managed to pull Sergio out of the room and close the door.

She said a few words in Spanish, as if bidding him good-by, and held out her hand. Sergio shook it mechanically. She turned away from him, went down the hall and opened a door about halfway down the corridor. So she lived in the same flat as Albina. Suddenly Sergio felt his face and ears flush with heat and the maniacal need to undress which he had felt all evening seized him again. He ran after the Mexican who was about to enter her room, and taking a pack of cigarettes from his pocket, he offered her one. She took a cigarette and, without a word, beckoned him inside and closed the door.

It was a square room, small and low-ceilinged, furnished with the same wretched, worn furnishings as Albina's. The only difference was that here, instead of a sofa, there was a proper double bed with a white spread and a headboard of black, whorled metal. The low, wide window seemed to open under a cornice and directly on a neon sign. This reflected light patterned the opposite wall and the ceiling, zebra-fashion, with red and purple stripes. The Mexican moved about the room, now talking without pause in a slightly harsh and reasonable tone of voice, almost as if she were offering maternal advice. It was as if she were saying, in that warm, hurried and sententious way of hers: "You really are a foolish boy. How could you not realize that Albina was only thinking of Luciano? But now you are here, with me . . . I'll make it up to you." He felt comforted by the voice although he could not understand a word she was saying, and he recalled how she had sung, feeling a surging need to hear her sing again. Meanwhile, the Mexican had disappeared behind a screen that seemingly concealed the wash-stand.

With infinite relief he began to undress. He took off his overcoat and then his shoes and socks. A freshness traveled upward from his hot, congested feet all the way to his head and, wiggling his toes, he looked down at them for a moment with delight. Then he took off his suit, his shirt and his undershirt and felt his body breathe again, as a moment before his toes had done. When he was naked, he sat on the bed, crossed his legs, lighted a cigarette and, for the first time during the entire evening, he felt comfortable.

But he had no desire to make love. He wished he knew Spanish so that he could tell the Mexican how much he wanted to hear her sing. He looked at the corner where the wash-stand was and noticed that the woman's clothes had been casually laid over the screen. Then she came out from behind it.

Completely naked, she seemed more squat and exotic than ever. As she came toward him across the room, walking over the black and red lozenges of the tiled floor, he felt he was being approached by an Aztec deity he had seen recently in a museum. Like that statue, the Mexican woman's legs were short and heavy, but so remarkably short and heavy that her feet seemed attached near the knee. Set on those legs, her too long torso was unnaturally upright. Her buttocks were flat, her belly round and prominent with the navel deeply imbedded in the flesh. Her breasts were oblong, like two gourds hanging heavy and solid against her. Atop her long neck around which snaked a thin braid of black hair, her face reigned immobile and expressionless, and her feet were flat against the ground, just as he remembered those of the divinity of her native land. She passed in front of the window and the neon light cast its red and purple stains over her face, her breast, like some vast, barbaric tattooing. She had a towel in her hand and held it out to him, indicating the screen, as if she were inviting him to wash himself. Sergio refused the towel, saying slowly: "No . . . not love . . . sing, sing," opening his mouth wide and placing a hand on his chest.

She understood at once and smiled with professional pride. She tossed the towel on the bed, leaned toward Sergio and taking his chin in her hand, as one does with children, said something to him in her warm, lively voice, as if she were praising him. Then she slapped him gently on the cheek. Sergio smiled gratefully. She sat on the edge of the bed, some little distance from Sergio, and reached over to take the hand he had rested on the spread. Her hand was large, rough and cool. She pressed his hand, crossed her short legs, looked for a moment straight ahead of her with her great, black, shining eyes. Then, swelling out her chest as if with sudden inspiration, she began to sing.

SAUCE FOR THE GANDER

John Howard Griffin

Born in Dallas, Texas, in 1920. John Howard Griffin had his schooling in Fort Worth, then went to France, where his musical studies led him to intensive original research in Gregorian chant at various monasteries. He served with the French early in World War II and spent thirty-nine months in the Pacific with the United States forces. As a result of wartime injuries, Mr. Griffin is now blind; he lives on a farm near Fort Worth where he breeds registered livestock, and writes eight hours a day. His first long novel, THE DEVIL RIDES OUTSIDE, was published in Fort Worth in the fall of 1952 (Smiths, Inc.). A second book will appear in the fall of 1953.

News of the aged friar's request spread throughout the cloister in no time. An early sun had already begun to distill October frost when the Father Prior of the Abbey of Dleifsnam puffed his way up the narrow stone stairs to the Father Abbot's study.

"Come, look out your window, Father Abbot," he said. The two monks gazed down into the sunlit courtyard which was surrounded by high stone walls, and beyond which the Flemish valley stretched serene to its hazy horizons.

"But what is happening?" Father Abbot asked. "Why is there such agitation among my monks? They run about the courtyard as though . . ."

"I don't really know," the prior replied soberly. Under his black robe, his chest still heaved from the long climb. Waiting a moment to catch his breath, he turned away from the window and looked about the Father Abbot's study, so peaceful with its scrubbed flagstone floor, its crisscross leaded windows ajar to let the sunlight pour in, and its sturdy oak table covered with rolls of parchment. "I don't really know, Father Abbot," he went on finally, "but I think it's because our decrepit old St. Clud begs to have audience with the Father Abbot and all the other Fathers in Chapter—on an urgent matter of morals."

"What?" Father Abbot's white head turned slowly, and his gentle blue eyes blinked in disbelief. "Now what could he possibly have on his mind?" Robes rustled in silence as the abbot inched feebly to his table, brushed some of the parchments to one side, and seated himself on the edge of it. He stared at the floor, his thin eyebrows lifted in puzzlement. "An urgent matter of morals? What can it mean? He's too dim to be tempted in the spirit, and surely he's too old to be tempted in the flesh. Why the poor old friar's done nothing but care for the hogs and waddle around babying those geese for the past twenty or more years."

It was true that St. Clud, as he was affectionately called by the other monks, was the menial of the monastery. It was he who performed, with seeming relish, those duties generally considered unpleasant and bothersome. He never tired, for example, of caring for his sick brothers, of tending the small herd of skeletal sows, or of driving the geese out into the open countryside for pasturage.

The other monks were occasionally disconcerted by his personal habits, for he had arrived at the monastery already a man of advanced age, too old to adopt that quality of discreet refinement usually associated with a religious vocation. He was completely unhampered by physical modesty, but in such an open, honest way, and with such childlike simplicity that indeed he made modesty seem almost a questionable virtue. But he was clumsy and noisy. He would blow his nose, even in chapel, with great honking sounds, and he had never learned to control the rich grossness of his language. However, all knew him to be a man of immense generosity and charity and they loved him for tending his menial tasks with such simple fervor.

While the Father Abbot and the Father Prior were discussing him, Friar Clud was in his cell, located in an old grange far to the end of the monastery properties, where he had been moved when the other monks had found it impossible to sleep because of his grotesque snoring. At this moment, he was sitting astride a squat three-legged stool, staring into space and cudgeling his poor brain to know what to do. He had long since forgotten about the world, and gradually, as his age had become very advanced, his entire manner of thinking had become centered around God and geese. Now, he was trying to remember how it was in the world. He sat with his elbows on his knees, his chunky hands holding each side of his head. He closed his eyes in prayer, mumbling his paternoster in provincial dialect. He prayed fervently for a moment, ruffling stubbed fingers through his sparse white hair.

Then a screeching honk outside made him open his eyes and wince with sympathy. He got wearily to his feet and shuffled across the doorstoop into a small enclosure that was surrounded on all sides by the monastery vegetable gardens. He bent down over a slat cage in which a giant blue goose was squatting. He reached in and fingered her bandaged leg, and noticed that she had not touched her food.

"You must eat," he coaxed gruffly. "You must try to forget. In about five days now, that thing'll be as pretty as it ever was and you can use it once more."

Moments later, the finest gander in all Flanders marched past, his plumage brilliant in the sun, his scarlet beak held high in the air. Beside him, a goose hen strutted, a very young hen. And the wounded goose once more raised her head to the sky and honked her heartbreak. Clud's watery eyes were stricken with an expression of pity. He looked helplessly from the caged hen to the gander and then back to the caged hen.

"It's all right," he soothed in a cracked voice. "It's all right. Here, eat a little, just a little. You know you'd best not get excited. You tear the wound open every time." But she honked her grief again, and the strangled cry pierced the aged friar's heart. He raised himself painfully into an upright position and turned on the gander, brandishing his stick with exaggerated gestures. "Go away. Get out. You old fool," he muttered. "All right, I can understand. You need a little friend maybe. That's understandable, but who ever heard of a gander changing his mate? She gets her little self hurt. Is that her fault? Is that any reason to pick up with the first loose wench that comes along? And then to strut in front of her like this, rubbing it in. Go on. Get out of here. You old fool!" Friar Clud's ruddy face turned scarlet above his white beard.

The aged friar did not drive his geese out to pasture that day. He went to Mass and prayed for guidance, after which he returned and sat with the injured hen until the late afternoon skies were filled with clanging vesper bells from the tower. Then he got to his feet and absently dusted off his bottom. After a last worried look at his charge, he headed through the cloister gardens, trudging between rows of gigantic purple cabbages, toward the chapel.

The others watched him, knowing only that the poor friar was struggling with a problem of morals, and their faces wore expressions of great concern and pity.

As soon as vespers were completed, all of the monks were called together in the Chapter Room to hear Friar Clud's distressing problem. Father Abbot was uneasy about some of the younger monks' hearing what might come from the old friar's untutored and indelicate lips. In his mind, he prepared a little lecture that would serve the occasion if necessary. He would explain to them how in advanced age, certain long-forgotten spiritual and physical phenomena might resurge with diabolic insistency. His meditation was interrupted by a slight wave of laughter. He looked up to see Friar Clud ambling across the room bowing to right and left, his uncertain grin revealing his three good teeth. Father Abbot studied that good-natured face with its goatlike eyebrows and its watery blue eyes, and felt a stirring of immense and compassionate affection. No matter what St. Clud had got himself into, he could not have done it viciously and he must not be judged too harshly. "After all," the Father Abbot told himself, "After all—" Usually, if he said "After all" a couple of times, some fine thought would come to follow it up, but this time no thought came to the abbot and he shrugged his shoulders in intimate irritation with himself.

When all the rustling sounds of monks settling themselves in place had died down, the prior, speaking in a voice of great gentleness, told Friar Clud that he might address the Fathers. The old friar rose from his bench, adjusted a pair of wobbly lenses to his snout, and with loud clearings of his throat he genuflected to all sides as though he were about to be knighted. Father Abbot's gavel rapped on the table and the tittering stopped abruptly.

"Reverend Fathers," St. Clud began, "as all of you know, I have been the menial of this monastery for a long time, with nothing to do but care for the hogs and drive the geese, so that in twenty and more years my poor brain has become as empty as an unused churn. That is why I begged this audience, for I am faced with a problem I do not know how to solve." The uneasy smile once again gummed itself across his face, and he wrinkled his forehead and concentrated on words with which to express himself. A blush seeped upward into his cheeks.

"Tell us simply what troubles you," the prior urged after a long time. "Do not be embarrassed."

"Well . . ." the old monk hesitated, cocking his eyes prayerfully in the abbot's direction. "This week something happened that never should happen."

A hush claimed the room instantly. Father Abbot's gaze softened with understanding and deep pity. "After all," he said to himself. "After all—" He was just opening his mouth to explain about natural phenomena resurging in senility, when Friar Clud went on in his unleavened voice.

"The goose, as you know, is the most moral of all animals. The goose mates for life and does not change mates."

Father Abbot's expression became sad and a little mystified. The poor old friar was rambling.

"Three days ago," Clud continued, "our finest goose caught the shameful portion of her leg in the garden fence, and now she cannot walk. Only three days, and now her gander has left her to go prowling after a much younger animal. This is unheard of. Now," Clud's voice became hoarse with emotion, "the betrayed hen will not eat. She is grieving herself to death and soon she will die. Her screams are heart-rending, Fathers. I'm sure you heard them at vespers. Unless some solution to this terrible situation can be found, I'm afraid I'll. . . ." His voice trailed off into confused silence. He squinted his simple blue eyes about him, seeking some expression of help from the surrounding Fathers. Most of them had their heads buried in their hands in concentration, their shoulders quaking.

Father Abbot tapped his mallet on the table once again. "What would you suggest we do, Friar Clud?" he asked patiently. "Couldn't you just find the bereaved goose another gander?"

The aged friar's face clenched into an expression of shock and disappointment. He shook his white head gravely.

"I see," the Father Abbot said with apology in his voice. "Well, it's up to you, but it seems to me that if the poor hen is going to starve to death, it would be better for you to kill her so that she can be cooked into a hash for one of our meals. Now, let's get back to this disturbing problem of morals, my son. You started to tell us about it a while ago. Don't be humiliated. You say this misfortune has already occurred?" The abbot fell silent as he saw Clud's shoulders sag. The old monk stood there in his brown patched robe, thunderstruck.

"But it was that," he protested, his blush deepening, "the gander going off. What must I do? In the world what do they do when a lecherous man leaves his wife for another wench?"

The prior's hand flew up and slapped his forehead with a loud smack. Father Abbot's face congested. Other monks stared dolefully at the ceiling and their mouths dropped open. Friar Clud was almost abject in his expression of bewildered misery. He allowed his hands to drop to his side in a forlorn gesture and tried to smile, but he looked more as though he were chewing.

Clearing his throat, the prior broke the silence. "I have told you before, Friar Clud, that you cannot judge animals from a human standard of morality. You have made this same error a—"

Father Abbot interrupted. "My son, if the goose is to die, persuade yourself to kill her so the cook can prepare her for our dinner. If there is some way to save her, you will know best. Now, go in peace, and do not let this torment you further."

The gumming movements of Friar Clud's mouth became more agitated, and his eyes half-blinked with great slowness. He seemed rooted to the spot. It was inconceivable to think of killing the hen he had so tenderly cared for. Kill her and let the other two go free? Some deeply engrained sense of justice made the solution seem monstrous to him, and he was stunned that such a fine man as the Father Abbot could make such a suggestion.

He stared about him helplessly for a long moment. Then he turned and walked slowly from the Chapter Room, his whiskered chin buried in his chest. Outside, late dusk enveloped the countryside in the soft blues and grays of twilight. First stars glistened pale. Friar Clud walked with great heaviness, swallowing back the forgotten nostalgias of all the years when dusk had been a time of quietness, of gentle acceptance—a time when he could sit on his stool in the door of his cell, surrounded by his animals, and rest after a long day's work. Tonight there was not that peace. Tonight he felt lonely and incomplete, and his loneliness was made more poignant by the placid countryside that rose on all sides from the valley, half-veiled in mists, chilled by hidden night breezes, lighted by brass chips of stars. All of those things that had made for peace in the past, seemed now to destroy the peace of the night.

He stooped and entered his cell. By the last vague light that filtered through his open door, he wetted some mashed grain for the injured hen. He fixed a new bandage on her leg and tried to force a handful of feed down her throat. But she pulled her head away and placed it under her wing, issuing sobbing sounds that wrenched his heart.

Later, after the last prayers of night had been chanted, Friar Clud remained alone in the darkened chapel and repeated endless paternosters in his childish patois. Again and again he prayed for guidance, abandoning himself into God's hands. Long after the last bells had reverberated throughout the cloister and the other monks were asleep, he stayed on his knees. He knew there must be a solution, and he wracked his poor brain to think of it. His heart turned cold at the thought of putting the hatchet to her. It was unthinkable. She was so pitiable, so completely blameless. The giant cacao-seed beads of his rosary dribbled through his fingers, one by one, as he concentrated on his prayers and tried to remember about justice and about how the heart works when romance is involved. Then, late in the night, he returned to his cell, burdened with the sadness of not having solved a thing.

All through the night monks rolled in their sleep and heard the grief-stricken honking. All during the prayers of matins and lauds, in the pre-dawn chill, they heard the pathetic sound. And then it stopped.

And there was more than one sigh of pity. More than one

heart became a little heavier for St. Clud, for despite his roughness, the monks loved him, and many of them felt that he had recesses of goodness and generosity that none of them could match.

During the morning, bits of fine down floated about the cloister courtyard, wafted here and there by a faint breeze. Under the bright sunlight, they looked like snowflakes.

At noon monks filed into the dimly lighted refectory and stood before tables of steaming goose hash. During the long *benedicite* attentions were divided. Glances were stolen in Clud's direction. Dampness made the stone room seem as somber as a cave, and spirits were heavy. Father Abbot made a mental note to have the cook prepare a pie for St. Clud. He knew the old man would never touch the goose hash. In fact, none of them felt much like eating it. A final "amen" echoed in hollowness throughout the long room, and benches scraped against the floor as monks took their seats.

The Father Abbot was waving to the cook when he noticed with astonishment that Friar Clud was gulping down hash with great hunger, making fantastic noises chewing with his three teeth, spilling it on his front with a trembling hand. Others watched and felt sure that the poor friar had taken leave of his senses from grief and worry.

And when lunch was over, and the short prayers were finished, some of them followed him back to his grange. They saw him enter the tiny courtyard and bend down over a slat cage. And inside the cage they saw a bandaged goose serenely eating her mash. Imprisoned with her, they saw a giant blue gander, his long neck stretched through the slats, flapping his wings and struggling to get out. They saw the gander reach over and bite savagely at the hem of Friar Clud's robe. But the old monk merely rubbed his hands together and beamed toothlessly.

During the night, by dint of much prayer and meditation, St. Clud of Dleifsnam had found his solution. The young wench was nowhere in sight.

LATE IN THE SEASON

Peter Matthiessen

A graduate of Yale, and formerly an instructor there, twenty-six-year-old Peter Matthiessen is a native of New York City. He now lives with his wife in Paris, where he is helping to edit a new literary magazine, The Paris Review, and is at work on a novel. His stories have appeared in Botteghe Oscure, in Cornhill Magazine, and in The Atlantic Monthly, where one was an Atlantic "First."

Cici Avery saw it first.

It was just at the edge of the late November road, a halted mass too large for the New England countryside, neither retreating nor pulling in its head, but waiting for the station wagon. Cici Avery saw it first, a dark giant turtle, as solitary as a misplaced object. As if it had strayed beyond its season, she thought, unrooted, like a leftover square of sod. She nudged her husband and pointed, unwilling to break the silence in the car.

Frank Avery saw the turtle and slowed. If he had been alone, he would have swerved to hit it, Cici decided, selecting the untruth which suited her mood.

The small eyes reflected the slowing car, then fastened on the man. The tail, ridged with reptilian fins, lay still in the dust like a thick dead snake, pointing to the yellowed weeds which, leading back over a slight crest and descending thickly to the ditch, were flattened and coated by a wake of mud.

Cici, hands in her trousers, moved in unlaced boots past her husband. The tips of the laces flicked in the dust like broken whip ends.

"Poor monster," she whispered to the turtle, "it's late in the year for you, you're past your season."

"Monster isn't the word," Frank Avery said. "I've never seen such a brute." He ventured a thrust at it with his riding boot. "It's not *really* a turtle?" he said.

"A snapping turtle," Cici said. She was a big untidy girl, whose straw-colored hair blurred the lines of her face like excelsior around a terra cotta head.

"A man-eater," he said. "It must be two feet across."

"It's a very big old monster," she said, sinking down on the crest behind it and stroking the triangular snout with her stick. The mouth reared back over the shell, its jaws slicing the stick with a leathery thump.

"Dear God!" Frank said.

Cici eased to her elbow in the grass, stretching the long legs in faded hunting pants out to one side of the turtle, and studied her husband. Frank Avery, precise in his new riding habit, stood uncertain beside the bull-like turtle, afraid of it and fascinated at once.

The very way he behaves with me, the thought recurred to her, as if I were some slightly disgusting animal, and yet he prides himself on his technique. The father of my children, except that his technique doesn't include having children. Romance is the watchword, but no children, not for a while. And then he is hurt because I don't love him. As if we were haggling over love as the stud fee, as if I had bargained with him for his manhood, she thought, and didn't realize until I took it home what a rotten bargain I had made.

Frank Avery stretched out his toe and sent the turtle sprawling on its back.

"Come on, you coward," he challenged it. "Fight."

The turtle reached back into the dust with its snout and pivoted itself upright with its neck muscles, then heaved around to face the enemy.

"Leave it alone," Cici said. "It can't help being a turtle."

"We should kill it," Frank told her. "It's disgusting."

We should kill it, she thought, because it's harmful on a farm, not for *your* reason. Lying there watching him badger the turtle, she felt a slow hurt anger crawling through her lungs, as if he had injured her over a period of time and only now she understood. Rebelling against him within herself, she was sorry for the turtle, for its mute acceptance of the riding boots which barred its way.

"You don't have to look at it," she said. "Besides, it's mine. I saw it first."

He turned to her, hands on hips, smiling his party smile.

"A fine thing," he said, and waited for her question.

"What is?" she obliged him, after a moment.

"Here we've only been married a year and now it's turtles. First it was kittens and puppies, and then horses, and now turtles. I appreciate your instincts, Cici, but you *can't* get weepy over turtles!"

He laughed sharply.

"Can't I?" she said. Unsmiling, she waited for the laugh to wither in his mouth.

Frank kicked suddenly at the turtle's head, but his toe shrank from the contact and only arched a wave of dust into the hard stretched mouth and the little eyes. When the turtle blinked, the dust particles fell from above its eyelids.

"Did I ever tell you about Toby Snead, Frank? When the other kids would torture a rat or a frog, Toby Snead would jump around, squealing and giggling. He loved it. He was skinny and weak, and he loved to see them pick on something besides himself."

"Was I giggling?" Frank said. His face was white.

I've gone too far, Cici thought, and I'm going to go farther. She felt exhausted, lying back in the natural grass, easing herself of a year of disappointment as calmly as a baby spitting up cereal, a little startled at the produce of its mouth, yet more curious than concerned.

"And you'll get your shiny new manly boots dirty, Frank," she murmured.

"I haven't been here every year to get them faded," he said. When she didn't answer, he added, "And pick up a local accent, and ogle the hired hand."

"The caretaker, you mean," Cici said, her eyes on the turtle. He's jealous, she thought, actually jealous; he can't admit that *he* made a rotten bargain, too.

"Oh Cici, let's skip it," Frank said. "I don't know what's the matter with you these days."

"I hope you find out," Cici said, turning her eyes on him, "before my change of life."

"Let's not start *that* all over again," Frank Avery said. His voice was tight, a little desperate. "I'm sick of it. And you'll catch cold, sitting on the ground."

"There's plenty between me and the ground," Cici said, grinning. She rose and, turning her buttocks to him, brushed the grass off with both hands.

"See?" she said, over her shoulder. "Besides, I've got *you* to keep me warm."

She stepped around the turtle and, taking Frank's face between her hands, kissed him with exaggerated sensuality on the mouth. When he tried to embrace her, however, she slipped from him.

"Cici, listen to me," he said, but she refused, stooping to the turtle.

"C'mon, monster," she said. "I'll take you home and mother you."

"Permit me," Frank said, and clowned a bow, but his heart was not in it. Circling behind the turtle, he seized it convulsively by the rear edges of its carapace and bore it like a hot unbalanced platter to the car.

"What do you want him for?" he said. Then, "Open the door, will you?"

"Monster's peeing on you," Cici told him, laughing in a way which suggested an alliance with the turtle against him. Watching his face, she was sorry she had laughed, but not for Frank's sake. Frank was an artist at revenge, he much preferred it to the messy temper which came to Cici so naturally. She knew him now, and she could expect reprisal with as much confidence as she had in his execution of it.

The turtle blundered to the rear of the station wagon and pressed its snout against the backboard. It seemed alarmed by this detour in its life, scraping its claws like harsh fingernails over the metal floor.

"Let's let it go, Frank," Cici said, afraid.

"No, no," Frank insisted. "I'm sure Cyrus would like to see it."

He was smiling.

Indoors, the turtle looked double its size. Cyrus Jone's boy Jackie had never seen anything like it. He trapped the turtle in the kitchen corner and dropped marbles on its head until Cici asked him to stop. Mrs. Jone, thin-armed in a cotton print, rushed over and slapped him in deference to Mrs. Avery.

Cyrus nodded shortly at Cici as if to excuse his remark, and said to his wife, "Not much sense in slappin' the boy if you haven't spoken to him first. He ain't a dog."

"I can't have him pesterin' folks," she whined, but retreated to the stove.

Cyrus Jone did not answer her. He said to Cici, "Your father telephoned, Miss Cici, he's comin' down tomorrow."

"Oh, that'll be nice," squeaked Mrs. Jone.

"Yes," Cici said. She was holding a baby Jone on her lap while its mother, one eye on the turtle, rummaged nervously with the supper.

Jackie, a large-headed child with prominent ears, goaded the turtle furtively. It renewed its effort to penetrate the corner.

"That's enough, Jackie," his father told him.

"I ain't doin' nothin'," the boy said, injured. "I just wanted to see if he was all right."

"He's all right," Cyrus said. He was a big man of strong middle age, whose hands rested tranquilly on his knees. His eyes were restless, however, and Cici knew he was watching her from the shadow of his corner; she glanced at his wife, already pressing a new round belly to the stove.

Frank Avery came into the kitchen. In his left hand he carried a .22 pistol, which he placed in the corner of the sideboard, in his right the whisky bottle from their suitcase. It was not quite full, Cici noticed.

"I'll have your dinner in a minute, Mr. Avery," Mrs. Jone

said. Her eyes switched rapidly from the bottle to the turtle to the pistol, coming to rest at last on Frank's forehead.

"Why don't we all eat together?" Cici said.

"And Cici can hold the baby," Frank said to her.

Cici did not return his smile, and only Jackie said, "Sure, we kin all eat together and watch the turtle."

"That's right," Frank said. "We might have a cocktail beforehand."

"I'm sure you folks'd rather . . ." Mrs. Jone began, terrified.

"What are you gonna do with the pistol?" Jackie demanded, touching it.

He's been drinking upstairs, Cici thought, I'll never placate him now, and I've missed my chance to let the turtle go. She had forgotten the turtle, she knew it did not matter to her, but suddenly its survival seemed identified with her own.

"Whatever you folks want'll do fine for us," Cyrus said. He rapped his fingers on his knees.

"Hey, what are you gonna do with the pistol?" Jackie repeated.

"Mr. Avery," Mrs. Jone corrected him.

"Mister Avery," Jackie said.

But Frank had gone to the pantry for ice. He returned in a moment with four glasses of it.

"Great," he said, pouring out the whisky.

In the moment of silence, the turtle pushed upward against the wall, then fell back heavily to the floor.

"Jackie wants to know what you're going to do with the pistol," Cici said.

"I was just about to ask Cyrus," Frank said. He passed the glasses and sat down.

"What's that, Mr. Avery?" Cyrus said.

"That turtle, Cyrus. I understand that kind of turtle is harmful, eats fish and young ducks and things."

"Frogs, mostly. That's right, though."

"Dangerous to swimmers, I imagine."

"I don't guess so. They're pretty leary, them hogbacks."

"Frank wants to kill the turtle, Cy," Cici said.

"Sure, let's kill'm!" Jackie said. "We kin shoot him with the pistol."

"Shush, Jackie," hissed Mrs. Jone. When Cici glanced at her, she hid her whisky glass among the pots on the back of the stove.

"I don't *want* to kill it, darling," Frank said. "I just don't think we should let it go."

"That's too bad, *dar*ling," Cici told him. "Because it's my turtle. I found it, and I'm going to let it go."

Her anger was sudden and quiet. The little boy watched her, open-mouthed, and Cyrus said,

"I guess I'd ha' killed it, had I found it, Miss Cici."

"You didn't find it, though," Cici snapped.

"You're being childish about it, Cici," Frank interrupted.

"No, I didn't, that's true," Cyrus laughed, as if Frank's remark were of no more consequence than the turtle's bumping in the corner. "But there's not much good in a brute like that one."

"That's right," Frank Avery said. Prematurely, he refilled all the glasses but Cici's which was untouched, and now sat down again. "We all agree it should be killed, Cici."

"I didn't say *that*," Cyrus said. "I don't guess one turtle could do much harm on a place this size, although I'd just as soon be rid of it."

The baby was stirring now in Cici's arms.

"I'll take it upstairs," Cici said, over the protests of Mrs. Jone. Her face, pressed to the baby's head, softened again to its usual fullness, but her mouth was set, and she did not look at her husband as she rose.

"Cici loves babies," Frank's voice said, pursuing her to the back stairway; it was followed by a laugh. "Babies and turtles."

Mrs. Jone's giggle tinkled like the cheap alarm clock over the pots on the stove.

She was still giggling when Cici returned and sat down to dinner.

"I *do* love babies, yes," Cici said to Frank.

"Well, I must say they're a terrible trouble," Mrs. Jone told her. "You don't know your own luck, Mrs. Avery."

"We have a baby every year," Jackie announced, but his mouth was already so occupied that nobody understood him except his mother.

She said, "Jackie!" and blushed.

Cyrus watched his wife, chewing his dinner without expression.

The turtle had found its way out of the corner and was dragging itself along the wall in the direction of the kitchen door. Cici listened. The belly plate touched the floor on alternate steps, a dull pendulum rhythm of tap and suspense which went unnoticed at the table.

"Yes, they'd certainly be trouble in *my* work, with all the traveling I do," Frank was saying.

"Oh, you'll have them, though, Mr. Avery," said Mrs. Jone. "Never you fear. Why, it's only nature."

"It's only nature, Frank," Cici grinned.

"Of course we will," Frank Avery frowned. Unlike Mrs.

Jone, he had brought his whisky to the table. "Right now, of course, it's inconvenient, but there's plenty of time. We're only thirty."

Cici did not comment, she had heard it all before, and to her it rang false and unnatural. Her time growing shorter, she had settled for Frank Avery and children. She had wanted to love him so badly, and now, in secret ways, he punished her failure. And having settled for less, she was to be cheated even of what she had settled for. It was all Cici could do to swallow, and sorry for herself, she permitted her eyes to cloud with tears.

She wondered if Catholic Mrs. Jone had been offended by his tactlessness. But Mrs. Jone was obviously too stimulated to be offended by anything, and Cici looked at Cyrus, who was now intent on the turtle's progress along the wall.

Very quietly, without turning toward her, Cyrus said,

"His pond must have dried out on him, he's after a new mud to winter in, this late in the year."

Cici nodded. The turtle was past its season, it had exposed itself to trouble. If only she could get it outside . . .

She watched her husband, who had heard Cyrus' voice but lost the words in the clatter of Jackie's fork, and was now glancing from one to the other with a half-smile, as if he wished to be enlightened.

The turtle was directly behind him.

Cici did not enlighten her husband, but offered instead a wink of innocence and duplicity which brought new color to his face. He glared expectantly at Cyrus, but Cyrus was absorbed with his mashed potatoes and did not notice.

Frank rose abruptly and went into the pantry for more ice.

Moving quickly, Cici horsed the turtle over the floor and out the kitchen door into the darkness, straining the precious seconds in her effort to be quiet.

"Oh boy," Jackie said, rising. "Let's go!"

"Be quiet," his father told him, his eyes on Frank Avery, who returned as Cici sat down. Frank's face was red with irritation, and he only glanced at her questioningly.

Cici smiled at him and said nothing. Her heart pounding, she cheered the turtle toward the bushes. The success of her coup was overpowering: like a schoolgirl, she was forced to bite on the insides of her cheeks to keep from laughing, trembling joyfully in the escape as in a childhood game of hide-and-seek.

"But it'll get away," Jackie whispered to his father, turning away sharply as if he hadn't meant to whisper it, it had just popped out, and therefore he was not to be blamed.

"My mashed potatoes are quite nice and fluffy tonight, if I

do say so," preened Mrs. Jone, and dropped her fork.

"But listen . . ." Jackie started.

Frank shifted his gaze to Cyrus, who, chewing placidly, returned it.

"When we're finished dinner," Frank said to Jackie, "we'll have to kill the turtle."

"I'm finished now," Jackie blurted. "It's going to get away."

And then there was silence. Finally, Frank Avery said, "Where in hell did it get to, Cici?"

"I let it go." The laughter jerked from her mouth.

"The turtle?" Mrs. Jone said. She stared at the empty corner.

"That was silly of you, Cici," Frank said. He was trying to control his voice. "You knew it should have been killed."

"Oh, relax, Frank," she said. "It doesn't matter."

"It *does* matter, damn it."

They watched him rise and take the pistol and, followed by Jackie, step out into the darkness.

"Jackie," his mother said, startled.

Cici rose and went to the door. "Frank," she called.

He came back into the light. "I need a flashlight," he muttered. Behind him, Jackie's voice rang through the darkness.

"Frank, don't. Please," she whispered. "It was mine. You're just killing it to spite me."

"You shouldn't have let it go," he said, pushing past her. "You've tried to make a fool of me all day."

When he came back through the kitchen, Cyrus watched him without speaking, but Mrs. Jone whispered,

"It's only just a turtle, everybody. Your dinner'll get cold."

Frank grinned tightly, saying to Cyrus, "We shouldn't let it go."

In the door, Cici blocked his way.

"You're being ridiculous, Frank. You're drunk. And who found the turtle? It's mine."

"God damn it," he said. "You knew I wanted that turtle killed. I'm your Goddamn giggling Toby Snead in disguise."

"Why?" she demanded, her whisper harsh as the turtle's sigh. "Why? Since when are you so interested in ducks and fish and things? They've kept going pretty well so far without any help from you, or the little boy you drag in to keep your courage up."

"You know . . ." he started, but did not bother to go on, because Jackie had found the turtle.

Defeating its own escape, it was pushing against the center of the nearest bush, its legs braced in the dirt; from the doorway, Cici saw Frank's dark hand reach across the flashlight beam and grasp the spiny tail.

Sick, she turned back into the kitchen. When Cyrus rose and went out, she snapped at Mrs. Jone,

"How can you sit there and let that little boy watch him?"

Mrs. Jone ran outside.

The shots came slow and unevenly—one, two three, four. The fourth shot drove Cici to the door.

The turtle was moving slowly in the dim light from the kitchen. Frank's back was to her, and through the excited shouts of the little boy and the shrilling of his mother, she heard a quieter sound.

"What are you laughing at?" she said, her voice hushed, but he was pointing the pistol again, leaning back, stiff-armed.

The turtle jerked a little, kept on moving away. One of its hind legs was paralyzed, and there were three black holes in the ancient shell.

"What are you laughing at?" Cici screamed, and the boy Jackie ran into the house after his mother.

"I'm sorry, darling," Frank's voice came. "I know it's not funny, but my shooting's terrible. I can't seem to hit its head."

"It's still moving," Cici whispered, as he turned to her. "You bastard. You perfect bastard."

"I'm sorry," he repeated, as if bewildered. "I must have been drunk." He put his hand to his forehead. "I didn't think you'd watch."

Cyrus came around the corner from the garage. He had a hatchet in his hand, and stopped the turtle with his boot. It opened its mouth, but could not close it again.

"Hell, mister, that's no way to kill a hogback," Cyrus said.

He bent and guillotined the turtle as Cici cried out.

The blood was black on the ground beneath the door light. Cyrus lobbed the head with its still-open mouth out of the light, then hoisted the carcass by the tail and, holding it away from him, moved toward the bushes. Its hind feet were still walking away.

Crying now, Cici slumped in the doorway. Frank Avery tried to approach her.

"It's still moving," she whispered, damning him with her horror. "You coward. And you couldn't even kill it."

"Cici, listen," he started.

"I hate you," Cici told him. "You're filthy."

The turtle fell in the invisible underbrush, a heavy breaking crash which jarred the night time into silence.

The returning steps of Cyrus Jone came from the darkness before them. Behind, the bright-lit kitchen waited in judgment, the empty chairs at angles to the cooling dinner. From an upper room, the little boy was crying.

B. Rajan

NONE SHALL ESCAPE

Born in Burma in 1920 and educated at Cambridge University, where he took his doctorate, B. Rajan was the first person in the history of Trinity College to be awarded a Fellowship in English, and was in charge of English studies in that college for three years. He is the founder and editor of *Focus*, a series of critical symposia on contemporary writing, and is a frequent contributor of poetry and criticism to British and American periodicals. Until his recent return to Madras Mr. Rajan was First Secretary in the Delegation of India to the United Nations.

FOREWORD. This poem is based on an episode in the *Ramayana* in which Sita, wife of the god Rama, is abducted by the demon Ravana, and carried off to Lanka (now Ceylon). Hanuman, prince of monkeys, who is Rama's friend, calls on his monkeys to make a causeway from India to Lanka. Over this the invading army marches, and in the battle which follows Rama kills Ravana in single combat. Doubting Sita's fidelity, Rama puts her to an ordeal by fire which she triumphantly survives.

In the ninth stanza I have described Rama as four-armed because he is conventionally so in paintings. Yama, in the eleventh stanza, is the god of death. Siva is the destructive aspect of the Absolute, and his third eye symbolizes his power of destruction.

The island's in mist
Like the curve of a smoke-ring
The causeway steps into
A perilous sea.
The lady of change
Sits exiled in Lanka
Where the demons are dark and
The revellers free.

The lady of change,
Changeless and enchanting,
The big, wicked uncle
And the sixty foot ape.
The beautiful hero,
With anger like rockets,
Who says "I am Rama
And none shall escape."

The castle of change
With the moat of its smoke-ring
The ring round the eyes of
The wide-awake sea.
The green and the gold of
The cape in the sunshine
But colourless, sinless
The lady and he.

The uncle possesses
The keys of the kingdom
The lady of change
Keeps her silences pure.
Svengali at Trilby
A snake at a rabbit
The uncle at Sita
But the lady's demure.

The hero regrets
He's allergic to swimming.
He can only get cracking
On the back of an ape.
The apes settle down
Like a necklace of pontoons.
The convoy goes over
And none shall escape.

With a honk of the conch and
A boom of the tabla
The bad man of Boloney
Gets ready for rape.
The bridges are down and
The eyes of the uncle
Are bigger than footballs
None Shall Escape.

But into the window
Gate-crashes the monkey,
Who says "I am Hanuman
I am His Will."
And into the doorway
The sword of the dancer,
Who says "I am Rama
The order is 'kill.' "

And silence comes down
On the lady of changes,
While Ravana dies on
The thread of her scream
And Sita looks into
The eyes of the dancer
Who says "Lady, your stillness
Must my anger redeem.

"Lady of change
The four arms of my wonder
Have taken you, held you
From heaven and hell.
Lady of change
In ecstasy changeless
You say you are constant
But fire must tell."

And the rose of the fire
That clustered around her
Protected the love that
Death could not obscure.
And the fire said fainting
"The lady is sinless
Who in heaven and hell keeps
Her silences pure.

"Pure even to God and
The king of his anger.
In presence of Yama
Where silences die,
The third eye of Siva
Erects her in beauty.
It is only you Rama
Whom changes deny."

And Rama looked up
And said "I am guilty.
God like, I am guilty.
The demon I drape
Is living in me and
The act of its murder
Must aways be endless
NONE SHALL ESCAPE."

STRANGE COMFORT AFFORDED BY THE PROFESSION

Malcolm Lowry

Born in Merseyside, England, in 1909, Malcolm Lowry was educated at Cambridge University. He and his wife, Margerie Bonner (HORSE IN THE SKY), have been residents of British Columbia, Canada for fourteen years. Best known for his extraordinary novel, UNDER THE VOLCANO (Reynal and Hitchcock, 1947), Mr. Lowry is also the author of numerous short stories and poems, and several other novels as yet not in final form. He is now at work on a collection of novellas and short stories, of which this story is one, to be entitled HEAR US OH LORD FROM HEAVEN THY DWELLING PLACE, to be published shortly by Random House.

Sigbjørn Wilderness, an American writer in Rome on a Guggenheim fellowship, paused on the steps above the flower stall and wrote, glancing from time to time at the house before him, in a black notebook:

Il poeta inglese Giovanni Keats mente maravigliosa quanto precoce mori in questa casa il 24 Febraio 1821 nel ventiseesimo anno dell' eta sua.

Here, in a sudden access of nervousness, glancing now not only at the house, but behind him at the church of Trinità dei Monti, at the woman in the flower stall, the Romans drifting up and down the steps, or passing in the Piazza di Spagna below (for though it was several years after the war he was afraid of being taken for a spy), he drew, as well as he was able, the lyre, similar to the one on the poet's tomb, that appeared on the house between the Italian and its translation:

Then he added swiftly the words below the lyre:

The young English poet, John Keats, died in this house on the 24th of February 1821, aged 26.

This accomplished, he put the notebook and pencil back in his pocket, glanced round him again with a heavier, more penetrating look—that in fact was informed by such a malaise he saw nothing at all but which was intended to say "I have a perfect right to do this," or "If you saw me do that, very well then, I *am* some sort of detective, perhaps even some kind of a painter"—descended the remaining steps, looked wildly once more, and entered, with a sigh of relief like a man going to bed, the comforting darkness of Keats's house.

Here, having climbed the narrow staircase, he was almost instantly confronted by a legend in a glass case which said:

Remnants of aromatic gums used by Trelawny when cremating the body of Shelley.

And these words, for his notebook with which he was already rearmed felt ratified in this place, he also copied down, though he failed to comment on the gums themselves, which largely escaped his notice, as indeed did the house itself—there had been those stairs, there was a balcony, it was dark, there were many pictures, and these glass cases, it was a bit like a library—in which he saw no books of his—these made about the sum of Sigbjørn's unrecorded perceptions. From the aromatic gums he moved to the enshrined marriage license of the same poet, and Sigbjørn transcribed this document too, writing rapidly as his eyes became more used to the dim light:

Percy Bysshe Shelley of the Parish *of* Saint Mildred, Bread Street, London, Widower, *and* Mary Wollstonecraft Godwin *of* the City of Bath, Spinster, a minor, *were married in this* Church *by* Licence *with Consent of* William Godwin her father *this* Thirtieth *Day of December in the year one thousand eight hundred and sixteen.* By me Mr. Heydon, Curate. This marriage was solemnized between us.

                      Percy Bysshe Shelley
                      Mary Wollstonecraft Godwin

In the presence of:

        William Godwin
        M. J. Godwin.

Beneath this Sigbjørn added mysteriously:

Nemesis. Marriage of drowned Phoenician sailor. A bit odd here at all. Sad—feel swine to look at such things.

Then he passed on quickly—not so quickly he hadn't time to wonder with a remote twinge why, if there was no reason for any of his own books to be there on the shelves above him, the presence was justified of *In Memoriam, All Quiet on the Western Front, Green Light,* and the *Field Book of Western Birds*—to another glass case in which appeared a framed and unfinished letter, evidently from Severn, Keats's friend, which Sigbjørn copied down as before:

My dear Sir:

Keats has changed somewhat for the worse—at least his mind has much—very much—yet the blood has ceased to come, his digestion is better and but for a cough he must be improving, that is as respects his body—but the fatal prospect of consumption hangs before his mind yet—and turns everything to despair and wretchedness—he will not hear a word about living—nay, I seem to lose his confidence by trying to give him this hope [the following lines had been crossed out by Severn but Sigbjørn ruthlessly wrote them down just the same: *for his knowledge of internal anatomy enables him to judge of any change accurately and largely adds to his torture*], he will not think his future prospect favorable—he says the continued stretch of his imagination has already killed him and were he to recover he would not write another line—he will not hear of his good friends in England except for what they have done—and this is another load—but of their high hopes of him—his certain success—his experience—he will not hear a word—then the want of some kind of hope to feed his vivacious imagination—

The letter having broken off here, Sigbjørn, notebook in hand, tiptoed lingeringly to another glass case where, another letter from Severn appearing, he wrote:

My dear Brown—He is gone—he died with the most perfect ease—he seemed to go to sleep. On the 23rd at half past four the approaches of death came on. "Severn—lift me up for I am dying—I shall die easy—don't be frightened, I thank God it has come." I lifted him upon my arms and the phlegm seemed boiling in his throat. This increased until 11 at night when he gradually sank into death so quiet I still thought he slept—But I cannot say more now. I am broken down beyond my strength. I cannot be left alone. I have not slept for nine days—the days since. On Saturday a gentleman came to cast his hand and foot. On Thursday the body was opened. The lungs were completely gone. The doctors would not—

Much moved, Sigbjørn reread this as it now appeared in his notebook, then added beneath it:

On Saturday a gentleman came to cast his hand and foot—that is the most sinister line to me. Who is this gentleman?

Once outside Keats's house Wilderness did not pause nor look to left or right, not even at the American Express, until he had reached a bar which he entered, however, without stopping to copy down its name. He felt he had progressed in one movement, in one stride, from Keats's house to this bar, partly just because he had wished to avoid signing his own name in the visitor's book. Sigbjørn Wilderness! The very sound of his name was like a bell-buoy—or more euphoniously a light-ship—broken adrift, and washing in from the Atlantic on a reef. Yet how he hated to write it down (loved to see it in print?)—though like so much else with him it had little reality unless he did. Without hesitating to ask himself why, if he was so disturbed by it, he did not choose another name under which to write, such as his second name which was Henry, or his mother's, which was Sanderson-Smith, he selected the most isolated booth he could find in the bar, that was itself an underground grotto, and drank two grappas in quick succession. Over his third he began to experience some of the emotions one might have expected him to undergo in Keats's house. He felt fully the surprise which had barely affected him that some of Shelley's relics were to be found there, if a fact no more astonishing than that Shelley—whose skull moreover had narrowly escaped appropriation by Byron as a drinking goblet, and whose heart, snatched out of the flames by Trelawny, he seemed to recollect from Proust, was interred in England—should have been buried in Rome at all (where the bit of Ariel's song inscribed on his gravestone might have anyway prepared one for the rich and strange), and he was touched by the chivalry of those Italians who, during the war, it was said, had preserved, at considerable risk to themselves, the contents of that house from the Germans. Moreover he now thought he began to see the house itself more clearly, though no doubt not as it was, and he produced his notebook again with the object of adding to the notes already taken these impressions that came to him in retrospect.

"Mamertine Prison," he read . . . He'd opened it at the wrong place, at some observations made yesterday upon a visit to the historic dungeon, but being gloomily entertained by what he saw, he read on as he did so feeling the clammy confined horror of that underground cell, or other underground cell, not, he suspected, really sensed at the time, rise heavily about him.

MAMERTINE PRISON [ran the heading]
The lower is the true prison
of Mamertine, the state prison of ancient Rome.

The lower cell called Tullianus is probably the most ancient building in Rome. The prison was used to imprison malefactors and enemies of the State. In the lower cell is seen the well where according to tradition St. Peter miraculously made a spring to baptise the gaolers Processus and Martinianus. Victims: politicians. Pontius, King of the Sanniti. Died 290 B.C. Giurgurath (Jugurtha) Aristotulus, Vercingetorix.—The Holy Martyrs, Peter and Paul. Apostles imprisoned in the reign of Nero.—Processus, Abondius, *and many others unknown* were:

> decapitato
> suppliziato (suffocated)
> strangolato
> morto per fame.

Vercingetorix, the King of the Gauls, was certainly strangolato 49 B.C. and Jugurtha, King of Numidia, dead by starvation 104 B.C.

The lower is the true prison—why had he underlined that? Sigbjørn wondered. He ordered another grappa and, while awaiting it, turned back to his notebook where, beneath his remarks on the Mamertine prison, and added as he now recalled in the dungeon itself, this memorandum met his eyes:

> Find Gogol's house—where wrote part of Dead Souls—1838. Where died Vielgorsky? "They do not heed me, nor see me, nor listen to me," wrote Gogol. "What have I done to them? Why do they torture me? What do they want of poor me? What can I give them? I have nothing. My strength is gone. I cannot endure all this." Suppliziato. Strangolato. In wonderful-horrible book of Nabokov's when Gogol was dying—he says—"you could feel his spine through his stomach." Leeches dangling from nose: "Lift them up, keep them away . . ." Henrik Ibsen, Thomas Mann, ditto brother: Buddenbrooks and Pippo Spano. A—where lived? became sunburned? Perhaps happy here. Prosper Mérimée and Schiller. Suppliziato. Fitzgerald in Forum. Eliot in Colosseum?

And underneath this was written enigmatically:

> *And many others.*

And beneath this:

> Perhaps Maxim Gorky too. This is funny. Encounter between Volga Boatman and saintly Fisherman.

What was funny? While Sigbjørn, turning over his pages toward Keats's house again was wondering what he had meant, beyond the fact that Gorky, like most of those other distinguished individuals, had at one time lived in Rome, if not in the Mamertine prison—though with another part of his mind he knew perfectly well—he realized that the peculiar stichometry of his observations, jotted down as if he imagined he were writing a species of poem, had caused him prematurely to finish the notebook:

> *On Saturday a gentleman came to cast his hand and foot*—that is the most sinister line to me—who is this gentleman?

With these words his notebook concluded.

That didn't mean there was no more space, for his notebooks, he reflected avuncularly, just like his candles, tended to consume themselves at both ends; yes, as he thought, there was some writing at the beginning. Reversing this, for it was upside down, he smiled and forgot about looking for space, since he immediately recognized these notes as having been taken in America two years ago upon a visit to Richmond, Virginia, a pleasant time for him. So, amused, he composed himself to read, delighted also, in an Italian bar, to be thus transported back to the South. He had made nothing of these notes, hadn't even known they were there, and it was not always easy accurately to visualize the scenes they conjured up:

>The wonderful slanting square in Richmond and the tragic silhouette of interlaced leafless trees.
>
>On a wall: *dirty stinking Degenerate Bobs was here from Boston, North End, Mass. Warp son of a bitch.*

Sigbjørn chuckled. Now he clearly remembered the biting winter day in Richmond, the dramatic courthouse in the precipitous park, the long climb up to it, and the caustic attestation to solidarity with the North in the (white) men's wash room. Smiling he read on:

>In Poe's shrine, strange preserved newsclipping: CAPACITY CROWD HEARS TRIBUTE TO POE'S WORKS. *University student, who ended life, buried at Wytherville.*

Yes, yes, and this he remembered too, in Poe's house, or one of Poe's houses, the one with the great dark wing of shadow on it at sunset, where the dear old lady who kept it, who'd showed him the news clipping, had said to him in a whisper: "So you see, *we* think these stories of his drinking can't *all* be true." He continued:

>Opposite Craig house, where Poe's Helen lived, these words, upon façade, windows, stoop of the place from which E.A.P.—if I am right—must have watched the lady with the agate lamp: Headache—A.B.C.—Neuralgia: LIC-OFF-PREM—enjoy Pepsi—Drink Royal Crown Cola—Dr. Swell's Root Beer—"Furnish room for rent": did Poe really live here? Must have, could only have spotted Psyche from the regions which are Lic-Off-Prem.— Better than no Lic at all though. Bet Poe does not still live in Lic-Off-Prem. Else might account for "Furnish room for rent"?
>
>Mem: Consult Talking Horse Friday.
>
>—Give me Liberty or give me death (Sigbjørn now read). In churchyard, with Patrick Henry's grave; a notice: No smoking within ten feet of the church; then:
>
>Outside Robert E. Lee's house:
>Please pull the bell
>To make it ring.
>
>—Inside Valentine Museum, with Poe's relics—

Sigbjørn paused. Now he remembered that winter day still more clearly. Robert E. Lee's house was of course far below the courthouse, remote from Patrick Henry and the Craig house and the other Poe shrine, and it would have been a good step hence to the Valentine Museum, even had not Richmond, a city whose Hellenic character was not confined to its architecture, but would have been recognized in its gradients by a Greek mountain goat, been grouped about streets so steep it was painful to think of Poe toiling up them. Sigbjørn's notes were in the wrong order, and it must have been morning then, and not sunset as it was in the other house with the old lady, when he went to the Valentine Museum. He saw Lee's house again, and a faint feeling of the beauty of the whole frostbound city outside came to his mind, then a picture of a Confederate white house, near a gigantic red-brick factory chimney, with far below a glimpse of an old cobbled street, and a lone figure crossing a waste, as between three centuries, from the house toward the railway tracks and this chimney, which belonged to the Bone Dry Fertilizer Company. But in the sequence of his notes "Please pull the bell, to make it ring," on Lee's house, had seemed to provide a certain musical effect of solemnity, yet ushering him instead into the Poe museum which Sigbjørn now in memory re-entered.

> Inside Valentine Museum, with Poe's relics (he read once more)
> Please
> Do not smoke
> Do not run
> Do not touch walls or exhibits
> Observation of these rules will insure your own and other's enjoyment of the museum.
> —Blue silk coat and waistcoat, gift of the Misses Boykin, that belonged to one of George Washington's dentists.

Sigbjørn closed his eyes, in his mind Shelley's crematory gums and the gift of the Misses Boykin struggling for a moment helplessly, then he returned to the words that followed. They were Poe's own, and formed part of some letters once presumably written in anguished and private desperation, but which were now to be perused at leisure by anyone whose enjoyment of them would be "insured" so long as they neither smoked nor ran nor touched the glass case in which, like the gums (on the other side of the world), they were preserved. He read:

> Excerpt from a letter by Poe—after having been dis-

missed from West Point—to his foster father. Feb. 21, 1831.

"It will however be the last time I ever trouble any human being—I feel I am on a sick bed from which I shall never get up."

Sigbjørn calculated with a pang that Poe must have written these words almost seven years to the day after Keats's death, then, that far from never having got up from his sick bed, he had risen from it to change, thanks to Baudelaire, the whole course of European literature, yes, and not merely to trouble, but to frighten the wits out of several generations of human beings with such choice pieces as "King Pest," "The Pit and the Pendulum," and "A Descent into the Maelstrom," not to speak of the effect produced by the compendious and prophetic *Eureka*.

My *ear* has been too shocking for any description—I am wearing away every day, even if my last sickness had not completed it.

Sigbjørn finished his grappa and ordered another. The sensation produced by reading these notes was really very curious. First, he was conscious of himself reading them here in this Roman bar, then of himself in the Valentine Museum in Richmond, Virginia, reading the letters through the glass case and copying fragments from these down, then of poor Poe sitting blackly somewhere writing them. Beyond this was the vision of Poe's foster father likewise reading some of these letters, for all he knew unheedingly, yet solemnly putting them away for what turned out to be posterity, these letters which, whatever they might not be, were certainly—he thought again—intended to be private. But were they indeed? Even here at this extremity Poe must have felt that he was transcribing the story that was E. A. Poe, at this very moment of what he conceived to be his greatest need, his final—however consciously engineered—disgrace, felt a certain reluctance, perhaps, to send what he wrote, as if he were thinking: Damn it, I could use some of that, it may not be so hot, but it is at least too good to waste on my foster father. Some of Keats's own published letters were not different. And yet it was almost bizarre how, among these glass cases, in these museums, to what extent one revolved about, was hemmed in by, this cinereous evidence of anguish. Where was Poe's astrolabe, Keats's tankard of claret, Shelley's "Useful Knots for the Yachtsman"? It was true that Shelley himself might not have been aware of the aromatic gums, but even that beautiful and irrelevant circumstantiality that was the gift of the Misses Boykin seemed not without its suggestion of suffering, at least for George Washington.

Baltimore, April 12, 1833.
I am perishing—absolutely perishing for want of aid. And yet I am not idle—nor have I committed any offence against society which would render me deserving of so hard a fate. For God's sake pity me and save me from destruction.

E. A. Poe

Oh, God, thought Sigbjørn. But Poe had held out another sixteen years. He had died in Baltimore at the age of forty. Sigbjørn himself was nine behind on that game so far, and—with luck—should win easily. Perhaps if Poe had held out a little longer—perhaps if Keats—he turned over the pages of his notebook rapidly, only to be confronted by the letter from Severn:

My dear Sir:
Keats has changed somewhat for the worse—at least his mind has much—very much—yet the blood has ceased to come . . . but the fatal prospect hangs . . . *for his knowledge of internal anatomy . . . largely adds to his torture.*

Suppliziato, strangolato, he thought . . . *The lower is the true prison. And many others.* Nor have I committed any offense against society. Not much you hadn't, brother. Society might pay you the highest honors, even to putting your relics in the company of the waistcoat belonging to George Washington's dentist, but in its heart it cried:—*dirty stinking Degenerate Bobs was here from Boston, North End, Mass. Warp son of a bitch!* . . . "On Saturday a gentleman came to cast his hand and foot . . ." Had anybody done that, Sigbjørn wondered, tasting his new grappa, and suddenly cognizant of his diminishing Guggenheim, compared, that was, Keats and Poe?—But compare in what sense, Keats, with what, in what sense, with Poe? What was it he wanted to compare? Not the aesthetic of the two poets, nor the breakdown of *Hyperion,* in relation to Poe's conception of the short poem, nor yet the philosophic ambition of the one, with the philosophic achievement of the other. Or could that more properly be discerned as negative capability, as opposed to negative achievement? Or did he merely wish to relate their melancholias? potations? hangovers? Their sheer guts—which commentators so obligingly forgot!—character, in a high sense of that word, the sense in which Conrad sometimes understood it, for were they not in their souls like hapless shipmasters, determined to drive their leaky commands full of valuable treasure at all costs, somehow, into port, and always against time, yet through all but interminable tempest, typhoons that so rarely abated? Or merely what seemed funereally analogous within the mutuality of their shrines? Or he could even speculate, starting with Baudelaire again, upon what the French movie director Epstein who had made *La Chute de la Maison Usher* in a way that would have delighted Poe himself, might have done with *The Eve of St. Agnes*: *And they are gone!* . . . "For God's sake pity me and save me from destruction!"

Ah ha, now he thought he had it: did not the preservation of such relics betoken—beyond the filing cabinet of the malicious foster father who wanted to catch one out—less an obscure revenge for the poet's nonconformity, than for his magical monopoly, his possession of words? On the one hand he could write his translunar "Ulalume," his enchanted "To a Nightingale" (which might account for the *Field Book of Western Birds*), on the other was capable of saying, simply, "I am perishing . . . For God's sake pity me . . ." You see, after all, he's just like folks . . . What's this? . . . Conversely there might appear almost a tragic condescension in remarks such as Flaubert's often quoted "Ils sont dans le vrai" perpetuated by Kafka—Kaf—and others, and addressed to child-bearing rosy-cheeked and jolly humanity at large. Condescension, nay, inverse self-approval, something downright unnecessary. And Flaub- Why should they be dans le vrai any more than the artist was dans le vrai? All people and poets are much the same but some poets are more the same than others, as George Orwell might have said. George Or— And yet, what modern poet would be caught dead (though they'd do their best to catch him all right) with his "For Christ's sake send aid," unrepossessed, unincinerated, to be put in a glass case? It was a truism to say that poets not only were, but looked like folks these days. Far from ostensible nonconformists, as the daily papers, the very writers themselves—more shame to them—took every opportunity triumphantly to point out, they dressed like, and as often as not, were bank clerks, or, marvelous paradox, engaged in advertising. It was true. He, Sigbjørn, dressed like a bank clerk himself—how else should he have courage to go into a bank? It was questionable whether poets especially, in uttermost private, any longer allowed themselves to say things like "For God's sake pity me!" Yes, they had become more like folks even than folks. And the despair in the glass case, all private correspondence carefully destroyed, yet destined to become ten thousand times more public than ever, viewed through the great glass case of art, was now transmuted into hieroglyphics, masterly compressions, obscurities to be deciphered by experts—yes, and poets—like Sigbjørn Wilderness. Wil—

And many others. Probably there was a good idea somewhere, lurking among these arrant self-contradictions; pity could not keep him from using it, nor a certain sense of horror that he felt all over again that these mummified and naked cries of agony should lie thus exposed to human view in permanent incorruption, as if embalmed evermore in their separate eternal funeral parlors: separate, yet not separate, for was it not as if Poe's cry from Baltimore, in a mysterious manner, in the manner that the octet of a sonnet, say, is answered by its sestet, had already been answered, seven years before, by Keats's cry from Rome; so that according to the special reality of Sigbjørn's notebook at least, Poe's own death appeared like something extraformal, almost extraprofessional, an afterthought. Yet inerrably it was part of the same poem, the same story. "And yet the fatal prospect hangs . . ." "Severn, lift me up, for I am dying." "Lift them up, keep them away." Dr. Swell's Root Beer.

Good idea or not, there was no more room to implement his thoughts within this notebook (the notes on Poe and Richmond ran, through Fredericksburg, into his remarks upon Rome, the Mamertine Prison, and Keats's house, and vice versa), so Sigbjørn brought out another one from his trousers pocket.

This was a bigger notebook altogether, its paper stiffer and stronger, showing it dated from before the war, and he had brought it from America at the last minute, fearing that such might be hard to come by abroad.

In those days he had almost given up taking notes: every new notebook bought represented an impulse, soon to be overlaid, to write afresh; as a consequence he had accumulated a number of notebooks like this one at home, yet which were almost empty, which he had never taken with him on his more recent travels since the war, else a given trip would have seemed to start off with a destructive stoop, from the past, in its soul: this one had looked an exception so he'd packed it.

Just the same, he saw, it was not innocent of writing: several pages at the beginning were covered with his handwriting, so shaky and hysterical of appearance, that Sigbjørn had to put on his spectacles to read it. Seattle, he made out. July? 1939. Seattle! Sigbjørn swallowed some grappa hastily. Lo, death hath reared himself a throne in a strange city lying alone far down within the dim west, where the good and the bad and the best and the rest, have gone to their eternal worst! The lower is the true Seattle . . . Sigbjørn felt he could be excused for not fully appreciating Seattle, its mountain graces, in those days. For these were not notes he had found but the draft of a letter, written in the notebook because it was that type of letter possible for him to write only in a bar. A bar? Well, one might have called it a bar. For in those days, in Seattle, in the State of Washington, they still did not sell hard liquor in bars—as, for that matter to this day they did not, in Richmond, in the State of Virginia—which was half the gruesome and pointless point of his having been in the State of Washington. LIC-OFF-PREM, he thought. No, no, go not to Virginia Dare . . . Neither twist Pepso—tight-rooted!—for its poisonous bane. The letter dated—no question of his recognition of it, though whether he'd made another version and posted it he had forgotten—from absolutely the lowest ebb of those low tides of his life, a time marked by the baleful circumstance that the small legacy on which he then lived had been suddenly put in charge of a Los Angeles lawyer, to whom this letter indeed was written, his family, who considered him incompetent, having refused to have anything further to do with him, as, in effect, did the lawyer, who had sent him to a religious-minded family of Buchmanite tendencies in Seattle on the understanding he be entrusted with not more than 25c a day.

Dear Mr. Van Bosch:

It is, psychologically, apart from anything else, of extreme urgency that I leave Seattle and come to Los Angeles to see you. I fear a complete mental collapse else. I have cooperated far beyond what I thought was the best of my ability here in the matter of liquor and I have also tried to work hard, so far, alas, without selling anything. I cannot say either that my ways have been as circumscribed exactly as I thought they would be by the Mackorkindales, who at least have seen my point of view on some matters, and if they pray for guidance on the very few occasions when they do see fit to exceed the stipulated 25c a day, they are at least sympathetic with my wishes to return. This may be because the elder Mackorkindale is literally and physically worn out following me through Seattle, or because you have failed to supply sufficient means for my board, but this is certainly as far as the sympathy goes. In short, they sympathize, but cannot honestly agree; nor will they advise you I should return. And in anything that applies to my writing—and this I find almost the hardest to bear—I am met with the opinion that I "should put all that behind me." If they merely claimed to be abetting yourself or my parents in this it would be understandable, but this judgment is presented to me independently, somewhat blasphemously in my view—though without question they believe it—as coming directly from God, who stoops daily from on high to inform the Mackorkindales, if not in so many words, that as a serious writer I am lousy. Scenting some hidden truth about this, things being what they are, I would find it discouraging enough if it stopped there, and were not beyond that the hope held out, miraculously congruent also with that of my parents and yourself, that I could instead turn myself into a successful writer of advertisements. Since I cannot but feel, I repeat, and feel respectfully, that they are sincere in their beliefs, all I can say is that in this daily rapprochement with their Almighty in Seattle I hope some prayer that has slipped in by mistake to let the dreadful man for heaven's sake return to Los Angeles may eventually be answered. For I find it impossible to describe my spiritual isolation in this place, nor the gloom into which I have sunk. I enjoyed of course the seaside—the Mackorkindales doubtless reported to you that the Group were having a small rally in Bellingham (I wish you could go to Bellingham one day) but I have completely exhausted any therapeutic value in my stay. God knows I ought to know, I shall never recover in this place, isolated as I am from Nancy who, whatever you may say, I want with all my heart to make my wife. It was with the greatest of anguish that I discovered that her letters to me were being opened, finally, even having to hear lectures on her moral character by those who had read these letters, which I had thus been prevented from replying to, causing such pain to her as I cannot think of. This separation from her would be an unendurable agony, without anything else, but as things stand I can only say I would be better off in a prison, in the worst dungeon that could be imagined, than to be incarcerated in this damnable place with the highest suicide rate in the Union. Literally I am dying in this macabre hole and I appeal to you to send me, out of the money that is after all mine, enough that I may return. Surely I am not the only writer, there have been others in history whose ways have been misconstrued and who have failed . . . who have won through . . . success . . . publicans and sinners . . . I have no intention——

Sigbjørn broke off reading, and resisting an impulse to tear the letter out of the notebook, for that would loosen the pages, began meticulously to cross it out, line by line.

And now this was half done he began to be sorry. For now, damn it, he wouldn't be able to use it. Even when he'd written it he must have thought it a bit too good for poor old Van

Bosch, though one admitted that wasn't saying much. Wherever or however he could have used it. And yet, what if they had found this letter—whoever "they" were—and put it, glass-encased, in a museum among *his* relics? Not much— Still, you never knew!—Well, they wouldn't do it now. Anyhow, perhaps he would remember enough of it . . . "I am dying, absolutely perishing." "What have I done to them?" "My dear Sir." "The worst dungeon." And many others: and *dirty stinking Degenerate Bobs was here from Boston, North End, Mass. Warp son*—!

Sigbjørn finished his fifth unregenerate grappa and suddenly gave a loud laugh, a laugh which, as if it had realized itself it should become something more respectable, turned immediately into a prolonged—though on the whole relatively pleasurable—fit of coughing. . . .

Albert J. Guerard

THE IVORY TOWER AND THE DUST BOWL

An Associate Professor of English at Harvard University, Albert J. Guerard was born in Houston, Texas in 1914, was educated at Stanford University and at Harvard. He is the author of three books of criticism, a critical survey and anthology published in Paris, stories and criticism which have appeared in various literary magazines, and four novels, the most recent of which is NIGHT JOURNEY (Alfred A. Knopf, 1950).

Let me say at once that I do not propose to tell novelists what they should write about this year or next. Nor am I going to ask why the novel is dying, since I do not think it is. But the journalistic question as to whether and why the novel is dying (which has surely been asked in every generation since Fielding) always has a mild immediate historical interest, and it can lead one to more serious matters. The changing terms of the question at least suggest the particular embarrassments and dilemmas of the novelist in one's own time. The saving preliminary reservation is to recognize that it is always difficult to write good novels, and that the novelist always has a "plight."

What lies behind the vague *malaise* of any number of journeyman reviewers in the presence of last week's new novels? Obviously they regret that "serious" novelists no longer try to write books like *Middlemarch*—comprehensive chronicles of a family or a community, "soul-satisfying" in their appalling completeness. This has become the province of the earnest second-rater, and a good writer (if he turn his hand to this sort of thing) produces *A Rage to Live*. The journalists regret too that novelists do not "sufficiently reflect man's dignity," which suggests a demand for moral optimism as well as compassion. And they regret the absence of humor and gusto—with better reason, perhaps, in this gray world we have to live in. Certainly they miss that narrative simplicity which (having passed over to the motion picture, radio and television) attracts so few good writers. Behind all this, I suppose, lies a regret for the placid undemanding form of vicarious living which traditional realism and even the outrages of naturalism provided.

The *malaise* is seldom expressed frankly, however. It is more common to say that the novelist is failing in his responsibility to the modern world. Withdrawn to some private world of guilt or fantasy, *he fails to document contemporary society*. He did not, with rare exceptions, document World War II faithfully. (Consider his unfairness to officers!) And he quite refuses to document this present and terribly important moment in man's history. Why have the last few years produced neither a *U.S.A.* nor a *Man's Fate* nor a *Magic Mountain* nor even a *Grapes of Wrath*? In their very different ways these four novels at least showed a comprehensive knowledge of what was going on. And this is the issue as Harold Strauss put it: the contemporary novelist does not know enough. In his crippled separateness and ignorance, he studiously avoids and evades the actual.

2

Admittedly the material is there and all around us—for great traditional fiction, for realistic novels ambitious in scope and massive in size. In our American scene alone there remain subjects enough for the novelist tempted by "subjects," for a younger Dos Passos perhaps: the tensions resulting from a sudden westward movement of population, the swift growth of an educated proletariat, the psychology of new generations whether silent or beaten, the tribulations of the lonely crowd. The larger horizon is of mass suffering (which is nothing new), but also of a mass uncertainty so diffused that the cold war can divide a Western European government from its people or a single family against itself. The possibility of guilt lies behind every act of political choice, even every feeling of preference. Is all this too anonymous to record? It is sometimes argued that the modern novelist is paralyzed by an absence of heroes, individual figures of a "certain magnitude." It would be truer to say that we have had altogether too many heroes for our comfort—Shakespearean heroes even, complete with their divided loyalties and tragic flaws. The Pétain-Laval-Darlan story cries out to be treated in five acts: an inward story which affected a whole nation. Or the story of de Gaulle (whether as Richard II or Henry V) with the novelist Malraux to observe it at close range. There is certainly, however one may interpret it, the story of Henry Wallace. And no plot ever conceived excels the Hiss-Chambers affair for psychological and moral interest, for drama and melodrama, for "collective" and "historical" interest. The *Witness* of Chambers has repeatedly evoked the name of Dostoevski. Yet the fact remains that all this seems, for the present, outside the manageable area of realistic or even Dostoevskian fiction.

I have read far too little recent fiction to venture to talk about dominant trends. Yet it seems clear enough that some of the best American novelists, young and old, decline to write realistic novels about the public crises of our time. It is hard to say how much of this is due to an already historic impatience with realistic techniques, and how much to the nature of reality itself. And of course it is always better to write good private novels than bad public ones. In any event, there is some basis for the charge of evasive withdrawal. There have been, recently more than ever, sensitive novels of childhood and adolescent guilt, and reveries of adolescent escape. There have been excellent novels of sexual tension and chronic self-destructiveness—two more subjects which go onward the same though dynasties pass. Novelists have rediscovered certain "subjects" and professions, bullfighting for instance, which have a timeless simplicity and fine intrinsic interest. Moreover, serious novelists have once again taken to writing historical novels about the American past: that simpler, greener past which yet carried its sufficient burden of neurosis, terror, violence. Finally, there have been stylized and nondocumentary visions of America, Wright Morris' summation of loneliness in *The Works of Love* or John Hawkes's wasteland of sexless apathy in *The Beetle Leg*. He would be rash who would condemn the authors for choosing these subjects. Yet the subjects did free their authors from any obligation to document whatever aspect of present crisis.

The tendency—perhaps a timeless generality, at least an evasion of social documentation—appears at the two familiar poles of the contemporary novel, Faulkner and Hemingway (though we must recall that both men have large works in progress). *Requiem for a Nun,* for all its pages of historical meditation, is a religious novel concerned with sin rather than crime, damnation rather than punishment. A glance back at *The Hamlet* or even at *Intruder in the Dust* will show how far this novel has freed itself from the need to document actual social pressures, mere material environment. By changing the date of Temple Drake's violation, Faulkner suggests that her story now exists outside time and even place. And so too *The Old Man and the Sea* exists outside both time and the modern world, with only Joe DiMaggio's heel-spur to remind us of the latter. What this novel suggests is a radical need to write about something very large and hence very simple and in any event something unaffected by modern history. It is a story of the Ideal Quest but also a minute record of what it feels like to be old. Does this fine little book really mean that Hemingway is "engaged" at last, after so many years of alleged nihilism? Or isn't it the ultimate act of disengagement from the modern world? (True. But if so many excellent novels show some form of evasion, perhaps we ought to limit the pejorative connotations of that word.)

Hemingway and Faulkner are stylists, though they are also a great deal more. Language itself may be a form of evasion—and here one must note the recent movement toward a richer, more complex and more personal prose. The old prohibitions against metaphor and simile and shaped rhythms and free meditative play of the author's mind have seemingly vanished, though an undertone of modern colloquialism remains. I am thinking not merely of verbal inventiveness and drive, the flashing imagery and Conradian word-play of Robert Penn Warren and Malcolm Lowry, but of something colder and more intellectual. The reaction may show itself in forms as different as the involutions of Buechner or Capote's thin grace. The new prose is very far from Hemingway's monosyllabic naming but also very far from the relaxed outpourings of Wolfe. It admits humor but also a dry ironic audacity —the shaped Jamesian wit of Mary McCarthy, Mark Schrorer, Isabel Bolton, Monroe Engel and others, the analogical surprises of John Hawkes. There is a renewed love of language—not a greater love than Hemingway's, of course, but a different one. A sudden elaboration of language may suggest a true decadence, as it often but not always did in the 1890s, a mere concern for prettiness. *And language may be used as a stick with which to beat inert matter into life. Or, it may serve to cover a poverty of subject.* This can occur even in Faulkner, who has the verbal power and ease to beat anything (even an ordinary suit of clothes, or a walk-on character) into grotesque and overwhelming life. To what degree is the contemporary novelist trying to cover his evasion of the actual and the political by (in Fitzgerald's phrase) "blankets of excellent prose"?

The suggestion may have its truth but it is certainly too simple. We have to deal with a generation far more educated than Hemingway's: college graduates and sometimes college teachers, followers of the James and Melville and Conrad revivals, readers of the *Kenyon Review*. They have lost that outraged naiveté which accounted, with European readers at least, for so much of their elders' appeal. But the reaction would probably have occurred anyway. As Milton and later Tennyson for a time exhausted blank verse, so Hemingway and his imitators may have exhausted the pure Hemingway style. This style has left its no doubt permanent mark, and even on Faulkner himself; it remains the greatest single revolution in the history of American prose. But Faulkner is the present master—and through his imitators one recognizes, at last, the close kinship of James's meditative irony. He has made respectable again Conrad's "prolonged hovering flight of the subjective over the outstretched ground of the case exposed."

I do not know the answer to my question as to how much of this concern for language is an evasion of ordinary dense reality. Style is not the subject, in the very best fiction, but it is of course *attitude*. Still, a total faith in the importance of one's subject matter may lead to a total disregard for style. Except for Stephen Crane the American naturalists—passionately convinced that the world could be changed—paid no attention to language at all, and hacked their way through their books. But also they were reacting against a feminine attitude toward art as its own end. The situation today is only remotely relevant. Rather than showing a simple evasion of seriousness I suggest that the novelist today is being thrust in upon himself and his own resources for seriousness. In a world which cannot be changed and perhaps not even be understood, in a role which has always been lonely and is now economically untenable, hedged in on all sides by the public abuse of emotive words, knowing now that the basic political and human drives cannot be explained simply—*the novelist's new dandyism of language perhaps represents not merely a pose but poise*. It is an act of resistance to machinery and brute process. Within some small chosen area the novelist is determined to make words express a great deal and also control a great deal. He shall—whatever the prohibitions of the 1930s—express his small human identity, the free play of his mind. Style can be an answer to surrounding ambiguity.

This leads us back, however briefly, to the novelist as a person and to his particular forms of "plight."

3

Much good writing is, as Conrad remarked, the conversion of nervous force into phrases, and he speaks of his twenty months' wrestling with the Lord for the creation of *Nostromo*. "These are, perhaps, strong words, but it is difficult to characterize otherwise the intimacy and the strain of a creative effort in which mind and will and conscience are engaged to the full hour after hour, day after day, away from the world, and to the exclusion of all that makes life really lovable and gentle—something for which a material parallel can only be found in the everlasting sombre stress of the westward winter passage round Cape Horn." At the end of his long task Conrad crawled away from his desk, not knowing where he was. Such concentration and detachment are very nearly impossible for the novelist today, even if he share Conrad's brooding skepticism. The daily outrage of the newspaper is a drain on energy and anger which can hardly be denied; the act of documentation becomes (for the social realist) tantamount to the act of creation. But so too the serious novelist must normally divide his time and energy between writing and whatever "second profession." I do not think the economic problem should be minimized, or the fact that serious novelwriting has ceased to be, after only a hundred and fifty years, a way of making a living.

I should like to see an honest and expert study of the economics of authorship and publishing, to which one might add a sociological study of the author as a person living in a small town and so isolated from the great world he is supposed to write about. But I can only mention them here as "environmental variables" which might tend to privacy and evasion. A further embarrassment lies in the serious novelist's naturally subversive role.

"The American novelist should face up to the responsibilities of the moment, and write about the things that matter: the present conflict and our place of leadership in the world today." Such a typical statement is embarrassing but not frightening. What is frightening is the corollary implication that one should not merely report but glorify our place of leadership. The average popular magazine will not cease to complain of the novelist's evasions until he consents to see the world as that magazine sees it, divided into black and white. And the novelist would indeed be fortunate (so far as creativity is concerned) who could accept our slogans with the assurance that Conrad accepted those of the Merchant Marine. And yet, even Conrad was in a minority; was on the losing side in the struggle to preserve tradition and authority. It is embarrassing for the novelist to be on the winning side, even though it may be the right one. For the great novelist (having freed himself from pity) advances into compassion; and the natural objects of both pity and compassion—inward division, ruin, poverty, suffering—happen for once to be on the other and losing side. In at least certain areas of the globe the American policy is to support abstract principle and the rectitude of minorities against the delusions of majorities. A hard one for the novelist to swallow, as a writer if not as a person. The example of Conrad is once again pertinent, who faced just this predicament when he wrote *Under Western Eyes*. He was honestly convinced of the democratic rectitude and cleanliness of the Swiss, the diabolic anarchy of the Russians. Yet he could not help but satirize that cleanliness; could not help but sympathize at least briefly with the disorderly and the fallen. He too, for a few pages, found himself on the Devil's side without knowing it.

I do not want to suggest that the great novelist must sympathize with evil. But I do think that the novelist's naturally subversive role means, simply, that he will decline to accept any division of the world into absolutes of black and white. The great creative mind, though it be as conservative as Conrad's or Faulkner's, is impelled to dissolve slogans and reject easy or merely pragmatic affirmations. It is a corrosive mind, and must win its way back to faith on its own terms of underground effort. It is by nature opposed to both the certitude and the glibness of the average writer of editorials.

So we shall have to assume that the true novelist would see the present conflict in grays, not merely in black and white. But the pressures militating against this healthy subversiveness are enormous and subtle. There is (for those who work partly for the motion pictures or the stage) that reasonable fear which Tennessee Williams has analyzed. And the novelist who makes his living through magazine sales may find himself suppressed as effectively. There is the mere problem of getting into print, however unprofitably. I wonder who would publish today a great novel by an avowed Communist, and openly hostile to the American cause? Publishers might reply that my preceding sentence contains a contradiction in terms; or, more plausibly, that such suppressions affect only a very few. The dilemma of the 'normal' subversive (a category in which I include most good novelists of the last hundred years, even Flaubert and Melville) is much subtler. He may fear that he is being duped, as so many have indeed been duped. Perhaps his detection of grays will give comfort only to those who cynically reverse black and white? Or he may, since he is human and has to live in a society, dislike the role of *seeming to be a dupe.* Beyond this he may experience that most depressing of all obstacles to creativity: the feeling that his voice will not be heard. And there is finally the aesthetic fact that the human spirit is at last wearied by irony and negativistic reporting. This remains true whether one chooses to document the Russian suppression of individual freedom or the less brutal American suppression of the freedom of action of western European governments. It is damaging to creativity to be frankly on the "winning side," doing one's best to convert slogans into human realities. But it may be still more crippling, for the novelist, to feel no hope at all; or to find oneself, for perhaps a lifetime of novel-writing, the realistic historian of hypocrisy, self-delusion and realist expediency. Whatever his political convictions, however sane or neurotic his view of the present conflict, the personal reasons for not writing about that conflict in terms of flat documentary realism seem compelling. But there are also—what a small "also"! —reasons inherent in reality itself.

4

Against the confusions of the year 1953 the events of World War II take on, in retrospect, a classical simplicity of line and motive. How easy it should have been: to dramatize the unambiguous impulses of those days, the collective enthusiasm and mass effort! And yet the important novels of the war dealt with a company, a platoon, a squad, a single soldier on leave. The great events of the war were in fact too complicated but also too dramatic to be manageable in realistic fiction, and the changes in emotion too swift and too crude. I saw the liberation of Paris but would never have conceived of it as "usable" in fiction, though a member of my company did (Stefan Heym, *The Crusaders*). By instinct or creative deficiency I chose two smaller events I had seen: a small absurd holding action on the Atlantic coast (*Maquisard*) and the liberation and immediate loss of a small town in Normandy (*Night Journey*). And even this second event and very small town would not lend itself to "realism." The important operations of the war had a surrealist character of absurdity and extreme which Malraux's China and Spain did not. A Harvard professor designed explosives to be concealed in donkey droppings in North Africa, so that the German army might be slowed down to a cautious zig-zag. And I understand the O.S.S. made plans to release phosphorescent foxes on the invasion beaches of Japan, to demoralize the defenders by these apparitions of the honored dead. Instead we dropped the atomic bomb. But what is *the realistic novelist,* the documentary novelist, to make of donkey droppings, phosphorescent foxes and the atomic bomb? In such a world the novelist competes on uneven terms with the journalist and the writer of nonfiction.

This reason has been mentioned repeatedly, in explanation of our war fiction and its limited character, and I think it is a valid one. Dealing with something already known, even the best documentary fiction is likely to seem contrived. And reporting, whatever its sins, has been schooled by Hemingway himself. The actualizing detail of one soldier's inarticulate discomfort, the tricks of understatement and irony, the emotional structure of the paragraph and the story, the pervasive sense of war's anonymity—all this (which was so exciting in the very early Hemingway) is available in one's morning paper. Journalism has been fictionized, and Hersey the novelist seems contrived beside Hersey the journalist. The instance of Arthur Koestler is striking. In *The Yogi and the Commissar* he tells the true story of a self-destructive flier named Richard Hillary, determined to die in the air for a cause he no longer believed in. The same story, transposed distantly in the novel *Arrival and Departure,* has lost its authenticity. So too Koestler's *Scum of the Earth* remains a convincing personal history of imprisonment. It has a compelling reality which *Darkness at Noon* lacks. There everything seems too mechanical: the interrogations, the tortures, the guilt feelings and their attendant toothache.

Today we still have an excessive melodrama, but also an excessive confusion. Some of the important problems—say the problem of how England can be induced to survive economically without an emigration of 25,000,000—are wholly outside the area of even the most ponderous fiction. As early as 1947 the war had become a war of words—monstrously distorted on the Russian side, but also distorted on ours. How much ambiguity can the novelist tolerate? My own experience was to try, in 1947, to write a realistic novel about what I had seen in France in 1945. I planned to document the tragedy of the displaced person, the black market, and Lord knows what else. But this realistic novel would not move. Then one day I read in the newspaper, *in adjoining columns,* a circumstantial account of fighting between Arabs and Jews and the report of an investigative commission saying that any rumors of fighting were unfounded. This was the fillip I needed, and this is how I came to write *Night Journey,* a novel laid some fifteen years in the future. The central fact of our modern history came to seem (often from the highest motives) a calculated and monstrous abuse of language. Later I read *1984* and *The Plague* and realized that those were the novels I should have written and had not.

However, I am not rash enough to suppose that I (or even Orwell and Camus) can "explain" our modern history. And this is a major problem for the documentary novelist of the 1950s, in contrast to the novelist of the 1930s. Not to mention the heroic days of naturalism when everything could be explained! For the André Malraux of *Man's Fate*, history could *still be explained*. History occurred in bedrooms, in the back rooms of little shops and over the luncheon tables of bankers, and it was prompted by man's self-destructive neuroses and fears. Equipped with such preconceptions, Malraux could still write a realistic novel of a complex three-way war, though he did telescope the events of several years into a few months.

The second major problem for the documentary novelist of the 1950s, compared with the novelist of the 1930s, is similar. For the Steinbeck of *In Dubious Battle* and *The Grapes of Wrath* there remained the illusion that history could *still be altered*—altered by the outraged individual voice of the observer. Behind the pessimism of the 1890 naturalists and the 1930 proletarians remained this genuine hope. What else but incorrigible hope could lead six different writers to document the Gastonia strike in novels?

At the risk of betraying further "failure of nerve" I must say that I do not think a documentary realistic novel of today could affect history very much. I refuse to acknowledge, on the other hand, that human will means nothing. The greatest present danger is that people will finally become inured to the universal abuse of words and finally come to accept as plausible and reasonable the plane of absurdity on which international relations are conducted and most newspapers written. A very great satirist in nonfiction may appear to save us, a Swift or a Voltaire. But in his absence there is much to be said for the novelist who reduces our present situation to absurdity through the classical methods of satire, whether of exaggeration, extrapolation or direct ridicule. I should like to suggest that one of the obvious modes of evasion—that of the "visionary novel"—may constitute the most effective form of responsibility. It cuts through and down to the truth as documentary realism cannot.

5

Visionary or symbolist novels of modern catastrophe are frequently summed up as "Kafkaesque"—not a very useful epithet when one considers the diversity of Kafka's own methods. All of these novels achieve their meaning through a distortion of journalistic actuality, and where their distortions coincide may exist some truth worth listening to. Perhaps they all remind us how easily one becomes accustomed to bureaucratic procedure and everyday horror; or how easy it is, today, not to live at all. But the tactics of the novelists (to take five significant examples) may vary greatly. Dino Buzzati's *The Tartar Steppe* (published in 1945 but the most recent to appear in English) is perhaps the closest to Kafka in conception and tone, a curious blend of *The Castle* and *The Burrow*. John Hawkes's *The Cannibal* is the only one to resemble surrealism in its freedom from logic and in its absurd crowding of event and image. George Orwell's *1984*, though the most inventive in terms of "machinery," is the closest to classical satire in essay form. Albert Camus' *The Plague* and Ennio Flaiano's *The Short Cut* lean heavily on a material reality to justify their visions, the reality of bloody rats and rotting mules. But these are also the most philosophical novels of the group. Of the five, only *The Short Cut* has a marked psychological emphasis. All five suggest a personal experience of World War II, and all five rest on a certain dry wit and tone of laconic understatement. (I hope it will be understood that I do not consider these five novels the most representative of "postwar novels.")

So far as I know the five novels were written independently, without benefit of mutual influence. It is therefore interesting to note the different ways in which they reduce our modern situation to absurdity. *The Tartar Steppe* is the story of Giovanni Drogo, who spends his entire adult life in a frontier fort, overlooking the northern desert. Across this steppe the Tartars will make their invasion . . . if there are any Tartars. The defenders, after years and then decades of waiting for this invasion, secretly hope for the "cold war" to turn hot. Part of *The Cannibal* is specifically dated 1945, a year in which a single enlisted man on a motorcycle occupies one-third of Germany, hurtling through the countryside on a mission he cannot hope to understand. Behind this journalistic symbol lies a larger vision of history as blind, inconsecutive and absurd, totally freed from human intention. *1984* refers much more specifically to "psychological warfare" and the universal abuse of emotive language, and suggests that governments make war to consume production and so keep themselves in power. The center of Orwell's system is "doublethink." His simple and contemporary point is that delusion and hypocrisy may at last become honest self-delusion.

The Plague is the story of an epidemic in the city of Oran in the 1940s. Allegorically it refers in some detail to the German occupation of Paris. But in larger and finally heroic terms it describes men's reactions to any undeserved and ambiguous disaster; the central symbol of the plague fluctuates easily from "war" to "evil" to the "cosmos." It too suggests man's capacity to bemuse himself; to pay himself off (as the French say) with words. In *The Short Cut* we have another inactive war, this time the Italian adventure in Abyssinia. The nameless lieutenant, like some character in each of the other novels, is degraded by the unchanging boredom of the war. But more importantly he raises—after committing an unintentional crime which leads to a chain of further crimes—the question of individual responsibility in an absurd world. The final vision of society is one of total ambiguity. Yet, ambiguity or no, the hero must follow through life the stinking trail of his individual guilt. The war itself is clearly purposeless, and the degradation of the civilian population, whether "liberated" or "conquered," is brilliantly suggested. Indeed (and unless we equate Camus' plague with the Germans rather than with war itself) the war in all five novels is purposeless.

All this is of course surface, though very important surface. Beneath this surface, as one looks for a deeper image of present plight, is the pervasiveness of ambiguity and illusion. Only for Camus does the enemy unmistakably exist, but whether *here* or *there* is difficult to say. Hawkes sees the Germans as unforgiving and incorrigible, but the true enemy is history itself . . . which simply and obscenely happens. One subject of Orwell's novel is man's capacity to fool himself; or, in Buzzati's terms, to mistake a bush or a riderless horse for an enemy column advancing across the steppe. In *The Short Cut* the ambiguity is universal. Does the white turban indicate a leper or a priestess? Are these sores leprous or psychogenic? What is this primeval valley to which the hero withdraws for forty days and forty nights? Flaiano imposes the most severe of the five trials and his novel is the least "political" of the five. Perhaps for that very reason his valley of rotting corpses most nearly suggests (in the unanswerable questions it raises) the daily ordinary world.

These five novels share a further image of contemporary man: an image of inertia and sexless apathy. In *The Plague* there is, as it were, no time for sex; the distant benefits of life and love become less and less important. The truly subversive act in Orwell's society, and the one which leads to Winston's arrest, is the act of sexual intercourse. As for the Germany of *The Cannibal*, sexual desire is maternal, mildly homosexual and even cannibalistic. The hero of *The Short Cut* does attack Mariam, violently and inhumanly and casually. Thereafter, in the presence of women, he lies in a stupor. Of the five novelists, Buzzati draws his moral most explicitly. Desexed by his years of garrison life, Drogo is helpless and isolated when he returns to the city on leave; and the heroism of his death lies in the quietness with which he recognizes that he has never lived at all. But still more pervasive than sexlessness is the inertia of daily and hourly living. Camus' leaders do act and resist. But the characters in these novels (even some of Camus') lie on their beds or in their various cages in an unexplained apathy—missing their few or many chances to live, as their own lives slip by.

These were (as I wrote my own visionary novel, and before I had read any of these books) the things I too seemed to emphasize: ambiguity, illusion and the corollary abuse of language; sexual indifference, regression or failure; a recurrent state of inertia. What the links may be between these things, as they will some day be spelled out, and what their obscure relationship to the events of our time, I shall not try to say. What one can add, as variously evident in these five novels, is that modern man seems to have lost his freedom of action. In *The Short Cut* he must take the blame, whatever the responsibilities of history, but only *The Plague* draws a clear distinction between those who co-operate with evil (history) and those who fight against it. And even in *The Plague,* the margin of choice is small. And as one looks beyond these five "visionary" novels to the modern novel in general, even to such a fine realistic work as *The Naked and the Dead,* doesn't the same message intrude: that the margin of choice is small? It is within the limits of the smallest conceivable world, and with all his material reward eaten away by sharks, that Hemingway's fisherman asserts his human dignity.

So one is forced to agree with J. Donald Adams and others that the modern novel does indeed see man as almost wholly bereft of freedom of choice; and one is forced to agree that some of these novels are depressing. And so? I should like to think of them also as "demoralizing" in the best sense. It is only when we come to recognize how completely we *have* lost our freedom, how monstrously we *are* the victims of political abstraction and inhuman historical process, how thoroughly we *have* been bemused by words—only then will we perhaps begin to feel (as flickeringly as these characters and their forgotten sexual desires) our almost extinguished longing for freedom.

The Directory

offered here is a partial listing of American book publishers and literary magazines which have been in recent years hospitable to new talent. Certain of the university presses which have made a special contribution in the fields of *belles lettres*, poetry and criticism are now listed. Addresses are given for the convenience of readers and writers alike, especially for overseas readers of *New World Writing* who do not have immediate access to the usual directories or catalogues of American publishers.

BOOK PUBLISHERS

Appleton-Century-Crofts, Inc., 35 W. 32nd St., New York 1, N. Y.
The Bobbs-Merrill Company, Inc., 730 N. Meridian St., Indianapolis 7, Ind. New York office: 468 Fourth Ave., New York 16, N. Y.
Cambridge University Press, 32 E. 57th St., New York 22, N. Y.
Columbia University Press, 2960 Broadway, New York 27, N. Y.
Coward-McCann, Inc., 210 Madison Ave., New York 16, N. Y.
Thomas Y. Crowell Co., 432 Fourth Ave., New York 16, N. Y.
Crown Publishers, Inc., 419 Fourth Ave., New York 16, N. Y.
The Devin-Adair Company, 23 E. 26th St., New York 10, N. Y.
Dial Press, 461 Fourth Ave., New York 16, N. Y.
Dodd, Mead & Company, 432 Fourth Ave., New York 16, N. Y.
Doubleday & Company, 575 Madison Ave., New York 22, N. Y.
Duell, Sloan & Pearce, Inc., 124 East 30th Street, New York 16, N. Y.
E. P. Dutton & Company, Inc., 300 Fourth Ave., New York 10, N. Y.
Farrar, Straus & Young, Inc., 101 Fifth Ave., New York 3, N. Y.
Harcourt Brace & Company, 383 Madison Ave., New York 17, N. Y.
Harper & Brothers, 49 E. 33rd St., New York 16, N. Y.
Harvard University Press, 44 Francis Ave., Cambridge 38, Mass.
Henry Holt & Company, Inc., 383 Madison Ave., New York 17, N. Y.
Houghton Mifflin Company, 2 Park St., Boston 7, Mass. New York office: 432 Fourth Ave., New York 16, N. Y.
Indiana University Press, Heighway House, Bloomington, Ind.
The John Day Company, 62 W. 45th St., New York 19, N. Y.
Alfred A. Knopf, Inc., 501 Madison Ave., New York 22, N. Y.
J. B. Lippincott Company, E. Washington Sq., Philadelphia 5, Pa. New York office: 521 Fifth Ave., New York 17, N. Y.
Little, Brown & Company, 34 Beacon St., Boston 6, Mass. New York office: 60 E. 42nd St., New York 17, N. Y.
Longmans, Green & Company, Inc., 55 Fifth Ave., New York 3, N. Y.
Louisiana State University Press, University Sta., Baton Rouge 3, La.
McGraw-Hill Book Company, 330 W. 42nd St., New York 18, N. Y.
David McKay Company, Inc., 225 Park Ave., New York 17, N. Y.

The Macmillan Company, 60 Fifth Ave., New York 11, N. Y.
William Morrow & Company, 425 Fourth Ave., New York 16, N. Y.
New Directions, 333 Sixth Ave., New York 14, N. Y.
W. W. Norton & Company, Inc., 101 Fifth Ave., New York 3, N. Y.
Pantheon Books, Inc., 333 Sixth Ave., New York 14, N. Y.
Pellegrini & Cudahy, 41 E. 50th St., New York 22, N. Y.
Prentice-Hall, Inc., 70 Fifth Ave., New York 11, N. Y.
Princeton University Press, Princeton, N. J.
G. P. Putnam's Sons, 210 Madison Ave., New York 16, N. Y.
Random House, 457 Madison Ave., New York 22, N. Y.
Rinehart & Company, Inc., 232 Madison Ave., New York 16, N. Y.
Rutgers University Press, 30 College Ave., New Brunswick, N. J.
Charles Scribner's Sons, 597 Fifth Ave., New York 17, N. Y.
Simon and Schuster, Inc., 630 Fifth Ave., New York 20, N. Y.
Stanford University Press, Stanford, Cal.
University of California Press, Berkeley 4, Cal.
University of Chicago Press, 5750 Ellis Ave., Chicago 37, Ill.
University of Illinois Press, 358 Administration Building, Urbana, Ill.
University of Michigan Press, 311 Maynard St., Ann Arbor, Mich.
University of Minnesota Press, Minneapolis 14, Minn.
University of New Mexico Press, Albuquerque, N. M.
University of North Carolina Press, Bynum Building, Chapel Hill, N. C.
University of Oklahoma Press, Norman, Okla.
University of Pennsylvania Press, 3436 Walnut St., Philadelphia 4, Pa.
Vanguard Press, 424 Madison Ave., New York 17, N. Y.
The Viking Press, 18 E. 48th St., New York 17, N. Y.
The World Publishing Company, 2231 W. 110th St., Cleveland 2, O. New York office: 119 W. 57th St., New York 19, N. Y.
A. A. Wyn, Inc., 23 W. 47th St., New York 19, N. Y.
Yale University Press, 143 Elm St., New Haven 7, Conn. New York office: 386 Fourth Ave., New York 16, N. Y.

QUARTERLIES AND LITTLE MAGAZINES

Accent, Box 102, University Station, Urbana, Ill. Quarterly. Fiction, poetry, criticism, reviews. Editors: Kerker Quinn, Charles Shattuck and others.

The American Scholar, Phi Beta Kappa Hall, Williamsburg, Va. Quarterly. Poetry, criticism, general articles, reviews. Editor: Hiram Haydn.

American Vanguard, Dial Press, 461 Fourth Ave., N. Y. 16, N. Y. Annual, in book form. Fiction, poetry, documentaries. Editors: Dr. Charles I. Glicksberg and Brom Weber.

The Antioch Review, Yellow Springs, O. Quarterly. Fiction, poetry, criticism, general articles, reviews. Chairman of Editorial Board: Paul Bixler.

The Arizona Quarterly, University of Arizona, Tucson, Ariz. Quarterly. Fiction, poetry, criticism, regional material, reviews. Editor: Albert F. Gegenheimer.

Botteghe Oscure, via delle Botteghe Oscure, 32, Rome, Italy; distributed in the U. S. A. by Farrar, Straus & Young, Inc. and Gotham Book Mart. Bi-annual. Fiction, poetry, criticism, *belles lettres* in French, English and Italian. Chief Editor: Marguerite Caetani.

discovery, Pocket Books, Inc., 630 Fifth Avenue, New York, N. Y. Poetry, fiction, criticism. Editors: Vance Bourjaily and Richard Aldridge.

Epoch, 252 Goldwin Smith Hall, Cornell University, Ithaca, N. Y. Quarterly. Fiction, poetry, criticism. Editors: Baxter Hathaway, Robert H. Elias, John A. Sessions and others.

Furioso, Carleton College, Northfield, Minn. Quarterly. Fiction, poetry, criticism, reviews. Editors: Reed Whittemore, Arthur Mizener and others.

The Hopkins Review, Box 1227, The Johns Hopkins University, Baltimore 18, Md. Quarterly. Fiction, poetry, criticism, reviews. Editor: Louis D. Rubin, Jr.

The Hudson Review, 439 West St., New York 14, N. Y. Quarterly. Fiction, poetry, criticism, reviews. Editors: Joseph Bennett, Frederick Morgan, William Arrowsmith.

Idiom, P.O. Box 86, Passaic, New Jersey. Quarterly. Poetry, fiction, criticism. Editor: Charles Gulick.

The Kenyon Review, Gambier, O. Quarterly. Fiction, poetry, criticism, reviews. Editor: John Crowe Ransom. Associate Editor: Philip Blair Rice.

Merlin, 35 Rue de la Bucherie, Paris 5e, France. Quarterly. Fiction, poetry, criticism. Editor: Alexander Trocchi.

New Directions Annual, 333 Sixth Ave., New York 14, N. Y. Annual, now in its fourteenth year. Fiction, poetry, criticism, *belles lettres.*

New Mexico Quarterly, University of New Mexico, Albuquerque, N. M. Quarterly. Fiction, poetry, criticism, regional material including bibliographical guide to literature of the Southwest, reviews. Editor: Kenneth Lash. Poetry Editor: John Dillon Husband.

New-Story, 6, Boulevard Poissonnière, Paris 9e, France. Monthly. Fiction. Editors: Jean François Bergery, Eric Protter, Robert Burford and others.

Partisan Review, 30 W. 12th St., New York 11, N. Y. Bi-monthly. Fiction, poetry, criticism, general articles, reviews. Editors: William Phillips, Philip Rahv.

Perspectives U.S.A., Intercultural Publications, 2 East 61st St., N. Y., N. Y. Quarterly. Reprints and new fiction, poetry, criticism, reviews.

Poetry, 232 E. Erie St., Chicago 11, Ill. Monthly. Poetry and criticism of poetry. Editor: Karl Shapiro.

Quarterly Review of Literature, Bard College, Box 287, Annandale-on-Hudson, N. Y. Quarterly. Fiction, poetry, plays, criticism. Editors: T. Weiss, Renée Weiss.

Quarto, Business Bldg., School of General Studies, Columbia University, New York 27, N. Y. Semi-annual. Fiction, some criticism and poetry. Editor: Norman Bonter.

The Sewanee Review, University of the South, Sewanee, Tenn. Quarterly. Fiction, poetry, criticism, reviews. Editor: Monroe K. Spears.

Southwest Review, Southern Methodist University Press, Dallas, Tex. Quarterly. Economic, political and sociological articles and reviews; Summer issue devoted annually to fiction, poetry, criticism, reviews. Editor: Allen Maxwell.

Story, A. A. Wyn, Inc., 23 W. 47th St., New York 19, N. Y. Semi-annual successor to *Story* magazine, in book form. Fiction. Editors: Whit and Hallie Burnett.

The Paris Review, 8 Rue Garancière, Paris 6e, France. Quarterly. Fiction, poetry, criticism.

The University of Kansas City Review, 5100 Rockhill Rd., Kansas City, Mo. Quarterly. Fiction, poetry, criticism, reviews. Editor: Clarence R. Decker.

The Virginia Quarterly Review, The University of Virginia, Charlottesville, Va. Quarterly. Fiction, poetry, criticism, general articles, reviews. Editor: Charlotte Kohler.

The Western Review, State University of Iowa, Iowa City, Ia. Quarterly. Fiction, poetry, criticism, reviews. Editor: Ray B. West, Jr.

The Yale Review, Drawer 1729, New Haven 7, Conn. Quarterly. Fiction, poetry, criticism, general articles, reviews. Managing Editor: Paul Pickrel. Editorial Board: William Clyde DeVane, Edgar S. Furniss, David M. Potter, Arnold Wolfers.

Zero, British Post Office, Tangier, Morocco. Quarterly—Fall 1952 issue to be published from 138-52 Elder Ave., Flushing, N. Y. A review of literature and art. Editor: Themistocles Hoetis.

OTHER MAGAZINES

The Atlantic Monthly, 8 Arlington St., Boston 16, Mass. Monthly.
Commentary, 34 W. 33rd St., New York 1, N. Y. Monthly.
Harper's Bazaar, 572 Madison Ave., New York 22, N. Y. Monthly.
Harper's Magazine, 49 E. 33rd St., New York 16, N. Y. Monthly.
Mademoiselle, 575 Madison Ave., New York 22, N. Y. Monthly.
The New Yorker, 25 W. 43rd St., New York 18, N. Y. Weekly.